THE LIGHTNING STONES

Jack Du Brul became a #1 *New York Times* bestselling author with Clive Cussler, co-writing the *Oregon* Files series, which has become a fan favorite. Du Brul is also the author of earlier bestselling novels featuring Philip Mercer. He lives in Vermont with his wife.

jackdubrulbooks.com

THE
LIGHTNING
STONES

THE LIGHTNING STONES

A NOVEL

JACK Du BRUL

ANCHOR BOOKS

A DIVISION OF PENGUIN RANDOM HOUSE LLC

New York

FIRST ANCHOR BOOKS PREMIUM
MASS-MARKET EDITION, JULY 2016

Copyright © 2015 by Jack Du Brul

All rights reserved. Published in the United States by Anchor Books, a division of Penguin Random House LLC, New York, and in Canada by Random House of Canada, a division of Penguin Random House Canada Limited, Toronto. Originally published in hardcover in the United States by Doubleday, a division of Penguin Random House LLC, New York, in 2015.

Anchor Books and colophon are registered trademarks of Penguin Random House LLC.

The Library of Congress has cataloged the Doubleday edition as follows
Du Brul, Jack B.
The lightning stones : a novel.—First edition.
pages ; cm
I. Title.
PS3554.U223L54 2015
813'.54—dc23   2015006983

Anchor Books Premium Mass-Market
ISBN: 978-0-307-45479-9
eBook ISBN: 978-0-385-54037-7

www.anchorbooks.com

Printed in the United States of America

10 9 8 7 6 5 4 3 2 1

For Cathy and Jim Saunders
No husband has had better in-laws

THE
LIGHTNING
STONES

PROLOGUE

Here she lay, in a tumbledown hotel on the edge of a jungle at the far end of the world. The knocks came soft and timid.

"Who is it?" she called, her voice husky with the sleep she so desperately craved.

"Miss Earhart?" a man asked tentatively.

Married to publishing magnate George Putnam for the last six years, she resigned herself to the fact that she would forever be known as Amelia Earhart, America's flying darling.

"Yes?" From her tone, she was clearly irked.

"Bert Hoover sent you a telegram and said I need to see you. I'm Mike Dillman."

It took her a few seconds to place the names. She'd received dozens of telegrams upon her arrival from Australia, mostly from George, but there were others as well, fans wishing her well. The cable the stranger just mentioned had taken her by surprise.

"Give me a moment," Amelia said, and slid out of bed.

She grabbed up her robe, a thin, diaphanous garment that weighed but a few ounces and was one of her few feminine conceits during the circumnavigation. She slipped it over her shoulders and looked to see her reflection in a small mirror by the silvery moonlight filtering through the hotel room's only window. She didn't think she looked much like America's flying darling just then, but there was little she could do about it.

She opened the teak door, a relic salvaged off an old steamer with slats on the bottom that allowed tropical air to circulate throughout her room.

Just enough light from the downstairs lounge reached the hallway for Amelia to see that Mike Dillman looked like he'd just crawled from the grave. His hair was lank and plastered to his sunken-cheeked skull. His eyes were nestled deeply in dark, bruised sockets, and while he was probably past fifty, his skin sagged like that of a man twice that age. She couldn't fathom a circumstance where this man and Bert Hoover traveled in the same circles, and yet Bert had vouched for this cadaverous stranger and had asked that she perform a favor for them both. She would have ignored the request had it come from a less important person, and seeing Dillman firsthand, she still might.

"We don't have much time, Miss Earhart," Dillman said, and coughed. He tried to suppress the rattling rail in his chest by hacking into the sleeve of his tattered shirt. When he moved it from his mouth, blood stained the cloth and a little clung to his lip.

She was instantly concerned. "Are you all right?"

"Not really," the shell of a man replied with a tired, resigned smile, "but it doesn't matter. Can you please get dressed and take me to your plane?"

Uncertain, a little frightened, and yet intrigued, she nodded. "I'll just be a minute."

She left Dillman in the hallway while she threw on a clean pair of riding britches and pulled her flying boots up along her calves. The boots were custom made. A gift from George, much like the entire heady existence she called her life. It was no secret that he used her fame as an aviatrix to sell newspapers, and she used the money he gave her for these wild expeditions to feed her addiction to flying. For surely that was what infected her so terribly and yet so fulfillingly. Wasn't that the definition of addiction, the unbreakable desire to do something you know is wrong, or dangerous, or immoral?

That was how she felt about being in the cockpit. She should be home raising a family, and not halfway around the globe from her husband attempting to be the first person, not just woman, but the first person to circumnavigate the earth near the equator. She had been the second person to solo the Atlantic, but the record books would tout her being the first woman, as if gender had anything to do with the ability to fly an airplane. Well, this time she'd have both titles and would make damn sure the headlines didn't commodify her sex.

She shrugged into a shirt over a bra that hadn't yet dried from its earlier washing. It felt like clammy hands were cupping her barely-there breasts.

Dillman was leaning against the wall, asleep on his feet and startled when she reopened her door. He suppressed another cough.

"I know this place seems like a backwater, but they do have a doctor here," Amelia offered.

"No," the disheveled man said. "I'll be fine."

Earhart shook her head and then led him downstairs and through the Hotel Cecil's quiet lobby. Men were still drinking in the adjoining bar, but none saw the pair exit out into the moonlit night. The hotel was located on the waterfront of this sleepy coastal fishing village. Earhart started walking north, where an airstrip had been carved out of the jungle and Guinea Airlines had erected a hangar. It was late enough that all of the houses were dark. Water lapped turgidly on the nearby beach.

"We have to go to my boat first," Dillman called, and preceded Amelia Earhart down to a lone jetty about two hundred paces east of the hotel.

Tied to the bamboo and teak dock was a thirty-foot single-masted sloop with a darkened hull and off-white deck. It looked as dilapidated as the man who had sailed it here. The deck was covered in various stains, and the hull looked like it was home to every barnacle and woodworm in the South Seas. She had no idea where he had sailed from, but she wouldn't trust this tub to take her across the lagoon.

"You're braver than you look, Mr. Dillman."

He looked at her queerly, not getting the joke. "I need a hand with the chest."

That's when Amelia noticed a tin steamer trunk resting on the deck next to the spindly ship's wheel. The case was battered and dented, and whatever color it had once been painted was chipped clear off. Parts of the trunk were blackened as though it had been rescued from a fire. It seemed fitting luggage for both sailboat and sailor.

"Is that what Bert wants me to fly to Hawaii?"

"Yes, a representative from the navy will meet you when you land and take possession of the trunk."

"I could fly it all the way to Oakland," she said.

"No. There will be too much publicity when you land there. Crowds can be controlled easier in Honolulu. Also, this needs to be put in safekeeping as soon as possible. It attracts lightning, Miss Earhart. I have it shielded as best I can, but you must avoid electrical storms."

"No problem there," she said, stepping aboard the sloop after Dillman. "I've been doing that since leaving the States in May. What's in the trunk?"

"Geological samples."

They both bent and lifted the case.

"Geesh, fella, I kinda have a weight limit, you know."

"This weighs sixty-four pounds exactly." He said this solemnly, because these sixty-four pounds had been his constant companion as well as hated burden for the better part of a month. And in all that time he'd fled from dark forces who wanted the contents of the trunk for themselves. "Can you make allowances for it?"

His voice was pleading, and his eyes were even more haunted. At that moment she understood that the responsibility of transporting the trunk, from wherever his journey had started, was likely what had so wasted the man. When he had started out, Mike Dillman had probably been a robust individual and not the withered husk standing before her. She also recognized that he no longer had the strength to continue and that she was the last hope for getting the contents of the trunk into the hands of the United

States Navy. Bert had cabled that this was of utmost importance to national security, but it was the fact that this man had sacrificed himself, and not the patriotic call to duty, that convinced her to see his labor completed.

"Sure, we can figure something out. Heck, I'm a good ten pounds lighter since starting this jaunt. Finding another fifty pounds should be a cinch."

They carried the trunk off the pier and through the sleepy village and finally into the metal-sided hangar at the edge of a primeval jungle. Her Lockheed Electra gleamed like a silver shark even in the dim light of the stars and low moon. Because she was a tail-dragger, her nose was pointed upward at an angle that reminded Amelia of a dog sniffing the air. The plane's big radial engines were nestled in cowlings along the wings and looked big enough to power a bomber. She loved this plane as no other before and still felt guilty about damaging it in Hawaii last spring on her first circumnavigation attempt.

Working by torchlight, Dillman assisted Amelia in removing some gear from the aircraft's nose storage locker. Some would need to be left behind, while other items, like the dozens of stamped souvenir folios, could be moved into the main cabin she shared with Fred Noonan. It took them about a half hour.

He escorted her back to the hotel, shook her hand, thanked her, and wished her a pleasant journey. He moved off into the darkness and allowed the night to swallow him whole.

Amelia felt an odd sense of superstitious dread, not for her safety but for Dillman's. She felt certain he was slated to die. She shook herself to dispel the chill and stepped back into her hotel.

"I thought you went to your room," Fred Noonan, her navigator, said. He was just leaving the bar and headed for the stairs to retire for the night.

Amelia studied him for a moment. Fred had a reputation as a heavy drinker, but she could see no obvious sign he had gotten himself drunk before the most dangerous leg of their trip. His eyes weren't glassy, he wasn't swaying, and his speech had the crisp diction of a trained aviator.

"Couldn't sleep," she replied. "I thought a walk would help."

Noonan smiled. "Nervous about tomorrow's hop?"

She laughed. "I have no reason to be nervous. All I have to do is fly the kite. It's you who has to find Howland Island, a speck in the otherwise endless Pacific Ocean."

"Piece of cake," he said with a cocky twinkle in his eye.

This truly would be a test of the navigator's arcane ability to discern their location. Howland Island, some twenty-five hundred miles away, was a coral atoll that sat by itself in one of the most uninhabited stretches on the planet. Off by even a fraction of a degree, they would fly on until their fuel ran out and die crashing into the ocean. Their lives were literally in his hands once they took off.

They climbed the stairs together, and Fred saw her to her room. She undressed in the darkness and slipped back between the sheets, making sure the mosquito netting was properly draped around her bed. Sleep was elusive. She tossed and turned until midnight before drifting into unconsciousness. Her dreams weren't of flying but of battling a massive storm in Mike Dillman's dilapidated sloop. He was with her but said nothing as wave after wave broke over the bows and sluiced through the cockpit.

She woke with a start when in the dream another in the endless series of swells doused her and Dillman, but when she cleared her eyes of stinging salt water, the cadaverous man was gone. She heaved in fast breaths while wrestling to get her heart under control.

Knowing how grueling the upcoming flight would be, she willed herself to calm down and at least rest until dawn.

She managed a few hours more sleep, but when the sun rose, she rose with it. She padded to the shared bathroom and got herself presentable before dressing and heading downstairs, where Fred was having breakfast with James Collopy, the regional director for Australia's civil aviation agency.

She greeted both men and ordered tea and eggs from Mrs. Stewart, the Hotel Cecil's genial owner.

"Looks like a good day to make some history, Miss Earhart," Collopy said in his melodious Aussie accent.

"What say you, Fred?"

"All the meteorological reports look good. The Coast Guard has the cutter *Itasca* in position off Howland to provide radio direction signals, so I say today is a fine day to make history."

Two hours later they watched as men from Guinea Airlines pushed the fully fueled Electra from their hangar. In the sunlight her skin gleamed like a mirror. She was loaded with over a thousand gallons of fuel, more than enough for the eighteen-hour flight even with the headwind they anticipated. Both pilot and navigator took one final turn in the restroom next to the airline office inside the hangar and then climbed atop the aircraft. The cabin doors had been sealed for added aerodynamics, so they had to crawl through a hatch cut into the roof above the cockpit and behind the direction finder's loop. Fred lowered himself first and plopped down into the navigator's station. Amelia waved one last time at the dozens of well-wishers lining the grass airstrip and slid into the pilot's chair.

In minutes she had the two radial engines humming nicely, with the props blurred to near invisibility. It was coming up on ten o'clock local time or midnight GMT. She waited until Fred gave a signal that his freshly calibrated chronograph read the hour, and she eased on more power. The overloaded plane waddled at first and then picked up speed. Though it was a grass field, it felt as smooth as tarmac. The plane continued to accelerate, and when they hit the spot where a road crossed the runway, the Electra bounced into the air and Amelia managed to keep her aloft. They flashed over the shoreline so low that the propellers threw rooster tails of water in their wake. Slowly and with patience beyond her thirty-nine years, the Lady Lindy flew the Electra up to a cruising altitude of eight thousand feet.

About ten miles from shore, the plane was still clawing to gain altitude when Amelia saw smoke rising from the ocean below. She grabbed a pair of binoculars and focused the lenses. It was a ship on fire—a sloop, in fact—and motoring away from it was another, larger sailing ship. She needed no imagination to realize the burning sloop was Mike Dillman's and that the haunted man was doubtlessly dead. It was quite likely that someone valued the samples Dillman had entrusted her with not in dollars and cents, but in human life.

She was torn. She should turn around and report what she'd seen, but an investigation would take days, or even weeks, and the military was waiting for the trunk. She allowed a debate to run back and forth in her head for a solid fifteen minutes, until she was far enough away from the burning sloop that she could justify her inaction and continue on. She didn't feel good about what she'd done—or not done—and rationalized it by telling herself it was what Dillman would have wanted. In truth it was her desire to finish the world-record circumnavigation that kept her from doing what she knew was right.

Fred was in the back of the cabin at the navigator's station, where he would be able to shoot the sun and stars out of a special window. He never suspected a thing.

At various times during the flight, Amelia would take the Electra down to five hundred feet so Noonan could judge their true speed over the water versus the airspeed indicated in the cockpit. All this was necessary to pinpoint their location relative to Howland Island, which was getting roughly a hundred and fifty miles closer with each passing hour.

After nightfall, he made his first star shot and calculated their position. He wrote a slight course correction with a grease pencil on a whiteboard, and flicked it toward the cockpit on the pulley cable rigged between his seat and hers. That was one of the things that so surprised people when they landed at the various airports they'd used around the world—the two of them didn't talk to each other during the flight. All communications were written down and passed back and forth.

Hours elapsed and the sun began to rise. Everything was going according to plan—everything, that is, except for the fact that they couldn't find their destination. Amelia had been able to communicate with the Coast Guard cutter *Itasca* a couple of times, but she could not get a radio direction signal on the predetermined frequency. She asked them to change to an alternate frequency, but the ship didn't respond.

By even her dead reckoning they had passed the tiny island a half hour ago. They were still picking up scraps of communication, but she couldn't raise the ship. She jotted a note asking what Fred thought they should do—keep going in the belief that the headwinds had been stronger than estimated and hope the island was still ahead of them, or double back and try to approach on a different vector. She also wrote down that they had an hour of fuel remaining.

Noonan took a few minutes to reply, but soon enough the pulley squealed behind her. He'd written, "I didn't screw up. Howland is ahead of us."

That was good enough for her. They continued onward, even after the chatter from the Coast Guard ship eventually faded to a static-laced silence.

Amelia Earhart and Fred Noonan flew into the pages of history and remain one of aviation's most enduring legends. Earhart flew true that leg of the flight, taking her modified Lockheed twin-engine beauty on the exact route Noonan provided. And for his part, Fred Noonan, once a navigation instructor for the storied Pan Am flying clippers, directed them exactly right according to the equipment he had.

What he didn't know, what he couldn't have known, was that an electromagnetic force was acting on his mechanical chronographs. Without accurate time, his sun and star shots were off by well over a degree within the first hour of the flight, and the error increased throughout the journey. The radio signals they'd picked up from the cutter *Itasca* had reached them over a freak skip across the ionosphere. They were never even close to Howland. And all this was caused by their cargo—what Mike Dillman had called "geological samples." They emitted the subtle electromagnetic force that turned what would have been a moderately interesting milestone in aviation history into an event of almost mythic proportions.

1

For the trapped miner the blackness was an absolute. It was his entire world. It filled every nook and cranny in the collapsed tunnel. It was a clammy presence on his skin, like he was pressed up against a corpse. The black had weight, like it was squeezing him as though he wore a too-tight diving suit. And that weight intensified every time he breathed, for the black invaded his lungs, crushing them, making him feel like he was taking in a warm liquid that he had to cough out. It coated the back of his throat like a noxious oil, slick and cloying. It filled his ears, jamming them so even when he screamed as loudly as possible, it sounded like a distant echo of a child's whimper.

The black. It was his entire world, and if rescue didn't come soon he was certain that it would begin to invade his mind as it had already subsumed his body.

Fifty yards and a world away, Hans Gruber, a taciturn German who was sick of the jokes people made about his name, picked his way past a jumble of crushed rock—detritus from the cave-in that littered the floor of the shaft some one thousand feet below the midwestern prairie. He wore heavy work clothes that were streaked and caked with dirt. An oxygen tank was strapped to his back although he and his team hadn't detected any poisonous gases. The LED lamp on his helmet cast a bright blue cone in the otherwise stygian realm in which he worked.

Making the going even tougher were the four-foot-long steel bolts that had once held the collapsed ceiling together. There were hundreds of them sticking up in the rubble that blocked the tunnel, and each one seemed to snag at his clothes and tear at his skin like skeletal fingers. The dust was mostly settled since the cave-in, but motes still hung suspended. The air was perfectly still—a sure sign that the ventilation was not working in this section of the mine. Another in a long string of omens.

Behind him the rest of his crew was busy with the screw jacks. A steel forest had grown in their wake. His men had erected dozens of polelike jacks to help stabilize the hanging wall over their heads and hold back, at least until they could finish with the rescue, the millions of tons of rock above them.

Three hours earlier, on what was otherwise a normal Tuesday in the mines, a crew was shoring up the roof in this section of tunnel by drilling holes into the ceiling and then using a pneumatic tool to twist the screw bolt into the living rock, binding the otherwise unstable matrix until it was no longer a threat to those who had to work under it. This mine was known for poor rock conditions, but men had worked it successfully for years without a fatality from a cave-in. The techniques and safety protocols were perfected and the men followed them to the letter, and yet Mother Nature and gravity care not for proper preparations. Without so much as a groan, a fifty-foot-long section of ceiling at least six feet thick had crashed to the floor of the tunnel. Fortunately the men coming behind the "screw crew" to fill the holes with grout to prevent the metal from rusting in the hot humid air hadn't yet reached the site of the collapse, so none of them were struck by the fall. But there were miners on the far side, and it was up to Gruber and his rescue team to reach them.

As the point man, it was Gruber who wielded the fifteen-pound steel bar and jabbed at the ceiling, prying at loose stones still hanging dangerously above them. The roof over their heads was a fractured mass of stone that could collapse at any second. With each poke and thrust, head-size chunks of stone fell to the scree-littered ground. Many times they would bounce toward Gruber, and he would need to jump aside.

It was hot, filthy work, and sweat cut runnels through the dust, smearing his face. He paused to check on the man directly behind him.

The second rescue worker gave him a nod of encouragement and a thumbs-up. "Yippee-ki-yay, Hans."

For once Gruber didn't mind the *Die Hard* reference. He got back to work, probing and jabbing and inexorably moving deeper and deeper into the collapsed section of the mine. There were three men waiting for him someplace ahead. Odds were they had been horribly crushed, their bodies nothing more than tissue stains, but there was always the chance one or more had been beyond the avalanche and unharmed. It was Gruber's job today to defy the odds and pull them out alive. It was the hope of rescue that allowed men to overcome the twin primal fears of darkness and enclosed spaces, and venture into the hellish mazes of underground mines. Like soldiers behind enemy lines knowing their buddies were looking for them, miners too needed that promise of salvation in order to hold out until help arrived.

Gruber jabbed at yet another weak spot in the ceiling and caused a mini-avalanche of loose rock and at least one boulder to fall. Pebbles rained off his miner's helmet, and for a few seconds the air filled with thick choking dust. He opened the tap on his air tank and took a few purifying breaths before stowing the mask. That air was for the men he was to rescue, he chided himself, not for his own comfort. He crawled on, climbing up and over a taller hillock of stones and debris, pressing himself nearly to the top of the tunnel, his heels scraping the hanging walls as he wriggled forward on his belly. The passage ahead appeared completely blocked.

So far they hadn't had to shift a lot of material, but it seemed now they would have to laboriously clear the tunnel one stone at a time.

Gruber reached and stretched and pressed hard against the wall of junk rock and felt the pile blocking the top couple of feet of the passageway shift. He dug his feet into the debris and pushed even harder, his gloved fists like the blade of a bulldozer as he used his tremendous strength to push the obstruction back and finally down the far side of the hillock.

Even as the rocks skittered and jumbled down deeper into the mine he heard a weak voice cry for help.

With a flash of excitement, Gruber realized he had reached the end of the cave-in.

"I think we have one!" the German shouted. He crawled faster, thrusting his head through the debris as though the earth itself was birthing him.

His light revealed that the tunnel beyond was all but unobstructed. Twenty feet farther in he saw the hulking pneumatic drill machine the miners had been using to bolt the ceiling. And between him and it lay one of the men. The miner's helmet was lying a few feet away, and it looked like one of his legs was pinned.

Gruber wiggled and fought until the rock finally released him, and he slid down the pile of shattered stone and crawled over to the trapped miner. Overhead, the ceiling appeared to be solid and undamaged.

"It's okay," he told the man.

The miner looked to be in shock. He'd been in darkness so long that Gruber's light seemed to blind him.

"Thank God," the man finally said. Gruber held a canteen to the miner's lips and let the man drink thirstily. So much so that he started to choke, and half the fluid he took down came back up again.

"Let's look at your leg. How does it feel?"

"It doesn't hurt," the miner replied with a cough. "It's just pinned."

"We'll have you out and in a bar before you know it."

"Can you find my helmet and turn on the light? It's been so dark . . ." The miner's voice trailed off.

"Sure thing, my friend. What's your name?"

Gruber stretched out to grab the man's helmet.

"I'm Tom Rogers."

Hans flipped the switch to turn on the lamp.

"Boom!" The voice was so loud it echoed.

"Vas?" Gruber gasped, and looked about.

"I said boom," the second rescuer repeated; it was the man who had given Gruber encouragement just moments before. "You just killed yourself, Tom there, and most importantly you killed me."

"*Nein,*" Gruber protested. "*Das ist bullshit.*"

"*Das ist nicht bullsheet,*" the man replied, mimicking Gruber's excited German accent. The second rescuer finished climbing through the tiny aperture and slid down to the tunnel floor on his butt, planting his feet firmly when he landed. When he spoke again any teasing in his voice had evaporated. "Check your gas detector."

Sheepishly, Gruber peeled back the cloth cover of the device hanging in a bag over his shoulder. The detector wasn't switched on for this training exercise, but pieces of paper like a tear-off pad had been affixed over the digital display. As they had progressed through the rescue, Gruber had checked the meter at various way points by tearing off the topmost sheet. The page below had always said "clear." This time he tore off the penultimate piece of paper. Below it was written "Methane at explosive concentrations."

"But I didn't cause any sparks," Gruber protested. "I left the pry bar up on top of the debris, and there is no metal on me that could cause a spark. The methane could not explode."

By now the "trapped" miner, Tom Rogers, had regained his feet and was dusting off his coveralls. Like Hans Gruber, Rogers was another trainee, and he leaned in eagerly to see what had gone wrong. Other than Hans giving him water too fast, which he'd spit back out to indicate the gaffe to his classmate, he thought Gruber had performed a textbook rescue.

"Look at Tom's headlamp," the rescue instructor said.

"The electronics are vacuum sealed," Gruber said. "The lamp cannot cause an explosion."

Philip Mercer pulled off his goggles and headgear, and fixed his gray eyes on Gruber in a serious stare. "That's why I said to look at it," he said with just a trace of irritation.

This was the twentieth time Mercer had led the miners on this, their final test, with each person taking point to show off what they had learned after two weeks of classroom instruction and field training. Mercer was justifiably tired.

Gruber examined the lamp under the white aura of his own. *"Scheisse,"* he cursed when he saw his mistake.

"That's right," Mercer said, pointing to the lamp. "The lens is cracked. That allowed methane to seep into the light, and when you flipped the switch the initial arc of electricity ignited, turning us into so much roast *schnitzel.*" He patted Gruber on the back. "Let's go back to the others."

Mercer let the two students precede him out of the seemingly isolated chamber and then clambered out himself. He was grateful that Hans had been the last of the nineteen men and one woman he'd agreed to train as he himself had once learned mine rescue techniques from South Africa's fabled Proto Teams.

Mercer had designed the curriculum himself, and with the help of the mine's owner had built several subterranean obstacle courses to challenge his students. He'd built this one by loading a particularly tall shaft with overburden brought down from the slag heaps on the surface. Another course he had rigged with smoke machines to simulate fire, while a third could be flooded using seep water pumped up from a lower level. In all, Mercer had shown them the basics of what they would find in a real-world mine rescue. He'd been in on enough actual rescues to know you can't plan for everything, and the ability to think on one's feet was as crucial as being well practiced.

Mercer still received cards from many of Los 33, the Chilean miners he'd helped rescue back in 2010, and expected he would for many years to come. It had been his gut call, in coordination with a local engineer, as to where to drill the escape shaft 2,300 feet into the bedrock in order to save the thirty-three men who'd been trapped for a record-setting sixty-nine days. In a life and career filled with proud moments, Philip Mercer had to concede that that was one of the best.

The rest of his students were waiting in a panic shelter carved into the side of a main tunnel about a hundred yards from where he'd constructed the "cave-in." The shelter had once been provisioned to last forty men a week in case of an emergency, but this former copper mine had been abandoned in the late eighties when it became too expensive to work profitably. An adjacent rock quarry was still going strong, but the Leister Deep Mine was played out.

The room was just barren stone walls and a smoothed-out rock floor. Power was supplied by a jury-rigged system using wires Mercer had run off a generator that he'd jacked into an old ventilation conduit. He wasn't sure if the exhaust actually made it to the surface a thousand feet above them, but carbon monoxide levels hadn't risen, so he figured he'd done something right.

These people had come from all over the world to study rescue techniques from him, and for the most part he'd been pleased with their progress. All of them were type A's, especially Kara Hawkins, the sole woman. She was a shift foreperson at a newly reopened Nevada silver mine who had arrived here on a Harley Softail Heritage Classic wearing full black leathers over her six-foot frame and dispelled any question of her sexual preference by sharing a bed with José Cabrillo, a mine engineer from Bolivia who looked and sounded like a young Ricardo Montalban.

"Well?" Gerhard Werner asked when Hans appeared with Tom and then Mercer. The two Germans were longtime friends who worked at the same mine back home.

Hans slashed a finger across his throat. "*Kaput.*"

"Gather round," Mercer called, wiping sweat from his face with a towel and then swigging from a water bottle someone had handed him. The water was cold thanks to the fridge they'd lugged down. And like a sports team they all took a knee to listen to their coach. "Half the class made the same mistake."

Gerhard interrupted, saying, "Hans turned on the lamp too."

"He did," Mercer said, "but that wasn't his main mistake. No, the mistake many of you made was listening to the victim. Think of this like saving someone who is drowning. Have any of you gotten lifeguard certification?"

He looked at the blank, sooty faces. Most of the miners were from rural coal country in whichever nation they called home. They were rednecks and hayseeds, and he didn't think fishin' holes and cricks had much in the way of swimmer safety. Still, he could tell they wanted to please him.

"Okay," he went on after a beat. "First thing they teach you is to always approach a drowning person from behind. Anyone want to guess why?"

A hand went up.

"José."

"If he see you he gonna try to drown you."

"Basically that's it," Mercer agreed. "The swimmer won't mean to drown you, but the human panic reflex when drowning is to grab anything nearby and climb on top of it, and that especially includes would-be rescuers."

"And you're saying that a trapped miner is like that drowning swimmer," another of the men said.

"I am. Now, why?" This time a few hands went up. "Jimmy."

The drawl was pure Kentucky. "'Cause he's gonna be all panic like and we're the calm ones. We know what's best for him 'cause we been trained."

"You do your holler proud, Jimmy," Mercer said with a smile. "For our foreign guests I will translate that answer into English."

A few of the other West Virginian and fellow Kentucky miners poked Jimmy Carson in the ribs. The students responded well to Mercer's style, a combination of patient indulgence with mistakes, vast knowledge of the subject, and an easy sense of humor. They had a good time but they were learning skills that might one day save lives.

"The miner you come across," Mercer went on, "has been alone and in the dark. He's hungry, thirsty, hurt, scared, and begging for his momma. It doesn't matter if he's been down there six hours or six weeks, since time is meaningless when you're facing the black. He wants out—and he may well see you as an impediment to his salvation rather than its harbinger. All of you have to remember to stay in command at all times, the way a cop or fireman would. Like them, we know the rules. The victims don't.

"Tom wanted his light turned on, but providing a victim additional light is not a priority. It might make him feel more secure, but that's not a necessity to save his life. Assessing the situation, the rock stability, gas levels, the victim's medical condition. These are the things you focus on first.

"If you take anything away from this training seminar it is these two things." Mercer's voice carried a serious tone that seemed to seep into the stone walls. "First thing is to thank the stars you're not a Chinese miner." This got a few dark chuckles as they had spent part of a classroom session going over the horrors of the Chinese mining industry. "But seriously, know that if you are ever called upon to use the skills we've worked on together, then some fellow miner is having the worst day of his life—and his life is in your hands. Don't make the situation worse by forgetting your training."

Mercer let them think about that for a few seconds before smacking his hands together to break the hypnotic mood. "Okay, children, I have taught you at least the basics, and despite a few gaffes that were not *bullsheet*, Hans . . . you've all passed the course." A round of spontaneous applause broke out in the room. "And," Mercer continued, "that means dinner tonight is on me."

The miners roared their approbation, even if the local eatery was a kitschy overdecorated chain restaurant. It had thirty kinds of beer on tap, and all of them were cold.

They started moving off in a raucous gang, like schoolkids anticipating summer vacation. Mercer stood, watching them go.

Teaching mine rescue techniques wasn't his primary job. Mercer was a prospecting geologist and mine engineer. He was the hired gun called in when big mining companies needed a second opinion before committing hundreds of millions of dollars to open a new pit or shaft, or when they needed guidance to maximize claims they were already working. Mercer was credited with finding billions of dollars' worth of extractable ore, be it something as ordinary as bauxite deposits for aluminum smelting, or as exotic as the sapphires from a mine in India that was producing some of the finest gemstones ever discovered. His career had taken him to almost every corner of the planet and had made him a wealthy man, but one who did not forget the roots of his success. Mercer felt a responsibility to his profession to give back a little of his hard-won experience. In fact, his pay for the weeks here in Minnesota was less than a tenth of what he earned consulting. But some things in life weren't about money.

"Dr. Mercer."

"Just Mercer, Tom," he said to the one student who'd hung back. "The doctor title is only used getting dinner reservations."

"I just wanted to thank you for everything. It's been real interesting."

"Well, let me say this with all sincerity, I hope to God you never need to use what you've learned."

It took a second for the young miner to catch Mercer's meaning. "I hope the same thing. Thank you."

They shook hands. Tom Rogers turned for the long walk to the mine head, where the lifts to the surface were located. Mercer didn't move. "You coming?"

"No," Mercer said. "I want to check out the science team that's leased out another part of the mine. I'll see you at the restaurant."

Mercer moved into a side chamber and killed the generator he'd rigged to run the lights and mini-fridge. The silence and darkness were profound. It was complete sensory deprivation—such an alien experience that most people couldn't stand it for more than a few minutes. Many panicked in seconds. Mercer could have stood there for eternity. He flicked on his helmet light and moved off down the tunnel, away from where his men had vanished around a corner. They were headed to the main lifting station. Mercer made for the auxiliary elevator shaft, his step light even in steel-toed boots.

The science team wasn't actually his primary interest. They were here at the Leister Deep Mine doing some research on climate change and cosmic rays. They needed to be underground and at this particular mine because the copper vein was situated below a thousand-foot-thick slab of iron ore. Though not commercially viable to mine, the ore acted as a shield to certain galactic rays while admitting others. It was, embarrassingly, a bit out of his field.

The problem with modern science, he mused, was that it had become so specialized that a geologist like him hadn't the foggiest idea what was happening in a related field such as climatology. Both were earth sciences, but so widely divergent that the men and women down here could be doing voodoo incantations as part of their research for all he knew.

No, Mercer's real interest was not in this particular research, but in Abraham Jacobs. Jacobs was one of the faculty advisers on the team, an éminence grise of Penn State University and later Carnegie Mellon, and was now retired but still consulted at a small private college in eastern Ohio. Far more than an adviser, Jacobs had been Mercer's mentor during his time at Penn State while he had earned his doctorate in geology.

When asked about his background, Mercer liked to quip he was African American. People looked at his white skin and storm-gray eyes and usually cocked a questioning eyebrow, until Mercer would explain that he was born in Africa, to an American father and a Belgian mother. His parents were killed in a forgotten uprising in a forgotten part of what was then Zaire, and he was raised by his paternal grandparents. They were wonderful people who tended to all his childhood needs, but it was Abe Jacobs who really became Mercer's role model and surrogate father.

They had drifted apart as Mercer's career skyrocketed, only to reconnect in recent years. The two men, master instructor and star student, had tried to see each other now at least once a year. It had been eighteen months since their last visit—and Mercer was further burdened by guilt because monthly phone calls had degenerated to occasional texts—so he walked with an eager step down the lightless tunnel.

Mercer had accepted this offer to teach mine rescue in the Leister Deep because he knew Abe would be here helping on the research project. According to their last communication, Abe would be arriving today, while the principal investigator and her postdocs and undergrads had been here setting up the experiment over the course of the past week.

Mercer came to a lighted nexus point where several tunnels came together. The secondary lift was a utilitarian cage behind a steel accordion door and was only in working condition because the bulk of the abandoned mine's upper levels had been turned into a climate-controlled storage facility totaling some eight million square feet. Down where Mercer had taught his course, and deeper still where the scientists worked, the air was too humid for storage, but since part of the facility was occupied, all of its safety and operations gear had to work properly no matter where it was located.

He stepped onto the open mesh floor of the lift cage and closed the door behind him. Below his feet was a profound blackness that seemed to want to suck him into its embrace. He depressed the control handle, and the elevator slid out from the glow of the subterranean crossroads and plunged downward. Had he wanted, Mercer could have brushed the rock of the shaft as the car dropped deeper into the earth. The stone was roughhewn, and it always amazed him that whoever had excavated this shaft had been the first creature ever to have laid eyes on this particular rock.

That concept gave him pause while he was in the field searching for the next mother lode, splitting open stones with a rock hammer and knowing that what he was looking at had never once seen the light of day. More than most, Mercer understood that humanity was a blip on the geologic timeline.

He descended another five hundred feet. From the dim light filtering up from below, Mercer could see that he was nearing the mine's deepest complex of tunnels. He eased off the controls to slow the elevator and flicked it off when the car matched the depth of another accordion door. Beyond was a well-lit chamber much like the one above. Unlike a commercial elevator with automatic safety clamps, this one bobbed for several seconds, a sensation first-timers found very disconcerting. Mercer paused so the tension in the fifteen-hundred-foot cable could equalize before sliding open the door and stepping out into the tunnel.

He had been given two gifts by genetic luck. One was a near-photographic memory, and the other was a spatial sense that allowed him to understand the three-dimensional mazes that were hard-rock mines, and the ability to move about them without fear of getting lost.

Unlike the level where he'd been teaching, there was a lot of equipment stacked about even though this was the secondary lift. The big main elevator was a quarter mile away and could easily transport the massive ore buckets that had once been pulled from this depth as well as the heavy equipment that had been lowered down to mine it. Human nature being what it was, it appeared the scientists preferred using this man-scaled lift to get to work versus the barn-size primary hoist that had transported much of their gear.

Mercer saw they had even brought down electric golf carts and a couple of Segway people movers with fat off-road tires to handle the rough floor. They were plugged into a charging station that ran off the mine's mains.

There's a first time for everything, he thought, as he looked around furtively. Mercer unplugged and then stepped onto one of the two-wheelers, thumbing the "start" button and almost killing himself because he was leaning back slightly and the Segway tried to lurch out from under him. He centered his weight better, and the gyroscopes stabilized the platform. He took a firmer grip on the handlebars, leaned forward, and was amazed at how smoothly the awkward machine moved. In seconds he was weaving it from side to side down the tunnel like a veteran rider.

This section of the mine had been carved using the "room and pillar" technique. Mercer thought it an odd choice, since usually coal was taken from the earth in that way. The rooms were vast, tens of thousands of square feet, and they were supported at regular intervals by pillars of unmined ore that formed columns to hold up the roof. Mercer zipped silently through several such yawning caverns, until he approached the side chamber where he knew the scientists had set up their experiment. Outside the chamber were a half dozen golf carts and Segways as well as mechanical transporters fashioned for use in low-ceilinged spaces. These were real mining machines, designed so the operator sat in a cage off to the side of the vehicle rather than a cab atop it. They were old and dented, with fading paint, relics of a time when the mine was in operation. Lord knew how the team of eggheads had gotten them running, but the flatbeds had been used to haul the bulk of their scientific apparatus from the main lift.

Mercer left his Segway next to the others and stepped over to look at one of the transporters. It had a forward cab with a diesel engine behind it, and an articulated bed that had to have been fifty feet long. There were multiple sets of small solid rubber wheels, which filled Mercer's mind with an image of a rudimentary mechanical centipede.

The thought was interrupted by a sudden sound—
one Mercer had first heard on the day his parents had
been mowed down by African rebels. He had heard
it many times since. It was the staccato ratchet of automatic weapons fire.

2

Instinct and experience told Mercer he was hearing machine pistols like an Uzi, but more likely the popular Heckler & Koch MP5s. The H&K was the preferred weapon of elite fighting forces like Delta or the SEALs. The weapons' sound had been suppressed with very good silencers, not some jury-rigged contraptions, but precision milled tubes with the correct sequence of baffles and discharge holes.

The incongruity of hearing suppressed gunfire deep in an underground mine didn't slow Mercer's reflexes. He had launched himself over the transporter's bed even before the machine pistols went silent. He snuggled up to the wheeled train as best he could, snapping off his miner's lamp and peering into the darkness between the close-set tires. His body was awash in adrenaline and his heart rate was spiking, and yet he was able to keep his breathing calm and deliberate.

Thirty feet ahead was the entrance to the antechamber where Abe and the others would be working. Mercer could just discern a lessening of the mine's

absolute blackness. To call it light was being too generous, but there was a faint corona far beyond the
opening and a few stray photons leaked out. Screams
echoed from the entrance, followed by another burst
from the machine pistols. Mercer saw the shadow of
flickering light, the telltale muzzle flash of autofire.

This time when the weapons fell silent, there were
no more screams. He had no idea what was happening and wished it was some elaborate joke, but he
knew it wasn't. Mercer remained motionless and silent, straining to see anything.

About one minute after the second burst and Mercer was beginning to move closer, when he saw a
sudden shift in the darkness. The patch of less-black
space—the entrance to the experiment chamber—
blinked four times. It was the silhouettes of four men
walking out of that room. They displayed no light
whatsoever, but the speed with which they emerged
and the precise interval between them told Mercer
they were acting as though they could see.

They had to be using thermal imaging, or they
were wearing light emitters in the ultraviolet band
with goggles that could distinguish it. With such
equipment, the tunnel would look illuminated while
the men themselves remained in absolute darkness.
The military used the system sparingly, because an
enemy with the right goggles could easily see the UV
light from the emitters.

Their shoes made barely a whisper as they jogged
through the massive room and disappeared into the
forest of support pillars. Mercer slithered from where
he'd hidden, moving cautiously in the dark. He didn't
dare turn on his headlamp. He inched closer to where
the gunmen had emerged, making certain each of his

footsteps was firmly on solid ground before trans-
ferring his weight. When he reached the entrance he
could better see the glow of distant light that had
found its way around several walls. He went down a
short corridor that twisted left, then right, and then
left again. Around each bend he was rewarded with
more light until he finally emerged into a circular
chamber with three sets of yellow construction lights
atop spindly tripods. One of them had been knocked
over and only shone a weak beam that still managed
to capture some of the horror. That lamp reflected off
a smear of blood on the stone floor as bright as lipstick.

The other lights painted a sickening tableau. There
had been six people down here. Four men and two
women. One of the women was nearest the felled
light, and it was blood from a wound in her neck that
was caught in its beam. By the slashes and swirls it
looked as though the woman had convulsed as her
heart pumped her life out of her shredded carotid.
The second woman had taken several bullets to the
chest, her body tossed back onto a table loaded with
computers and scientific gear so that her feet dangled
above the floor.

The men had fared just as poorly. Two looked like
they had been hit in the back, most likely during the
opening pulse of lead when the gunmen had entered
the chamber. Another appeared to have been running
laterally across the room and took several shots into
his thigh, hip, and torso before augering into a stack
of gas cylinders like those used by welders.

The fourth man was Abe Jacobs. It looked to
Mercer like he had tried to use his body to shield the
woman who had bled out. His chest was a bloody

mess, and his full beard—a source of pride that hung down past his neck—was stained like red steel wool. In the middle of the room was a heap of thick glass that had been shattered. Hoses ran from the pile to a central mixing control that looked like an oilfield manifold, which itself was fed from several of the gas cylinders. These were the remains of a cloud chamber they were using in their experiments. Nearby was a copper box with a hinged lid whose function he couldn't guess.

Mercer took all of this in with a quick sweep. He rushed to Abe's side, dropping to his knees and grabbing for the old man's hand, but it was futile. Abe had probably been dead even before his body had hit the hard stone floor.

Mercer expected tears but none came. Instead he felt a hot anger building in the pit of his stomach. He stood and quickly checked the others. Had there been a chance to save any of them he would have remained to dress wounds and comfort the victims, but there was nothing he could do for any of these people. At least, not by sitting in this chamber.

With hands made sticky by blood, Mercer ran out of the room and back into the main chamber. His miner's lamp couldn't penetrate more than a couple of feet, so the darkness beyond the beam was an unknown world of inky shadow where one of the gunmen could be lurking in wait for any sign of pursuit. Mercer glanced above his head and saw that the science team had strung lights from the main shaft to their science chamber. These people weren't miners accustomed to the black. They would want as much light down here as possible.

The assault team had smashed the bulbs as they

approached, which told Mercer they were likely retracing their steps using thermal imagers tracking the still-hot filaments. Mercer wore thick coveralls that trapped a massive amount of heat, and his body was only about fifteen degrees cooler than the mine's musty air. The commandos wouldn't be able to see him until he was practically on top of them.

He leapt aboard the Segway and leaned as far forward as he dared, the gawky wheeled platform taking off, if not like a shot, then a lot faster than Mercer could run for the mile he needed to cover to reach the main lift. The wind across his face told him he was moving at a good clip.

Now it was calculations of relative speeds and distances. How quickly would the gunmen want to make their escape without making noise? Full tilt, would be Mercer's guess. Meaning they would be running flat out, hampered only by the need to wear the thermal imaging goggles. Call it a seven-minute mile. They had a two-minute head start even before Mercer went to check on Abe and the others. Another minute lost.

The math was irrefutable. He couldn't catch up to them. His only hope was they were somehow delayed in getting into the three-story-tall main lift cage.

Mercer finally saw lights up ahead. At this level, the area around the lift station had been carved into a massive cavern, with roads leading off into the rock strata as well as ramps and chutes to feed the multiple levels of the personnel lift or the tall ore skip. The support structure around the elevator looked like a quarry's loading platform, with three stories' worth of steel and tangles of piping and ore processors. There were simply too many lightbulbs for the commandos to smash, so they left the chamber alone.

Mercer slowed to a stop just before he burst into the cavern and jumped from the Segway. He hadn't thought through what he would do if he succeeded in catching the murderers. He was completely unarmed. The best he could hope to accomplish was to warn the top-side lift crew to trap the shooters in the elevator until the police could be called.

He edged out of the blackened tunnel and took up a position behind a small tracked excavator that had been abandoned decades ago. The machine had been stripped for spare parts so it resembled an insect's husk after being devoured by ants.

He spotted the gunmen right away. They were climbing the scissor stairs on the side of the loading platform, heading for the top tier of the three-story elevator car. There were four of them dressed in black tactical gear. Each had high-tech goggles pushed up on his forehead, and they carried silenced machine pistols. These weren't MP5s as he'd surmised but something newer and even more sinister, weapons designed to do one thing and one thing only—kill humans. One of the men also had a large pack over his shoulders, and judging by his posture it appeared its contents were heavy.

The elevator car was already in position. The men needed only to step into it, close the grate, and send the signal to the operator up on the surface. Once they were up the shaft a few hundred feet, Mercer planned to break cover and reach the intercom mounted just outside the lift doors.

His plan changed a moment later when the lead gunman mounted the loading platform and nonchalantly shot out the intercom. Even as the muted echoes of the silenced shots faded, Mercer could see the panel sparking and sputtering.

He didn't think. He acted.

Mercer rushed from his hiding place and ran as fast as he could, while above him the men were stepping into the elevator cage. He ignored the ground-level loading platform and instead threw himself down a set of stairs that gave access to the bottom level.

A gunman slammed the gate closed on the top compartment, and a second later a bell toned. Mercer reached the last step. The gate was closed in front of him, and he could just see the bottom of the thirty-foot-tall elevator begin to rise.

With this lift, unlike a commercial one, Mercer could open the gate to gain direct access to the elevator shaft itself. Miners were well trained in elevator safety and could be trusted not to kill themselves by doing anything deliberately stupid. Like Mercer was doing now.

The elevator was a functional three-chambered steel cage attached to a hoist on the surface. Simple signals told the operator at which level to stop the lift. They were at the lowest level, and Mercer knew this elevator was going straight for the surface.

A cable dangled in a loop from under the car. It was a standard armored metal electrical wire that had worked itself loose from a couple of brackets. Below it, the shaft dropped another twelve feet into a sump to collect rainwater seepage. A nearby pump kept the water at manageable levels.

Mercer didn't break stride or think through what he was doing. As the monstrous elevator car began its ascent, he jumped for the cable just before it rose out of reach. Mercer barely got his fingertips around the steel before his momentum slammed him against the rough-hewn shaft wall and nearly wrenched his shoulder from its socket. He scrambled to get a better grip as he pendulumed beneath the fast-rising elevator. He finally got his second hand onto the wire and chanced looking down. The light from the loading station appeared as distant as the glow of a celestial constellation. And even as he watched, the elevator rose high enough for the light to fade completely. Darkness sucked at his dangling boots.

Mercer wriggled an arm through the cable loop to take the strain off his hands, and another of the riveted brackets securing the cable to the car snapped. The pop couldn't be heard over the mechanical grind of the car, but Mercer's sudden gasp as he fell a few inches sounded to him like a thunderous scream. Not twenty feet above him were four heavily armed men who showed no compunction over committing murder. With a good flashlight, they could easily see Mercer through the car's floor and ceiling grates.

He readjusted his position, gaining a better grip on the cable, which for now seemed to be holding. He looked up. Two of the shooters held lit flashlights, but neither was directed downward. They were already five hundred feet up from the bottom of the shaft, with another thousand to go. Had there been sufficient light, Mercer probably would have started panicking. As it was he forced himself not to think of the widening chasm between his bicycling legs and the ground far below.

The elevator continued to rocket upward, rattling and scraping in a trip that never seemed to end. They shot past the level where Mercer had been teaching mine rescue. There were no lights to mark the opening, but he felt the brief change in air pressure as they soared beyond it.

Mercer's arms were beginning to tire as lactic acid

built up in muscles that were already sore after a day spent crawling through simulated cave-ins. He swung his body just enough to throw a leg over the loop, and he hung there like a lemur, alternating hands to give each a rest.

He had no idea how he was going to get out of the shaft once he reached the top, but for now all that mattered was keeping close to the shooters. It struck him that the killers had probably shot their way into the mine in the first place, and the operator above was likely at gunpoint.

With a loud pop Mercer's weight caused another bracket to let go, and the downward jerk on the cable snapped two more in rapid succession. His snug little perch, where he could use a hand to steady himself against the elevator's underside, now became a wild swinging ride that saw each arc grow in amplitude and frequency. Mercer's heart raged in his chest as he desperately clutched the cable. The jerkiness made him lose his leg grip, so once again he was hanging over the void with only his hands—which burned with fatigue and felt as though the tendons were going to erupt through the skin.

Thirty agonizing seconds later, the elevator began to slow. It wasn't the staid deceleration of a skyscraper's ergonomically designed lift, which felt as gentle as a jetliner's final approach. This was the brutal jarring slowdown of a military transport dropping into Bagram when the Afghans were launching SAMs at every inbound flight.

Momentum nearly slammed Mercer into the underside of the lift.

The car came to a stop a moment later. The top of the Leister Deep's main shaft was housed in a huge warehouselike building, surrounded by a massive concrete pad. There was just enough light for Mercer to see that below him was a yawning porthole to the abyss, and a drop of more than fifteen hundred feet.

His hands were shaking.

He had to get himself clear as soon as possible. The exit gate was above him. There was only one way to reach it, and that was free climbing in the cramped space between the elevator car itself and the side of the shaft.

Mercer positioned himself so he could contort his body and begin to sway back and forth, building up speed with each turn. He timed it at the height of one of his looping swings and reached out one hand to grab the edge of the car, his fingers fitting into the metal grate. He let go his other hand and quickly threaded it into the grate too so he'd only taken the strain on one hand for a second.

The shooters were talking quietly as they shuffled off the elevator. Had Mercer led the team, he would have sent the elevator back into the depths and disabled it, as well as the smaller secondary lift, so that the murders wouldn't have been discovered for the days it would take to repair them.

He got lucky that the gunmen weren't so thorough.

He heaved and struggled to raise himself in the narrow gap between the shaft wall and the lift. There was barely enough room for his head, and he had to deflate his lungs to get his chest to fit. Blood flowed from where the steel had cut into his fingers. Mercer ignored it all. The killers were already out of the elevator and headed, he supposed, to a getaway vehicle. He had to move fast or he was going to lose them.

He slithered his way to the lowest of the personnel platforms and unlatched the accordion gate. He slid it open just enough to squeeze through. He could hear voices above him. He slowly climbed out and up to ground level. Across from him and up in a control booth was the lift operator's station. It had a large plate-glass window that overlooked the loading platform. The window was spattered with blood, and the body of the operator was slumped in his chair. The blood was still running and oozing down the glass. The local mine worker had done his job by operating the lift, as ordered, and was summarily executed.

A fifth gunman clad in black tacticals was waiting for the others next to a tall rolling door and an idling four-door Ford F-350 pickup. Mercer noted the rear license plate had been removed. He assumed the truck was stolen.

The four men who'd gone down into the mine linked up with their surface support guy. He made a big deal of the backpack, and then they loaded themselves into the dually pickup. In seconds they had pulled out of the building and vanished around a corner.

Mercer launched himself from the stairwell and raced after the truck. He pulled up short when he got outside. It was late afternoon and a cold rain was falling. It was mid-April, but the bitter air held March's chill. The truck was already being swallowed by the gloom. Its taillights flashed as it slowed to let a bucket loader from the nearby gravel quarry pass. And then the truck started to pull away.

The access road to the mine complex was only a mile long, but it went through several tight hairpins as it descended down to a valley where it tied in with a local two-laner. Mercer ran for the bucket loader. It was as large as a semitrailer, with tires that stood as tall as he did, but the excavator moved slowly enough for him to catch up and then vault onto a ladder leading up to the operator's cab.

The driver was shocked when Mercer suddenly appeared and opened the door.

"What the hell do you think you're doing?" he asked angrily. "You could have gotten yourself killed."

"Do you have a cell phone?"

"No reception up here . . . I don't bother. Who are you?"

"I don't have time to explain. That truck that just went past you. The men in it killed six people down in the Leister Deep as well as the hoist operator. Get to a phone and call the police. It's a Ford F-350 dual rear-wheeled pickup with five men in it wearing black tactical uniforms. There's no rear license plate."

The driver took one look into Mercer's slate-gray eyes, recognized the determination behind them, and chose to believe the bizarre story. He cranked the bucket loader's joystick control and added on some more power.

Mercer reached across and chopped the throttle controls back to idle. "I don't think you understand, pal. I'm going after the truck. Get out and run."

"No way, man. I can't let—"

That's as far as Mercer let the operator get. He threw a right fist into a spot below the miner's left ear. His head snapped around and his eyes went glassy. Mercer popped the quick release for the safety belts and hauled the driver out of his chair as the bucket loader continued to slow.

The man was groggy but not out. Mercer frog-marched him down the rear deck to the stairs mounted over the back tires. The driver was starting to come to his senses. Mercer could feel him becoming more resistant. Rather than hitting him again, Mercer collapsed the driver's knee so that he fell back into Mercer's waiting arms. He lowered the operator to the deck and unceremoniously pushed him down the stairs. He rolled like a log and then fell into the mud in a dazed heap.

"Call the police! Have them stop that truck!"

Not knowing what the driver would do, Mercer raced back to the cab and threw himself into the operator's seat. He was in a Caterpillar 990. Not their largest front-end loader, but not too far off the mark, either. He was very familiar with how to drive it, and nearly every other piece of iron that came out of Cat's Peoria, Illinois, plant.

He cranked up the throttle and marveled at the throaty boom of the 625-horsepower diesel. The machine lurched forward. Mercer had no intention of trying to catch the fleeing pickup. He had a quarter of their top speed. What he had, though, was a real off-road capability they could only dream about.

Rather than steer down the broad dirt access road, Mercer directed the 990 over the edge of the plateau where the mine and quarry were located, avoiding the S-shaped switchbacks altogether. The grade was steep, better than forty-five degrees, but there were enough small trees and undergrowth to keep the eighty-ton monster from plunging out of control. Mercer worked the joystick control like a fighter pilot, juking the loader around the larger trees that it couldn't simply bowl over. Saplings as thick around as baseball bats vanished under the massive tires, and branches whipped at the cab, one shattering the side glass.

The loader emerged onto the haul road once again, halving its distance from the speeding pickup that had yet to notice it was being stalked. Like a rampaging elephant, Mercer drove the loader across the road and down another embankment. This time there wasn't anywhere near the same amount of vegetation, and the big machine began to slide on the loose rock and dirt. Mercer fought the instinct to apply the brake and instead hit the gas to straighten out. The back end tucked in behind the front, and he continued to steer down the slope. He hit the next section of flat haul road and was nearly tossed through the windshield by the impact, and for a moment he feared the blow had been enough to dislodge the front axle. But the machine ran on, a snarling testament to American design and construction.

The pickup had just passed by. Mercer could clearly see the marks on the ground from its doubled-up rear tires. The loader sped across the road, and when Mercer put its nose over the next slope, he could see the truck steadily accelerating out of the last hairpin turn. And a sharp-eyed gunman must have seen him too.

A rear window in the dark truck's cab slid down, and the stubby barrel of one of the machine pistols appeared. They must have figured the big Caterpillar machine was chasing after them, and they were taking no chances. The range was extreme for such a weapon, but that didn't stop the shooter from unloading a thirty-round magazine of 9mm Parabellums.

A few shots might have hit the loader. Mercer couldn't hear any strike over the engine's roar, but for good measure he raised the bucket and tilted it outward so that the cab was protected. He urged the machine over the precipice. This time there were bushes and trees, but they were thicker than upslope and Mercer was forced to use the loader's massive weight as well as its powerful engine to bull his way down the mountain. He was forced to lower the bucket and use its lip like a blunt ax to scythe through the scrub and topple trees that rose forty feet or more. His speed was cut in half, and he felt frustration mounting. There was only one more switchback before the haul road met the local byway. Within a quarter mile of the entrance to the mine, there were any number of turnoffs. Even if the loader's driver had called the police, once the shooters reached the public roads they'd vanish inside of a couple of minutes.

If Mercer couldn't stop them, he had to find a way to delay them.

He had the engine roaring like a rhinoceros defending its territory, and the dense copse of trees, saplings, and brush disappeared under the loader's tall rubber tires, but the Ford pickup was also under full power. The driver knew what he was doing, because he power-slid into the last hairpin, letting momentum and centripetal force slew the big truck around onto the final leg of its escape.

They were now charging for the spot where Mercer would emerge back onto the road from his crazy dash down the treacherous slope. If Mercer was late and they made it past, it was over. They would be gone.

The Ford's engine was racing, and Mercer knew it was going to be close. In the last few seconds before he hit the road, the vegetation gave way to knee-high grass and the Cat picked up just enough speed. But then came the hail of bullets. Four guns opened fire simultaneously. One of the shooters had crawled into the pickup's open bed and was firing over the cab.

Other rounds came from the passenger window and from the two guys in the backseat.

The onslaught of lead was overpowering, and their aim grew more accurate as the gap between the two vehicles narrowed. Mercer didn't have the protection of the big steel bucket as these shots were coming from his right-hand side.

The windshield and remaining side glass disintegrated, showering him with diamond-like shards. Bullets pinged off metal and ricocheted past his head.

Mercer had no choice.

He levered a booted foot onto the operator's seat and threw himself out the left window. He rolled as he landed on the decking from which he had tossed the driver moments earlier, and used his momentum to leap bodily off the earthmover.

Mercer landed in the grass and tucked his head as tight to his shoulder as he could. He rolled and tumbled a half dozen times, shedding speed with each jarring impact with the frost-hardened ground. The loader thundered past him, its tires churning just feet from where he had somersaulted. Bullets continued to pummel its thick steel hide.

And then the machine hit the flat of the road just in front of the pickup. Had Mercer remained at the controls things would have worked out differently. The impact with level ground wasn't evenly distributed between the two front tires. The left hit first, which caused the machine to veer sharply to that side. The bucket swung crazily at the same time the pickup's driver laid on the brakes and threw the truck into a sliding skid, before kicking it around in the opposite direction like a matador torqueing away from the enraged bull. The earthmover's bucket clipped the

F-350's rear quarter panel with enough force to put the truck up on its outside wheels. The driver cranked the steering to the opposite lock, and as quickly as the vehicle almost flipped onto its roof it was back down on all six wheels and accelerating away.

Mercer lay in the wet grass while the loader crabbed across the road and fell down into the final ditch at the bottom of the access route. The engine kept power going to all four tires, but the bucket had buried itself into the swampy ground. The wheel spin managed to kick up an impressive amount of semi-frozen mud, but the loader wasn't going anywhere.

He heard the Ford hit the public road and begin a long, smooth acceleration away from the mine. They had gotten away with murdering seven people. Mercer had no idea what they'd stolen in the backpack—some part of the experiment, no doubt. He couldn't begin to speculate what would be worth the cold-blooded murder of so many innocents.

All Mercer could do was lie on his back in the rain, knowing he'd failed to bring justice for his mentor. He ached everywhere.

Mercer was still there, six minutes later, when he finally heard sirens approaching the mine. By then, he had already decided what he had to do. It would have nothing to do with justice. It was too personal now. What came next was revenge.

3

A state cop took Mercer's statement while a female paramedic patched up some abrasions on his left shoulder and right knee. He'd hit the muddy ground hard enough to tear the thick fabric of his coveralls and flay open good-size patches of skin. An ankle was also sore, but it was something a few ibuprofen and a couple of vodka gimlets could handle. A dozen more cops had descended on the mine while a team from the ME's office had removed the body of the hoist operator from his cab. Forensic people photographed the blood spatter and the arc of shiny brass shell casings that had spewed from the machine pistol that had killed him.

"Come on," the state detective said incredulously. "You expect me to believe that you hung on to the bottom of the elevator cage as it rose fifteen hundred feet?"

He spoke with a midwestern flatness, and his suit had come from a discount chain store. His name was Paul Gerard and he was about fifty, with a silvery crew cut and a drinker's florid nose. The skin around where he'd once worn a wedding ring was still slightly puckered. Divorced less than a year. Self-made cliché was Mercer's estimation.

They were sitting in a glassed-in cubicle near the main lift hoist that had once been offices when the mine was open.

Mercer winced when some spray was shot into his shoulder wound. "We've gone over this. I discovered the bodies, and the driver confirmed I borrowed his bucket loader. Bill—"

"Gundersson."

"Right. Gundersson. You've seen the bullet holes on that thing for yourself. That alone proves the gunmen wanted to stop me, right?"

Gerard refused to respond. Mercer plowed on anyway. "I followed them from the experiment chamber, and the only way I could have reached the surface in time to keep after them was to hold on to the underside of the elevator cage."

The detective looked down at his little notepad and changed subjects.

"How was it you happened to be there at the right time?"

"Right time?" Mercer couldn't believe the cop would use such an idiotic phrase.

"You know, right after these shooters show up and kill six people down there."

"Abraham Jacobs just arrived here today. I assume he was the primary target." Mercer paused. "Correction. He and the others were collateral damage. Whatever they took away in the backpack was the primary target."

"Any ideas what was in it?"

"None whatsoever," Mercer replied. He gave a

grateful nod to the paramedic after she'd applied a wide adhesive bandage to his shoulder.

"How are you on your tetanus shot?" she asked, closing up her large orange medical case.

"Two years out, so I'm good."

"All right, I cleaned out the wounds and gave you some topical antibiotics. If you start showing signs of infection like redness or purulence, or if you suffer fever or chills, please consult a physician."

"I will. Thank you." Mercer turned his attention back to Detective Gerard. "It shouldn't be too difficult to figure out what was stolen if you go through the computer down there. It'll have detailed descriptions of what they were up to."

"And it was this Abraham Jacobs running the show?"

"No. He was lending a hand. The lead researcher was Susan Tunis. I think she's a PhD in chemistry or atmospherics or something. As I understand it, Abe was just an adviser."

"So why did you chase the gunmen?"

It was a reasonable question and one that Mercer had been asking himself for years because this wasn't the first time he'd encountered armed men. Far from it. "Why did I go after them?" he repeated Gerard's question. "I did it because if I hadn't, no one else would have."

"You some kinda hero?" the detective sneered, with a cop's offense at civilians taking the law into their own hands.

Mercer didn't want to antagonize the police, so he bit back an angry retort and lied to the man instead. "No, Detective, I just saw the murdered corpse of an old friend and lost my judgment for a few minutes."

Gerard, given the answer he wanted to hear, nodded. "Let me ask you something else. Do you think this was terrorism?"

"Does my opinion really matter? With seven people gunned down by men toting automatic weapons, the FBI will be calling this terrorism just so they can go after the shooters. ATF will get involved, as will every other acronym-happy division of Homeland Security. You're only asking me questions now because the feds haven't rolled in from the Twin Cities, and those agents, in turn, will be supplanted by the big boys flying here from D.C. But I'll tell you the truth, Detective Gerard. This was a robbery, pure and simple. They were after whatever Abe Jacobs had brought with him this morning, and they killed all the witnesses. As to your inevitable follow-up, again I have no idea what it was or why they attacked here and not at Abe's lab back at his school." Mercer paused. "Are we done?"

Gerard closed his notebook and slipped it inside a jacket pocket. The pen he kept fiddling with. "You were right about the feds. I'm just babysitting the scene until they show. The guys that went down into the mine are there to secure the scene. They can't touch dick."

"Piss you off?" Mercer asked.

"Soon as I got the call and heard automatic weapons were used, I knew I was gonna be low man on the totem pole."

Mercer wasn't unsympathetic. "I've worked with a lot of feds over the years. One-on-one they're okay. It's when you face them as a bureaucracy that they all begin to suck."

Gerard snorted. "That's it exactly. I thought you

said you're a mining engineer. How'd you ever tangle with the FBI?"

"I'm a favorite target of some pretty extreme environmental groups." Which was true, but not the real reason Mercer had so much experience with terrorism and counterterrorism techniques. That mostly came, like today, from being in the wrong place at the wrong time but still willing to do something about it. He asked the state detective, "How'd you like to do me and this investigation a huge favor?"

Gerard looked guarded once again. He cocked an eyebrow.

"The feds are going to need twelve to eighteen hours just to get the ball rolling, time that this investigation can't afford. You and I both know the gunmen's pickup has already been dumped and the shooters have scattered. There won't be any fingerprints or DNA, so that'll be a dead end. The only real clues are going to be in Abraham Jacobs's lab."

"And you don't think the feds know this?"

"They might, but since Abe was second banana here they're going to tear apart Susan Tunis's life first."

"I could tell 'em what you told me. About how you believe the attack was timed to coincide with when your friend got here."

Mercer shook his head. "That won't make a bit of difference. They have procedures, and once they figure out the ghost of Osama bin Laden didn't murder those people, and that this is a robbery and not terror related, they're going to lose interest and pull resources. They might not get around to Abe's place for two, maybe three, days."

"So what's your favor?" Gerard asked as if he didn't know.

"Let me go," Mercer said. "Keep me out of this. Make Bill Gundersson a hero by telling the FBI that he tried to ram the pickup when he saw all the guns."

"You know that's not going to happen."

Mercer sagged a little in his seat, deflating.

"On the other hand," Gerard said. "Suppose I went outside to have a smoke and you happened to sneak on outta here?"

"You'd do that for me?" Mercer asked, hoping against hope.

"Nope," Gerard said, putting on a ridiculously large cowboy hat and getting to his feet. "But I would do it for a state cop killed about twelve years ago who approached a disabled vehicle not knowing the driver was wanted by the FBI. Seems it wasn't information they were willing to share. Our guy took three to the chest. His vest stopped two of the slugs, but the third tore into his heart. The perp stole his cruiser and kept going for another three hours before he was taken down at a roadblock."

Gerard straightened his jacket. "The feds are going to think I'm a rube no matter what. You're just another witness as far as my notes will show." He had spoken seriously all through their conversation, but now his voice took on a flinty edge. It would have been clichéd had the state detective not been so earnest. "You're going to see this thing through, right?"

Mercer answered as simply as he could. "To the bitter fucking end, Detective."

"I'll be back in ten."

Paul Gerard stepped out of the office and ducked through the towering sliding doors and into the rain, a cigarette pursed between his lips and the brim of his hat ready to shield his smoke from the drizzle. Mercer waited a beat and followed the state cop. Gerard was at the far corner of the warehouse, chatting with the guy they were using to replace the dead hoist operator. Judging by the cloud of smoke wreathed around their heads, Gerard had shared from his soft pack of Marlboros.

Mercer would have loved to take the opportunity to clean up. He still wore his filthy and torn coveralls and steel-toed boots, but there wasn't the time. Gerard had given him a limited window. He left the building and made his way to a nearby single-wide trailer painted white with a faded blue stripe. The trailer had first been towed off the dealer's lot sometime in the late sixties, and the old mine represented the last in a long string of incrementally more dismal homesteads. Inside the reconfigured structure were shower stalls, lockers, and a kitchen with seating for eight. Mercer and his students used the mobile home to change after each day's lesson before they drove down to the motor inn where they were all staying.

Three of them were at the table with a state trooper, held over because they had seen the gunmen's pickup. All four men had the glazed eyes of extreme boredom.

"Hey, Mercer, what's going on?" Hans asked.

"No talking," the cop said automatically.

Mercer addressed the crew-cut patrolman with the Smokey Bear hat and Sam Browne belt. "Detective Gerard said he's done with me and I can take off. He also said to give him a few minutes before sending over the next witness."

"Did he say who he wanted?" the young officer asked. He'd been trained to be in control of any situation, and yet he felt himself automatically deferring to Mercer.

"He said to leave it up to you," Mercer replied. He recognized the kid's inexperience and gave him an outlet to show he still had some authority.

The young trooper had no idea how easily he'd been manipulated. "Okay. If Detective Gerard has your contact information, I guess it's all right."

"Thanks." Mercer addressed his students, "Sorry about all this, guys. We'll finish up our last lesson tomorrow and have our party afterward."

One of the men was about to correct Mercer but then caught what their teacher was doing. He wanted to buy some time, and they would be more than happy to give it to him.

"*Ist nicht kein Problem,*" Hans said, stressing his accent to the point of parody. He'd keep Gerard busy for hours playing up the language barrier in case the state cop changed his mind about letting his star witness go.

Mercer grabbed his civilian clothes from a locker, fished the keys to his rental from the front of his jeans pocket, and strode out of the trailer without a backward glance.

Hertz had given him a GMC Yukon, an SUV only slightly smaller than the steam dredges that once plied its namesake river in search of placer gold. Mercer slid into the driver's seat, grateful that he'd gotten insurance because the stains he'd just transferred from his coveralls to the fabric seat looked permanent. The big V8 rumbled to life, and he pulled out of the parking lot, carefully threading his way around the haphazardly parked state and local cop cars. The low clouds reflected the hypnotic blue and red flashes of all the rooftop lights.

One cop detained him for only a moment at the

gate and waved him through when Mercer explained that Gerard had said he could leave. Driving down the access road he could see the wanton path of destruction he'd carved with the big Caterpillar front-end loader. It really did look like some mechanical animal had gone on a rampage.

At the base of the haul road, a group of cops had cordoned off the bright yellow earthmover while a couple of guys in wet Tyvec suits were examining the bullet-riddled machine. No doubt they would be admonished by the federal forensic teams for not waiting.

Mercer was waved through by another miserable-looking state patrolman in a rain-slicked poncho who'd likely been radioed from above. Mercer turned in the opposite direction from the shooters, knowing no answers would be found in that direction. He wasn't even sure what questions he needed answered at this point. All Mercer knew for certain was that he had not lied to Gerard. He was going to see this through, all the way to the end.

—

The distances in the American heartland were vast, something he'd forgotten from his occasional cross-country trips when he was in Boulder at the Colorado School of Mines and drove back to visit his grandparents in Vermont. He had left the Leister Deep at nearly six at night. The sun was well down and the miles were mesmerizing. By midnight he felt like he'd covered most of the Midwest but realized he was less than halfway to his destination. He saw why the snobs in New York and D.C. called this flyover country. You sure as hell didn't want to drive it.

He knew he should pull over into one of the brightly lit oases of civilization that flanked both sides of the four-lane interstate, each promising several multistory hotels with recognizable names, chain restaurants not unlike the ones he'd left back in Minnesota, and twenty-four-hour gas stations abuzz with truckers hauling hard for the coasts. He passed several such sanctuaries, all nearly identical, but when he finally realized he was becoming a danger to himself and others if he remained behind the wheel, the next exit was as dark and deserted as an abandoned logging road, forcing him down several miles of twisty macadam until he came across a town that was nothing more than a crossroads with a building at each corner. One was a two-story storefront that housed a closed diner, a lawyer's office, and a barbershop below, while above was a sign for Sukie's Dance Studio in a large window so caked with dust that even in the darkness it looked like it hadn't seen a student since the Lindy was the rage, or at least the Hustle. Opposite that was another, larger commercial building set back from the road and surrounded by small farm machinery for sale: skid-steers, tines to convert front-end loaders into forklifts, mechanical splitters, hoers, reapers, and tractor attachments whose purpose Mercer could merely guess. The words *Feed Lot* were written over the large windows, and the gravel parking area was crisscrossed with spilled winter wheat seed. Another corner of the town was a low ambling building with two identical wings of darkly painted doors off a central office/reception area that had been made to look like a bell tower, though the belfry was faded paint and the bell was just a plywood outline. Across the street, a gas station's spiderlike canopy hovered in the sodium-vapor glow of its own lights, like one of the alien spaceships in *Close Encounters*. That's how Mercer described it to himself, and he recognized the depth of his exhaustion by the way he was torturing metaphors in his head. Another sign of fatigue was how the dingy roadside motor court, with its cheesy bell-tower motif, looked to him as inviting as the Ritz Paris or New York's Mandarin Oriental.

He pulled in, the four-by-four's tires crunching over broken glass and the grit laid down atop the previous winter's snow and ice. Light from the office spilled out just enough for him to see a woman emerge from a back room, her hands to her face as she knuckled sleep from her eyes. Mercer thought she must have been the employee of the year to hear him pull up and be ready before he stepped into the lobby, but then he saw her pick up a blanket-wrapped bundle from behind the counter and gently place it against her shoulder above her heavy breasts. He could now hear the faint bleats of a crying infant.

Mercer killed the engine and grabbed the bundle of clothes he'd taken from the trailer back at the mine. His eyes felt as gritty as his skin, and he hoped this place had enough hot water for its—he counted: ten, eleven, twelve—twelve rooms, because he planned on using it all.

He opened the glass door softly so the bell attached near its upper hinge didn't disturb the child, who'd quieted during his approach. The girl, no more than nineteen, had bad skin and a rather bovine expression. She said nothing by way of greeting.

"I'd like a room," Mercer finally said in a quiet whisper.

"Sixty bucks," she replied, "but you're like filthy. I can't let you stay here."

Mercer looked down at his coveralls. They were a mess, but then he doubted she would have cared much if it wasn't her responsibility to clean the room in the morning after he'd gone.

"Tell you what." He peeled two hundred-dollar bills from his wallet. "This is for the room and any damage. I doubt there's much in this place worth more than one forty."

For some reason that made the girl giggle.

"I just need a shower and a few hours rack time."

"I need your name for the register," the girl said, flipping open a dog-eared registration book.

Mercer placed the cash on the scarred counter, leaned past her, and pulled a red plastic fob and its attached key from a cubbyhole behind the desk. He'd taken a room close to the center of the building—and, he hoped, its hot water supply. "My ID is on the two bills. My name's Ben Franklin."

She said nothing more as he turned and headed back out. He parked the truck two doors down from his own room and let himself in with the key. The lightbulbs had been replaced with low-watt fluorescents, so the room remained cloaked in shadow and murk. He couldn't care less. He allowed himself a half hour under the hottest water he could stand, needed three of the threadbare towels to properly dry himself, and collapsed onto the sagging full-size with the tapioca-colored spread and mismatched pillows.

No sooner had his head hit the low-thread-count cotton than he knew he'd been kidding himself. It was true he shouldn't be driving, but there was no way he was going to sleep. His mind didn't work that way. He'd tried to outrun his feelings by pouring on mile after mile, but the fact remained that his friend was dead along with six others and he'd been unable to stop any of the slaughter. Mercer wasn't Catholic but he understood guilt better than most. It was his motivator and anchor at the same time. To assuage it he would go to any lengths even when, more often than not, the guilt was not his to shoulder. It was a burden he took up out of duty rather than true responsibility. This meant sometimes he could not forgive himself things for which he was wholly blameless. A shrink would have told him his feelings dated back to his parents' death, and the fact that he'd been unable to prevent the tragedy. Now Mercer felt he should have stopped Abe's vicious murder, so the guilt weighed especially heavy.

That hadn't been the case when a then twenty-something Philip Mercer had gone back to Penn State for his doctorate, following two years at the Colorado School of Mines.

Over Christmas break that first year into his PhD studies, Abe had secured a research grant to take a few of his best students to West Africa for a ten-day trip to assist in a mineral prospecting expedition. The grad students would essentially be unpaid load bearers and Sherpas for the field team, but they had jumped at the opportunity.

The first week of the trip had gone off without a hitch. The team of eight Westerners, including Abe and his three top students, plus four armed native Cameroonians, had scoured streambeds and exposed rock formations for interesting geological markers. They were investigating the belief that this particular region in the highlands contained coltan, a mineral necessary for the newly burgeoning cellular phone market. They hadn't yet found any of the dull metallic ore, but that hadn't dampened any spirits, especially among the grad students.

Their final day dawned cool and misty. The camp stirred to life slowly, but soon cooking fires were lit and instant coffee was being passed around. A breakfast of powdered eggs was about to be served when dark shapes flitted through the surrounding mist, and a staccato solo of mechanized death rang out. There had been talk of rebels in this area, but they were supposed to be across the border in Nigeria, over forty miles away.

One of their Cameroonian guards was hit in the opening barrage. He went down as if body-slammed, with blood and other matter oozing from a gaping hole in the back of his head. By all rights, Mercer should have been frozen where he sat, opposite Abe and another student from California named Lance. This was similar to the ambush that took his parents; all that was missing was the battered pickup his mother was driving with his injured father in the back when they were gunned down.

But Mercer didn't hesitate. In that first split second, Abe became the parents he hadn't been able to save. Mercer didn't think about himself, didn't consider the danger at all. He had failed to prevent two parents being lost to the violence of this savage continent, he wasn't going to lose a man he now considered a third. He just moved on adrenaline-fueled instinct to protect Abe Jacobs, or die trying.

Mercer leapt through the flames of the cooking fires and tackled both his fellow student and Abe as fresh bursts of automatic fire ripped through the camp. He pressed the two into the loamy ground with his body weight as strings of bullets crisscrossed over their heads. Off to one side, it sounded as though another one of their guards had fled into the jungle.

One summer years earlier, Mercer's best friend, Mike, had been given a .22-caliber rifle by his father. The two fourteen-year-olds had spent the summer working every odd job they could think of in order to feed that little rifle's insatiable appetite for ammunition. No sooner had the boys been paid than they were at a local gun shop buying boxes of rounds, much like some teens hung out at convenience stores hoping someone would buy beer for them. Then it was off to an old gravel pit where they took turns shooting the gun as though they were movie action heroes. When school and then winter finally ended their shooting trips, they had both pumped thousands of rounds through the .22, damaging its barrel so it no longer shot true, and yet both had become superior marksmen from every shooting position they had studied in an old World War II–era army training booklet they'd found at the gun store.

Mercer pushed down on the two Americans for good measure and rolled through the short grass for the dead guard. The mist was lifting, and he could see the muzzle flashes of at least five shooters moving in on the camp. The two remaining guards were pinned behind a craggy bit of rock that jutted from the jungle floor. Their cover would vanish in another thirty seconds as the shooters advanced.

He reached the dead guard and pulled the AK-47 from his lifeless grip and two spare magazines from a pouch on the man's chest. His name was Paul. He had taken to Mercer because he had a son named Philippe.

Although Mercer had never fired an automatic weapon, muscle memory from those teenaged shooting trips left him feeling comfortable with the Kalashnikov in his hands, and he used it as though it were an extension of his own body. From an awkward prone position he loosened a short burst that caught one of the shooters just as he stepped into the clearing where the prospectors had made their camp. Mercer could tell the man was dead even before he fell, so he switched his aim toward the muzzle flash of another attacker who was still hiding among the trees and semitropical shrubs that surrounded them.

The unseen gunman screamed when his body was raked by the burst, then fell into a silence so profound that it could only mean he was dead.

The two hired guards, sensing a shift in the battle's momentum, popped up from their cover position and added their combined fire to the hail of lead exploding all around the camp.

Mercer's eyes never rested on one spot for more than a few seconds while he scanned for additional targets. He also checked that the AK's bolt was closed, meaning there was a round in the chamber, and he quickly changed out the magazine. His fingers were a little less sure than they'd been on the old Ruger, but he got it done.

Another of the attackers went down when targeted by the two guards. He screamed even louder than the man Mercer had taken, and it seemed his high keening cry for help was enough to unman the remaining attackers. Their guns fell silent as they retreated into the forest. Mercer sprang from where he'd been crouching and started after them. He felt certain that whoever led the guerrillas would reorganize them quickly and they'd be back. He raced into the jungle, the AK held low on the hip, his finger ready to squeeze the trigger. One of the many things he'd never anticipated about a firefight, despite what he'd seen on television, was the unimaginable level of noise. The multiple discharging guns had left him deafened, his ears ringing as though he were standing next to some enormous electrical generator.

Mercer reached another small clearing two hundred yards from where they'd camped. He spotted four men across the way, maybe thirty yards out. Three were armed natives dressed in street clothes and battered tennis shoes. The other two wore paramilitary camouflage with matching packs and slouch hats on their heads. They didn't carry Africa's ubiquitous weapon of choice, the Kalashnikov. They were fitted out with black assault rifles, mounting scopes, and boxy twenty-round mags. These were Western guns, expensive and recognizable as the tools of professional mercenaries. In the murky light of dawn it was hard to be sure, but Mercer felt the two dressed as soldiers were white men, not black.

He skidded to a stop. The other men saw him and their guns all came up, but Mercer was already set to fire and even with the AK down low, he sent a scything barrage across the clearing. The two Africans died immediately, and one of the white mercenaries took a round that spun him in place and he dropped from view. The other got his gun to his shoulder and opened fire. Mercer had no cover, so he dove back into the jungle, his finger still on the trigger, the AK's bolt slamming back and forth like an industrial loom stitching out bullets.

He never took his eyes off the target, so he saw in the flash from the other man's gun that the shooter was white, not much older than Mercer himself, and had a port-wine birthmark covering part of his left cheek. He stood up to the wild blast Mercer had fired at him because he was used to dealing with poorly trained boys who thought the sound of a machine gun was as deadly as its aim. But in an instant one of Mercer's bullets struck him in the center of that purplish mark, and blood formed a halo around his head as he was knocked flat by the kinetic shock.

Mercer reached to reload his empty weapon only to realize the second spare magazine had dropped from his back pocket somewhere on the trail from camp. He looked back at where the men had been. The first white mercenary he'd tagged was getting to his feet, and one of the native gunmen was also stirring.

Wounded game was especially deadly, and injured men were no exception. Mercer moved back into the jungle and retraced his steps until he'd returned to the camp. Abe was tending to an injured prospector, while one of the remaining guards gathered equipment. The other man watched over the camp warily, his rifle at the ready. There was no sign of the guard who'd run away. Someone had already draped a tarp over Paul's corpse.

"Mercer," Abe cried. "What happened?"

"I don't know," Mercer said, panting and a little shaky. "I caught up with them about two hundred yards out. I got a few of them, but two are injured and they might regroup and come back—we should get going."

Mercer grabbed a spare banana mag and rammed it into his AK, racking the slide to chamber a round as if he'd done it a million times.

He looked at Abe working on the prospecting geologist, but all he saw was his own parents dying while he ran away with his nanny. Abe looked up with a smile, relieved that the injured man would be okay, and that his star student had saved their lives. Mercer hadn't failed this time, and he vowed that to the best of his abilities he would never do so again.

They made it to their predetermined rendezvous without incident and met the truck that was waiting to take them out of the wilderness. The guard who had run away at the outset of the attack was never seen again, and the company that had hired the guards made certain Paul's widow and child would be provided for. They never learned for certain what was behind the deadly attack, but rumor was a local warlord was trying to exert control over the territory for its mineral wealth and had hired white soldiers of fortune.

It was this incident that a few short months later would make Abe recommend his best pupil for a mission into Iraq when the CIA needed a geologist to help an insertion team assess whether or not Saddam Hussein had enough domestic uranium ore to start an enrichment project. That mission was the pivot point for Mercer's career to veer as much into countering terrorism as into finding Earth's natural resources. So much of what Mercer was proud of, and also that for which he was most deeply ashamed, had its genesis in that one incident when he had saved Abe's life. Losing him now didn't change his past, but it did make him regret not thanking his old mentor one last time.

As a scattering of cars hissed by the road outside the Bell Tower Motor Court, and dawn started creeping past the sheer drapes, Mercer replayed the mine attack in his head again and again and again. He recalled, too, the incident in the jungle. One battle a victory, the other a defeat. Bookends to a friendship that ended too soon.

By six thirty, Mercer knew everything he could about his new enemy. He'd watched their assault in his head a hundred times. Three of the shooters were harder to discern in his mind, but not the fourth, the leader. Mercer would always know that man by the way he held his head and moved. All four commandos were pros, but the leader—he was a warrior by nature more than training. Mercer had paid with a sleepless night, but in reward his target had crystallized in his mind. When their paths next crossed, Mercer planned on putting him down without so much as a warning. He was responsible for Abe's death, not Mercer, but until Mercer killed him, he would carry that weight like a stone in his heart.

4

Marcel Roland d'Avejan's hand tightened on the smartphone until his knuckles went white and an unconscious part of his brain realized he might crush the device.

"You did what?" he demanded in a rising shout, his normally accent-free English showing its rural French roots.

"It got out of hand," the man in America replied. "What can I say? They're all dead." It sounded like he was sucking on a piece of hard candy. His speech was garbled and wet.

"You can say," d'Avejan ranted with little-suppressed fury, "that you are a complete moron who can't follow instructions. You were supposed to steal some goddamn rocks from a bunch of academics, not gun them down."

The caller was a professional and knew that part of his job was calming clients when things didn't go their way. A great deal of that process was just letting them vent. Corporate types like d'Avejan were the worst. They thought they ran in a hard and cruel world, but when the true levels of human depravity were opened up to them, they whined like frightened children. His opinion wasn't swayed either way by the fact he'd been in d'Avejan's exclusive employ for the better part of two years as special facilitator for his company's global security arm.

"I will not say it was strictly necessary," the ex-soldier replied. "However, their deaths will slow the investigation."

"You can't be serious," the Frenchman scoffed.

"They are looking into a mass murder, not a theft. Totally different type of investigation. Trust me. For the first week the FBI will be turning over every rock in Minnesota looking for Al Qaeda operatives. Part of my team has already crossed into Canada with the sample and will be airborne in less than two hours. We will finish up here in the States and be out of the country no later than tomorrow at noon. The feds from D.C. won't even have landed in St. Paul by the time we're clear."

Several long seconds passed. The security contractor knew exactly what was going through Roland d'Avejan's mind. It was the same thing that had gone through his when the newest member of his team had opened fire hours earlier, without orders. The young security contractor thought one of the students had been reaching for a weapon. Of course there was no weapon. These were college kids and a couple of doddering professors. No matter the mistake, he realized even before the last victim bled out that he had no choice but to accept the circumstances and make the best of them. Accept, adapt, and overcome. It was a motto learned long ago.

He could almost feel his employer's anger moderating as he came to understand there were some circumstances beyond his control. The quicker he recognized this, the quicker he could move on to the next phase of their operation.

"Are you sure no one followed you?" d'Avejan asked. He was once more in control. He was over the initial shock of being an accessory to a number of murders even if he hadn't been directly complicit.

"Someone on a loader tried to ram us, *meneer*," the mercenary admitted. "He missed and we left him in a ditch. We abandoned the truck two miles from the target site as planned and took to our secondary escape vehicles. No one saw them and we were well clear by the time the police were called in."

"I don't like the idea that a workman tried to stop you," d'Avejan said.

"I wasn't too keen either," the man in America admitted. "I don't know how he knew to come after us, but he was hell-bent to keep us from leaving."

"Could he have seen what happened down in the mine?"

"No way." On this point the security specialist was adamant. "Most likely he was responding to the shooting of the hoist operator and believed for a minute that he was Rambo. In the end his efforts were inconsequential. This was nothing to worry yourself about, *meneer*."

Marcel Roland d'Avejan finally relaxed his grip on the smartphone. Not that it mattered if he crushed it. He treated the four-hundred-euro phones as burners, the way drug dealers used prepaids from a corner *tabac*. One and done. As in one call and toss the phone and its associated number.

"Call when your task is complete." D'Avejan

killed the connection and forcibly smashed the phone open to remove the battery before feeding the pieces into an industrial-style shredder behind his desk. The machine made an awful sound for just a few seconds and yet rendered the electronic marvel into so much ruined solder, copper, and plastic. The battery went into a recycling basket next to the shredder. Just because he trashed a few of these phones a week didn't mean he wanted to trash the environment.

After all, saving the planet was what this whole mission was about.

He took a few breaths. His hands were shaky, and his stomach suddenly felt like it was filled with coiling snakes. Men were dead because of a decision he had made—not as the result of a horrible accident at one of the many industrial facilities d'Avejan controlled, but because they had been murdered. Gunned down in cold blood, for the simple fact they were witnesses and it was easier to kill them than deal with them.

One of the snakes lurched up his esophagus, forcing him to choke back a searing bolus of vomit. He ran for his office's marble en suite bathroom and just reached the commode before his stomach heaved again and his breakfast spewed into the bowl. He gagged and spat, trying to clear his mouth as if he could also clear his conscience. His stomach heaved again, a powerful paroxysm that seemed to tear through his gut but produced nothing but a thin rope of foul liquid that he had to wipe from his mouth with a wad of tissue. He flushed away the evidence of his guilt but remained on his knees, repeatedly spitting into the bowl as his saliva seemed to have soured as much as the contents of his stomach.

Two full minutes elapsed before he hauled himself

to his feet and brushed his teeth at the nearby sink. Only when he was finished rinsing with a swig of antiseptic mouthwash did he look at himself in the mirror in front of him.

D'Avejan was fifty-four, and thanks to regular tennis with two different pros, he remained in good shape. His hair, still more pepper than salt, had needed help, so he had the most expensive plugs money could buy, not that anyone could tell, and his skin remained taut thanks to subtle yet frequent bouts under a surgeon's knife.

D'Avejan's goal was to maintain what nature had molded him into on his forty-fifth birthday. He had read that was the peak age for many men. They had strength and masculinity, as well as the fine wrinkles and depth of expression that came with maturity and acquired wisdom. D'Avejan had set about stopping the hands of time, and had succeeded for the most part. He looked a decade younger than his actual age, and many of his friends teased him, saying that he kept a moldering portrait of himself in an attic to age for him. He would chuckle at that and also cross his mouth with a finger, entreating the person to keep his or her silence on the subject.

Today his looks were betrayed by a pallor that had washed away the tan he'd recently honed following a business trip to Dubai. And his normally bright blue eyes, undoubtedly his best feature, were haunted and red-rimmed as though he'd been crying. He touched a finger to the corner of one eye and felt liquid transfer to his skin. He had been crying, only in his gastric distress he'd not noticed.

He coughed, embarrassed by his appearance. Marcel Roland d'Avejan—he detested being called Marcel, and only allowed his wife to call him Rollie—was a self-made mega-millionaire. He had inherited a specialty welding company decades earlier from his bachelor great-uncle and turned it into one of the largest industrial combines in the European Union. Thanks in part to owning old rights to titanium-cutting machinery, the company had been poised to enter the lucrative aerospace business when d'Avejan's aging uncle had succumbed to a strange immune system deficiency that would only later be known in France as SIDA—and as AIDS in the English-speaking world.

Young Roland had been his uncle's right-hand man, and took over the rebranding of what had up until then been Nantes Metalworks, as named by d'Avejan's great-grandfather upon his demobilization following the First World War. Roland d'Avejan shifted focus and built the company into Eurodyne, a conglomerate with annual sales of four billion euros and nearly eighty thousand employees in five distinct corporate divisions. Eurodyne dominated the manufacture of nearly all the jet turbine blades used in most of Europe's military and civilian aircraft. Under his stewardship the company had long ago branched out from metals manufacturing into precision hydraulic systems, rail stock for freight and passenger service, consumer appliances like vacuum cleaners and refrigerators sold under a number of trade names, as well as energy production—following the acquisition of a power company running four nuclear plants in France and another in the Czech Republic.

In his climb to success, Roland had blurred countless ethical lines. He'd even paid, early on, to have a competitor's son beaten in order to intimidate the rival and force him to relocate. Of course he'd cheated on taxes, raided workers' pension funds, price gouged, engaged in price fixing, bribed, blackmailed, and knowingly sold defective equipment, but being party to murder was something he never would have considered.

Now that line had been crossed, and there was nothing for him to do but accept it and move on. He felt steadier. He noticed a few rust-colored vomit stains on his shirtfront. He worked himself out of his jacket, slipped the knot of his two-hundred-dollar tie, and peeled off the shirt. One of his many foibles was the fact he only wore a shirt once. It had started out as a bit of bravado when he first started making money, as if to say "look at me, I am so successful that my shirts are always new."

Recently, though, as business stresses mounted, his onetime affectation was now the most visible sign of a burgeoning fear of germs. He had a grip on it, for the most part, but when people weren't around to judge he would indulge in long showers with the most corrosive soaps he could find. Through an OCD Internet chat room he discovered a specialist who made custom lye-based cleaners that were barely fit for human use and would leave his skin rapturously parboiled.

When he was forced to be around others, he kept water-free hand sanitizer on him at all times. If questioned, he would explain he had developed a skin condition that caused him to break out at the slightest brush with unnatural chemicals. Given his well-established credentials as an environmental crusader who had turned Eurodyne "green" before it had been fashionable, people gave him a pass as a bit of an eco-kook and never mentioned it again.

From an eighteenth-century ormolu-accented bureau in a closet near the private en suite he plucked out one of twenty identical bespoke shirts with his monogram on the right cuff and real bone buttons. The cotton was so smooth it felt like silk against his skin. His wife had been out with friends the night before, so d'Avejan had taken one of his special showers. His torso looked like it had been scoured with a commercial sandblaster.

He dressed, knotting his tie so that the dimple was precisely centered, and stepped back out into his main office. The picture window from his thirty-fifth-story corner office looked out from Paris's commercial center of La Défense over the Bois de Boulogne, the city's second-largest park and home to the famous Hippodrome de Longchamp horse-racing track, and afforded him a spectacular view of the Eiffel Tower. It was midmorning. The roads were snarled with traffic, the Seine teeming with early-season tourist boats, and yet the city had never looked fresher or cleaner.

D'Avejan helped himself to a Perrier from the wet bar tucked into a low credenza under the window and belched out the last of his inner turmoil. So what if the science team with Jacobs was dead? He didn't know any of them personally, and their deaths would save untold millions, even billions of people in the not-too-distant future. Was their sacrifice high? Even d'Avejan was sorrowful that they had paid the ultimate price, but it was for a better future for the rest of humanity. He further assured himself that they hadn't suffered. His special facilitator was too professional to have prolonged their agony. He imagined clean kill shots and vowed not to read any media accounts in case that wasn't what had actually transpired. Better for his conscience if he could maintain the illusion that they had quick deaths rather than discovering the six scientists had died slowly over time.

He tossed the empty green bottle into the recycling bin and turned his attention to the Bloomberg terminal standing on a rolling cart he could hide away when he had guests. The high-tech portal into the financial world was an invaluable tool but ruined the elegant decor of his office suite with its industrial functionality. Better it remained out of sight when not in use.

He checked the latest price on Eurodyne and made the inevitable comparison to its peak a few years earlier. They were partly the victim of the credit crunch that followed the global real estate market implosion, but the steady downward spiral of his company's worth could also be blamed on a feckless society that couldn't see the woods for the trees. Eurodyne had been in position to become a world leader at the forefront of energy production, distribution, and storage. Instead, the energy arm of Eurodyne was slowly eroding away the profits made by the other divisions and dragging the company into the red. Share prices were down another half euro this morning because a contract with a Spanish utility was being "reevaluated," which in the real world meant canceled.

No sooner had that sour thought raced across his mind than his private secretary buzzed him on the intercom. "Monsieur d'Avejan, Monsieur Pickford is on the line for you. As always, he claims it is urgent."

D'Avejan's eye gave a spasmodic tic. Ralph Pickford was a bottom-feeding parasite in the energy market. Or at least that's what Roland liked to tell himself. In truth, the American billionaire was one of the shrewdest speculators in the business and happened to be the largest shareholder in Eurodyne outside of d'Avejan's own voting bloc. It was why the Texan had unfettered access to the Frenchman and why he let his secretary's "as always" gibe go without comment. She hated the abrasive American even more than d'Avejan did himself.

D'Avejan let out a frustrated breath, cleared his throat, and barked, "Put him through, Odette." He didn't wait for Pickford to say anything. "Ralph, this is not a good time. If you are calling to tell me the Spanish are pulling out of the deal, it is something I knew last night but could not divulge as it was an inside secret. I also know the stock is down another half euro, and I need not be reminded that if the price falls a further ten percent you will sell in order to claim the loss on your taxes, *and* that your withdrawal would have catastrophic consequences for my company. Have I hit all the highlights?"

In the six years since the oilman from Houston had acquired such a large stake in Eurodyne, Roland d'Avejan had been cordial at worst and obsequious at best to Pickford. He had no idea where he'd gotten the wherewithal just now to speak so forcefully to a man who could effectively ruin him with a single phone call.

It was obvious that Pickford hadn't expected such a forceful greeting either because the line buzzed with stunned silence for several long seconds. "Well," Pickford drawled, drawing out the word for several long, chuckling syllables. "Sounds like someone found a pair in their briefs this morning."

Having spent so much time around Americans, d'Avejan understood the insult immediately.

"I wear boxers, Ralph, and my testicles have been there all along. Do you have anything constructive to say this morning or are you just calling to complain that you've lost fifty million dollars since the opening bell."

"Don't kid yourself, Roland. I lost fifty on your stock but made a hundred shorting the Spaniards. That info wasn't insider at all. The writing's been on the wall for a month that they were going to back out at the last minute. That country's broke, but they can't afford to piss off their trade unions, so they make sweetheart deals worth all kinds of bucks to the labor wonks, then yank the plug and plead poverty and blame outside forces.

"They did it to you today just like they torpedoed that Chinese solar firm two months ago. You might recall that company went tits-up as a result, and the CEO had the good sense to wash down a bottle of sleeping pills with a fifth of vodka. When the Chicom government is your biggest backer, it's better to off yourself when you torch a few hundred million yuan betting on a bunch of lazy-ass spics from the mother country."

"All very colloquial and interesting, Ralph, but what's your point?" Again, Roland was surprised that he was holding firm against his biggest shareholder. That suicide reference would have normally had him at least apologizing about the Spanish deal.

"Point is"—Pickford began getting a little hot, his Texas drawl much more clipped—"I've had my accountants going over Eurodyne's records again, and for the life of them they can't figure out what happened to the eighty-seven million dollars you spent buying something called Luck Dragon Trading of Guangzhou, China, eight months ago. Luck Dragon was created the day it was acquired, and as far as anyone can tell it has no assets other than a box number at the Guangzhou central post office."

"Luck Dragon is to be our entrepôt into southern China," d'Avejan said with a trace of boredom at such a nothing question. "Since it's you and I talking and I know this is a secure phone, the seven million was for the legitimate trade name and all the other typical bullshit needed to set up a business in China. No surprises there. The rest, however, is to pay bribes. Some now and some doubtlessly in the future. However, it is better to have the slush fund in place on the outset than have to create it down the road."

"Seems pretty damned steep to me," Pickford groused.

Roland tried to put it in language the American would understand. "China has come a long way in the past decade. You can no longer secure the locals' cooperation with a handful of beads and some pretty cloth, the way your forefathers bought America from the Indians. The Chinese play some of the meanest hardball on the planet. Trust me. Anything less than a hundred million is a steal, and I am referring to euros and not your severely devalued greenbacks."

"And what do we get for this money?" the oilman asked dubiously.

"Manufacturing rights with labor at roughly forty cents per hour per employee, a dollar an hour for supervisors and semiskilled techs, and absolutely no environmental oversight during construction. Further, we will be able to label the building a green project and use its operation as a carbon offset to one of our factories in the European Union."

"How do you get the green certification? I thought there had been a crackdown on scam companies claiming bogus carbon credits on projects that had already been built or that had no environmental sustainability."

"There was," d'Avejan told him. "What do you think we're buying with that eighty million? On carbon credits alone we should pocket that much by our third year in operation."

"And what do we plan on manufacturing?" Pickford was beginning to understand the deal, but like any old-school capitalist, he distrusted revenue streams he didn't fully comprehend. Being paid not to produce carbon dioxide was something he hadn't yet been able to get his mind around.

"Doesn't matter," the Frenchman replied. "The credits are already built into the numbers. We could make solar panels or rubber dog crap and the money is guaranteed through the ETS." This was the Emissions Trading Scheme, the Europe-wide cap-and-trade system to limit dangerous levels of greenhouse gases from entering the atmosphere. To some it was a way to save the planet from catastrophic global warming, to others it was a waste of nearly $300 billion, and to others still it was a new playing field for questionable but lucrative financial transactions.

Men like Roland d'Avejan saw it as a little of all three. Being eco-minded didn't mean one couldn't game the system a little and turn a profit. He went on. "Ralph, as I have said on more than one occasion, if you question my handling of Eurodyne I suggest you put me up for a vote of no confidence with the board of directors. If I lose, then I might have time to see my family for a change. My wife tells me my daughter has just been awarded a scholarship to the University of Basel in Switzerland and that my son is set to race a full season in Formula 3000 in hopes of attracting the attention of a Formula One team for next year. The last I really recall of them, my daughter was thirteen and in love with all things horse, and my son believed he was a black American rap star and called himself Jay Hop or Lil Hop or something equally ridiculous. So either call the directors or let me run my company as I see fit, and I will have the stock back up to its highs within twelve months."

"Is that a promise?" Pickford asked a little snidely.

"This is business, Ralph. There are no promises except the tax man always wants his cut, and some asshole always thinks he can do your job better than you. I have to go now. *Au revoir.*" Roland d'Avejan hung up the phone before Pickford could say anything.

D'Avejan sat stunned for several seconds, half tempted to buzz his secretary and have her deflect the call if the Texas oil baron rang back, but in his gut he knew Pickford wouldn't. He'd been soundly told to go to hell, and for the time being that's exactly what he would do. It took little thought for Roland to understand where his newfound confidence had come from.

He felt stronger than he had in a long time, more vibrant, like he'd just come off his greatest tennis victory or had just sent his mistress to a screaming orgasm and she still begged for more. His member was even a little tumescent. He wouldn't have time to see his mistress tonight, but Odette hadn't been hired solely for her typing skills.

He had to force his mind back to business. That Pickford had spotted the anomaly surrounding the Luck Dragon Trading deal wasn't too surprising. Despite his vast financial holdings, the American knew where every one of his dollars, dimes, and pennies was at any given time. No doubt he would spend the day harassing CEOs of other companies he had a stake in, cajoling and chiding and fighting for any edge he could get to increase his worth just that tiny bit more. The man was a greedy pig, but a smart one, and eventually he would wonder why Luck Dragon posted no more business.

D'Avejan opened a top desk drawer and pulled out a fresh cell phone from the pile. He had to call a legitimate number, but at least his end of the conversation was entirely anonymous. He dialed and waited while the signal bounced halfway around the globe, switching from phone to satellite feed to radio transceiver and finally through an antiquated PBX machine tucked into the dim corner of a ship's radio room.

"Where are you?" d'Avejan asked by way of greeting. He spoke in English, the only language he and the man he had phoned shared.

"At my desk doing paperwork. What about you?"

"Don't get smart, Lev. Are you still in Vladivostok?"

"*Nyet,*" replied the captain of the *Akademik Nikolay Zhukovsky.* "We left about five hours ago."

"Is everything set?" D'Avejan regretted asking the question as soon as it passed his lips. Lev Shukov wouldn't have slipped out of Russia's easternmost port had he not been ready.

Fortunately the taciturn sea captain kept his biting retort to himself and simply said, "Everything except the most important thing."

"Yes, yes, I know," the Frenchman responded quickly. "I'm working on it."

"You might want to work quicker. We have a hard deadline for the first shot, and so far the ionizing medium we have aboard won't—how you say—cut it. I can pump terawatts of energy into the stratosphere, but without the right medium is like pissing through a fire hose. Try all you want, you will not put out fire."

"Lev, it's not as bad," d'Avejan countered. "Our lab-grown crystals are just slower. But as of today we have another piece of real crystal. I will make arrangements to chopper it out to the ship while you're en route."

"And you? Do you come to see your triumph?"

"I don't know yet. My real triumph won't happen for months. But I might join you anyway to at least witness the beginning of this historic endeavor."

"Either way," Shukov grunted, "send Marlboros. I could not find any in Vladivostok, and I'm stuck smoking these Turkish cigarettes that taste like donkey ass."

"You'd know, Lev," d'Avejan teased, obviously relieved that the ship was away and now beyond Pickford's reach. Unbeknownst to but a handful of people at Eurodyne, the whole Luck Dragon Trading deal was cover to acquire the specialized Russian ship and finance certain modifications to her.

"Ha, you French and your sense of humor. For record, Jerry Lewis is not funny and neither is that douchebag mime."

"No arguments there." Roland's father had loved Marcel Marceau. Roland had hated both his father and his given name, and thus France's most beloved street performer as well. He turned serious. "Just make sure you get into position on time. There's too much riding on this operation to blow it now."

He clicked off the phone and fed it to the shredder. He was pleased. Things were in motion now, and soon momentum would reach a point where they couldn't be stopped. He brushed a hand down the front of his suit pants, felt his arousal becoming even stronger than before, and reached for the intercom on his desk. "Odette, would you please lock the outer door and come in here."

5

It was eight thirty in the morning when Mercer rolled up to Abe Jacobs's little faux-Tudor house just outside a side gate of the college where he'd last taught and had chosen to retire. Apart from the surrounding stone wall, the school was indistinguishable from the charming town of Killenburg, Ohio. Located on the banks of a feeder stream to Raccoon Creek, which eventually drained into the Ohio River, Hardt College had just celebrated its one hundred twentieth year. Its founder, Konrad Hardt, was a German émigré who had never spent a moment past his tenth birthday in a classroom, but had been a genius of mechanical design. His inventions streamlined industrial manufacturing in such diverse businesses as cigar rolling, railway lanterns, and thread bobbins.

Hardt had recognized the importance of education, and upon his death bequeathed a grant large enough to buy virtually the entire town of Killenburg and create what he thought a liberal arts college should be. He modeled it somewhat on the nation's first coeducational college across the state in Oberlin, Ohio. Hardt College had been coed since its founding—its namesake had seven daughters and no sons and was rumored not to have had a choice in the matter. The school had grown over the years and now had a total of two thousand students, as opposed to its first graduating class of just thirteen.

The town was as much a part of the school as the school was of the town. In fact Killenburg would have long since become a ghost town when an upstream hydro project siphoned off half its stream—and thus the motive power for the two mills that had once employed its citizens. The presence of the school was what kept the town alive, and it remained a quaint enclave. If not for the changes in clothing styles and the makes of cars, Mercer could imagine Killenburg looking much like it had fifty, even a hundred years ago.

As with the rest of the town, the street in front of Abe Jacobs's house was lined with stately oaks that would provide ample shade in the summer and coat the ground in a Technicolor carpet come autumn. Spring was still far enough off that the trees were just skeletal silhouettes against a cloudy sky. The steeproofed Tudor was of tan stucco with real wood-beam accents and late-Gothic-style mullioned windows.

His old mentor had chosen Hardt because several friends from his days at Carnegie Mellon had settled here. For its size, the private college had a strong science program, thanks to an endowment that had allowed it to construct a dedicated building four years earlier with state-of-the-art labs and enough high-tech toys to keep even Abe and his coterie of aging geeks enthralled.

Mercer imagined that Abe's final years had been happy ones. Some men retire to golf courses or fishing holes; Abe Jacobs would have retired to an experimental laboratory. That's the kind of man he was.

Mercer killed the engine and forced his hands to relax on the wheel of his rental. He stepped from the SUV. The air was oddly colder here than in Minnesota, and still carried the hoary blade of winter. Thick snow covered much of the lawn and any other spots that hadn't been hit by plow or shovel. Though Mercer hadn't visited Abe since he had come to Hardt, there were certain things he knew would remain consistent, and one was the moldy cement frog crouched next to the front door. Beneath it, as he knew after doing this countless times at Penn State, was a spare front door key. In some categories, Abe was lacking in originality—security and decorating among them.

The house smelled of pipe tobacco and was outfitted in a style likely called midcentury bachelor. The heat had been absentmindedly left on, so it was at least seventy-five. The furniture was all too big for the spaces and had been shoved against walls, so little paths ran from room to room. The prints and paintings on the walls were all garage-sale rejects that Abe had owned forever. His favorite, an aerial shot of Jerusalem, hung over a brick fireplace with a blackened mantel. Off the living room was a kitchen done up in harvest-gold-colored appliances and a dappled linoleum floor that looked like the mummified hide of a long-dead giraffe. A Formica table and 1960s vintage chairs designed to impart some futuristic vision of mankind's seating needs took up much of the floor. The table was spread with old newspapers, trade magazines, and loose envelopes.

Most of the drapes were at least partially closed, so the house remained dim even as the sun struggled to burn through the morning clouds. There were two other rooms on the downstairs floor—a formal dining room that hadn't seen a meal served since McDonald's recorded their billionth, and Abe's study, which Mercer decided to search last. He climbed the narrow stairs, sending a cadence of creaks through the home. Off the tiny landing at the top of the steps was a bathroom so dated the toilet tank was affixed to the wall a good four feet above the bowl, and the mirror over the pedestal sink was losing its silver backing, so that Mercer's reflection appeared in sepia tones. Somehow the old looking glass made him smile. Abe would have looked better with a few of his wrinkles blurred by the mirror.

The master bedroom was dominated by an antique four-poster that Mercer didn't recognize and assumed had come with the house. A matching chest of drawers was tucked under the window, and atop it in cut-glass bowls was Abe's collection of cuff links, one of his many idiosyncrasies. The bed was neatly made and the room didn't smell musty, which made Mercer think the old man had had a housekeeper.

It was the guest bedroom that revealed the house's greatest surprise. The bed not only was unmade, it was occupied. A woman lay in it. She had shucked off most of the bedcovers, and her white T-shirt had ridden high enough on her thighs that had he chosen, Mercer could have deprived her of her last shot at modesty. She lay facedown, and her dark hair spread across the pillows in a wild mane that brushed far past her shoulders. By her slim form and the tautness of her skin he knew she was young.

A red leather jacket was tossed over a nearby upholstered chair, while the girl's jeans lay on the floor to the side of the bed. Mercer quietly retreated from the room. He partially closed the door and, from the hall, loudly cleared his throat to rouse her.

She startled awake with a sharp intake of air.

"Hello," Mercer called out softly. "I'm a friend of Abe Jacobs."

"What? Who's out there?" she snapped in fear-tinged aggression. He could hear her shift on the bed, doubtlessly covering herself with blankets.

"I didn't mean to frighten you," Mercer went on. "I am a friend of Abe's."

"How did you get in here?" she demanded.

"Abe always leaves a key under the decorative frog next to the front door. I let myself in. My name is Mercer. Professor Jacobs was my adviser when he taught at Penn State."

Her next demand was "What are you doing here? Professor Jacobs is out of town."

"I know," he replied patiently. "Could you please come downstairs so we can talk without having to shout through a door? I'll see if I can make us some coffee." Mercer turned away without giving the girl a chance to ask further questions.

As he got an old kettle of water onto the hideous yellow stove, he heard the toilet flush upstairs and another rush of water from the bathroom sink that made the thin walls sound like they were holding back a biblical deluge. A few minutes later came the creak of feet padding down the stairs, and then she turned into the kitchen.

Mercer guessed she was in her mid-twenties, a grad student most likely, and saw that she was very pretty with nearly black hair and the dark sloe eyes to match. She hadn't had time to put on makeup, but she didn't need any. Her skin glowed with youth while her mouth was bright-lipped and generous. She'd tamed her mane of hair into a thick ponytail that fell in a rope down her back, but loose tendrils still danced around her face and forced her to either paw at them or blow at them with charming bother.

She sported a red leather jacket over a V-neck sweater and jeans. A small black knapsack he hadn't noticed in the bedroom was slung over her shoulder. She didn't step into the kitchen but positioned herself against the wall dividing it from the living room so that she was much closer to the front door than to Mercer. She was cautious but not overly alarmed.

"Who are you again?" she asked. Her voice had a rasp like she was a lifelong smoker, but she hadn't smelled of cigarettes and she made no effort to light one.

Mercer found milk in the fridge, noted the date was still a day away, and pulled a jar of instant coffee, another of Abe Jacobs's hallmarks, from a cabinet as well as two mismatched mugs. Spoons he found in a drawer. He set everything on the table. "My name is Philip, but people mostly call me Mercer. Abe was my academic adviser when I was at Penn State. We've been friends ever since. Who are you?"

"I'm his niece, Jordan Weismann."

Mercer was stirring granulated coffee into a cup and looked up at her, his expression more severe than the neutral one he had wished to present. Given the circumstances he couldn't be blamed, though. He said, "Abe doesn't have any nieces, and if your next answer is another lie I'm calling the police."

Her expression changed only slightly. It was a look of contrite embarrassment, not deception. "Look, I grew up calling him Uncle Abe—well, at least when he and my dad both taught at Carnegie. They were in the metallurgy department. I said that niece thing because I wanted you to know I belong here."

"And why are you here?" Mercer asked.

"He's letting me watch his place while he's off on some experiment. I forget where. I'm . . . Hey, can I get in on that coffee?" Mercer nodded and handed over the mug he'd prepared for her. She added enough milk to cloud the brew before stepping back again. "I'm kinda between jobs right now and, well, between homes too. Uncle Abe's doing me a huge favor."

Mercer got a mental flash of the gunmen fast approaching. He had no real evidence that they were coming here after murdering Abe and the others, but it was something he couldn't discount out of hand. He'd kept his SUV moving well above ninety for most of the drive from Minnesota, and had only caught a couple hours of rest. The shooters wouldn't need to stop for sleep if they shared driving duties, but they would not speed so as not to draw attention to themselves. Mercer estimated he had a thirty-minute cushion, and decided he shouldn't waste it chatting with one of Abe's old family friends.

"Jordan," Mercer began, "I don't know how to say this, so I am just going to come out with it." He was a stranger to her, and yet societal evolution had imparted an innate understanding of the tone he used. She blanched.

A hand went to her chest in a universal gesture of self-protection. "What happened to him?"

"He was killed," Mercer said as kindly as those words could ever be uttered, then added, "Shot dead by men who might be coming here."

It was like a rug had been pulled from beneath her

feet. She slid down the wall, landing with a thump on her backside, her instant café au lait falling from her fingers and splashing across the hardwood floor. She tried to keep her eyes on Mercer, but her head fell to her chest. For a moment he thought she had fainted, but then her face rose once again and her eyes brimmed with tears.

"Why would you say something like that?" Gone was the mature huskiness in her voice, replaced by a lost little girl's plaintive cry.

"I am sorry. But it's true. I chased the men who killed him, but they got away. Like I said, it's possible they are on their way here. You need to leave. Right now."

"But I just talked to him the day before yester—"

Mercer recognized that she was about to spiral into denial, followed by every other stage of grief, and he didn't have time to usher her through her sorrow. "Jordan, please. Pull yourself together. Do you have a car?"

She had managed to sniffle back tears, and focused all of her attention on him. He was now her anchor, and her eyes stayed with his as he crossed the room and offered her a hand back to her feet.

"Car?" he prompted again.

"Yes. Um, no. I mean I have a car, but it died when I got into town. It's at a garage out by the interstate."

"I have an SUV outside. Get whatever stuff you have here and hop in. I'll be there in a minute."

She didn't move. "My bag is in the trunk of my car. I forgot it yesterday and then Abe left and I was planning on walking out there today to get it. But now . . ." Her voice trailed off.

She was handling the news worse than he had expected, but then again he had no idea how close she and Abe had been. That he hadn't heard of her didn't mean the two hadn't been as tight as real family.

He made a quick decision. "Okay. Just follow me. This won't take a second."

"What are you going to do? If the men who killed Abe—" This time she choked off her own words because saying Abe had been killed was the first step in accepting he was gone.

"Don't worry," Mercer said with a smile and gripped her upper arm. She was so thin his fingers almost met despite the leather coat. "Like leaving a key under the frog, Abe was a creature of habit."

He found what he was looking for in the tiny closet off the room Abe Jacobs had used as an office/den. Mercer well remembered the old desk and swivel chair that squeaked only seconds after being oiled, and the club chairs that sat in front of the desk, chairs Mercer had lolled in through many, many evenings while deep in discussion back in Happy Valley. This room was a little smaller than that at Penn State, the view out the window a little more bucolic, but this was exactly like the den Mercer remembered from all those years ago, and he felt certain that Abe had replicated it wherever his career had taken him. In the bottom of the closet was a scuffed Samsonite suitcase made of a hideous blue indestructible plastic. Mercer pulled it free from under a mound of other detritus and set it on the desk. He pressed open the locks and levered up the lid.

Inside were all sorts of old papers, some stuffed in binders, others loose or in yellowed envelopes. There were some black-and-white photographs of people who were long dead and whom Abe had never discussed. There were a couple of books, including a Hebrew copy of the Talmud and a partial field guide for the maintenance of a Sherman tank's L/40 75mm M-3 cannon. At the bottom of the suitcase was a dirty rag rolled around a flat object about the size of a hard-cover book.

Mercer unrolled the rag, and into his hand flopped a brown leather holster for a German P-38 pistol, made not by the fabled Walther Company but under license by Spreewerke and marked by the letters CYQ. Abe's father had landed in Normandy as a tank's driver, and by the time he had battled through the Ardennes he was its commander. He had taken the pistol off a dead German officer following the Nazis' last major pushback against the Allied forces. Below the pistol was a small strongbox. Mercer knew that inside it were Mort Jacobs's medals, insignia, and military discharge papers. An entire gruesome chapter of both a man's youth and a continent's agony neatly tucked away.

"Is that a gun?" Jordan Weismann asked with a mix of revulsion and fascination.

Abe had first shown him the weapon when Mercer was an undergrad, and it had been Mercer himself who convinced Jacobs to allow him to clean the then rust-bound automatic. Abe would never be convinced to actually fire the pistol—he was a New York–born intellectual first and foremost—but out of respect to his late father he let his young protégé restore the P-38 to its original condition. What he didn't know was that the spare magazine tucked into a slot under the holster's flap had been loaded all those years before with eight rounds of Federal Premium 124 grain 9mil.

She watched with glassy eyes as Mercer pulled both the pistol and the spare magazine from the holster and allowed the tough old leather to drop back into the Samsonite. He thumbed the release to eject the empty magazine from the pistol's butt and rammed home the loaded one with a precise slap. He flicked the safety off, jacked the slide to chamber a round, thumbed the hammer back down, and reengaged the safety once again. The gun vanished behind his back and under his bomber jacket.

The cool ease with which he handled the deadly looking black gun brought a flush of unexpected arousal to Jordan's cheeks. She looked at him in hopes he hadn't noticed. He had, but his expression didn't change, for which she was grateful.

"This was Abe's father's," Mercer said. "He brought it back from World War Two. Abe hated the thing. He hated all violence, but he also couldn't part with it, so he's been lugging it around from one campus to the next just like that stupid cement frog and the picture of Jerusalem over the mantel."

Mercer took another look around the study. If there were any clues as to what Abe Jacobs had been doing in the mine to get him killed, they likely weren't here. Abe kept all his important research material and files in a campus office near his lab. At least he always had. The look on Jordan Weismann's face was one of doubt and uncertainty. She had to be wondering how a former student of stolid old Abe Jacobs could be so comfortable around a handgun. He wished he had time to explain, but the mental clock in one corner of his mind continued to wind down. The gunmen couldn't be that far away.

"I need to check out Abe's office on campus. Do you know where it is?" He took Jordan's hand, and they started out of the house.

She shook her head. "No, I'm sorry. I just got here

yesterday. Uncle Abe was in a hurry to leave, so I didn't get a tour of the school or anything."

"Okay. I'm going to stash you someplace, and then afterward you are getting out of town. Where are your parents? Still in Pittsburgh?"

"No," she said with a defiant edge to her voice. "My mom died three years ago from cancer, and my dad and I aren't exactly close."

Mercer paused just shy of the open front door and swung Jordan around so that he was looking her in the eye. "I don't know you from Adam, but you were a friend of my friend and that's good enough for me. Take some free advice and do yourself a favor. Unless your father is some sort of monster, there will come a time in your life where you are going to regret not having him around. I lost both my parents when I was twelve, and not a day goes by that I don't think about the relationship we were supposed to have. Reconcile with your father."

Her eyes tightened, and a crease formed between her well-maintained brows. "My life is none of your business."

Undeterred, Mercer said, "I'm sure Abe gave you this same advice on more than one occasion. He had no family, so I know he took on students as surrogates. I was one and so were you. He was a father figure and now he's gone, Jordan, and your real father is the only one you have left."

He was about to go on, but movement over her shoulder drew his attention. Jordan was tall enough for him to need to push her out of the way a little to clearly see the tree-lined street. A compact car—a Honda Fit—was driving by much too slowly for the time of day. Mercer had never seen the driver and the man had never seen him, but they both recognized each other as being someone out of place.

The driver was in his late twenties, blond and fit looking. His eyes widened at seeing a couple stepping from the house. Mercer tried to hide his surprise at seeing Abe's house being cased by an ex–Special Forces type. The driver turned his attention back to the road and buried his foot in the floorboards. The little car didn't have much in the power department, but it was nearly lost from view by the time Mercer launched himself at his SUV.

He had noticed the car had an Indiana license plate. It had doubtless been stolen by the gunman as he made his way south from the Minnesota mine. The man's apparent youth also suggested he wasn't a seasoned professional and was therefore not likely to be alone here in Killenburg. The lead man, the man Mercer had vowed to kill, was here too. Most likely at Abe's office while he sent his subaltern to search the less conspicuous house.

Mercer felt the SUV's passenger door slam as he jammed the key into the ignition. Jordan Weismann whipped an arm across her shoulder to buckle her seat belt. She didn't look over at Mercer, but he could see a tightening of her jaw and the ferocity at one corner of her eye. He knew women enough to know that asking her to get out would be a complete waste of time. Intellectually she knew the risks. He assumed she had never faced a barrage from an automatic weapon, so in a practical sense she had no idea what she was doing, but she had made a choice, and Mercer wasn't going to talk her out of it.

The big V8 roared to life, and arcing jets of slushy snow blasted from beneath all four wheels. Mercer balanced the heavy pistol into his partially unzipped bomber jacket.

"Do you have a plan?" Jordan asked, finally turning to look at him as the Yukon plowed through part of a snowbank in pursuit of the little Honda.

"Run this guy down and find out why he killed Abe and the others," Mercer said.

"Are you sure he's one of them?"

"I never got a good look at them all, but the way he just reacted tells me everything I need to know. He's one of the shooters."

The SUV had an automatic transmission, but Mercer worked the column shifter like a NASCAR driver, eking out the engine's maximum torque and using the motor to assist the brakes through the neighborhood's tight turns.

The light green Honda juked around a sharp corner a second after Mercer spotted the nimble little four-door. He cursed. It was like chasing a jackrabbit. The Honda Fit was more agile, had better acceleration, and the driver had the advantage of knowing where he was going. Mercer felt like he was guiding a hippopotamus, the Yukon lumbered so. It rolled into the corners like a sailing ship heeling in a gale wind.

The fleeing Honda took yet another sharp right turn, and Mercer suddenly understood what the gunman was after. He had flushed the SUV away from the target house, and now he was doubling back.

Mercer cranked the Yukon's wheel hard over and slotted the big SUV between a couple of pine trees and the corner of a mid-block house. The Yukon turned the front fence into so much wooden kindling as it blew through. They had no problem with the snow, bulling over drifts like a tank. They passed the house, and a nice glassed-in back atrium where the startled owner had been enjoying the morning paper and a coffee before an SUV barreled through his backyard. The truck tore apart a more substantial back fence and sped across some other poor suburbanite's lawn. This one abutted a raised ranch with a back deck draped in snow like white bunting. Mercer guided the truck through a high-speed slalom, avoiding copses of trees and an aboveground swimming pool. He didn't see a large plastic sandbox buried in the snow and tore across it in an unexpected explosion of sand particles as fine as diamond chips.

They careened past the ranch house and raced across the owner's front lawn. There were no more fences to crash through, but Mercer managed to accidentally clip the trailer hitch of a boat sitting in the driveway. In their wake the trailer's front jack collapsed, and a nice eighteen-foot bass boat tumbled to the frozen ground and capsized.

In a four-wheel drift that taxed the Yukon's suspension, Mercer threw the truck back onto Abe Jacobs's street. He'd managed to cut deeply into the Honda's lead but not nearly enough. The car was stopped in front of the Tudor house, driver door open, and the man was running from the house back toward the car. He saw the Yukon's sudden appearance, only a half dozen houses away, and dove back into the idling car.

The driver didn't wait to see his handiwork. The street was too wet with snow melted by the municipal salt trucks to peel out the tires, but he managed to get the car twitchy as he rocketed up through the gears.

For a breathless second, Mercer glanced at the house, and noticed the front window was broken. Then came a shattering explosion that blew the remains of the living room window across the lawn like a cannon blast from a ship of the line discharging grapeshot. The front door resisted the overpressure for only seconds before it, too, blew off its hinges and flew like a playing card into the street. Mercer stopped the SUV. Flames quickly engulfed the front of the house, licking at the stucco and igniting the decorative oak beams.

The explosive device the Honda driver had thrown through the window must have contained an accelerant. Gasoline would be easy enough, thought Mercer. Abe Jacobs's quaint Tudor home was about to become a charred pile of cinders and ash. The conflagration grew before their eyes. Smoke and then flame started pouring from the upstairs window above the front room. The house, and whatever clues Abe might have left behind, were moments away from being a total loss.

6

Mercer pulled his cell from his back pocket and slammed down on the accelerator once again. He tossed the phone to Jordan. "Call 911."

"About the fire?" Jordan asked, her fingers poised.

He knew the consequences would be dire if he was wrong, but he couldn't take the chance. "No. Tell them they need to lock down Hardt College. There are armed men on campus."

With so many school shooting tragedies in recent years, it was a threat law enforcement would not take lightly.

She hadn't yet spoken to a police operator when Mercer drove through the campus gates. There were few students out, thankfully most were in class, but a few people were walking the paths between the stately buildings. The structures were an odd assortment of clapboard and brick, Federal style and classical, built not so much to blend with each other but to showcase architectural taste at the time they were erected. One dorm had the glaze of blued glass and orange-dyed anodized aluminum popular in the late 1960s, while another was simple unadorned brick that had likely gone up during the austere war years.

Mercer saw a sign for the Lauder Science Center with an arrow pointing off around the imposing plantation-style mansion that had once been the entirety of the college. The roads were plowed enough so that Mercer couldn't tell if the green Honda was already here, but he felt certain it was. The road curved past some neglected gardens and around several more academic and administrative buildings, the largest of which was labeled Nichols Gymnasium—Home of the Brown Boars.

Mercer couldn't imagine a more uninspired name for a sports team. To add insult to injury, the mascot on the sign looked more like a South American tapir than a European boar.

They rounded a hill and continued following the signs for the science building. It had to be one of the school's newest construction projects. It stood four stories and was sheathed in dark glass with modernist touches including a grand atrium held up with struts like a giant Erector set. Inside they could see a large mobile in the shape of the solar system. Rather than traditional internal stairs, enclosed glass ramps looped along the outside of the building like the handles of an Etruscan vase. Jordan and Mercer watched students inside the ramps bustling along, and it reminded them both of gerbils in those elaborate plastic Habitrail cages.

Without warning, the students near the entry started running in panic. An instant later, Mercer saw beyond the large windows that the green Honda was racing into the building. It slipped right through the main doors and was careening across the tiled atrium, headed for the main ramp up to the second floor. The tube was more than large enough to accommodate it, but students either had to flatten themselves to the curved glass walls or try to race ahead of the car.

Mercer watched it speed up the ramp. Two students, a male and female, were struck and hurled against one of the tube's large curved windows. The coed left a smear of blood on the glass as she slid to the floor. Two more alert students who had pressed themselves flat to avoid the hurtling car quickly crossed the tunnel to help.

Mercer didn't yet know the driver's intention. But now that the other man knew he was being pursued, he would have no choice but to change his original plans. If Mercer had to guess, and he'd been thinking about little else during his long drive, the gunmen were here to steal anything pertaining to what they had already taken back in the mine. If that failed, their next priority would be to destroy any remaining evidence. The car might have been used to haul away material like notebooks or geological samples, but the eight or ten gallons of gasoline in the fuel tank could also ensure a fire of epic proportions.

There was a wide plaza in front of the science building. Some students were still running out the main doors, while others stood and stared after where the little Honda had vanished. They all reacted when Mercer ground his fist into the SUV's horn and steered the truck up the four steps onto the plaza. He now saw marks in the snow where the Honda had sped up a handicapped access ramp that was too narrow for the big GMC. Students scattered and Jordan was beginning to scream. Mercer ignored it all and guided the truck toward the entrance doors, slowing enough to give stragglers time to get clear before he rammed the truck into the opening. Though there were double doors, the entry was too narrow for the SUV. Aluminum jambs buckled and glass shattered when Mercer rammed the vehicle through.

More people reacted to the pandemonium. One hysterical woman stood with her hands clutched to her mouth and shrieked maniacally. Others ran for a set of internal stairs. The last of the students who'd been in the ramp made it to the atrium and scattered.

"What are you doing?" Jordan yelled.

"Not sure," Mercer told her.

The ramp was too narrow for the SUV, but following the Honda wasn't Mercer's intention. The sides of the truck were scraped down to raw paint, and both mirrors had been torn off by the entry doors. There was little additional damage Mercer could do to the SUV by slamming its nose into the tunnel entrance. The four-by-four actually made it deep enough that the front fender wedged against where the ramp began to curve out and up. There was no way the Honda could make it past them. Nor could he open either his or Jordan's door. He fumbled for a button to hydraulically open the rear gate.

"Go," he told Jordan. "I'm right behind you."

She needed no further prompting and quickly wriggled between the two front seats and legged over the back bench seat. In the rearview mirror Mercer saw her jeans stretched tight across her backside before his attention was grabbed by a new rush of frightened students running down the ramp, casting panicked glances behind them.

They reached the stuck SUV but paused at the obstruction for only a moment. Like lemmings, the students climbed over the hood and on top of the roof, forcing down the rear tailgate before Jordan could escape the trapped vehicle.

"Mercer," she cried from the cargo area.

The last student leapt onto the truck's hood, looking goggle-eyed at Mercer before scrambling up the windshield and onto the roof. Seconds later he slid down the back of the SUV and vanished across the science building's atrium.

Mercer was just reaching for the tailgate button again when the Honda came roaring down the ramp. There was a passenger sitting next to the driver this time. It was the team leader. He was in his forties with weathered lines around his eyes and a strong jaw. Any woman would have considered him handsome. His hair was just a little longer than a military buzz cut, and under a dark coat and thick sweater his chest and shoulders appeared broad.

That was all he saw of the gunman. Mercer might have thought he had trapped the killers in the building by blocking their escape, but the Honda's young driver was nothing if not adaptable. He cranked the wheel to the left, and the nimble car smashed through a laminated wood handrail and then the ramp's curved glass wall. The panes exploded in an eruption of shards that dusted the ground below. The car chased after the glittering avalanche. It had been doing less than twenty miles per hour and yet flew a remarkable distance before crashing to the ground in a dustup of white powder that cushioned the eight-foot drop. The driver kept the momentum going, the front wheels spinning wildly as the vehicle grabbed and fought to find traction.

Mercer swore. He hadn't anticipated that. While

the Honda reached a shoveled pathway and its tires found purchase, he dropped the GMC into reverse and pulled the SUV free of the ramp with the piercing whine of nails on a chalkboard.

He threw the Yukon into a tight K-turn, knocking over an abandoned reception desk and a bunch of ferns in a concrete planter.

"Hold on!" His warning came too late to prevent Jordan Weismann from being tossed around like the marble in a can of spray paint.

He jammed the gas pedal again and laid on the horn. By now all the students had wisely sought cover away from the chaos, and he had a straight shot for the main doors. Mercer misjudged slightly, and the big truck pinballed through the tight opening, breaking more glass and leaving behind curls of chrome trim on the floor.

The shooters were pulling away, but not too quickly. Their crazy stunt of launching the car off the ramp must have damaged the Honda somehow. It was going nowhere near its top speed. Mercer and Jordan had a chance. He took off after the gunmen, his eyes slitted against the glare of a newly shining sun. The Honda was headed for a back gate out of the fenced campus, and Mercer calculated angles and speeds and felt he had a good shot at catching them before they reached it. Jordan wedged herself back into her seat next to him, her expression as determined as his. It took just a few moments for the rampaging V8 to close the gap. Mercer felt the comforting weight of the P-38 still nestled in his jacket.

He hadn't taken any professional driving courses, but he'd talked to enough law enforcement to know how to spin out a car while in pursuit. The maneuver had more to do with momentum than the relative weights of the cars, but here, with a GMC SUV versus the little Japanese import, the advantage was all Mercer's.

Until the Fit's sunroof slid open and the team leader emerged, cradling a wicked-looking black machine pistol with a thick silencer. Just the day before Mercer had faced a full-on assault of four such weapons while driving a massive bucket loader. The shooters couldn't miss, then. Here, the ground was even rougher, there was only one gun, and despite its size, the Yukon was tiny compared to the Caterpillar 990 loader.

Mercer was confident that in the most vulnerable seconds before they rammed the car, the gunman's aim would be thwarted by his weapon's inherent inaccuracy, his bouncing gun platform, and the fact his target was hopping and jouncing as well. Mercer was just about to commit to his attack when he studied the small weapon's barrel and not the hurtling car and realized the 9mm aperture was rock steady. The shooter was so well trained and so proficient in this, the most difficult of shooting situations, that he had a dead bead on his pursuers.

"Down!" Mercer shouted, reaching across the center console to haul Jordan below the dash while he cranked the wheel sharply left, hurling the Yukon through a split-rail fence.

Half of a thirty-round magazine emptied into the SUV in as much time as it took Mercer to yell his warning, but his driving reflexes had been quicker than both his mouth and the gunman's finger, because the bullets stitched a trail across the top of the SUV's windshield and peppered a line down its flank. None of them hit where the shooter had been aiming—a tight slashing burst across the windscreen that would have decapitated driver and passenger alike.

While the Honda wove through a small forest of pines, its taillights growing more distant, Mercer fought to regain control as the Yukon fishtailed wildly in the middle of what appeared to be an open meadow. Having never been to the school before, he didn't understand the significance of the split-rail fence they had blasted through and didn't know something was seriously wrong until he heard the first moaning cracks of ice giving way under the truck's nearly three tons of steel. The open field was a pond surrounded by a fence so students didn't wander too close. Mercer chanced a look into the rearview mirror and saw that the ice in their wake was bobbing in great broken slabs that had dark water lapping at the back wheels.

Even farther behind he saw a bursting eruption of red and orange flame leap out of one of the science center's second-story windows, followed immediately by a rolling cloud of black smoke that climbed the side of the building toward its flat roof. Moments later came the jarring sounds of the detonation, the dull boom of the initial ignition, and the follow-up blast of overpressure powdering glass and concussing the cold winter air.

For now, all Mercer could do was curse again and concentrate on steering them out of this mess.

The far side of the pond, if the fence line was to be trusted, was a solid three hundred yards away. Knowing that ice near the shore is thicker than ice toward the center of a body of water, Mercer was sure that at the rate they were traveling, they were going to crash through. Their only chance was the frozen-over stream that fed the pond. The tiny lake's discharge was too well hidden by the snow, but he could see the silver husks of rushes sticking up where the feeder entered the pond. As gently as possible he turned the wheel, dropping his speed ever so slightly. As he'd experienced while working in the Canadian Arctic for DeBeers, too much speed on an ice road could build a sine wave of water under the truck and split the ice even before the front wheels hit it. He couldn't speed up, and with the ice breaking in their wake, he couldn't slow down either. It was a delicate balance.

Jordan finally realized their predicament and went ashen. "Mercer, we're on a pond."

"I know," he said tightly, easing off on the turn when the Yukon's nose was pointed between the two stands of water plants. He had been so easy on the wheel that the back end didn't so much as twitch on the grease-slick surface. The stream was about eight feet wide and would be shallow enough for the truck to remain in the clear should they crash through its crust of ice.

And as he neared the stream, the ice beneath the truck grew thicker. It still cracked under the SUV's crushing weight but didn't shatter. Snow lay deep around the edges of the pond, windblown into drifts of inestimable height. The front of the SUV plowed into one such drift just as they were exiting the pond and entering the feeder stream. Again, Mercer's lack of knowledge about the campus was his downfall. The pond was an artificial construct, the stream a man-made channel that fell into the usually bucolic water body from a three-foot-high brick-and-mortar waterfall that currently lay hidden under a mantle of powdery snow.

The wall was just high enough to catch the underside of the front bumper, and they were traveling hard enough to accordion the Yukon midway down its hood. Airbags deployed with explosive efficiency. Mercer just managed to keep from having his nose broken by one, while a still unbuckled and discombobulated Jordan bounced into hers with a shoulder and tumbled to the passenger-side footwell. The collision was enough to break the ice under the truck, and frigid water quickly began seeping in around the doors and rear gate, which had popped open once again.

Mercer's first concern was his passenger. "Jordan, are you okay?"

"Jesus, this water's cold." She quickly hauled herself up onto her seat. "And your driving sucks."

He almost smiled. That she could complain was a sign that she indeed was all right. "You wanted to come with me. Remember?"

Her dark eyes hardened. "You could have warned me you were nuts."

"You should have figured that out the moment you met me." Mercer lowered his window and flattened the already deflated airbag against the steering wheel. He pushed his body out of the truck and onto the door, making sure Abe's pistol was still tucked into his jacket. The front tires were fully submerged and had grounded on the bottom. The SUV's lighter back end still floated amid the broken chunks of ice. He swung up and out onto the hood.

The Honda continued to race for the back gate, probably unaware that the chase had ended, the sound of its trick exhaust diminishing with every passing second.

"Give me my phone," he said to Jordan as she

climbed over the center console and made ready to join Mercer on the Yukon's wrinkled hood.

"Remember when I said the water was cold?" she asked. "Yeah, well, I had my hand in it as I tried to rescue your phone from a watery grave."

"What about yours?"

"A melted puddle by now. I left it charging in Abe's kitchen."

It really didn't matter now. Mercer could make out the Doppler whine of approaching sirens. The authorities knew something had happened at Hardt College and were racing to investigate. Even if he somehow got a cop's attention and reported the fleeing Honda, the local authorities didn't have the manpower to secure the campus and go after the gunmen. Besides which, in the next ten or so minutes the shooters would steal another car and be making their way anonymously out of Killenburg, Ohio.

Mercer helped Jordan climb onto the hood. The metal was warm under their bodies, and he could hear the engine hissing and bubbling as it bled heat into the stream still trickling under all the ice and snow. He looked over at the Lauder Science Center expecting to see the wing where Abe Jacobs must have kept his office fully engulfed in flame.

Instead he saw wisps of white smoke coiling out of some shattered windows and icicles forming on the outside of the sills from the sprinkler system's discharge freezing against the cold metal framework.

There was hope of salvaging something from this mess after all. He yanked Jordan off the truck. "Come on. We're not done yet."

7

The sound of sirens grew steadily louder as the pair raced hand in hand across the campus. The snow was deep enough that Mercer needed to hold on to Jordan so he could help tow her through the taller drifts. If he hoped to find anything before the cops shut down the campus he would have to hurry. And because Jordan had spent time with Abe more recently, even if she hadn't been to his office here at Hardt, she might see anomalies that he did not, so he didn't consider abandoning her and sprinting ahead.

Mercer had no idea how long they would have once they reached the science center. Units from nearby towns would roll in to assist, and eventually county and state cops as well. Still, Mercer figured ten minutes at least before one of the responding officers left their cordon and actually swept the Lauder Building. After that, everything would become a crime scene, and they'd be faced with the same bureaucratic obstacles he'd managed to avoid in Minnesota.

Students had scattered from the building. Many were rushing across the rural campus for the purported security of their dorms. Others remained hidden behind cars in the adjacent parking lot. As they approached the battered front entrance doors, Mercer made sure no one could see his weapon and start a fresh wave of panic. A boy and girl huddled behind a bench on the cleared flagstone plaza in front of the modernist building. The science center's fire alarm wailed in rhythmic pulses that beat in on Mercer's brain.

He approached the duo hiding behind the bench. "Listen. I'm an off-duty cop," he said, and let them see the butt of the pistol. "When the uniforms arrive, make sure they know we're inside."

The wide-eyed girl and the goateed boy both nodded, not questioning why an off-duty policeman would need to bring a civilian woman into the building with him.

Mercer led Jordan inside. The lobby was a mess, with broken furniture, ruined carpeting, and junked bits of the SUV scattered on the floor. It was also thankfully deserted. But as loud as the alarm had sounded outside, now that they were in the building, the shriek was enough to make the two of them physically cringe. It was nearly impossible to talk.

Wordlessly, Mercer took Jordan's hand again and together they mounted the external ramp, mindful of where the car had smashed through the handrail and window. The floor was littered with glass shards, and a cold wind blew in through the jagged hole. Farther up and around they climbed until they reached the second-floor landing. To their left was a balcony that overlooked the main atrium and afforded a great view of the dangling solar system mobile. From the railing the installation's details stood out beautifully. Earth's moon was covered in miniature craters, and Saturn's rings were rendered in fantastical colors.

To the right was an open space littered with overturned couches and chairs that showed the tire tracks where the Honda had turned around. Leading away was a broad corridor lined with a series of closed doors that Mercer guessed were classrooms. Three-quarters of the way down the long hallway he could see fire-blackened Sheetrock, and he watched the spray of water pouring from the overhead sprinklers. The pressure wave from the initial explosion had blown the covers off most of the fluorescent lights and shattered the bulbs, so the hall was dimly lit but flashed brilliantly every couple of seconds when an emergency strobe light fired off in time with the siren. The effect was like that of a creepy fun house. Mercer yanked out his pistol when a student dashed from the shelter of one of the classrooms and raced past them without as much as a sideways glance.

He watched the student vanish down the ramp, bent low in a naturally defensive crouch, and then Mercer turned back to check the hallway again. He spotted movement—a shadow shifting behind the gray curtain of water pouring down through the fire suppression system. Mercer could understand a reluctant student hiding out in a classroom six doors down from the explosion, but not someone lurking just on the far side of where the blast occurred. The outline paused its pacing of the hallway and seemed to study them through the falling water.

Instinct and experience took over. Jordan was a pace or two ahead of Mercer. He launched himself at her, throwing his left arm around her waist and twisting her to the floor. He rolled over her as they landed, extending his right hand so that her body was covered by his and his pistol was aimed at the mysterious figure. Jordan was just taking in a breath to shout her angered protest at being manhandled when the hallway filled with the mechanical crash and subsonic judder of a silenced auto pistol discharging its deadly load.

The air in the corridor came alive with plaster dust and gunpowder smoke and a heavy mist of water blown sideways by the fusillade fired through the sprinkler cascade. Bullets chewed everything they touched, showering the couple with shredded batting from the ceiling acoustical tiles and bits of plastic from a fluorescent light cover.

Compared with the silenced machine pistol, Mercer's P-38 roared like a cannon in the hallway's confines. It was an assault on all the senses and one he tried to repeat, but the pistol jammed after firing just the single bullet, a hasty shot he hadn't aimed as much as hoped had gone in the direction of the shooter.

The analytical side of his brain knew that the eighty-year-old spring inside the pistol's magazine no longer had the yield strength it once possessed. In effect the magazine spring had been crushed flat over the years by the bullets Mercer had loaded so long ago, and could no longer bounce back into its original shape. The weapon fired the first round with no problem, but the next bullet in line didn't rise high enough out of the grip to be caught by the slide and chambered. Mercer would have to pop out the bullet and refeed it manually.

He thought through all this even as he peeled Jordan off the floor and half dragged her into a classroom. They just reached cover when another burst of autofire raked the corridor, some rounds thudding into the classroom's wooden door and others pinging off its frame. Mercer quickly noted that there were doors connecting this room to the next and, he assumed, to those farther down the hallway. This room was a chemistry lab, with long parallel rows of workstations stacked with beakers, pipette racks, and ceramic crucibles suspended over unlit Bunsen burners. He pressed Jordan flat to the floor behind one of the rows.

"Stay here."

"Don't worry," she panted. "I'm never following you again."

"Smartest thing you've said all day."

The connecting door was closed but unlocked. Mercer first cleared his pistol's jammed action and inserted another round into the chamber. He then thumbed all the remaining rounds from the defective magazine and held them ready in his left hand. He gave little thought to the fact he was facing a machine pistol with what amounted to a single-shot gun, and that his adversary knew he was armed. He needed answers, and taking this guy down was the only way he was going to get them.

He checked the next classroom before committing himself. It was a typical schoolroom, with a teacher's desk and lectern in front of a blackboard that faced about twenty students' desks. A few posters lined one wall while the other was windows looking out over a quad. Police cars were careening into view, their strobes flashing against the morning snow.

Mercer went on through the next room, and then the next. In this one, a clone of the previous, he could hear the roar of water still sluicing through the overhead pipes and discharging into what was presumably Abe Jacobs's office. The gunman hadn't fired again, and Mercer wondered if he was still waiting just beyond the veil of water. He wondered too why the gunmen had left a man behind. The only reason was that he and Jordan were the shooter's intended quarry. The driver had to have warned the leader that he had been made, and a hasty trap had been set here at Abe's office to not only destroy the scientist's work but to take out whoever it was who'd been dogging them since Minnesota. The lone gunman could then escape in the pandemonium.

He had to give it to these guys. It was a good plan that very nearly worked. He was just about to go through to the next room when behind him he heard Jordan Weismann scream.

He'd been flanked!

Mercer whirled and ran back as hard as he could. He streaked through the intervening rooms without seeing them and burst back into the chemistry lab. For a moment it looked like one of the students had taken Jordan hostage. The gunman had a smooth baby face and a thatch of dark hair slicked down to his head by a dousing under the sprinklers. He looked no more than seventeen but was probably twenty or more. A silenced Mini Uzi dangled from a sling off his shoulder while he held a black automatic pistol to Jordan's temple, his other arm snaked around her neck in a choke hold that barely allowed her toes to touch the floor. He doubtless expected Mercer to stop or at least slow his headlong charge.

The shooter was too young to have learned the lesson that you never play chicken with someone with nothing to lose.

Mercer kept coming at a full sprint. He watched

the gunman's eyes widen when he realized his tactical mistake, and he was just pulling his pistol from Jordan's temple to aim at Mercer when Mercer brought his own gun to bear and fired the only round he would need. The 9mm bored a hole through the shooter's forehead and erupted out of the back of his skull in a gout of pink and white and gray that splattered the wall behind them like an obscene imitation of a Rorschach test.

The gunman was punched back by the impact and nearly dragged Jordan to the floor as his body fell. She managed to disengage herself from the crumpling figure, and when she saw the ruin that was the back of his head she screamed into the echoes left in the gunshot's wake.

Mercer ran to her and took her up in his arms, turning her so she couldn't see the stain seeping from the corpse's head into the tile floor. Over the shrieking fire alarm he told her she was okay . . . it would be okay . . . meaningless platitudes, but as so often in the past they did the trick. Jordan soon stopped shuddering and gave him a hard squeeze before straightening out of his embrace.

"That was a hell of a risk to take with my life," she said, trying to sound tough, but she was obviously rattled and unsure whether to be grateful, angry, or to just give in to her terror.

"By the time I pulled the trigger, I was only about twelve feet away. I could have made that shot at twice the distance."

"Who are you? Seriously. What geologist can shoot a gun like that?"

"One who spends too much time in dangerous places" was all Mercer had the time to tell her. "Someone must have heard the shot. The police are going to be swarming this building in minutes. Come on."

They made their way down the hallway. Icy wind blew in from shattered windows, and there was no way to avoid ducking under the streaming sprinkler heads. The water felt like it was just a couple of degrees above freezing. Their leather jackets protected their bodies, but both had water streaming down their faces and under their collars after just a few seconds' exposure. Mercer withheld telling Jordan that the dousing had washed some of the shooter's blood and brain from the back of her coat.

Mercer had feared Abe's office had taken the brunt of the makeshift explosive's force but was pleased to find that the devastated room just off the hallway seemed to be a receptionist's office, with banks of three-drawer filing cabinets, a sofa and coffee table, and a large desk that had once been covered in papers. Those files lay sodden and charred like giant confetti all over the antechamber's floor. The sofa had been blown against the wall and flipped, while the remains of the coffee table were four stainless-steel legs and a metal framework standing in a sea of broken glass. The fire the gunmen had hoped to start never took root. Even without the multiple sprinkler heads pouring a constant rain into the space, the finishes and furnishings were too institutional to burn.

Each of the three doors opposite the entrance was made of solid wood, and one of them remained locked. The other two had been ripped off their hinges by automatic fire, the area around their handles shredded by high-powered rounds until the doors simply fell open. Each office beyond had windows that overlooked a parking lot, and each had been ransacked enough to prove that it hadn't belonged to Abe Jacobs. In one, Mercer saw the framed diplomas for a Professor Judith Murray. The other office was the work space for Dr. Anthony Wotz. Both rooms had suffered blast damage, ruined windows especially, but it was the gushing sprinklers that had caused the most destruction.

Mercer assumed that his and Jordan's arrival had stopped the gunmen from accessing the last office, Abe's no doubt. They must have known his office was located off the reception area but didn't know the exact suite number, and it was dumb luck they chose the wrong two doors first. A rare piece of misfortune for the gunmen, and Mercer knew well that fortune not only favored the bold but also the prepared.

He loaded another round into the P-38 and held the weapon at an angle at the spot where the lock entered the jamb outside of Abe's office and pulled the trigger. As before, the report was an assault on the ears far beyond even the wail of the alarm. Mercer kicked open the door and stepped into Abe Jacobs's campus office.

The room was packed floor to ceiling with boxes of papers and books. More paper spilled off a couch onto the floor in a long avalanche of data and notations. Abe's desk was buried under heaps of scientific journals and spiral-bound notebooks. An ancient computer monitor took up one corner of the desk, with a monstrous CPU sitting on the floor next to it, twenty-year-old tech that would not recover from the shower of water pulsing from the overhead pipes.

Mercer didn't know what to expect when he'd gotten here. A clue perhaps about what was going on. Instead he faced a mountain of possible clues. Any one of the notebooks, any single article in one of the hundreds of journals, could indicate what had gotten Abe and the others killed. He had first feared there wouldn't be enough to go on from here. Now he realized there was too much information to sift through in any meaningful time frame. Even if the authorities gave him unfettered access starting at this moment, it would take a month to sort all the boxes and files and tote bags and baskets and piles of paperwork that Abe had surrounded himself with.

There was only one logical move he could make since he and Jordan were out of time. He grabbed the trash can that had sat next to Abe's office chair. He dumped out about a gallon of water and saw that the can was about half full of random papers and one blackened banana peel. Whatever was in there likely included the last items his mentor was working on before he left for Minnesota. If Mercer was going to catch a quick break, he figured it was in Abe Jacobs's trash can.

"We've got to go."

"The trash," Jordan said archly. "That's all you're taking?"

"Feel free to load up on old copies of the *International Journal of Powder Metallurgy* or some of these other outdated rags," Mercer replied as he retreated back through the reception room and into the corridor. By now he was soaked to the skin and shivering. He looked back. Jordan was right behind him, her hair plastered to her head and her lips white and bloodless. The phrase "drowned rat" came to mind. He imagined he didn't look any better.

Rather than retrace their steps down to the atrium, they went deeper into the building. Mercer took a moment to hide Abe's pistol above the ceiling tiles in a classroom at the end of the corridor. He also emptied the trash can and stuffed the sopping contents minus the banana peel under his coat and led Jordan down a set of fire stairs to the main floor. There they found an emergency exit and stepped out into the chaos of a campus on lockdown.

"Keep your hands up and limp like you hurt your leg," Mercer warned as they started walking toward a parking lot.

"What? Why?"

"So the police don't shoot us and so we can get a ride out of here before anyone figures out we're suspects in all this."

"But we didn't do anything wrong," Jordan protested. Then her voice rose to a cry when she tried to lift her arms over her head. "Oh, shit. Ouch."

"What is it?" Mercer asked, instantly concerned. He turned to see her beautiful dark eyes widening in pain and confusion. She couldn't raise her left arm above her shoulder.

"I don't know. My arm. I did something to it. It's killing me."

He looked around. In a distant parking lot, police cars were blocking access to the science building, while behind the cordon, ambulances and other emergency vehicles were lining up to treat the unknown number of victims. A uniformed policewoman standing next to her cruiser spotted them and started waving them to her. Her partner covered the building from the other side of the black-and-white with a twelve-gauge pump action up to his shoulder, as if a shotgun would be any use at that range.

Mercer studied Jordan's arm for a second. There

was no outward sign of damage. Her scarlet leather jacket hadn't been holed by a bullet, nor was it camouflaging any sign of blood. He suspected that when he tackled her upstairs he had bruised or dislocated her shoulder or broken her collarbone. None of these conditions was life threatening. "Ignore it for now," he said as kindly as he could. "I know it hurts, but we need to get out of here as quickly as we can or we'll be stuck for days. Okay?"

She bit her lower lip, a gesture Mercer found irresistible in women. Her eyes were brimming with tears, but she nodded bravely. As more adrenaline wore off her pain would only increase.

Mercer took on an exaggerated limp as they shuffled first past the snowdrifted lawn surrounding the science center and then into the parking lot, where the police had lined up.

"Hurry," the female cop said as they approached, her hair tucked under her peaked cap and her eyes hidden behind mirrored shades. She directed them to the back of her car so that its bulk was between them and the building with its unknown number of shooters.

"I hurt my knee," Mercer said as soon as they were safely behind the cruiser.

"What happened?" The cop ignored his claim of injury.

"I don't know." Mercer spoke fast and put a high-pitched manic edge to his voice as if he was barely keeping it together. "We were on the second floor. We heard something downstairs and then this big explosion. We had to run past the office that blew up and then we heard gunfire. Well, I think it was gunfire—it sounded weird, muted like. Well, then two big booms. Bang, and then a few seconds later bang again. We were in the stairwell by then. That's where I fell and hit my knee. I tripped Jordan here. She says her shoulder's hurt too." He turned to her. "I am so sorry, Jord."

"We're out and safe," Jordan said, rubbing his arm as if he needed soothing to calm down. "That's all that matters."

"Did you see anyone or anything?" the woman cop asked. She eyed Mercer as if he were a suspect. For his part, Mercer slowly unzipped his jacket so she could see the strange bulkiness underneath was caused by the batch of wet papers from Abe's trash.

"No. Nothing." Mercer acted as though he just realized the papers he had tried to protect were sopping. "Goddamnit. I need these."

"Please, sir, stay focused," the officer said.

Jordan piped up, "Um, like, my arm is freaking killing me." She rubbed the joint theatrically.

"We'll take care of you in a second, ma'am," the cop said, and turned back to Mercer. "Are you sure you didn't see anything? We have reports of a car chase across campus."

Mercer kept his attention on the wet bundle of papers and answered distractedly, "Ah, no we didn't see anything. Like I said, we were in a second-floor chem lab. There was some kind of disturbance downstairs and then this really loud explosion. Jordan and I ran for it as soon as the sprinklers put out the little bit of fire that was in the hallway. Then the gunshots and we fell in the stairs and now we're here." He looked at her with the innocence of a child.

For her part, the cop seemed a little less suspicious of this slightly hysterical man and the woman who needed to keep touching him so he'd stay calm. In her non–politically correct mind she figured he was gay and the woman had more balls than him. "Do you have ID, sir?"

"Upstairs in my briefcase," Mercer said without hesitation.

The officer was about to ask a follow-up question when her radio blared. She listened to the acronym-laced call and spoke into her shoulder mic. "No, nothing since. Just students and faculty exiting the building." She listened again. "Roger that." She made a dismissive gesture in Mercer and Jordan's direction. "Get back behind the fire engines. There are EMTs and ambulances to take you to Presbyterian if your injuries are bad enough."

"Thank you," Jordan said. She looped her good arm under Mercer's shoulder, pressing up against his body so she could help him walk behind the police barricade.

"You'll get an Oscar for sure," Mercer whispered into her ear as they struggled another block away from the science center.

"I played Mrs. Higgins in high school," Jordan told him.

"Who?"

"*My Fair Lady*? Mrs. Higgins? Henry Higgins's mother?" Seeing she wasn't getting anywhere, Jordan gave up. "Your acting wasn't too bad, either," she said.

"I was channeling my inner Harvey Weinstein from *Independence Day*."

"That was Harvey Fierstein," Jordan corrected him. Her face was pale and not from the cold. She couldn't stop herself from cradling her bad arm with her good. "Harvey Weinstein is a movie producer."

"I'll take your word for it." By the time they reached the rows of ambulances and fire engines swarming with emergency personnel, Mercer had all but abandoned his fake limp so that he wasn't drawing attention to himself. Jordan shivered against him, and even he had to admit the chill was creeping into his bones. They needed dry clothes.

A pair of EMTs saw them coming and marched to them with blankets ready to throw over their shoulders. "Are you two okay?" one asked. He was short, with a cheesy mustache but a genuinely concerned expression.

"Hit my knee," Mercer said quickly, "but it's feeling better. Jordan's the worst off. She has a sore shoulder. Not sure why."

At that the two paramedics all but ignored Mercer and bustled Jordan to the ambulance's open doors, where heat blasted from the vents in an almost visible wave. They sat her on a gurney, and the medics peeled back the blanket and started manipulating her shoulder joint, asking her over and over what hurt, where, and how badly. While they worked on her, Mercer found spare scrubs in a locker next to the emergency vehicle's side door. No one was paying him any attention, so he sat on the threshold and pulled off his boots and jeans. Even exposed to the cold air his skin felt warmer being out of the wet denim. He slid on two layers of the thin cotton pants, drawing the waist strings tight. He used a pair of ACE bandages to fashion himself some socks and soon had his boots back on. Moments later he had a scrub top on under his sweater and jacket and felt almost human again. The scrubs had been sealed in a clear plastic bag. He wrapped the still-wet papers inside it before sticking them inside his coat along with all the stuff he'd had in his jeans pockets. The jeans he folded into a bundle around his damp socks.

He approached the EMTs still huddled over Jordan. "What's the verdict?"

"If she'd let us cut away her jacket we can confirm," the mustached paramedic said, "but I think her collarbone is broken."

"Hospital, then?" Mercer asked.

"Most likely."

Jordan chimed in, "Listen, guys, I don't doubt that it is broken, but I don't want you wasting your time on me."

She looked past the two hovering EMTs and gave Mercer a wink. He could have kissed her. She intuitively knew they couldn't be taken to the ER in an ambulance because there would be no escape once they were logged into the hospital's system.

She went on, "After an explosion like that there are probably a lot of hurt kids in there, and the gunmen are still on the loose. I don't want to be responsible for some injured cop or gut-shot student not making it to the hospital because I took his or her ambulance."

The men were obviously torn between helping an attractive, though mildly injured woman and the possibility of saving a life during a crisis. In the end, many EMTs are adrenaline junkies and want to be there for the dramatic rescue, so after exchanging a knowing look with his partner the spokesman of the pair said, "As long as you promise to go straight to the hospital." He glanced at Mercer. "You have a car?"

"Two-minute walk from here," Mercer assured him, not adding that it was currently half submerged in the pond, and cops were probably approaching the stranded rental as if it were John Dillinger's getaway car.

"Okay. You know where Presbyterian Memorial is?"

"I was born there," Mercer lied.

The EMT nodded. "Take her straight there. If she thinks her arm's sore now, give it more time and it'll get worse without treatment."

They swaddled Jordan in several blankets and helped her out of their ambulance. "Thanks," she said. "You guys are wonderful."

"Just take it easy from now on."

She rewarded them with another smile and let Mercer lead her away. Out of earshot she said, "We don't have a car and you have no idea where the hospital is. I've stuck with you this far, but I am not kidding when I say my arm is really hurting."

"Trust me," Mercer said. "We'll be on our way in no time."

News vans were starting to pull onto the campus but were being held back behind a second police cordon. Mercer and Jordan passed through this one without being questioned and were soon in another parking lot where students were aimlessly milling around. He approached one kid sitting in a parked car with its engine running. The door was open while he listened to a live news broadcast from a radio reporter standing about twenty feet away.

"How would you like to be a hero?" Mercer asked when he was within speaking distance.

The student looked up at them. "Huh?"

"A friend of ours was just taken to the hospital, but we weren't allowed to ride in the ambulance with her and we're hoping you can give us a ride."

"Where'd they take her? Presbyterian?" the kid asked. He was clean-shaven and dressed in an expensive overcoat, although his jeans were ratty and his shirt was wrinkled. Mercer guessed the coat was a recent Christmas gift. The white late-model BMW station wagon was likely a hand-me-down from his mom.

Mercer shook his head. "No, they mentioned another hospital. I'm sorry, we're not from around here."

"Presbyterian is the closest, but there's also St. Agnes about ten miles farther east."

"That's the one!" Mercer crowed. "St. Agnes. That's where they took her. The ambulance guys said something about an orthopedic specialist on staff there."

"Please," Jordan said, giving him a pout with promise.

Any doubt the kid had vanished in her liquid dark eyes. "Sure," he said. "Um, hold it a second, I need to clean up a little." He shoved used takeout wrappers and water bottles from the front seat into a plastic FoodLand bag and tossed it into the back cargo area. Mercer helped situate Jordan in the front seat and got her belted, explaining to the kid, who said his name was Alex, that she hurt her arm in the stampede outside the science building.

A minute later they pulled out through Hardt College's main gate, and thirty minutes after that Jordan was explaining to an emergency room doctor at St. Agnes Hospital that she had slipped on some ice in her driveway and she thought she had broken her arm. When the subject of the attack on the local school came up, she and Mercer pled ignorance. Two hours later, Mercer delivered Jordan, in a fresh white sling, into a newly rented Hertz SUV he had ordered sent to the hospital parking lot.

She was on enough painkillers that she didn't respond when he asked her if she wanted to get anything out of her car. He figured she shouldn't be alone for the next couple of days, but Mercer wasn't about to hang around Kellenburg, Ohio, playing nursemaid, so he just let her sleep and turned the Chevy in the direction of his home near Washington, D.C. When she was up to it, he'd get her back to pick up her car somehow.

He placed a mental wager that by the time he arrived at his brownstone, the FBI would have made the connection between the parallel attacks by running the registration for the vehicle he'd abandoned on the campus pond.

He made a call to an old friend, hopefully to forestall a trip to the Hoover Building. Being proactive, rather than reactive, was a philosophy that had always served him well.

8

By a quirk of fate, Philip Mercer still lived just outside of Washington, D.C., in the urbanized suburb of Arlington. He'd been there since soon after earning his PhD in geology from Penn State and accepting a job with the U.S. Geological Survey. That particular bit of employment hadn't lasted long. He was too independent-minded for government work and soon branched out as a consulting geologist for private mining concerns. His first major contract netted him more money than he'd ever thought possible. He liked money as much as the next guy, but it had never been his prime motivator. Mercer thrived on the challenge rather than the reward, which explains why he had left the USGS so quickly. Not knowing what to do with his newfound wealth, he'd listened to the landlord in the brownstone where he rented a one-bedroom apartment. The man had convinced him that real estate was the only true measure of long-term wealth, and had sold Mercer the six-unit building at what truly was a very good price.

What the previous owner had failed to mention

was that being a landlord, even to just five other families, was as thankless a job as a Mumbai sewer shoveler. His first 1:00 a.m. call about a leaky faucet convinced him to hire a management company, even though they sopped up 20 percent of the building's revenue. It mattered little. The other tenants knew he owned the brownstone, which somehow gave them the right to bother him at all hours of the day or night, for repairs both big and small.

After six months of near-constant pestering, Mercer had finally had enough, and he converted the brownstone into a single-family dwelling, of which he was the sole occupant. His life had taken some wild turns since then, but the brownstone had remained his one safe harbor, and he had kept to a vow made all those years ago that he'd sleep on the streets before ever becoming a landlord again.

He steered the rental onto one of the few remaining original residential streets in Arlington, right across the Potomac from the nation's capital. Mercer smiled when he saw the car parked in his customary spot at the end of the block. He'd just taken delivery of it the day before heading out west to teach the class in mine rescue techniques. It was a Jaguar F-type hardtop in black with black interior and the hottest wheels he could find. This was the V8-powered S version with an eight-speed automatic transmission that could smoke any manual off the line and had the added bonus of not deadening a driver's clutch leg in D.C.'s notorious traffic. He had been toying with a replacement for his venerable XJS for a while, testing Porsches, Maseratis, and some of the slinkier BMWs, before settling on another of England's premier sports cars. This particular model was as sleek and beautiful as its namesake South American jungle cat and was a fitting tribute to its ancestor, the E-Type Jag, which set the standard in the 1960s for all supercars that followed.

Jordan Weismann had awoken several hours earlier but had been quiet, her head resting against her window, her gaze fixed on the nothing they had passed. Mercer could tell her pain was back and that she was resisting taking anything for it. Though he himself would have done the exact same thing, he thought her stubbornness especially pointless. There was no shame in taking a couple of painkillers.

"We're here," he announced. It was after rush hour, so the block was relatively quiet. He found a spot for the rental behind an incongruously parked school bus.

What gave Mercer even more joy than the beautiful sports car was the three-story brownstone. It was a sanctuary from the world, a space he had created where outside pressures did not exist. Usually once he passed through the front door and into the towering foyer he could forget everything but finding his center once again. With Abe's death so fresh on his mind and the questions swirling about the motive for his murder and the identity of the people behind it, he knew he would find little solace here—but it still felt good to be back.

He stepped out from the truck. The air in Washington was twenty degrees warmer than it had been in Ohio, and there wasn't a bit of snow on the ground. Despite the proximity to the city and the high rises that surrounded the little residential enclave, the evening smelled like spring. He helped Jordan from the SUV. Her mood, if anything, had soured further. It seemed as if it wasn't just the physical pain of her broken bone, but the emotional toll of losing Abe as well as the adrenaline hangover of nearly being killed. Mercer predicted from his own experiences that she would not eat tonight and would sleep for the next twelve hours, but then wake up as ravenous as a bear coming out of hibernation.

He sensed something was wrong as soon as his fingers curled around the front doorknob. Mercer instantly regretted ditching the P-38 pistol for fear he and Jordan would be searched following their escape from the Lauder Science Center. There was a slight vibration coming through the door, and even as he realized what was happening, his wariness waned and anger flowed in.

The door was unlocked, most every light in the house was on, and the wireless speakers were belting out a raucous Gene Krupa drum solo from the 1938 Benny Goodman Carnegie Hall concert. There had to be twenty people dancing in the open-plan living room and around the billiards table that occupied what should have been the dining area. Others stood on the antique spiral staircase that corkscrewed up to the second- and third-floor balconies overlooking the atrium, their feet tapping in time to the primal drumbeat. And in the middle of it all was Harry White, resplendent in a zoot suit straight out of an old gangster movie. He twirled one elderly woman into the arms of a gentleman while a second blue-hair awaited her turn in his studied embrace. He saw Mercer and mouthed, "Oh shit."

Harry's new dance partner must have sensed his consternation because she turned and saw the youngest man in the room by three full decades in the company of an even younger woman. They had just come in the front door, and while the pretty woman looked confused, her handsome friend looked beyond mad.

Dev Hindle, who had been standing with his wife, Marta, at the second-floor library balcony, recognized the home's rightful owner and quickly retreated to the stereo rack in the rec room to kill the throbbing big-band swing. Judging by the look on Mercer's face, Dev realized that old Harry hadn't gotten permission to invite the Oaklawn Retirement Community's Saturday Socialistas over for a midweek dance. Dev knew Harry from when they both worked for Potomac Edison and had met his young friend Philip Mercer at a local bar called Tiny's on a few occasions.

The silence crashed in on the party as soon as he muted the stereo. A few people muttered their surprise, but most looked at their watches and assumed it was time to return to the bright yellow bus for the ride back home. No more than a minute after Mercer opened the front door to find Harry re-creating scenes out of *Cocoon,* the last of his guests shuffled past a still-irate homeowner. And then a couple in their seventies who had been necking in an upstairs bedroom came down the stairs in a breathless huff.

Mercer glared at Harry when the trysting couple dashed past, the man's collar smeared with lipstick and her knee-high support hose down around her ankles.

"In my defense," Harry said when the door closed after his last guest, "you weren't supposed to be back until tomorrow." His voice sounded like railroad spikes drawn across a rusted iron plate, a rasping sound earned through sixty-plus years of cigarettes and Jack Daniel's.

"And *you* weren't supposed to use my house as the venue for some golden years bacchanalia."

"Bacchanalia?" Harry scoffed dismissively and

rubbed a hand through his silvery crew cut. "Only a few of us had anything stronger than sugar-free diabetic punch, and there's no way Betty Norris let Jim Peters get past second base."

"Mercer, what's going on?" Jordan asked peevishly. She was pale and trembled, and he realized she was spiking a fever. "Who is this?"

"Sorry. This is my, ah, my—" Mercer paused, trying to decide how to describe his best friend. "Harry White."

The old lothario didn't miss a beat. "I was his Harry White. From now on I will be your Harry White."

"Harry," Mercer continued. "This is Jordan Weismann. She grew up knowing Abe Jacobs."

Despite the drinks he had doubtless consumed, Harry detected an undercurrent in Mercer's voice. "What happened?"

"Abe's dead," Mercer said, exhaustion suddenly making his eyelids feel like stones. The shoulder he'd scraped leaping from the bucket loader suddenly started to ache too. "He was shot in Minnesota. His lab in Ohio was blown up and his house burned down. The shooters nearly got Jordan and me a couple of times."

"Ah, Christ," Harry spat. "I only met him once, but I liked the old guy." It was lost on Harry that he was fully ten years older than Abe Jacobs had been. In fact he was twice Mercer's age but somehow saw the two of them as contemporaries.

White pulled a half-crushed pack of Chesterfields from the pocket of his baggy suit pants and was about to light it when he caught Mercer's disapproving glance. They'd both made sacrifices recently, and he was still getting used to it. He stuffed the pack and an old Zippo back into his pocket.

"Jordan," Mercer said, turning to her, "give me a few minutes to make sure one of the guest rooms is done up and you can hit the sack. You need to take some meds for the pain or you'll never sleep, and I'll get some ibuprofen for that fever."

She said nothing. Her eyes, usually bright and inquisitive, were dull and listless. She finally showed a spark of interest when movement caught her attention. It was coming from down a corridor that ran past the kitchen and Mercer's home office to a set of back stairs. The movement was accompanied by the click of something hard against the marble floor. From the shadows of the dimmer part of the house emerged what appeared to be a parti-colored child's golf bag laid on its side with four stumpy legs for support. At the rear end was a tail that flew at half-mast, while at the front was a blocky head with a silvered muzzle the length of a toucan's bill and two enormous ears that swept the ground with each tottering pace.

"Is that a basset hound?" Jordan asked of the decrepit canine.

"That's Drag—he's half basset, half Hoover canister vacuum," Harry said proudly. "Drag, come here, boy, and meet your future stepmother."

Nearly twenty years earlier, Mercer had found Harry on a bar stool at Tiny's the first night he'd moved into the neighborhood, when he had gone out as a distraction from unpacking. A decade later, Harry had found Drag rummaging around a Dumpster behind that same seedy dive. Mercer had always felt that he had drawn the short stick in this deal, while the mangy dog had won the damned lottery, especially since developers had recently bought Harry's nearby apartment building, evicted all the tenants, and torn it down to make way for a secondary parking structure for a local mall's expansion. For the past five months Drag and Harry had been Mercer's houseguests, and since Harry had yet to start looking for a new place and Drag didn't appear too eager to move either, he suspected the pair had now morphed into permanent roommates.

Drag ambled over to Jordan, who bent at the knee and extended a hand. Because of his sensitive nose, the dog had already determined she was okay though devoid of any decent food scents, so he ignored her proffered hand and flopped next to her like a walrus, exposing his ample belly for immediate attention.

"He's adorable," Jordan said despite her mounting misery, a chunky plastic bracelet jangling as she scratched Drag and the hound's leg went into paroxysms of pleasure.

"Don't let him hear you say that or he'll never leave you alone," Harry said. He turned to Mercer. "Don't you have work to do, innkeeper?"

Mercer called Harry a bastard under his breath and climbed the antique corkscrew stairs to the second floor while his octogenarian friend and his broken-down dog helped Jordan forget the past fourteen hours. He had never been more grateful to the unlikely duo than he was right now.

Few people ever experience how truly ugly terrorism can be, and Jordan had just been given a very personal dose. People see it on the news or read about it in the paper, Mercer thought, but it's different when it happens close by because it is no longer an abstraction happening to others. The guns are meant to kill you and the explosions are meant to tear into your body, and even if you survive you are forever changed. That is one of terrorism's hidden aims—to mentally scar those left in its wake so that they never feel safe again and always fear the light. It is therefore up to the survivors to defy the killers and show that they will not be victimized. The old man and his equally ancient pooch were subliminally guiding Jordan on her journey back from the darkness, and Mercer knew she couldn't have been in better hands; those two had done it for him on more occasions than he cared to remember.

The second-floor landing was Mercer's library, and the shelves were lined with countless first-edition science books and texts. Collecting them had been a passion for many years, and while he enjoyed looking at them he admitted to himself that the desire for acquiring more had waned. Bifurcating the shelves was a set of French doors that led to the rec room, a large space decorated in oaks and brass, and brown leathers and forest greens. A well-stocked bar ran along the right wall, and a large flat-screen hung on the wall opposite the doors. This was the heart of Mercer's home, where he spent the lion's share of his time. The seat of one of the bar stools fit his butt like a glove, while to his chagrin another fit Harry's even better. Long before losing his apartment, Harry considered Mercer's place his own, and that went doubly for the ranks of liquor bottles behind the bar.

Mercer crossed the room, noting that Harry had stayed true to his word and not smoked in here since he'd been away. That was the aged letch's price for room and, if not board, at least a half gallon of Jack Daniel's per week—he had to smoke outside. Mercer really didn't care about the smell. Harry had been smoking in his house for so long he was immune to it, but it was his way of urging his old friend to cut back on the cancer sticks.

He didn't kid himself that he was adding years to Harry's life by making his nicotine habit a little harder to feed—the guy was on the hard side of eighty-five, after all—but it was a gesture of concern, a male way of showing he cared without actually admitting it.

Beyond the rec room were two guest rooms connected by a Jack-and-Jill bath. This was Mercer's real concern. Jordan would be sharing a bathroom with an eighty-plus-year-old man with an enlarged prostate, poor eyesight, and shaky hands—also known as the filthy john trifecta. To his amazement, the bathroom sparkled and smelled of air freshener and a hint of vanilla from a recently snuffed candle.

Mercer's natural suspicion rose, and he guessed that in a day or two he'd be getting a bill from the maid service Harry had hired in anticipation of tonight's geriatric debauch. He double-checked the bedroom Harry wasn't currently occupying. It was functional if a bit bland, but the sheets were clean and there were fresh towels in the closet. Mercer unplugged the telephone extension on the nightstand from Jordan's room so in the morning it wouldn't disturb her, and he dumped the phone in the hall closet where he kept spare linens and the wand and hose for the central vacuum cleaner.

He found some pills in the medicine cabinet and brought them with him back to the bar. Harry had coaxed her up the stairs, led her to a leather sofa, and pulled a wool lap robe up to her shoulders. She was shivering with the ague of her fever. Harry was behind the bar mixing himself a Jack and ginger.

"Get some water for Jordan, then make me a double," Mercer ordered and crossed to her side. Drag had levered his tubular body onto the couch next to her and packed his considerable bulk against her to add warmth.

He sat near her and stroked a feather of damp hair off her forehead.

"I feel like crap," she said without opening her eyes.

"You'll be okay. It's just your body telling you to stay still for a while and rest."

"It could have just texted me and not given me the chills, aches, and general crappiness."

"Yeah, well the human body can't text just yet."

She opened one eye to look at him. "Did I just say my body should text me?"

"You did."

Jordan giggled. "I'm sorry, but I don't think I know what I am saying anymore. Sorry about all this."

"No need to apologize. God knows what would have happened to us both if we hadn't met."

She gave him a queer look, as though she hadn't considered their meeting being so providential, but she couldn't maintain any level of concentration and her face relaxed once again. Harry handed Mercer a glass of water and went back behind the bar to mix a double vodka gimlet. Mercer woke Jordan and got her to sit upright so she would take the ibuprofen. He also got her to swallow two of the prescription pain tablets she'd been issued in Ohio.

He then slid one arm under her knees and another under her shoulders. Like many women, she hated being picked up lest her weight be judged, but Mercer had her up and against his chest so quickly and so effortlessly that she mewed softly, then rested her head against his shoulder while he carried her through to the bedroom.

He laid her on the bed and regarded her face. Her mouth was tight as she fought against the fever and her skin was pale, almost translucent. Though wet with perspiration, her hair was still thick and so dark it almost had sapphire highlights, like the wing of a raven. Her bone structure was flawless.

Looking down at Jordan Weismann as she once again sank into deep sleep, Mercer felt the stirrings of attraction, which he discounted quickly. What man wouldn't be attracted to a smart, beautiful twenty-something woman who was fifteen years his junior? She was every guy's fantasy girl . . . but Mercer wasn't so hard up as to try to seduce her. He tucked the blanket tighter around her wan face and brushed her hair off her forehead again, then killed the light and shut the door behind him before making his way back to the bar.

"First of all," Harry said and saluted him with a recharged Jack and ginger. "You have brought some beauties home over the years, but this one takes the cake. I thought the one from a few months ago, ah . . ."

"Cali."

"Right. Cali. She was fine and all, but she didn't have much up top and you know I like a woman with a little more blouse bounce. Even with her arm in a sling I can tell Jordan has a rack on her that'd shame a moose."

Mercer wasn't sure if he heard Harry correctly, but fearing that he had, didn't ask for clarification.

"Of course," White continued and handed Mercer his drink, a twinkle in his rheumy blue eyes, "she is a little old for my tastes."

Mercer shook his head and slid onto his bar stool. He gave his old friend a reprieve from their roommate contract by saying, "The smoking light is on, go ahead and light 'em if you got 'em."

"Much obliged," Harry replied and pointed to the already smoldering butt in an ashtray. He knew Mercer needed to talk tonight and rightly assumed he didn't want to wait for him to go outside for a smoke. Harry took his customary seat next to his best friend and affected a studied slouch. Where once he had been a tall, straight man, years had rounded his shoulders and put some thickness around his waist. His face was wrinkled by time and abuse, but there was a merriment and kindness to him, the type that children and women see intuitively. It was why Drag had followed him home after God knew how many others had tried to help the mangy beast. It was also what made these two men such great, if unlikely, friends—these were quiet traits both shared but never boasted about.

"So what's her deal?" Harry finally asked, blowing a jet of smoke ceilingward.

Mercer told him everything that had happened since he first heard the shooters open up with their automatic weapons in the Leister Deep Mine, all the way to his phone call to Dick Henna, an old friend who had once been the director of the FBI. Mercer had been forced to leave a message—Henna had become withdrawn ever since his wife, Fay, had died of a sudden stroke. He had hoped to catch Dick and stave off a full FBI assault on his house.

His backup plan was to call the D.C. field office in the morning and explain who he was and what had been happening. Though he loathed government bureaucracies, the FBI was the agency best equipped to check the papers he had recovered from Abe Jacobs's trash. That evidence was still sealed in the scrubs bag in order to prevent the fragile paper from drying out and disintegrating.

"Any idea who is behind all this?" Harry asked when the story and second pair of drinks were done.

"None," Mercer conceded. He had hoped the re-telling would give him some sort of insight. "With his office ruined by the sprinklers and his house more than likely leveled, looking into Abe's connection is a dead end unless we get something from the papers we salvaged."

"What about the scientist he was helping? Any-thing on her?"

"Susan Tunis was her name. I don't know anything about her other than Abe agreed to assist in her re-search. And don't ask me what that was, because he never told me. All he did was hint that it was some-thing revolutionary."

"Apparently revolutionary enough to kill for," Harry added.

Mercer then realized the mistake he had made. He had figured the timing of the attack had coincided with Abe's arrival at the mine, so he had concentrated his efforts on investigating his old friend. He hadn't considered that another team of gunmen would have gone to wherever this Susan Tunis worked and sani-tized her home and office as they had done to Jacobs's. Mercer could chalk it up to exhaustion or the need to protect Jordan Weismann, but he knew the truth was he'd screwed up. He should have forced that state cop, Gerard, to use whatever pull he had to get the feds to Tunis's known addresses as soon as possible.

Mercer knocked back the last of his drink so that the ice cubes rattled against his lip.

Maybe he was kidding himself. A Minnesota state policeman didn't stand a chance of getting the FBI to change their entrenched procedures. The gunmen had a large window in which to operate before any real pursuit coalesced. Maybe he'd get lucky and some sharp agent would have added two and two and gotten four, but he wasn't optimistic. Hell, they hadn't even figured out his role in the attack at Hardt College.

Mercer debated having a third drink, won the debate, but only made it a small one. While he was sipping it, Harry shrugged into a blue windbreaker and unfurled Drag's leash. The dog heard the leash's rattle, cocked one ear, and lifted one sagging eyelid but otherwise didn't show the slightest interest in moving from the couch.

"And this is why," Harry said as he clipped the leash to Drag's collar, "I didn't name you 'Walk.'" He had to skid the stubborn dog across the slick leather for a ways before Drag gained his feet and jumped off the sofa.

It took a full minute of cajoling and dragging to get the basset to the front door, Harry muttering good-natured curses the entire way.

9

They had to have used lasers on the windows to detect the glass vibrations and translate that into voices and sounds, because they knew someone was coming to the front door. Harry's hand was inches from the knob when the door blew inward. Immediately, dark shapes swarmed into the foyer. They must have realized the layout of the house with its towering ceiling made tear gas all but useless and flashbangs were too loud in such a tight neighborhood, so they came instead with overwhelming force.

Harry went down under the weight of three men wearing forty-odd pounds of tactical gear including vests and riot-shield helmets. Drag went berserk as soon as his master fell to the hard marble floor. He clamped his jaws on the nearest target, which turned out to be one of the men's butts. The guy howled at the pain while Drag tried but failed to find purchase on the slick Carrera tile so he could tear out a chunk of his gluteus.

Mercer heard the commotion and ran past the library to the balcony. Even with three men already atop

Harry White, more poured through the front door, assault rifles and shotguns held high and at the ready.

Drag was either shaken off or more likely lost interest because he let go and moved out of the way of the tactical assault team. There were eight in total. Three held Harry, and three others kept their weapons trained on Mercer while two more spiraled up the stairs, never taking their sights off Mercer, who had wisely dropped his barely touched drink and laced his fingers behind his head.

"Mercer," Harry wheezed from the bottom of the pile. "Someone at the door for you."

At that moment two more strangers entered the house, a man and a woman, both wearing dark suits, though hers appeared of better cut and quality. Both had automatic pistols in their hands. The woman, blond and about forty, held hers low and relaxed, while her partner kept his up by his head, alert and seemingly eager to pop off a few if the need arose.

"Stand down," Mercer shouted, trying to regain some modicum of control. "There is a third person in the house. A woman. Jordan Weismann. She is asleep here on the second floor in a back bedroom."

"Who the hell are you?" the man in the suit hollered up.

"Philip Mercer, the guy you are here to talk to. The eighty-year-old you so righteously took down is a friend. You are FBI, right?"

By then, the tac-team members who had come up the stairs forced Mercer to his knees, frisked him, and cuffed his hands behind his back with a zip tie. Satisfied they had him secure, another agent mounted the stairs to take charge of the prisoner, while the first pair went to search the rest of the house.

The men pinning Harry to the floor finally started to get back to their feet. They looked sheepish and knew tonight's exploits would be the source of a great deal of teasing once they returned to the Hoover Building. It took a trio of them to wrestle some geezer to the ground, and one of them had a tooth-marked ass thanks to the old man's fat dog.

"Got one," the tactical guy yelled from the upstairs bedroom. "It's a woman and she's out cold."

"Be careful," Mercer warned him. "She has a broken collarbone."

"Are you Philip Mercer?" the male agent asked, all bulging eyes and puffed-up chest.

"I just said I was no more than ten seconds ago," Mercer snorted. He turned his attention to the female agent. He could tell by her suit and bearing that she was actually in charge and not her testosterone-fueled partner. "You could have just called me, you know."

"True," she said and holstered her boxy Glock automatic, "but where's the fun in that?"

"Where exactly is the fun in all *this*?" Harry spat. His clothes were a mess, his lip was bloody, and in all the excitement Drag had peed on the floor. White motioned to the offending puddle with a cuffed hand. "It's your fault he had an accident, so one of you tinhorns is going to clean it up."

"Shut up, you old fart," the male agent barked.

Harry whirled on him, his mouth a grim, tight line, and his eyes so focused the FBI agent couldn't turn away. He was like a chicken mesmerized by a cobra.

"Just so you know, Sunnybuck"—Harry's voice was hard, grating, like some Old Testament prophet raging at the furies—"when your daddy was still sucking your granny's tit and long before he realized his little mushroom prick could do more than piss in his diaper, I was in the goddamned merchant marines convincing kamikazes to dance with the wrong end of my fifty-cal. So fuck you and your 'old fart' crack and clean up my dog's pee." Still in a huff he turned to Mercer. "This kind of shit keeps up around here, and I think I'm gonna get my own place again."

Mercer replied without hesitation, "I'll help you pack."

A cell phone buzzed in the awkward silence that followed. None of the agents, especially the two seniors in their suits and button-downs, expected such detachment in the face of overwhelming force and firepower. The old man was more concerned about his dog and was practically foaming at the mouth in righteous indignation over the poor thing, while Mercer himself was as icy calm as a surgeon. If anything, there was a spark behind his eyes as if he knew this was some sort of practical joke that only he was in on. The female agent pulled a sleek black phone from her jacket pocket, and her eyes widened and her mouth tightened when she saw the calling number on its display.

If Mercer's suspicions were right, her self-control was impressive. He figured if this particular call had come to the male agent, he would have had an accident far worse than Drag's.

She swung the phone to her ear and turned away. The sonic blast of the caller's voice forced her to pull the cell away from her head, but she was aware that the two prisoners could hear the verbal broadsides coming through the tiny device and clamped it back again. Mercer felt a bit of regret. Because of the culture within the FBI, the chewing out she was now receiving for a screwup that wasn't her fault could set her career back significantly. Mercer made a mental note to call Dick Henna once more and make sure she and the tac team were protected from the inevitable bureaucratic furor. The male agent could fend for himself.

Though he couldn't hear the man berating her over the phone, he could listen in on her responses, each one preceded and postscripted by "Sir."

"Sir, yes, sir . . . Sir, a few minutes ago, sir . . . Sir, Mike Gillespie and Tom Walsh's tactical team, sir. Sir, two others, a female and an older male, sir. Yes, sir, one moment, sir." She clamped a hand over the cell's microphone and said to Harry, "Sir, is your name Harry White?"

Wary, Harry said, "Who's asking?"

"My boss about five times removed, Deputy Director William Higgins."

After a moment's thought Harry's wizened face brightened. He had met Higgins years earlier when the FBI had placed a protective detail at Mercer's house following a murder attempt linked to a radical environmental group. Higgins had been an agent on the rise and had obviously done very well indeed. "Tell Billie it's old Harry all right and that I haven't forgotten I still owe his grandmother a night out on the town."

"Yes, sir. It is White and he says he owes your grandmother a night out. Sir? Yes, sir, I will be sure to tell him. Yes, sir. Thank you, sir. You will have my report by nine o'clock tomorrow morning. Sir? Yes, of course. Eight o'clock. Good night, sir."

She clicked off her cell but remained turned away

from the men for a moment, no doubt composing herself following what must have been the worst drubbing of her life. She took a deep breath, raked her fingers through her hair, and turned. She pointed a long finger at the leader of the tactical assault team. "Tom, uncuff everyone, and you and your guys can stand down."

"Yes, ma'am," the FBI commando replied and nodded to his men to carry out her order.

She then looked to Mercer. "Obviously we have gotten off on the wrong foot. Would it really smooth things over and let us start fresh if we pick up the dog pee?"

Mercer took a moment to delight in the mental image of her knuckle-dragging partner on his knees with a wad of urine-soaked paper towel in his hands. It was a nice fantasy, but he would be better served by not antagonizing the agents any further.

"No," he said at last. "We can take care of it. For the record, I am Philip Mercer, this is Harry White, and the woman upstairs is Jordan Weismann. The dog's name is Drag, but short of torture through starvation you won't get much out of him."

Her brief smile was partially at the joke, but mostly it was gratitude for not making her order her subordinate to pick up Drag's mess.

"I am Special Agent Kelly Hepburn and this is Special Agent Nate Lowell." Both whipped shields and credentials from their belts and flashed them perfunctorily. "At the outset, let me apologize for this intrusion. It was not our intention—"

Mercer cut her off. "Agent Hepburn, it most certainly was your intention to barge into my home, so please don't apologize. You are sorry because I happened to know the former director of the FBI, and he finally got around to talking to your bosses about who I really am. You are sorry for unfortunate timing. If Harry had waited ten more minutes to walk his dog, Drag probably would have peed in the house anyway, but Deputy Director Higgins would have called in time to warn you not to treat me like a typical suspect and to just knock on my front door. Am I right?"

This time her smile was one of respect. "Yes, sir. You are."

"You will find my home office is in the back of the house just past the kitchen. I'm going to check on Jordan and I'll meet you two there in a minute. If you're so inclined there's a Keurig in the kitchen. Coffee and cups are above it in the cabinet, but I doubt the milk in the fridge is less than a month old, so I'd take it black."

"Don't forget the party," Harry said, tugging at Drag's leash to get him out the front door. "There's some fresh soy milk in there. A few of my guests were lactose intolerant." He added with a wrinkled nose, "And a few didn't care they were."

Jordan was still drugged enough that her being dragged from her bed and deposited on a wingback chair in the library overlooking the foyer didn't register in the slightest. She was sound asleep, and for a second time Mercer scooped her into his arms and carried her back to the bedroom, then shut off the lights. He took a few more minutes to brew a coffee from the old machine behind the bar that was dialed to his masochistic tastes. He grabbed the plastic bag containing the evidence from Abe Jacobs's office and joined the two agents in his office. Nate Lowell sat in one of the chairs facing the desk, trying not to look like a leashed and muzzled pit bull. Agent Hepburn resembled neither of the actresses with whom she shared a surname but was attractive in her own right. She was bent over a geological sample Mercer kept on a credenza to the side of his desk. The gray-green stone was unremarkable and rather crumbly, and anyone who wasn't a geologist would dismiss it as nothing.

"That's kimberlite," Mercer said, swinging past her and lowering himself into the chair behind his leather-topped desk. "Named for Kimberley, South Africa, where the first industrial diamond mine was located."

"Is it valuable?" she asked, taking the chair next to Nate Lowell. She activated the recorder function on her smartphone.

"No," he replied. "It's just a souvenir."

Technically he wasn't lying. The hunk of kimberlite was practically worthless. The large, gem-quality diamond embedded on the underside was another matter entirely. He placed the plastic scrubs bag onto his desk.

"Why don't you start from the very beginning," Kelly Hepburn prompted.

"Before I do, has anyone thought to secure the home and offices of Dr. Susan Tunis, the lead scientist on the project that was attacked in Minnesota?"

The two agents exchanged a look that Mercer had little trouble deciphering.

Hepburn said, "Both her office at Northwestern University and her home in Evanston were destroyed. Her husband was lucky and only slightly injured when he tried to enter the burning house." She added,

"It happened about five hours after the murders at the Leister Deep Mine."

Mercer did the calculations in his head. They had hit Dr. Tunis outside of Chicago on their way to Abe's home in Ohio. The time they spent ransacking her office and residence was why he had beaten them to Hardt College. Otherwise they would have driven through the night and struck Abe's long before he arrived. Had that been the case, he was certain Jordan Weismann would have been killed.

"What about her research?" Mercer asked, purging himself of emotion so he could focus on the investigation. "And we need anything you can recover from the computer servers at Hardt College too. Whatever they were working on is what got them killed."

"We already have people on that, Dr. Mercer," she assured him. "Please, why don't you tell me everything from the very beginning."

He went through his story again, giving as much detail as he could. Kelly Hepburn seemed impressed by his escape from the mine and subsequent chase in the big bucket loader. Nate Lowell looked at him as if it were all bullshit.

"You can verify my story with Detective Paul Gerard of the Minnesota State Police," Mercer concluded, not caring what Lowell thought. The guy was a grade-A mouth breather.

"We've seen his report," Hepburn confirmed, "though we aren't entirely sure why he didn't keep you at the mine as a material witness."

Mercer gave a little lopsided grin. "Don't blame him. I snuck off a minute before he made my presence there mandatory. Also, this bag on the desk contains everything I recovered from Abe's office. I'm sure your people are going over the space yourselves, so add the contents of his trash can to the other piles of evidence."

"Hey, asshole," Nate Lowell snarled. "Whatever you took from the crime scene has already broken chain of evidence. It's now considered tainted and is worthless to our investigation."

Mercer kept his anger in check. "Agent Lowell, what I saved from certain ruin from water damage will not help in the slightest in getting a conviction for Abe's murder, so chain of evidence is moot. What it might provide is a direction to pursue, a clue perhaps as to what he and the others were working on."

Lowell leaned forward, his jaw working like he was gnawing on his next words before spitting them in Mercer's face. Mercer ignored him and pegged Kelly Hepburn with his storm-gray eyes. "I am going off the assumption that Abe brought a geologic sample with him to the Leister Deep Mine. My hope is that whatever box or bag or carton it had once sat in was dumped in the trash when he transferred it to a more secure travel case. I could be way wrong here, but it makes logical sense."

"What makes logical sense here—" Lowell started, but Hepburn pressed a restraining hand against his shoulder.

"Dr. Mercer makes sense, provided that the trash wasn't emptied after Abraham Jacobs left for Minnesota."

"Abe arrived the morning he died, and I was in his office less than twenty-four hours later. Also he's the only one to use this trash can." Mercer lifted the bag and its sodden contents. "All this crap didn't get in here by magic."

Though she'd recorded Mercer's statement on her phone, she had also taken the time to jot down notes in a small spiral-ringed booklet. She flipped back a few pages. "You said that yesterday was the first time you met Jordan Weismann?"

"Yes, that's correct." Mercer leaned back a little in his chair, noting Lowell's hackles were back down.

"But you hadn't heard of her before?" Hepburn asked with a touch of doubt in her voice. "She says you share a mutual friend."

"Trust me, Agent Hepburn, Abe Jacobs was the most generous person I have ever known. He collected friends his entire life, and there are hundreds if not thousands of former students and colleagues left in his wake. I know just a handful of them—and even in those cases I probably haven't spoken to them in years—so before you ask your next question, no, there is no way I can verify that Jordan and Abe were friends. I suggest finding out who her father is and pursue her relationship with Abe from that direction."

The agent wrote down Mercer's suggestion. "We would like to speak to her, of course," she said, lifting her pen from the pad.

"No problem to me," Mercer replied, "but she is asleep and spiking a fever. If it hasn't gone down by tomorrow morning, I am probably going to take her to a doctor."

"Would you have a problem if I leave an agent here?" Hepburn asked.

"None whatsoever, provided it's not Agent Lowell."

Lowell bristled once again and his jaw went into overtime. "Relax," Mercer said, waving a dismissive hand. "It's for your protection. You see, Drag has gotten a taste of FBI ass and would go after yours if he had half a chance."

The agent came out of his chair, propelled by his well-muscled arms and a bruised ego. "You son of a bitch."

"Stand down, Nate," Kelly Hepburn shouted. "That's an order." She shot Mercer a look that asked if provoking her partner had been strictly necessary.

Mercer shrugged. He had done it because if he hadn't, Lowell would have been assigned protective detail, and at some point the guy would have crossed a line and Mercer would have been forced to deck him. Nate Lowell looked to be the kind of bully that would stand behind his shield if he got his ass kicked, and Mercer would be facing a striking-a-federal-officer rap. He didn't want to push his friendship with Dick Henna that far. Better to provoke a Pavlovian response in front of his partner and have Lowell sent home. One of the tac-team guys could come back and babysit.

"Go outside and get some air," she ordered hotly.

Lowell pivoted on his foot and marched from the office. From Mercer's perspective the situation got a little funnier because he could hear Harry and Drag coming through the front door as the FBI agent was trying to leave. Harry kept his old dog from biting at Lowell, but Drag barked it up like he was Cujo's long-lost cousin. Mercer smiled at the ruckus, and even Kelly Hepburn snickered.

"Sorry about Nate," she said. "He was recently medically DQed from working HRT and hasn't adjusted to being a regular field agent."

"Excuse?"

"Explanation."

"He has the look of a door kicker," Mercer admitted.

"A damn good one until he took a nine-millimeter

to the gut. He's recovered enough to stay with the Bureau but his door-kicking days are behind him." Kelly Hepburn stood to leave. Mercer also got to his feet. He picked up the bag of wet garbage.

"One last question," she said. "What is your relationship to Jordan Weismann?"

"My relationship? I don't have one with her. She was in trouble. I bailed her out and now she's asleep in my guest room. End of story."

"Where does she go from here?"

"That's not up to me. Call me tomorrow to see if she's up for questioning and ask her yourself." He found himself hoping her curiosity on this subject was more personal than professional. He presented the bag to her like a date proffers flowers. "Don't say I never gave you anything, Agent Hepburn."

"I'll be in touch in the morning, Dr. Mercer." She shook his hand with a firm up and down motion, and she was out the door with the evidence slapping against her leg. Mercer heard Harry rumble something to her, and a second later the front door closed for a final time.

Mercer met Harry and Drag on the spiral stairs, the pair of them struggling mightily. Drag's slow pace was something Mercer was used to. He was a little concerned about Harry until he remembered the impotent lecher had been dancing for God knew how long before he came home. The old bastard hadn't been hurt in the scuffle. He'd worn himself out partying.

"Hell of a night," White said.

"Amen to that," Mercer agreed noncommittally.

"Hot girl in the guest bedroom, another just in your office, and you're going to be sleeping with a flatulent basset hound who hogs the covers."

Mercer chuckled. "You know, I wish I liked at least one of my friends. That's all I ask for. Just one. See you in the morning."

Harry moved off onto the library balcony. Drag didn't miss a step and continued up, following Mercer for his spot on the more comfortable king-size bed on the third floor.

"Damn Judas of a dog," Harry muttered jealously. He called up after his pet, "No wet food for the rest of the week, you mangy traitor. It's kibble or nothing."

He may not have understood the words, but he at least understood the tone. Drag ponderously turned himself around on the sweeping stairs, backing like a semitrailer to make the swing, and dutifully tottered off to bed after his real master.

10

Mercer was at Jordan's bedside when she woke the following morning. Her eyes expressed the full gamut of emotions in a fleeting second, before drooping in abject misery. Mercer pulled a moist compress from her forehead and resoaked it in a bowl of cool water. He wrung it over the bowl so the clear water dripped musically and placed the towel on her fevered brow.

"You're going to a doc-in-a-box if your fever doesn't break in the next hour," he told her.

Jordan struggled up against the headboard so that she was slightly elevated. Her hair looked brittle against the pillows, and she shivered. He held a glass of water with a flex straw to her lips, and she drank greedily. He pulled it away before she took in too much too quickly.

She coughed, and when she spoke her voice rasped like Harry's after a three-day bender in an Atlantic City casino. "For once in my life, I am not going to argue."

"How are you feeling?"

"Like chilled death. Why am I so feverish?"

"Trauma and shock," he explained. "Your body doesn't know how to fight either, so its default response is a fever. I've seen this a few times. It'll break eventually, but you'd be more comfortable if we can get you something stronger than over-the-counter meds. How's your arm?"

She moved it without thinking and winced. "Sore, but not as bad as it could be. Why are you being so nice to me? You don't even know me."

He smiled down at her. "For one thing, you needed help and no one else was volunteering for the job, so it fell on me. Also you were a friend of Abe . . . and that makes you one of the good guys, so I'd help you no matter what. And finally I am helping you because Abe and I hadn't seen each other in too long, and I hope that you have some idea what he'd been up to lately. I need to figure out what put him in the cross hairs of a group of trained killers."

He could see her cloud over with confusion and a lack of anything concrete to provide him. "Don't worry about it now," he said. "We can talk when you're feeling better. And I don't want to heap anything more onto your plate, but an Agent Hepburn of the FBI is here and wants to talk to you too."

"The FBI?" It was clear she had no recollection of their visit the night before. "What do they want me for?"

Kelly Hepburn had been just outside the bedroom listening to make sure Mercer didn't try to coach her or influence anything Jordan might say. She came around the corner and said, "I need you to corroborate the statement Dr. Mercer provided last night, Jordan. I'm Special Agent Kelly Hepburn."

She flashed her badge and entered the guest bedroom. Mercer had to hand it to her. Harry had just told him that Jordan was coming around less than two minutes earlier. The tac guy, Simmons, who had spent the night sitting at the bar in the rec room, had radioed that information to whoever was outside, and Kelly Hepburn had knocked on the front door twenty seconds afterward. She was making certain her witnesses spent as little time together as possible without making it seem they were under suspicion.

Mercer had already noted when he'd let Hepburn into his house that she was wearing a more flattering suit than the night before, and a silk rather than cotton blouse. She wasn't so obvious as to use more makeup, but her jewelry was better and he guessed her shoes were the best her closet had to offer. Despite this, her handshake had been cool and professional, like the night before, and her eyes hadn't lingered on his any longer than was polite. He was left to assume that she was dressing for someone back at headquarters or one of the tac-team guys in the van outside. Since there was no sign of no-neck Nate Lowell, he could at least cross her partner off the list.

Jordan glanced quickly at Mercer, unsure. And then she found a little of the strength she had so ably demonstrated the day before. "My dad was our family's big disappointment," she said, helping herself to another sip of water. "He became a scientist while his two brothers both went into law. One is a senior partner in Pittsburgh, and the other is a municipal judge in Philadelphia. I've learned enough from them to know not to talk to the authorities, especially the FBI, without a lawyer present."

"As is your right, Miss Weismann," Kelly Hepburn agreed. "However, neither you nor Dr. Mercer are under suspicion at this time, and I will not make any notes or recordings of this conversation. How about that? All I want is to verify what Dr. Mercer told me last night and I will be on my way." She was hit by a sudden thought and turned to Mercer. "I was going over my notes this morning, and I can't believe I didn't ask you what happened to the automatic pistol you took from Abraham Jacobs's house. Where is the Walther P-38?"

Mercer looked at Jordan, not correcting Hepburn's mistake as to the gun's manufacturer. "Tell her where, and it should mostly satisfy her that we aren't the second coming of Bonnie and Clyde." He saw Agent Hepburn stiffen. "I said mostly satisfy."

The woman from the FBI relaxed.

Jordan said, "Mercer hid the gun in the ceiling of one of the second-floor classrooms. I think it was either 212 or 214."

"Room 214," Mercer verified. "I didn't know what the police outside the building were doing, so I thought it best not to walk out armed to the teeth."

"Prudent," Hepburn remarked casually. "And, Jordan, why exactly were you at Hardt College and, more specifically, at Abraham Jacobs's house?"

She looked a little sheepish. "I was being a bum, really. I, oh hell. Okay, I lost my job about five months ago and my savings ran out and I was just evicted from my apartment. I asked my dad if I could move back in with him, but he said no. *Quelle surprise.* He and I are no longer close since my mom died. He buried himself in work and I . . . had other distractions."

Neither Mercer nor Agent Hepburn needed her to elaborate on the point.

Jordan continued, "Abe and my dad worked together back when they both taught at Carnegie Mellon, and he was always like another uncle to me, so when Dad told me I had to make it on my own, I copped out and begged a bed from Abe until I can figure out what I am going to do next. Abe was only supposed to be in Minnesota for a few days, and he hinted he might be able to get me something at Hardt when he came back."

"What did you do for work?" Hepburn asked.

"I was a planning and zoning researcher for the city of Scranton. Budget cuts killed my position."

"Is that what you studied in school?"

"Not exactly. I was an environmental studies major." She gave a wan smile of unrealized dreams. "I had planned on saving the world, but that didn't work out either."

In mock horror Mercer said, "Dear God, a tree hugger."

Jordan laughed until she coughed. "Sorry. And don't worry. Two years working for a crumbling municipality has crushed any youthful optimism out of me. I haven't hugged a tree in a long time."

"What is your father's phone number?" Kelly Hepburn asked.

"You said you weren't going to take any notes," Jordan pointed out.

"I'm not, but I have a pretty good memory for numbers and I just want to verify your story."

"I wish you wouldn't call him," Jordan said, not exactly pleading but uncomfortable with the idea. "He doesn't know I went to Abe's, and I'm afraid with Abe's death and me being at his house, my dad might, I don't know, like hold me responsible or something. I know it sounds crazy, but he would jump to a conclusion like that."

"I will be circumspect, Miss Weismann," Agent Hepburn assured her. "Why don't you try describing the men who attacked you."

Jordan immediately looked to Mercer for help. Hepburn was seasoned enough to know that now was the time to separate the two of them. Under the best of circumstances, witness testimony was notoriously unreliable, and Jordan's could be influenced by Mercer's body language and micro-expressions. "I'm sorry," she said. "Dr. Mercer, would you be so kind as to give us a few minutes alone?"

He immediately understood the reason behind her request. He also recognized how adroitly the agent had gotten Jordan talking. He gave Jordan's good shoulder a squeeze. "You'll be all right. Just tell her everything you remember, and if it gets too much for you, you can stop at any time." Mercer glanced at Hepburn for confirmation, and the attractive agent nodded. "See you in a few minutes."

Mercer burned the time sitting at the bar in the rec room with Harry, who was three-quarters of the way through the *Washington Post* crossword. Mercer decided against another cup of coffee. He hated waiting but knew there was no other choice. It would take hours before the FBI had anything preliminary from the trash and perhaps longer still to garner any information about the nature of Susan Tunis's research project. Mercer had developed the habit of polishing lengths of old railroad track as a way of freeing his mind so he could think clearly, but right now even that distraction seemed frivolous.

He had to admit that for the first time in a long time he was an outsider. Since the last national election he had lost his role as special science adviser to the president of the United States, a job that required very little of him but opened doors all over Washington and beyond. Now he was just another citizen, and even though his friendship with Dick Henna had bought him a little professional courtesy, he held no illusions that Agent Hepburn was obligated to keep him in the loop. She needn't share anything with him about her investigation even though he desperately wanted in on this. He wanted justice for Abe's murder but just as badly he wanted to understand the bigger picture. There were other layers to this crime, shadows lurking deeper in the background. Someone had paid a great deal of money to get at whatever Abe had brought to that subterranean chamber, and they didn't care who died in their quest to possess it.

The civilian death toll so far was limited to Abe, Dr. Tunis, and her people, and the hoist operator, but it was a miracle that the only fatality at Hardt College had been one of the gunmen. Still, there were dozens injured, some critically, and until Mercer unraveled the mystery he felt certain the butcher's bill would continue to rise.

Thirty minutes later, Kelly Hepburn backed out of the guest bedroom and softly closed the door. She came into the rec room just as Harry pushed the completed puzzle away from himself and stood. It was noon and time for the first drink of the day.

"Can I get you anything, sweetheart?" White asked as he stepped around the mahogany bar to prepare his drink. Behind the rows of liquor bottles on the back bar was an antique-looking world map stuck with pins of various colors. It was a map of the places Mercer had traveled, and it looked like with the exception of Antarctica there weren't many corners of the earth he hadn't visited.

"A Diet Coke, if you have one," she said and took a seat next to Mercer, "and the understanding that if you ever call me 'sweetheart' again, Mr. White, I will shoot you."

"We only have regular Coke," Harry fired back, peering into the refurbished fifties-style lock-lever fridge, "and I suppose calling you 'honey' is out too."

"Regular is fine, and you're very perceptive for a guy with one foot firmly in the past and the other inching toward the grave."

Mercer nearly choked on his laughter, and even Harry, the butt of one of the better zingers either had heard in a while, had to laugh.

"I thought FBI training was supposed to remove any vestiges of humor," Mercer finally said, still chuckling.

Kelly Hepburn shrugged out of her suit coat and hung it from the back of her bar stool. "That's usually the case, but I was absent that day."

Harry placed an ice-filled glass in front of her and a can of soda. "Touché," he said and tossed her a wink.

"Is Jordan asleep?" Mercer asked.

"Her fever is starting to break, so she's drifting in and out. I was done questioning her anyway." She poured cola into the glass, the ice popping and crackling as it chilled the beverage, and then she took a long swallow, wincing slightly as the carbonation hit her nose. "Dr. Mercer—"

"It's just Mercer," he told her. "I only use my title to impress girls and maître d's."

She arched an eyebrow. "I don't count?"

"Only if you can get us good tables," Harry muttered without looking up from his drink.

Hepburn smiled. "Okay, Harry. We're even. Mercer, I think by now you can tell that this is no longer an FBI priority."

"I figured that would happen sooner or later. This isn't terrorism in the traditional sense, so the urgency faded as soon as the shooters vanished again."

"Afraid so. I even requested a doctor come with me this morning to see Jordan and was turned down. Your and Harry's friendship with higher-ups aside, I can only get a preliminary examination of the trash you recovered. Any detailed analysis will have to wait. Same thing with the computer servers at Hardt College and Northwestern. If we can't get anything about Dr. Tunis's work within a day, it gets dropped down the urgency list for a couple of weeks. I know this is personal for you, and I wanted to be honest, if nothing else."

Mercer nodded. "I appreciate that and I know you're doing your best."

"There isn't a whole lot to go on, not unless these screws strike again."

"And because they got what they needed from Abe and erased all the evidence from the two colleges, they're long gone."

"Yup." She took another long sip.

"I assume this also means the case isn't doing your career much good," Mercer pointed out.

"That shit hit the fan when your buddy, former director Henna, rained down on my boss four times removed."

"Sorry about that," Mercer said. "I was trying to prevent a misunderstanding from turning into my public lynching."

"You were just trying to protect yourself and Jordan. Can't blame you for that." Agent Hepburn took another mouthful of soda and stood. She shrugged her jacket over her shoulders and fitted it around the Glock in its flat kidney holster. "Before I forget, I need a few hundred bucks."

"Excuse me?"

"This isn't a shakedown. Jordan is in no condition to travel, and she needs some stuff. Unless you want to comparison shop in the feminine hygiene aisle at Walgreens, I advise you pony up the cash and don't ask any more questions."

Mercer hastily peeled two hundred-dollar bills from his wallet and handed them over.

She reached across and took another. "I should get the prelim from forensics about the trash this afternoon. I'll be back then with whatever news they have and the stuff Jordan asked for."

———

While Harry and Drag watched *NCIS* reruns in the bar and Jordan fought her fever in the guest bedroom, Mercer spent the rest of the day in his downstairs office, first contacting the owners of the Leister Deep Mine. He needed to tie up loose ends pertaining to the mine rescue class he had taught, ensuring final payment for renting part of the mine was sent and insurance coverage canceled. Then he wrote up the performance reviews for each member of the class, which occupied most of the afternoon.

Jordan woke in the early evening, her fever broken but more exhausted than before. She managed a quick shower while Mercer and Harry changed her sweaty sheets, and she ate a few mouthfuls of soup before drifting off into a deep trouble-free sleep.

Agent Hepburn called at around six and asked if it was too late for her to come over and review some of what she'd discovered. She arrived a half hour later just as Mercer was returning with bags of take-out food.

Hepburn set several shopping bags on the floor near the hallway to the back bedrooms, a large one from CVS and the others from the Nordstrom at the Pentagon City Mall. It appeared that Jordan Weismann planned on being here for a while, which Mercer didn't mind at all.

"Can I offer you something stronger than a Coke this time?" Harry asked.

"Is that Johnnie Blue?" she asked, eyeing the distinctive bottle amid lesser brands of Scotch on the back bar.

"Aye, lassie," Harry said in an atrocious brogue.

Knowing how expensive it was, she asked Mercer if he minded. "Not in the slightest," he assured her. "If you ask me, Scotch tastes like a blend of . . ." He was going to say "yak urine and iodine" but held his tongue. "Let's leave it that I don't drink the stuff and you're welcome to all you want. Harry, get me a gimlet while you're back there, will ya?"

"On it."

Mercer pulled sandwiches, salads, and soups from the takeout bags and even conjured real silverware from a drawer behind the bar. He gave Agent Hepburn the latest on Jordan's condition and said that he felt she would be up and around the following day. For her part she told Mercer and Harry that Jordan's father confirmed he had once worked with Abe Jacobs but questioned why his name came up in the course of investigating the retired metallurgist's murder. Hepburn told him it was routine, but the man became even more suspicious when asked about his estranged daughter. He did say that Jordan and Abe had been friendly when she was younger, but neither had seen Jacobs in years. When he pressed Hepburn about how and why this was pertinent, she hid behind national security and quickly ended the telephone interview.

"So her story checks out," Kelly Hepburn concluded. "You both are clear as far as the Bureau is concerned. Like you in Minnesota, she really was in the wrong place at the wrong time."

"Didn't think it was otherwise," Mercer said, "but it's good to know. What else have you found out?"

"Everything I didn't need to know about wax paper, for one thing."

"Come again?"

"Wax paper. The tech guys went through all the garbage you recovered from Abe Jacobs's office. Everything was pretty standard—basic computer paper, candy wrappers, an empty applesauce container, opened envelopes with addresses that all check out as legit, paper coffee cups, junk mail, broken rubber bands, as well as a large square of wax paper that according to the nerds is yellowed enough and shows enough signs of the paraffin's degenerative long-chain molecular blah blah blah so it is at least fifty years old, possibly much older."

Mercer stopped chewing his roast beef. "That might mean something."

"Thought you'd think so." Amid the shopping bags was a slim leather case, almost like a laptop bag but smaller and much more stylish. Agent Hepburn grabbed it and brought it to her place at the bar. From it came a notebook stuffed with photographs and a

tablet computer. She fired up the tablet, flicked her
finger through a few apps and a few screens, and presented it to Mercer.

It was a picture of wax paper all right, dingy yellow compared to the fresh milky sheets he doubtless
had in his kitchen and had never used. The paper was
crinkled and curled like it had been wrapped around
something irregular and maybe the size and shape of
a carrot. He could see there was faded printing on
one part of the paper, and try as he might he couldn't
make it out, even by tightening in on it using the tablet's zoom.

"Any idea what it says?" he asked.

She took the computer back, flicked through a
couple of other pictures, and presented it to him once
again. It was a close-up and digitally enhanced image
of the faint writing. "Best they could do."

It read:

camole 681
ne b l oorer

"Any idea what it means?" Kelly asked when Mercer had been studying it for nearly thirty seconds, his
brow tight over his gray eyes and his mouth held firm.

"Could your people make anything out of it?" he
asked back.

"No. Nothing. As a favor—remember this is now
low priority—one of the lab rats sent it through a
decryption program and some handwriting analysis
logarithms but got nowhere. And that is about all the
tech support I'm going to get unless we can find some
definitive link to international terrorism. And don't
bother with Google, Bing, or Yahoo. I spent a couple

hours on them and turned up all kinds of crap but nothing relevant."

Harry had shrugged a pale blue windbreaker over his oft-laundered white button-down and was just unfurling Drag's leash when he walked behind Mercer and Kelly and looked at the tablet's screen. "Did you look up 'sample six eight one' instead of 'camole'?"

"What are you talking about?" Agent Hepburn asked.

"When the paper creased through the first line it cut off the bottom curve of an *S* and the bottom tail of the letter *p*. It's not 'camole 681.' It's 'Sample 681.' And in the second line, the letters *o-o-r-e-r* are rarely ever seen in sequence except in proper names like Moorer."

It took Harry nearly fifteen minutes to get Drag out of the house and to a spot in the neighborhood he deemed worthy to soil and finally back indoors. By then, Mercer and Kelly had checked out several dozen people with last names ending in *oorer* online. The only one that seemed a remote possibility was the former chairman of the Joint Chiefs, Admiral Thomas Moorer, even though he'd been dead for more than a decade.

Harry laboriously shucked his coat and settled back onto his bar stool. Kelly wrinkled her nose at the smell of Chesterfield cigarettes clinging to him. "Any luck?" he asked, sipping at the watery remnants of his third Jack and ginger of the day.

"Not much," Mercer admitted.

"Figured you wouldn't. Names ending in *oorer* aren't that common. That's why I think the first *r* isn't an *r* at all."

Mercer groaned. He should have known Harry

would have figured something out. The octogenarian had been doing crosswords for over sixty years and any number of other word games as well. He had once seen Harry guess a *Wheel of Fortune* puzzle with only a single letter showing and only three others eliminated from play. Where the FBI's brain trust and computer logic failed, good old-fashioned experience could prove invaluable.

"I think that first *r* is a *v*. It's *oover*, not *oorer*."

"Okay," Hepburn said. "That leaves us with Nebl Oover." She typed quickly. "And it's meaningless."

Mercer finally saw the pattern that Harry must have picked up on. "The first letter isn't *n*. Remember how the bottom of the *S* got cut off in 'Sample.' Same thing here. The top of the first letter is missing. I think it's an *H*." Mercer's eyes suddenly widened as everything came home in a clarifying rush. He knew the name written on the paper, and it made perfect sense even if he didn't yet know why it was there. "Cross the *l* so it's a *t* and then tell me what you get.

She typed "Hebt oover" into a search engine, and the tablet kicked back the answer that had eluded her best nerds for most of the afternoon—Herbert Hoover.

11

"Herbert Hoover, the president?" she asked, confused by the result.

Mercer nodded. "Before going into public service during World War One by running a charity that basically saved every man, woman, and child in Belgium from starvation, Bert Hoover made millions as a mining consultant and entrepreneur. He had businesses in China, Russia, and Australia. A few other places, too, I think."

Harry said, "He was Mercer before Mercer was Mercer. Of course, Hoover was a Quaker, which means no booze, so I guess he was a more sober version of Mercer before Mercer was Mercer."

"Thank you from the peanut gallery," Mercer said and refocused on Kelly. "Sample 681 could be something geological he collected during his career. This could be the break this case needed."

"How?"

"The Hoover Presidential Library," he explained. "I have no idea where it is, but it should have archived everything there is to know about Hoover before, during, and after his presidency. If he collected this Sample 681 or had anything to do with it, the researchers there should be able to find it."

She worked at the tablet for a moment. "It's in West Branch, Iowa. That's closer to Iowa City than Davenport, if that helps."

"My knowledge of Iowa geography is limited, so I'll take your word for it. Any contact information?"

"I have a phone number and e-mail address. How do you want to handle this?"

Mercer had suspected all along that this case would hinge on the science behind whatever Tunis and Jacobs were doing, so he wasn't surprised that she was asking his advice on how to proceed. "We'll call in the morning and simply ask if they know anything about a geologic sample labeled 681 that Hoover either collected or owned at one point in his life."

"Simple as that?"

"Sometimes it can be," he replied. "Have your people been able to get anything from the university servers about what kind of experiment they were working on in Minnesota?"

She shook her head in disgust. "Even if I had more people on this, both schools are in a panic, which means they've swung their legal departments into full battle mode. Neither administration will let us on their campus without warrants, or even talk to us without their lawyers present. We need subpoenas to get a look at any computer archives or research material, and right now we are having a hard time finding cooperative judges."

"That pesky Constitution," Mercer teased.

Hepburn threw up her hands in a gesture of surrender. "Hey, I get it and am all for it. I even swore an oath to defend it. But it pisses me off when people use it to cover their ass rather than defend someone's rights, you know. These college lawyers are more afraid of being sued by a relative than finding out the killers' identity."

Mercer couldn't argue the point. "In that vein, it makes sense I call the library rather than you. Pardon the expression, but we don't want them thinking we're making a federal case out of this. Better it comes from a civilian doing some innocuous research."

It was clear Kelly didn't like it, but she saw the wisdom behind his idea and nodded. She continued, "We did get a few people to talk off the record. Dr. Tunis was a climatologist, and apparently the experiment she and Abe Jacobs were working on was to be some sort of paradigm-shifting event in the field. One guy said if they were right about something, Al Gore was going to have to give back his Nobel Prize. Not sure what that means or if that's good or bad given how serious climate change is."

Mercer did his best not to roll his eyes. As a trained geologist he tended to think someone claiming to have found a trend in an earth system, especially something as chaotic as climate, with just a century or two, and sometimes much less, of actual data was at best fooling themselves—and at worst intentionally fooling others. He said mildly, "It's an emotionally charged subject for a lot of people, and there are billions upon billions of dollars riding on research, so schools tend to be circumspect. You should keep on it, but I think our best bet is going to come from the Hoover Library."

Agent Hepburn finished her smoked turkey sandwich and the last of her Scotch. "What time are you going to call them?"

"They're an hour behind us, so ten thirty our time."

"I'll be here to listen in. You want anything in the morning? Doughnuts? Bagels?"

"Chocolate doughnuts," Harry said excitedly.

"Nothing"—Mercer overrode him—"but thanks."

"I'll walk her out," Harry volunteered, fumbling for his coat and Drag's leash as a pretext. Mercer knew he was going for the hard sell on morning doughnuts. Mercer had done his part to limit Harry's smoking, but he guessed there wasn't much he could do if the octogenarian wanted to put himself into a sugar-induced coma. "Hello," Jordan Weismann said seconds after Hepburn left. She padded into the library wearing one of Mercer's old Penn State T-shirts. It came to just above midthigh. She had to have been awake for a few minutes because her hair had been tamed into a ponytail, and she'd managed to wash the puffiness from her sloe eyes. Her arm sling flattened one of her breasts while nearly forcing the other from the top of the shirt, and Mercer tried not to stare.

"Hi," he said thickly, dragging his eyes up to hers. "How are you feeling?"

"Better, thanks. I'm still tired, but I feel a lot more human."

"You certainly look less zombie-esque," Mercer joked. "Can I get you something?"

"I'm thirsty. Do you have any ginger ale?"

"I've got plenty, just don't tell Harry I'm breaking into his private stash." Mercer moved behind the bar while Jordan laid herself on the couch and pulled up the antique steamer robe.

"Whenever I was sick as a little girl, my mother always gave me matzo ball soup and ginger ale. To this day I equate the soup with not feeling well and only drink ginger ale when I'm under the weather."

"It's the same for me and bouillon cubes," Mercer said, bringing over an iced glass and a mini bottle of Schweppes. "Just the smell reminds me of having the flu when I was a kid and makes me nauseous."

"Thank you," Jordan said, snaking an arm out from the blanket to accept the glass he'd poured. A long sip cleared a little of the raspiness from her voice. "Where's Harry?"

"He and Drag just walked Agent Hepburn out." Mercer pointed to all the shopping bags. "Which reminds me, she bought out CVS and Nordstrom's for you."

"I needed some essentials," Jordan said quickly. "But it was awfully nice for her to do this for me." She pushed off the blankets and scissor kicked herself off the couch, giving Mercer another glance at her shapeliness.

It was a guileless maneuver that still managed to catch Mercer's breath in his throat.

Jordan grabbed up all the bags and didn't return for nearly thirty minutes. Harry didn't return either, which told Mercer he and Drag had stopped by Tiny's for a nightcap or two. When Jordan finally stepped out from the bedroom she wore a man's white cotton oxford and some makeup, and her hair was brushed out past her shoulders. She looked at once sexy and vulnerable.

"So fill me in. What's been happening since I've been out."

"Our garbage run into the science building back at Hardt College has paid off. There was a piece of wax paper in the trash can. We were able to figure out it was once wrapped around something called Sample 681 and that it had something to do with Herbert Hoover. We're going to call his presidential library in the morning to see if they can shed any more light on the mystery."

"So no idea what this sample was or how it ties in with Abe and that other professor from Northwestern?"

"Neither school is talking officially," he told her, "but the rumor mill has it they were working on some cutting-edge climate research."

"One of my favorite topics," Jordan confessed. "I wonder what they were doing."

"I've been thinking about that for a while now, and the only reason I can see they were in that mine would have been to do an experiment where cosmic rays and other background radiation sources have been blocked by the earth. I think this dovetails into other work done at CERN to gauge the importance of cosmic rays in cloud formation. This isn't really my field, but I recall the work may be part of an alternative theory to carbon dioxide being the sole driver of global warming over the past hundred years."

Jordan's eyes suddenly narrowed, and she sat up a little straighter on the couch. "No way. I know about that theory and can tell you it has already been debunked. Man-made carbon pollution is causing global warming, and anyone who says otherwise is a climate denier."

As Mercer had told agent Hepburn earlier, climate change was an emotionally charged subject, and he could see that Jordan Weismann was more passionate than most. What amused him was how activists thought they were defending a scientific theory, when it was actually their own political and philosophical beliefs they fought to protect to the exclusion of all alternatives.

Normally he didn't engage people in debates about their beliefs, but as a scientist he couldn't let her last

sentence stand without comment. "I don't really follow the climate debate that closely, but I want to point
out something you said that tells me you're reading
propaganda bullet points and not the literature produced by scientists." Her eyes narrowed even further,
and her entire body language became defensive. Mercer plowed on anyway. "Carbon pollution is not a
scientific term. Even calling carbon a problem is an attempt to demonize something by association. People
hear 'carbon pollution' and they think of dirty piles of
ash or soot. We are not talking about coal dust or industrial slag. The topic at hand is carbon dioxide, the
invisible gas you exhale about twenty-two thousand
times a day and your houseplants breathe in. Calling
it just carbon or carbon pollution is a PR stunt.

"Your second point of calling someone who questions the theory of global warming a 'denier' is dis-
ingenuous at best and deceitful at its worst. Most
thinking people understand that greenhouse gases
will raise the temperature of the planet. That is not
really part of the debate. The question is by how
much and what do we do about it. By labeling those
who question the dogma, you are trying to reframe
the topic so as to prove the other lie that gets tossed
about all the time—that the science is settled. Science
is never settled and anyone who says otherwise is
lying."

"Hold on one sec—"

Mercer cut her off. "Before you say anything, I
am not questioning your belief in global warming or
climate change or climate disruption or whatever the
current name is. You have every right to believe whatever you want. What I don't like is how some people
try to spread the gospel with innuendo, half-truths,
and smears."

Jordan took a couple of calming breaths before she spoke. "Saying you believe in climate change is the same as saying you believe in evolution or that smoking causes cancer. These are scientific facts."

"Completely true," Mercer agreed. "The faith I mention comes into play when researchers try to project out a hundred years what the earth will be like. Evolutionary biologists don't extrapolate the future from the fossil record to convince the public they know how the common gray squirrel will change over the next hundred years. The more activist climate scientists attempt that all the time. And any oncologist worth his salt will tell you they don't know how the chemical triggers in smoke actually cause lung tissue to turn cancerous, only that they do.

"The earth has been warming since the middle of the Victorian age. That is a fact. How and why are up for debate and what happens in the future is pure guesswork and usually not very educated guesswork at that. A cleaner environment, using less fossil fuel, saving forests, and reducing consumption in general are all noble and lofty goals, but people can't be guilted or frightened into wanting to realize them. Nor lied to. Groups who think creating ever scarier future scenarios will change society are deluding themselves and ultimately delaying more fundamental and obtainable environmental objectives."

He could see Jordan's hard flinty edge beaten dull by his words, and it was his turn to take a breath.

"Okay," she said, drawing out the word to show she recognized she'd hit a nerve. "Why don't we talk about something less controversial, like the Middle East or abortion?"

He chuckled. "Sorry. Sometimes I get on my soapbox when science is used to push an agenda because then it is no longer science . . . it's marketing."

They sat in silence for a moment, until Jordan finally gave him a mischievous grin and said, "So . . . Sample 681?"

"Yes," Mercer replied. "Back to the topic at hand. The Hoover Library. Hopefully there will be something there that lays out exactly what's going on and what makes Sample 681 worth so many lives."

"You're sure you've never heard of it?" Jordan asked.

"No. That name sounds like a catalog number from a mineral collection and not a scientific description. I can envision it sitting on a dusty shelf somewhere wedged between Samples 680 and 682."

"Any idea how Abe came to have it?"

"None. It could have been loaned to him or to Hardt College. It could have been something he brought with him from Carnegie or Penn State. Hell, it could have been something he found in a garage sale two weeks ago. Agent Hepburn is working on subpoenas to look into computer archives. I'll ask her tomorrow to add information pertaining to Sample 681 to the list. Could be it's something Dr. Tunis heard about at Northwestern. Then she discovered Abe had it and asked him to bring it to her underground laboratory."

"I guess there's no real point in trying to speculate, is there?" Jordan said, a little dejected by the enormity of what they didn't know.

"We're just getting started," Mercer assured her. "That's the problem with the Internet. People today are used to having their questions answered with the click of a button. We can't get discouraged yet. It's still early times."

She chuckled. "E-mail was too slow growing up, so we started texting and then edited that down to just tweeting. Now a hundred and forty characters are too much so no one looks beyond the hashtag."

"We were still passing handwritten notes when I was in school, and the only phone anyone had hung on the wall in their kitchen." Mercer looked at her in the silence that followed and finally said, "I guess I didn't need to remind you that I grew up in the Dark Ages . . . I think I'm going to call it a night."

Jordan got off the couch and met him in the middle of the room. Her eyes were now soft, and she touched his arm with her good hand. "I want to thank you again for taking me in. I remember now that Abe talked about you once or twice, and I can see how you made such a lasting impression on him." She turned to head to bed but paused and looked at him once more. This time there was an impish lift to her lips. "And trust me when I tell you that there are women out there who kept the notes you gave them as girls, and they wish whatever you wrote on them was still true."

Before Mercer could think of anything to say she ducked into her room and closed the door.

———

Mercer waited until quarter of eleven the following morning to call the Herbert Clark Hoover Presidential Library. He hadn't yet heard from Kelly Hepburn and his call to her cell had gone to voice mail, so he went ahead with the investigation without her.

It took a few minutes to establish his bona fides and to track down a staffer who could help him with his rather esoteric request. He was finally put in touch with a researcher named Sherman Smithson who'd been a fixture at the Iowa institution for years.

"I am not familiar with that particular sample, Dr. Mercer," Smithson said in a pinched nasal accent, "and most of what we have here are paper archives and not bits of rocks and minerals, but I can check some databases for you so long as you understand that most people actually come to us to do primary research of this nature."

"I appreciate that, Mr. Smithson." Mercer recognized that had he been overly familiar and used the man's Christian name, Smithson probably would have ended the call on a pretext. "And I am certainly grateful for your help. There actually might be a law enforcement connection to this piece, so whatever you can do will be a tremendous help."

"Law enforcement?"

Mercer could picture Smithson wrinkling his nose at something so beneath the lofty tower of pure academic research. He'd taken the wrong tack trying to whet the archivist's interest. He made up the blandest story he could imagine. "Well, I might have exaggerated about law enforcement, but a certain Ohio college might be receiving a stern letter from the dean of the geology department at a university in Pennsylvania if what I suspect is true and Sample 681 was taken some decades ago without permission or even a formal requisition."

"Ah, I see." Smithson seemed mollified that this was about nothing more than an old tiff between schools. "Well, let's hope we can set this straight. What is it exactly you need from us, Dr. Mercer?"

"Anything you can tell me about this Sample 681,

but mostly I'm interested in where it came from and when it was collected."

"Do you suspect President Hoover collected it himself?"

"It's possible, but it's just as likely it came from someone else on his behalf, or was sent to him so he could assess its value. At this stage I really don't know."

"Very well. I know of two places I can check quickly and a third that might take some time. How about you leave me your telephone number and I will call by this afternoon with anything preliminary. Is that satisfactory?"

"More than," Mercer assured him, rattled off his cell number, and thanked him before ending the call.

"Good morning," Jordan said, stepping into the rec room.

Mercer had heard her showering twenty minutes earlier and had been expecting her entrance. She wore new jeans and an American Eagle hoodie with plain white sneakers. For being bought by someone else, the jeans and sweatshirt fit her perfectly.

"Morning," Mercer greeted her. Harry just waved from his perch at the bar. It was Friday and the crossword was getting tough. "How are you feeling?"

"So much better," she said.

"Want some coffee?"

"God, yes. And to tell the truth I'm starving."

"We were supposed to have doughnuts," Harry said, glancing up from the newspaper, "but Kelly isn't here yet."

"You'll have to check the fridge. I have no idea what Harry's guests brought over for their octogenarian orgy the other night."

"Octogenarian? Bah," said Harry with a disdainful wave of his hand. "A couple of those silver foxes were barely into their seventies. As to orgy? Well, those weren't blue M&M's you saw being passed around."

Jordan winced. "And on that note I am officially no longer hungry."

"I'm never going to eat again," Mercer agreed.

Harry smiled like the Cheshire cat and then stood. "Come on, honey," he said to Jordan. "There's plenty of food downstairs, and no one brought anything blue other than their hair. Mercer, get her coffee."

He set a steaming mug onto the table in front of the couch and placed a newly bought half-gallon milk jug and some sweetener packets swiped from some restaurant long ago next to it. While he waited he dialed Kelly Hepburn's number, and this time someone answered. He was pretty sure he recognized the voice. "Agent Lowell?"

"Yeah, who is this?"

"It's Philip Mercer. Why are you answering Agent Hepburn's phone?"

"'Cause she can't," he said bluntly. "She was in an accident this morning. Her cell got crushed. The phone company's now routing her calls to me."

Mercer was filled first with dread and then anger. With everything going on, there was no way Kelly Hepburn had an accident. But before he voiced his suspicions, he asked about her condition.

"Don't know yet. She's in surgery at George Washington University Hospital. From what I hear from the EMTs who drove her, her leg's busted and she took a blow on the side of the head."

"Hit-and-run?" Mercer asked, suspicious that the driver was one of the shooters from Minnesota, possibly even the team leader.

"No. It was an eighteen-year-old coed named Samantha Rhodes rushing from her job at a Starbucks to class at the University of Maryland."

"No shit," Mercer said, shocked and oddly relieved. He had pictured men dressed in black tactical gear with silenced machine pistols held just out of view as they rammed into Kelly's car.

"Yeah, no shit." Lowell sounded a little rattled by what had happened to his partner, but he was quickly regaining his distaste for Mercer. It was in his tone.

"What did happen exactly?" Mercer asked, feeling more on an even keel. This really could be just a weird coincidence. Though he hated them with a passion, he was enough of a realist to know they happened.

"The District PD says the girl swerved to miss a cat that had run into the road and plowed into the side of Kelly's car. Kelly's leg was broken, and she slammed her head into the side window hard enough to shatter the glass. That's the injury the EMTs were most worried about. She's conscious and all, but groggy, you know."

"Concussion," Mercer said.

"Sounds like it," Lowell agreed. "Why are you calling her?"

"I'm following up on a lead from the trash I recovered from Abe Jacobs's office. I have a call in to the Hoover Presidential Library about this Sample 681. Did Kelly tell you about it?"

"Sounds like bullshit to me. That piece of wax paper could have been wrapped around his lunch for all we know."

"It was over fifty years old, according to your own experts," Mercer countered.

"There's nothing there, Mercer. Take what I'm

about to say any way you want, but our part of the overall investigation is a sideshow, you get me? The real work is being done at the crime scenes in the Midwest. Not here in Washington. Agent Hepburn was only letting you stay involved so you could feel you were doing something to help your dead friend. As soon as we finished our interview of you and that Weismann girl, we were officially done. Understand?"

"No," Mercer snapped. "This could lead to something."

"It would be a waste of critical manpower. Let the FBI do the investigating and we'll leave the rocks and shit to you." Lowell killed the connection.

Mercer wanted to toss his cell across the room but calmly thumbed it off and slipped it back into his jeans pocket. There was nothing less imaginative or more risk averse than the bureaucratic mind. He retrieved his phone and dialed the hospital only to be told that the FBI, in cooperation with her immediate family, was withholding all information on Agent Hepburn as a matter of policy.

He pocketed the phone again and slumped onto a bar stool. He glanced at Drag. The dog gave a half-hearted wave of its tail and closed its eyes. Harry and Jordan trooped up from the kitchen with plates laden with leftovers including lobster mac and cheese, brisket, and some homemade bread that still smelled like it was fresh from the oven. "Looks like someone stole your lollipop," Harry said.

"Kelly Hepburn was in a car accident this morning." Mercer continued speaking into the astonished silence. "She has a broken leg and what sounds like a concussion. I can't get word from the hospital because of an FBI blackout, but Lowell was kind enough to share the fact that the Bureau doesn't much care about our inquiry with the Hoover Library. For all practical purposes we're dead in the water."

"Shit," Harry spat.

"That about sums it up, yes."

"What about the people who killed Abe?" Jordan asked.

"The FBI is going to keep investigating, of course, but from what I gather from Lowell, we're no longer relevant."

"What about calling Dick Henna again," Harry suggested.

"It's one thing to use him for some protection, it's another to ask him to interfere with an active investigation. I just can't do that."

Jordan asked, "What happens now?"

"Not sure. I guess it depends on what we learn from the archivist at the library. If it's something credible we pass it on to Lowell, I guess, and hope they follow up." He didn't add that no matter what they passed on, he was not going to back off his own inquiries.

—

It was nearing four o'clock when the phone rang. Mercer recognized the Iowa area code. He clicked it on before it could ring a second time. "This is Mercer."

"Dr. Mercer. Sherman Smithson here."

"Mr. Smithson, glad you could call back so quickly. Thank you."

"Not at all. It has been my pleasure," the archivist replied, a little less reserved and fussy than he'd been earlier. "Doubly so because I think I have been successful."

"Really?"

"Indeed. President Hoover was in possession of something he called Sample 681. It was sent to him by a man named Mike Dillman some time after World War One but before Hoover became president. I am sorry I can't be more specific than that."

"Do you know anything about this Dillman character?"

"No, I am sorry to say. I've never heard of him before today, and I did perform a cross-reference check for you through our databases. He appears nowhere else in President Hoover's papers. On a lark I also checked for him on the Internet. I turned up dozens of people with that name, but none appeared in any historical context. This may be something you would wish to pursue further."

"I will, of course," Mercer said. "How about anything more on Sample 681?"

"There you run into a bit of luck. It was the president who gave it that number classification for his personal collection of geological samples. Mike Dillman called it a 'lightning stone' in a letter he wrote to the president that came with the sample. In it he gives longitude and latitude reference lines for where he found it. At least that's what I think they are."

Mercer opened Google Earth on his computer. "Would you read them to me, please?"

"Certainly."

Mercer's fingers entered the numbers as soon as Smithson rattled them off. The stylized globe on the flat-screen display rotated and then began zooming in on the precise location. Mercer let out a groan before it was even halfway to the coordinates.

"What is it, Dr. Mercer?" Smithson asked.

"Sample 681 came from south-central Afghanistan."

"Ah, that explains the last line in the note Dillman sent along."

"What does he say?"

"He writes, 'Mr. Hoover, many places claim to be the navel of the world—Delphi and Jerusalem to name but two. I can assure you, however, where I found this sample is Earth's one and only anus.' That seems apt from what I've heard of the country."

"And just my luck," Mercer said without enthusiasm, "I get to play planetary proctologist."

12

The man who met Mercer at the Kabul International Airport just north of downtown looked like an ordinary Afghani, with three notable differences. He was almost a full head taller than the other drivers clustered outside the terminal building clamoring for fares. He wore Western-style combat boots with high ankle support and steel toes. And his skin was about two shades darker than any other man within many miles. This dark countenance split into a broad grin when he saw Mercer cut through the multitudes that congregated around airports in every Third World city he'd ever visited.

They embraced when they met, and the black man shook the single rucksack slung over Mercer's shoulder. "I see you still pack like a teenage girl heading to summer camp."

"Half of what's in here is for you, Book. A fifth of Maker's Mark because you and Harry just have to drink different whiskeys, and a carton of duty-free Marlboros because they're as good as dollars when it comes to baksheesh."

"Ever since the Fed started quantitative easing, the locals want to be bribed in euros." Booker Sykes placed two fingertips to his lips and gave such a piercing whistle that everything around them seemed to pause for a beat. A four-door Toyota pickup detached itself from a line of similarly dusty vehicles and approached them. Armed soldiers stationed outside the terminal watched warily, always on the alert for a suicide bomber striking at so many soft-target foreigners.

Sykes had spent a lifetime honing his body into a force of lethality; when he moved, he did so with the grace and reserve of an apex predator. He swung open the truck's passenger door but paused there until Mercer had settled into the backseat before easing his bulk into the truck. His eyes never stopped scanning the crowd.

"Welcome to Kabul," he said over his shoulder, his basso voice easily outclassing the Toyota's rusted-out exhaust. "I still can't believe you're here."

"Neither can I," Mercer agreed.

He thought of the world map behind the bar back home, with pins stuck in over seventy countries documenting his work as a consulting geologist in some of the remotest locales on Earth. Mercer was familiar with how much of the population lived in grinding poverty among the ruins of failed states. Ten minutes into his first visit here and he could tell Afghanistan, and in particular Kabul, was no exception. What struck him most on flying into the country and again now out on the streets was the near-monochromatic scenery. The roads, the mountains, the buildings, the camels—everything was hued in a muted brown palette.

The exceptions were the yellow-painted taxis that

made up the majority of the cars on the streets, and the bright blue of the women's burkas. The Afghan women moved like wraiths, consciously unseen by the men jostling along the sidewalks. It made no sense to Mercer that the vividness of their costumes should make them stand out against the dull background, when the sack-like burkas were meant to hide them entirely. It was like going into combat wearing safety orange rather than camouflage.

Mercer laughed. "I guess it's better than if the sample had been found in North Korea."

The traffic was insane. The roads might have had lines painted on them at some point in the distant past, but the brutal summer heat and biting winter winds had scoured them away. Drivers maneuvered any way they chose. The only thing they all did consistently was try to drive around the worst of the potholes, some of which were deep and broad enough to hide an Abrams tank. Young men on motorcycles and bicycles wove in and out between the stalled cars, often using a fender or tire to rest a leg if things slowed to a stop. Carts led by horses and donkeys, many full of manure, were as common as the gaily painted trucks with Pakistani license plates bringing in goods from over the Khyber Pass.

"I chuckle," Booker said, "when I hear people bitching about traffic on the D.C. Beltway. It ain't shit compared to this furball."

"How much longer are you here?" Mercer asked.

"Two more weeks, then I am stateside. They want me to come back, obviously, but I'm not so sure. Stacy would prefer I take an office job, and I'm starting to think I can compromise and become an instructor someplace."

This was the first Mercer had heard about this. "So she has her hooks that deep into you?"

"She sure as hell beats coming home to Harry White and that stinky old dog of his."

That was an unarguable point.

Booker Sykes was once among the elite soldiers in the world. From Rangers to Special Forces and on to the indefatigable Delta, his exact number of deployments remained a national secret even after his retirement from the army, but he had seen as much combat as anyone alive—and in places the American public had no idea their nation had a military interest. He had just last year retired after putting in his twenty, to take a much more lucrative job with a private security contractor with the intentionally innocuous name of Gen-D Systems. He was essentially being paid ten times as much for one-tenth the danger of what he'd been doing with the army. What he hadn't expected was to fall hard for one of the company's in-house lawyers. Sykes had one failed marriage already, a casualty of his constant deployments, but he wasn't the same stupid twenty-seven-year-old he'd been then, and he recognized that he wasn't going to do any better than Stacy Grantham—and that maybe it would be best if his war fighting days were behind him.

"Just tell me where you two are registered and I'll get you something nice."

Sykes casually gave Mercer the finger over his broad shoulder, his attention never far from their immediate surroundings. In the bustle of the city anything and everything could be rigged to explode, from the broken-down truck on the side of the road with one of its tires off as though it was being replaced, to the twelve-year-old boy standing at a crosswalk with his hands thrust deep into his pockets.

Mercer would have never considered this trip if it weren't for his friendship with Book Sykes. The two had met when Sykes was still with Delta and on a training rotation at the air force's notorious Area 51. Mercer had been there leading a group of miners who were tunneling underground as part of a top-secret physics experiment. He had used Sykes and his team's unique abilities once or twice since then under the auspices of his role as special science adviser to the president, but since Mercer had lost that job the two met only as friends. Sykes still lived outside of Fort Bragg, Delta's HQ in North Carolina, and near Gen-D's offices as well, but he managed to get to Washington whenever he was back in the States.

A day earlier, as soon as he'd gotten off the phone with the Hoover Library, Mercer had called Book's satellite phone here in Kabul. Sykes then cleared it with his bosses to take Mercer on as a short-term client, but could do nothing about getting him a "friends and relatives" discount. To hire Sykes and three of his men, plus transportation for just a couple of days, ate up the better part of fifty grand. This was a heavy price, but Mercer had been well paid over the years— and to get a crack at Abe's killers he was willing to pay far more.

It was only after arrangements had been made with Sykes that Mercer reached out to Nate Lowell. As Mercer knew would happen, the FBI agent listened with the studied disinterest of a tollbooth attendant on retirement day, promised to include Mercer's information from the Hoover Library in his report, and hung up before Mercer could ask about Kelly Hepburn. As Agent Hepburn had said, hers wasn't the main thrust of the investigation, so to expect anything out of Lowell was a waste of time.

Mercer had then told Harry and Jordan exactly where the next leg of the investigation would take him. Harry was unmoved. He'd been around to see Mercer jet off halfway around the planet too many times to care. On the other hand, Jordan was stunned. It appeared in just the few days they had been together she'd come to rely on his steady presence. He had assured her that the gunmen couldn't possibly know their identities, so they were perfectly safe—but that wasn't it. It seemed as though she liked knowing he was nearby, that she could call his name and he'd be there.

Mercer had given Jordan an indulgent smile. There was something about her that excited him—her youthful beauty, her intelligence, her vulnerability . . . perhaps all three. "Twenty hours flying there, forty on the ground, tops, and twenty back. Let's call it four days just to be sure. Then I'll be back—and hopefully with the answers that will end this nightmare."

"Maybe . . ." Jordan had said. "But it's not safe, Mercer, and you know it." He nodded understandingly, and told her a couple of stories about Booker T. Sykes and his exploits, knowing it would make her feel better to know he had someone like Sykes watching over him.

Upstairs on his closet floor, Mercer kept a packed go bag. The only items he dumped from it, since he was flying commercial, were the folding knife and the Beretta 92 pistol. He trusted Booker could get him replacements in country. Less than sixty minutes after learning where Sample 681 had been unearthed, he was ready to go. He would fly first to London, then New Delhi, and on to Kabul, where Book would meet him and escort him the last couple hundred miles. He didn't bother shaking Harry's hand. They were long past that. The old bastard didn't even get off the bar stool. He just tossed a casual wave over his shoulder without a second glance. Drag greeted Mercer's departure with even more sangfroid, and snored on while Mercer left the rec room.

Only Jordan had walked him down to the front door, her arm still held against her chest by the sling. Mercer stooped to kiss her on the forehead, but she recoiled from him, a strange look on her face.

"Just how old do you think I am?"

The question shook him and he sputtered a bit before she rescued him by saying, "I know I look really young, Mercer . . . it's been a drag most of my life, but I figure when I'm forty it's going to be awesome. I'm twenty-eight, not eighteen, so if you want to kiss me properly I won't think you're a perv or anything."

He ran the numbers in his head and found her math to be impeccable. He was gentle with her arm, but firm as he pressed her hard body against his and his mouth to hers. With her sling between them it was awkward, but nonetheless rewarding. He had one hand at the base of her neck, tilting her head, the other at her waist and nearly encircling half her body. Her knee pressed gently between his legs, nuzzling, teasing.

He broke the kiss before he no longer had the will to do so and stepped back, panting, sheepish, and more than a little awestruck.

"Wow," Jordan said, slow to open her eyes.

"Yeah, wow," he replied, smiling. "I guess I'll see you in a few days."

"And we will definitely pick up where we left off."

He gave her one more short fierce kiss, and then he

was out the door, hooking it with an ankle in a practiced maneuver that gave it just enough momentum to close with a solid clunk.

That had been nearly a full day earlier. "Mercer," Sykes called, startling him back to reality. Sykes pointed to their driver. "I want you to meet Hamid. Hamid, this sad white boy is Philip Mercer, and trust me when I tell you that danger follows this man like the goat stench after a Taliban. Hamid's brother is our chopper pilot, and Hamid works as a mechanic as well as a driver."

"What kind of helo?"

"A Mil Mi-2 that's about ten years older than you or I and goes through as much oil as gas," Booker said with a sardonic smile. "That is one thing I do miss about being on Uncle Sam's dime. We had Blackhawks that were maintained by boys who ate and breathed all that techno shit."

Mercer was familiar with the Mi-2, a Soviet-era workhorse found in many of their former client states but now maintained without the patronage of the Soviet/Russian Mil bureau. He'd flown on some in Africa, where they had used flattened paint cans to patch the bodywork, and duct tape and baling wire to hold other parts in place.

"I never said you weren't brave," Mercer said.

Book grinned again and repacked his cheek with chewing tobacco.

Gen-D Systems rented a warehouse not too far from the recently renovated Ghazi Stadium, where the Taliban once held public stonings and beheadings. It was now home to several football clubs.

Hamid sounded the Toyota's horn midway down the block from their destination, alerting the guards that they were coming. This part of the city was relatively safe, but these men took no chances with security. As they neared the razor-wire-topped gate, an Afghan employee inside drew it back on its rollers to let the truck slip through and then just as quickly rammed it home again so that a steel locking bar fell into place. Hamid needed to slam on the brakes in order to avoid hitting other vehicles parked in Gen-D's tight lot, or any of the shipping containers that seemed to make up half the structures in the city. Here they were storage. Elsewhere they were homes.

The warehouse was battered by weather, and some bricks looked as crumbly as dust, while there were huge stains on the cracked asphalt lot and several of the cars dotting it had been picked clean for spares. In all, it reminded Mercer of an East L.A. chop shop, only when he got out of the truck the music he heard from a boom box atop an oil drum wasn't Latin pop but some Indian synth music that sounded like cats fighting in a burlap bag.

"Home sweet home," Sykes said, unfolding his considerable frame from the Toyota.

"Has a nice postapocalyptic vibe," Mercer said. "I like it."

"I am not wasting my per diem on a room at the Intercontinental. I'll show you where you're crashing, and then we'll see to that bottle of Maker's Mark."

The living quarters, though spartan, were adequate, and they had installed a shower with a high-pressure head and enough hot water to soak out twenty-two hours of stale airline air and cramped muscles. Because of the short notice, there had only been coach seats available on the long leg from London to New Delhi.

Mercer met Sykes and three other Americans in the operations room, which also doubled as their lounge.

There were mismatched sofas facing a flat-screen TV hooked to a satellite dish on the roof, and a Sony PS-4 console on the cement floor. The walls were covered with travel posters, mostly bikinied women on sugar sand beaches, but also some maps of the country as well as detailed ones of the city of Kabul and the surrounding suburbs. Light came from yellow construction lamps aimed at the ceiling.

The warehouse had once belonged to a spice merchant, and even years later the air still carried the tinge of Eastern flavors—saffron, cinnamon, and of course the aroma of raw opium, which had been the man's real business.

The bottle of Maker's Mark was on a sideboard the men used for their bar, among other bottles of spirits he'd never heard of—but in a country where only foreigners could buy alcohol, Chinese vodka and Japanese gin worked just fine. Mercer squeezed two limes into a glass and poured in the vodka. There was no ice.

"Grab one of those liter bottles of water," Book ordered and waved his bourbon glass in the direction of the flats of water stacked next to the bar. "We're at nearly six thousand feet and we'll be even higher tomorrow. I don't need you puking from the altitude."

He was sitting on a recliner covered in colorful dyed cotton tapestries since its original upholstery had long since been worn away. "And, Mercer, I hope you don't take offense—operational security requires that you not know the other guys' real names. But these are the men going south with us tomorrow. Do you remember the code name I gave you when we jumped into that monastery in Tibet?"

"Snow White," Mercer said dejectedly, hating the

moniker of a newbie but knowing he'd never earn a real operator's nickname.

"Snow it is"—Sykes laughed—"and these three are Grump, Sleep, and Sneeze. And of course, I am your host, Doc."

"You're also an unimaginative prick," Mercer said. He shook the men's hands. They all had the calm eyes and easy demeanor of elite soldiers, men who had been pushed so far beyond the limits of endurance that they no longer needed to show how tough they were. If you didn't immediately recognize it, you weren't worth their time. Mercer knew he would never have the time to gain their respect, but Sykes must have told them a little of his and Mercer's exploits because they looked at Mercer with slightly more regard than they would have offered a regular civilian.

"First off, I want to say thanks. I know it's more money in your pockets, but Book said you all volunteered for this mission without really knowing the risks. And neither do I. With any luck it'll be nothing more than a quiet day in the countryside with us back home in time for supper. On the other hand, we could be heading into an area crawling with insurgents or drug smugglers. The satellite pictures I've seen only show an area of canyons and valleys that are so steep the bottoms are in shadow for all but an hour a day." He looked to Sykes. "Have you gotten any intel on the region?"

"We've asked around," Booker replied. "It's pretty remote even by Afghan standards, but it is close enough to the Pak border that there could be smugglers—and those bastards have a hell of a lot more fight in them than the Taliban because they're better paid. That said, no one has anything solid going on down there.

I even reached out to my contact in the Company. She said everything appears quiet. The Tali's spring offensive is still a few weeks away, and it's still a little early to catch them moving supplies into position."

"So what's the plan?" Mercer asked.

"Nothing's changed since yesterday. We'll chopper in to as close as we can, then hoof it the rest of the way. You do whatever you need to do while we cover your sorry ass, and then it's hot feet back to the LZ and we bug out. The only pucker factor is Ahmad, that's our pilot, is going to need to dust off and refuel in Khost, so that leaves us on our own for the better part of three hours."

"And what about you?" the operator nicknamed Sleep asked Mercer. He was African American like Booker but spoke with a deep southern accent. "What are you doing here exactly? Book says you're a geologist."

Mercer nodded. "A few days ago a friend of mine was killed over a mineral sample that was discovered in our target area. I have no idea how long ago or what the sample was. I don't even know if there's any left there, so I guess we can consider this a fact-finding mission."

"If my read of history is right," Grump said, spitting some tobacco juice into a soda can, "the Vietnam War started with fact-finding missions."

"Don't worry," Book told his men. "To the best of my knowledge Mercer has never actually started a war. Right?"

Before Mercer could reply, the earth jolted under them enough to rattle the bottles on the bar and send peppery dust raining from the building's exposed rafters. The men looked around and then down at the ground. Concerned but not alarmed.

Mercer finally had to ask, "What was that?"

"IED," Sneeze told him. He was a slender man with dark hair and a beard who could easily pass as a native. "Sounds about two miles away and fairly large. More likely a truck bomb than a suicide vest."

Seconds later the sound of sirens penetrated the warehouse's thick brick walls.

"The Taliban is letting the government know that they're coming soon," Sneeze went on. "And once they take over, the opposition will swing into action with the exact same tactics. No one can rule this country, because the lines drawn on their hundred-year-old colonial maps don't mean squat. The idea that there really is a nation of Afghanistan is as much a myth as saying there are such places as Shangri-la or Atlantis."

A boy of about twelve dressed in traditional clothes came in from another room. He was pushing a trolley cart that looked like it had been stolen from a hotel. On it were stainless serving dishes, a stack of cheap china plates, and cutlery.

"Ah, good," Book said. "On that happy note, dinner is served. Mercer, this is Hamid's son, Farzam. Farzam is our batman when he's not in school, and his mother is our cook. The best in Kabul, right, Farzam?"

"I am that, Mr. Book," the boy said in what was obviously a routine they did often.

"I was talking about your momma."

"Her as well." The boy grinned and settled the cart next to the bar.

There wasn't much conversation with the meal. The men lined up cafeteria style, served themselves from the rice and goat bowls, and then sat to shovel food into their mouths the way railroad workers used to feed coal into locomotives. Afterward they drifted to their individual rooms, basically cubicles made of plywood with hinged doors that maintained a level of privacy.

"You good, sleepwise, for tomorrow?" Booker asked Mercer when his men had gone.

"Good enough for the trip there and back, but I pity the poor SOB sitting next to me on my flights the next day—unless he's deaf or otherwise immune to snoring."

"Fine. I'll wake you at zero-five-thirty for breakfast and kit up. We head for the chopper at six and hope to be in the air no later than six thirty." Booker reached behind his back and removed a sleek black pistol. He popped the magazine from the butt and racked the slide to eject the round already jacked into the chamber. He thumbed the brass shell back into the mag and rammed it into place once again before handing it over to Mercer, grip first and the barrel angled away. "We never let principals carry weapons on protection detail because ten times out of ten they're civilians here doing charity work or part of some rebuilding effort and don't know a Beretta from a hole in the ground." He heaved himself off the couch. "You, on the other hand . . . Just don't shoot any of my boys."

13

The sun was not yet up when they left the compound. They drove in a large SUV that sloshed on its suspension whenever they went around a curve, telling Mercer the Suburban was heavily armored. Hamid was behind the wheel with Book in the passenger seat. The three other shooters, Mercer, and all their gear were jammed into the back.

"We would have picked you up from the airport in this beast," Booker explained, "but another team was using it to ferry a couple of Silicon Valley types who are here trying to persuade people who've just stopped living in caves that they now need 4G Wi-Fi."

"How'd they do?" Mercer asked as they raced through the predawn darkness, their headlamps the only light visible except for the setting moon.

"They're still alive," Book said. "That's all I care about."

It sounded like a flippant comment, but Sykes was speaking from the heart. The successful completion of the mission was all that interested him.

It was dark out, and cold—two factors that sapped

the spirits and eroded will, and yet as they rocketed through the deserted streets, Mercer felt confidence surging through him. The truck smelled of the inevitable spices from their headquarters, and of gun oil from their assault rifles, but there was another scent in the vehicle. It was the musk or the pheromone that bonded parties of hunters since humanity's days on the plains of ancient Africa. It was what gave them the courage to face enemies armed with tooth and claw and speed and stealth. Prey that was larger than them, better able to defend itself. Prey that was not prey at all, and yet those proto-humans with their sticks and rudimentary language not only eked out their existence on the grassy plains but thrived to eventually inhabit every corner of the globe.

At the most basic level the men in the truck were no different from the primitive hunters. Their weapons were better, their language more refined, but they were imbued with that same antediluvian courage that left them buoyed of spirit and eager to face whatever challenge may come.

The chopper was hangared at the far end of the international airport, well away from the commercial airliners and the meager aircraft of the fledgling Afghan Air Force that used the airport. The Mi-2 had been rolled free of the building and into the brightening sky. It was so utilitarian and boxy it reminded Mercer of a panel van with a tail stalk and rotor blades, and a huge forehead bulge that was its two turbine engines.

The pilot was already in the front seat busy with preflight checks, while another Afghan waited by the open cargo door to help the passengers load their gear. Booker's men didn't bother with hard cases for their weapons but carried them in the open. Mercer had no idea what bureaucratic nightmare had to be negotiated for this to happen, but there were a couple of soldiers nearby and Sykes approached them with a handful of the Marlboro cigarette packs Mercer had brought into the country. He suspected that this was just simple wheel greasing and not the true bribery that let Gen-D Systems operate as its own army. The soldiers immediately lit up their cigarettes, standing under a bright No Smoking sign written in Pashtu as well as English and in symbols so basic a child could understand them.

Sykes introduced Mercer to the pilot, Ahmad, and then the two talked about the latest weather report for their intended route. Rain was a possibility, which neither pilot nor team leader liked, but it would only hamper their operation, not force its cancellation. They discussed the fuel situation, and Ahmad reassured Book that he had a reserve supply waiting in the city of Khost.

"All right," Sykes said and his voice boomed. "Let's mount up."

The men wore a patchwork of Western gear hidden under Afghan clothing that was surprisingly comfortable and warm. Mercer carried about thirty pounds of equipment. Some was for technical mountaineering: Mammut Duodess climbing ropes, rock bolts, and a sling of carabiners and belay clamps. The rest was extra ammunition magazines for the team's M-4A1 assault rifles and some geology tools he had pilfered from Gen-D's motor pool workshop. The claw part of the hammer would work as a pick, but he had doubts about the tensile strength of a two-foot pry bar he'd borrowed. The Beretta 92 9mm pistol

Book had loaned him was strapped to his thigh in a low holster that made him feel a little like a gunslinger out of an old Western.

They settled into the chopper as the old turbines wailed into life, one after the other. The engines bogged down when Ahmad engaged the transmission to start the big rotors turning overhead. Yet in minutes the entire chopper was bucking and shaking like a washing machine about to tear itself apart. The sensation wasn't unknown to Mercer. This was an older helicopter, after all, but it seemed to take forever before the blades were beating the air with sufficient speed to haul the ungainly machine into the air.

Like a rickety elevator, the Mil struggled and wheezed and made all sorts of terrifying sounds as it climbed into the dawn. The sun was just beginning to paint the mountain peaks that dominate the skyline to the north and south of the capital city. The snowy crests flashed impossible shades of gold and red when struck by the pure light of such an unpolluted place, and for a moment Mercer could forget the poverty and dinginess of the city sprawled below them.

Only Ahmad and Sykes next to him had headphones, and the Mi-2 was too loud to hold anything short of screaming matches, so Mercer settled in for the two-hour flight toward the tribal regions spanning the Afghan-Pakistan border. In all of recorded history it was one of the few places in the world that could boast it had never been fully conquered.

As they cleared the city, he was reminded of Buzz Aldrin's line about the moon being "magnificent desolation." The same could be said of Afghanistan. There was little below them but rock and valley, hilltop and hardscrabble villages scraping by on the edge of fields that were more gravel lot than life-sustaining grove. It was too early in the spring for anything to be in bloom, so the landscape was a patchwork of earth tones that bled and ran into each other in a drab mosaic that stretched to the silvery mountains in the distance. As well traveled as he was, even Mercer had a hard time recalling such a harsh and unforgiving land.

They thundered on. Two of Sykes's men slept, or at least had their eyes closed. Another scanned the ground to their right, while Booker in the left front seat watched for anything suspicious coming at them from that direction. They were safe enough at altitude and speed from an RPG, and not even the Taliban had any working Stinger missiles left over from the post–Soviet invasion days, but years of being immersed in combat zones made the men rightly cautious.

Mercer continued to push fluids into his body as they flew higher into the mountains. Altitude sickness was a real concern. He'd never really been struck by it in the past, but he would be pushing himself hard over the next twelve or so hours without giving his body the proper amount of time to acclimate. As a precaution, he popped a few Tylenol, knowing headache was usually the first symptom. Their overwatch sniper, Sleep, saw him do this and flashed a diver's "okay" sign. Mercer responded in kind, and the shooter tucked his cap farther over his dark brow and nodded off again.

Ninety minutes later, Mercer felt Booker Sykes tapping him on the shoulder. He turned in his rear-facing jump seat and stretched his upper body into the cockpit. "What's up?"

"We're nearing your coordinates," Book called over the beat of the rotor and scream of the turbines.

"Thought you should see what we're flying over to get a better picture than those satellite shots."

Mercer nodded, preoccupied by worry. There was a danger to this mission he had considered from the moment Sherman Smithson rattled off the longitude and latitude coordinates for what Michael Dillman had claimed was the location where he had discovered Sample 681. The danger was that Dillman could have been dozens or even hundreds of miles off target. Since the minerals were obviously collected long before modern navigation aids like GPS, Dillman was working with a sextant, a chronometer that might not have been calibrated in weeks or months, and making best-guess estimates of a slew of other factors in determining his location.

Dillman had dutifully written out the coordinates for the sample's origin to a very precise degree, one that Mercer could pinpoint decades later on a satellite photograph as a tight valley that looked like it petered out into the side of a mountain. However, that didn't mean the written coordinates marked the actual spot where the man had found Sample 681. Mercer had to hope Dillman was accurate enough to get them close, so that his own knowledge of geology and geography could lead them to where X really marked the spot.

The ground below the speeding chopper was a crosshatch of canyons and ridges that had no discernible pattern. It was all chaos but with monotony of color. Rather than brown, like around Kabul, here the world was shades of gray, from nearly black to almost white. It was ugly terrain, and one that he didn't relish having to march across because the shortest distance in terrain such as this was never a straight line. It also didn't help that the promising dawn they had left in

Kabul was now a leaden sky that seemed to hover scant feet over their heads.

Booker split his attention between the panorama unfolding beneath them and a handheld GPS device that he'd programmed with their destination. Mercer had eyes only for the topography, while behind him in the cabin, Sleep, Grump, and Sneeze watched out for any movement that could betray a Taliban position. Occasionally, Mercer could see Sykes mouthing orders to Ahmad to correct their flight path.

A minute later, Book made an emphatic gesture pointing his thumb down, and Mercer could read his lips as he said to the pilot, "Hover here."

Mercer studied the ground for anything that looked familiar. At first all the arêtes and gorges and talus slopes looked the same, and then the landscape resolved itself to the images he'd studied earlier. This was where Dillman claimed he'd found the mysterious mineral he'd called a lightning stone, which Herbert Hoover later classified numerically for his collection. As with the satellite pictures, nothing about this location struck Mercer as being geologically significant. It looked like every other godforsaken part of this country, bleak, desolate, totally uninviting and uninhabitable.

Prospects didn't improve when Sykes handed him a pair of military-grade binoculars. Ahmad kept the Mil in constant motion so they didn't become an easy target, but Mercer had no trouble studying the ground and for five minutes he peered intently at everything but saw nothing.

"Give me a five-mile perimeter," he yelled at Book. Sykes nodded and relayed his order to the Afghan pilot. As had been discussed earlier, they only had fifteen minutes' flying time before Ahmad would need to off-load their extra weight in order to make it to Khost and refuel.

They spiraled out away from the exact coordinates Michael Dillman had provided. Mercer had known not to expect a big glaring sign that advertised an excavation of some sort, but the farther they flew from Dillman's purported spot, the fewer were their chances of actually finding anything. In searches, one either looked at one locale precisely or combed a massive area; there really wasn't much by way of middle ground.

He kept the binocs snug to his eyes as the chopper circled the rugged massif, intent on catching every detail he could in the few minutes remaining. Each ridge and hillside looked identical. There were no individual reference points, nothing distinctive to help orient the search. He wasn't sure what he was looking for exactly, so he wouldn't know it if he actually saw it. There was little of interest at all, and yet that in itself might be what he sought. It was maddening, and he started to think this whole trip had been a colossal waste of time.

He decided they should head back to the coordinates, land, and hope for the best. He was reaching to tap Book on the shoulder to tell him when he saw something that caught his attention. It was a crease in the side of a mountain at the head of a narrow canyon. The only way it was recognizable would be by standing at its base or high above as they were now.

He pointed it out to Sykes. "See the top of that one mountain covered in snow that looks like an octopus's tentacles? Look below that and to the right. That narrow valley. What does it look like to you where those two rounded parts of the mountain meet?"

Sykes used the verbal waypoints to spot the anomaly. He grinned wolfishly. "Looks like a butt crack."

"Remember what I told you Dillman wrote? The sample came from the anus of the world. Bet you a case of whiskey there's a cave where those two lobes of the hill come together."

Booker nodded. "As long as all you geologist types have childish senses of humor."

"We do. That's our spot."

Sykes told Ahmad, and the pilot scouted the ground for a suitable place to let them off. They got lucky in that there was a flatland on top of a mountain not four miles from the site Mercer selected. He flew them there after Booker programmed their new destination into the GPS.

Ahmad approached the LZ like he was going to buzz right past it and only flared the chopper at the last second, reining it back like a horse so that it was almost standing on its tail rotor before leveling it out a foot off the ground and at zero indicated airspeed. It was a masterful tactical maneuver, and the men didn't waste it by congratulating him. Mercer felt like he was being borne by a massive crowd as the men poured from the back of the Mil in a rush to get clear. Seconds later, the lightened chopper sped off again, emerging from a filthy cloud of rotor wash and climbing hard.

When the dust cleared, the four operators were prone on the ground, ringing the LZ and watching the valleys and nearby peaks for any sign their landing had drawn attention. Mercer also stayed put and waited for Sykes to give him the all clear. The *whop whop* of the receding helicopter faded to silence before the former Delta commando was satisfied they were alone.

Though confident they were secure, the men never stood to outline themselves against the sky as they moved off the flatland and down the crumbly side of the hill. These mountains were among the most seismically active in the world, so that nothing on the surface appeared to have been exposed enough to weather much. All the stones were hard-edged and flinty, like natural knives that would shred unprotected skin without mercy. Apart from all the other gear Booker Sykes had loaned him, Mercer was thankful for the Kevlar combat gloves. He kept his sidearm holstered, but Sykes and the others swept the terrain with the barrels of their weapons in constant arcs that seemingly missed nothing. Sykes took the lead with the others strung out behind him at fifteen-yard intervals. They would bunch up or spread out as the terrain demanded.

For the first part of the trip off the mountain, their descent was a barely controlled slide. The loose rock shifted under their boots, releasing miniature avalanches with every step. It was only when they hit against a larger rock buried in the scree that they could gain some sense of influence over their movement.

But they did not head straight to the valley floor; that was tactical suicide in Afghanistan. They found an old game trail midway down the hill and started moving parallel to the crest and now heading toward their destination. The air remained cold and damp, almost thick enough to be considered a drizzling mist but not quite. It wasn't even enough to dampen clothes yet, but it didn't bode well for what might come.

The one trail petered out, forcing them to move along loose rock again, exposed to the opposite side of the valley and anyone with a sniper rifle. The terrain across the valley looked as forlorn and barren as where they were walking. However, Mercer knew a good sniper could dig into almost any background and remain hidden for days. Mercer asked himself if he felt eyes on him, and honestly he wasn't sure. He walked a little quicker and stooped a little lower.

It took a careful hour to move to within a mile of their target. Sykes called a break and ordered their sniper, Sleep, up to higher ground to get a better look. Mercer scarfed down some more painkillers and water. He was panting hard in the thin air but didn't feel himself succumbing to altitude sickness. His vision was acute, his head felt fine, and he had no nausea. He felt better, in fact, than on a Saturday morning following a night out at Tiny's with Harry.

The sniper returned fifteen minutes later. The men hunkered down in the protection of a small grove of stunted pines that clung to the rocks at the very terminus of the timberline.

"The target valley is still a ways off," Sleep said, the butt of his long gun resting on his thigh. "But we might have a problem. I heard bells."

Grump cursed.

"What's that mean?" Mercer asked, though he had a good idea.

"Goats," Sleep said. "Locals put all kinds of shit on their goats, including bells."

"And lipstick," Sneeze joked, "don't forget lipstick."

"Direct approach is out," Sykes decided, guessing the goats, and their human minders, would stay down in the valleys where there was more vegetation. "We'll keep to the hills and circle around to the head of the valley. That's our target anyway."

It took another long hour, moving slowly, always scouting ahead and straining their senses to perceive anything out of the ordinary in the gathering storm. They heard nothing resembling goat bells and collectively decided that the danger was passed. A new problem was approaching; the clouds that were rolling in were black and heavy with rain. If they let loose before the mission was over, Ahmad might not make it back until the storm dissipated, and no one relished the idea of a night spent out in the open.

Mercer pulled his headscarf tighter to keep out the dribbling rain. He had started a slight cough in the past twenty minutes, nothing more than a deep tickle that he could mostly suppress, but the first time one escaped his lips Sykes had looked at him sharply. They both knew what that single inexorable exhalation portended. He also had to admit that the Tylenol was doing little for the pressure building in his head and behind his sinuses.

He was breathing far harder than the others, a fast pant like a dog in the summer heat.

"Slow it, man," Grumpy said. "Force yourself to take slow, even breaths. That's it. Nice and deep. Give your lungs time to absorb the oxygen you've already taken in rather than suck in O_2 that ain't there."

A few seconds later, Mercer felt the pressure under his diaphragm ease and the rope tightening around his skull unknot. "Thanks," he said, feeling a bit more human.

"It ain't nothing, bro."

They continued on. Their target valley started wide and then narrowed and steepened, so that sheer cliffs lined its two-hundred-yard width. From what Mercer had seen from the chopper, it would widen out into a circular bowl near where he saw the cleft that looked like human buttocks. If he were to guess, he would assume local shepherds used the protective bowl when the weather turned foul to shelter themselves and their animals. So far there had been no ringing of bells or scent of a watch fire in the misty air, but Mercer had to admit that the strain of being constantly alert for such signs was exhausting. The fighters protecting him could go for days on extended combat patrols, but he was nearly spent after a couple of hours. He had always admired Sykes and men like him, but this experience was boosting his admiration to a new level.

The darkest of the clouds rolled past without shedding their store of rain. Mercer's woolen outer smock, though heavy with accumulated dew, had kept him warm and dry as such garments had done for hundreds of years in these rugged mountains. They reached the head of the canyon. From here the cliffs were sheer and virtually featureless. Only occasional tufts of grass found a crag in which to root, and there were but a few spots where birds had nested and permanently streaked the stone with their droppings.

Mercer and Sykes hid behind a slab of stone that had sheared off a cliff aeons ago while the men covered them, both studying the ground below for any sign of a cave that Michael Dillman had dubbed the anus of the world. The molded contours of the mountain at the valley's head and the long vertical crease that ran down it looked even more like a butt now that they were closer. It was flattened somewhat, and a little shaggy with grasses, so Mercer thought of it as a guy's ass rather than the shapely curve of a woman's. And just where it would be anatomically on a human, there was a darkened cave entrance where the two lobes of stone met and doubtless inspired Michael Dillman's anatomical reference.

"I'll be damned," Sykes said when he spotted the six-foot-wide cave entrance. He whispered to Mercer, "What now, we put you in a big body glove and lube you up?"

"You are no longer allowed to comment on my sense of humor."

Because of the cave's height, thirty feet above the valley floor, and the way the cliffs curved, Mercer would not be able to free climb up to it. Also he had to admit that in the thin air he probably didn't have the strength. There was a flat plateau about fifty feet above and to the right of the cave entrance, and it looked like an easy march up a goat trail to reach it. From there he could rappel down and spider crawl to the cave mouth while the others provided cover. He told Sykes his plan, and after a few minutes studying the terrain through binoculars the former Delta officer agreed.

The trail was just wide enough for them to place one foot in front of the other and walk with their shoulders torqued around, but the grade was manageable and soon the men were eighty feet up the two-hundred-foot cliff face and on the shelf Mercer had seen from the ground. A chunk of stone the size of an automobile engine had broken off the cliff and made a perfect belay point for the safety rope Mercer would pay out as he climbed across to the cavern.

Sykes and Sleep helped with the line while Grump surveyed the entire scene through his sniper scope, and Sneeze did the same over his M-4A1's optics. There was some passable cover behind other chunks of rock that had dislodged and settled on the shelf over the years, but this was still an exposed position and countersniper procedures were necessary.

While Booker tied off the line, Mercer shucked his pack and quickly hauled out the extra ammo, spare canteen, MREs, and other gear so all he would carry in it for the climb were the rock hammer, the short pry bar, sample bags, and a flashlight.

"I don't like it here," Sykes said, giving the rope a final, brutal pull. "Get over there, do your thing, and get your ass back. We are way too exposed for my taste. Got it?"

"What is it you guys say? Hooah," Mercer replied.

"Hooah," Sykes called back softly, and Mercer climbed over the makeshift barricade and started down the rock face.

The strain on his arms and legs immediately made him want to cough, but he suppressed the urge and concentrated on his tenuous grip on the stone. It was ice cold and greasy from the rain turning a coating of dust into something as viscous as pond slime. The climb also put added pressure on his abdominal muscles, which were toned into hard bands, but when they tightened on his stomach, it brought the first wave of altitude-induced nausea. The men above kept the rope from getting in his way as he crawled down, and also across the right cheek of the buttocks-shaped formation. The mountain was very young in geologic terms and erosion hadn't yet smoothed out the face, which provided plenty of hand- and footholds, but still he was racing his own body's negative reaction to being this high up in the oxygen-depleted air.

As part of his mine rescue work, Mercer was an accomplished climber, even if he never saw it as a thrill sport. He moved surely and steadily, his technique flawless in execution and adherence to safety protocols. His fingers were cold but not yet cramping, and only once did the toe of his boot slip from a knuckle-size projection when he asked it to take his weight. Because of the rock face's outward curve, he could not see the ground directly below him, which wasn't a problem, but when the wind picked up, whipping around the horseshoe-shaped valley head, Mercer felt a small stab of concern. It came around so fast that it got between him and the stone and tried to peel him off the mountain with surprising force. He had to tighten his hands into claws and curl his toes to keep a precarious grip on the rock, attempting to press his body back against the face while Mother Nature tried to send him tumbling into the void.

Fighting for every millimeter, Mercer was able to mash himself to the rock in a lover's embrace. He suddenly gave in to his body's need, and he coughed so deeply it almost felt like he'd torn tissue. He spat some watery saliva, but it wasn't stained with blood. That would likely come later.

The wind dropped a minute later and he kept going, ever downward and moving to his left, approaching the cave entrance with each step. Because it was so high off the valley floor it wouldn't be home to any predators; snow leopards, though rare, still haunted these forsaken mountains, and they were high enough in elevation that bats wouldn't likely call it home, but there were some large bird species that hunted the Hindu Kush, and Mercer wasn't keen on encountering one bursting out of the cave as he tried to enter.

He was still five feet above and ten feet to the right of the cave when he paused, pulled out a handful of pebbles he'd collected just prior to the climb, and threw them at the shadowy cave entrance. Several pattered down the face of the cliff, but enough found their mark that had a vulture or eagle or other raptor been roosting inside, it would have burst out in a riot of feathers and angered cries.

Mercer finished his descent and soon found himself standing at the cave entrance. The floor was littered with the bones of tiny creatures—mice and voles and other ground mammals that were the favored meal of the indigenous birds of prey. Powdered guano also blanketed the floor while more recent streaks splattered the walls. The cavern remained wide and tall for only a short distance into the mountain before the ceiling dropped and the walls narrowed. Mercer unhooked himself from the line, tying it off around a chunk of stone almost as large as the upper anchor point.

Only ten feet in, and he was down to his hands and knees and needing the flashlight to peer into the stygian blackness ahead of him. There was nothing remarkable about the geology; the mountain was granite of poor quality judging by the numerous cracks and fissures. It wasn't handling the shock load of so much seismic activity, and if he were to guess he'd have to say the cave would most likely collapse in another couple thousand years.

A further twenty feet in, and he was forced to remove his backpack and push it ahead of him and commando crawl. He saw no evidence that anyone other than the raptors had been here before him. The sandy cave floor showed occasional animal tracks, but no telltale human spoor. This didn't bode well and Mercer started feeling the first pangs of doubt. He had just

been guessing that this cave was what Dillman refer-
enced. They could be miles from the actual target. He
moved on, forced even flatter by the constricting rock
walls and lowering ceiling. No matter how carefully
he crawled, he still kicked up a cloud of fine dust particles that made their way deep into his airways and
triggered another coughing fit, only this time the surrounding stone seemed to squeeze in on each spasm
and redouble the pain in the delicate oxygen-deprived
tissues of his lungs. Each cough was like a full body
blow, and no matter what he tried he couldn't seem
to catch his breath. Mercer worried that in seconds
his hind brain would overwhelm his logic center and
blind panic would ensue. He fought to control himself, to calm down and take easy shallow sips of air,
to forget the tons of rock pressing in on him, and the
tickle at the back of his throat or the coppery taste of
blood in his mouth.

Booker and his team were hanging exposed on
the side of a mountain in the middle of Taliban country, and they were relying on him to get the mission
done as quickly as possible. He took as deep a breath
as possible and forced himself to hold it, forced the
muscles around his diaphragm to relax. He held on
to that breath until his vision pixelated and dimmed
so it looked as if his flashlight was dying and he was
being left in the pitch-darkness of that Afghan cave.
He kept at it until he was moments from passing out,
and maybe he even did for a second, but then he let it
go, nice and easy, no need to panic. When his lungs
were empty he took another, normal breath and this
time there were no spasms. The air was still filled with
dust, and it irritated his nose and throat, but it wasn't
getting so deep as to convulse his entire body.

He was sixty feet into the mountain, and the tunnel remained snug but not impassable. He saw no signs that animals ventured this deep. In fact he saw nothing at all except the futility of what he was attempting. Rather than mourn the loss of Abraham Jacobs as a proper friend should, and attend his funeral and swap stories about a great man with others who had loved him, Mercer had turned Abe's death into a quest, a personal obligation to find those responsible. Here he was, in the bowels of a desolate mountain in the middle of one of the most dangerous places on Earth, putting his life and the lives of the others in jeopardy because he couldn't face Abe's death head-on. As he had so often in the past, Mercer had taken a tangent when faced with one of life's roadblocks, and this time it had gone too far afield even to try to justify. Mercer realized the tightness in his throat and the burning behind his eyes had nothing to do with the dust.

Feeling as distraught as when he saw Abe's crumpled body in the Leister Deep Mine, Mercer shifted so he could start sliding back out of the hole. His light swept across the rough wall and something caught his eye—a smudge on the wall at the very limit of its glow. Unsure about anything, he slithered forward and saw what looked like letters painted onto the wall, as crudely as if they were drawn by a child. It was the black crustiness of the medium that made him realize they had been drawn with human blood.

They read: MD.

14

Michael Dillman. It had to be. Mercer scanned the ceiling of the cave just a few inches over his head, and he saw the rock protrusion where Dillman had hit and subsequently split open his scalp.

Mercer's doubts evaporated, and he knew now more than ever that he was on the right path—not just the physical trail of the lightning stones, but also the goal of avenging Abe Jacobs. Mercer needed this wrong to be righted. Someone had murdered his friend, possibly for what was to be found in this cave, and Mercer owed it to him to see this through, no matter where it ended and what it cost.

He moved now with renewed vigor, the near hypoxia he'd been experiencing almost forgotten as adrenaline saturated his blood. Mercer squeezed deeper into the tunnel-like passage, forcing his body through the constricted space and allowing his cave training to take over. Fifteen feet farther, and the walls and roof suddenly opened into a chamber about the size of a small bedroom. The ceiling wasn't quite the standard eight feet, more like six for the most part, but in one corner it had collapsed into a pile of loose stones with a hole above it. No light made it down from the surface, but Mercer could feel air being drawn up through the ceiling as if from a chimney. It was cold enough for him to see his breath.

Three other things caught his attention as he swept the flashlight beam around the room. One was the odd jagged stripes radiating from the hole in the ceiling and etching their way down the walls and across the floor. It looked as though the gray stone had been painted with snaggy black lines. The second thing was the grotto at the far end of the room. It was a natural formation, about four feet high and two wide, and it seemed most of the black scorch lines terminated at its entrance. The final thing, and the one that held his interest, was the body.

The corpse was obviously ancient. It was little more than black parchment skin drawn over a skeleton that had shrunk and shriveled over time. The dead figure was sitting in the meditative lotus position, with wrists resting on its knees and feet crossed over onto the opposite thigh. The only incongruity was that while the corpse maintained this most Eastern of poses, it was actually resting on its side, so one bony knee stuck up in the air and the head had detached from the neck after it no longer had support. Mercer immediately understood that the body had once sat guarding the entrance to the grotto and someone, Dillman most likely, had moved it out of the way by simply setting it aside without any thought to repositioning it.

Looking more carefully, he saw that ragged holes had been punched through the body at random places and that the skin had discolored around these spots in zigging streaks of darker char. He looked again at the pattern of lines on the walls and the spokes of darker coloration coming from the hole in the ceiling and shooting for the grotto, and he finally understood what was taking place, or at least had taken place here.

He trained the light into the grotto to verify that with a storm still expected topside he was safe, and saw the hollow behind the grotto was empty. The grotto was, in fact, a large geode, and someone— Mercer had to assume Michael Dillman—had removed the crystals that had once lined its interior. Left behind like empty honeycombs were the sockets in which the crystals had formed, and judging by their size the crystals themselves would have been the size of bananas or larger. He flashed back to the wax-paper wrapping recovered from Abe's trash can. It had spent decades encasing something tubular about the size of a carrot. One of these crystals, he was certain.

As to the rest of the mystery, whatever molecular composition and atomic structure had gone into the crystals' formation, they had interfered enough with the surrounding natural geomagnetic forces to turn the geode into a big fat lightning rod. The cave had been hit so many times over the past millions of years that the shock had cracked the ceiling, and the natural bolts of searing electricity had scarred the stone and eventually punched holes through the body of a Buddhist or Jain mystic who had decided to crawl in here to die, at what must have been considered a sacred place.

Dillman's moniker for the stones now made sense.

This all came with another, troubling realization. Mike Dillman had plundered the cavern completely. Mercer scanned every inch of the phone-booth-size geode with his light, contorting his body and craning his neck to see each square inch of its otherworldly interior. There wasn't a trace of Sample 681 left anywhere.

The locals who settled this area would have experienced the lightning striking this particular piece of mountain. Maybe they had explored the cave, but seeing the corpse had persuaded them to leave the site alone. But Dillman came along, a field geologist who, if he was anything like Mercer, would take local lore and custom into account when prospecting. He figured there was something underground attracting an inordinate amount of lightning, and he came in to investigate. Mercer didn't know if Dillman had cleared it all out in one trip, or taken a few samples and only returned later when it was found the crystals had real value. Either way, Mercer thought as he slashed his light back and forth one last time, Dillman had been very thorough in cleaning out the cache of crystal gems. The bastard. Mercer had quickly developed a distinct dislike for the old prospector. Mercer was decades if not a century or more too late.

His light rested on the macabre remains of the long-dead mystic. The cave was too tight for someone to have dragged the body down here and set it in its current tableau, so the swami had come down to accept death willingly. Mercer wasn't too sure of the rites of Buddhists or Jains, but he didn't think suicide like this was strictly forbidden as it was in Islam or Christianity. He considered the spiritual and physical path this man must have taken to reach this point. He would have seen the mountain take strike after strike every time the sky opened up with bolts of blue fire. That had to have had some higher meaning to him, so the shaman came here to learn why this happened and decided this was such a sacred spot, a womb within the living rock, that he wanted it for his sepulcher. He had to recognize that it was the crystals that attracted the sky fire, so they were the real power here.

So what would he do? Just sit down and wait? Come here hoping to be struck by lightning?

"You wanted to go out in a blaze of glory, didn't you?" Mercer said to the capsized corpse. "And to make sure that happened, I am willing to bet . . ."

He let his voice trail off and examined the claw-like hands, fully expecting to see the spindly fingers curled around one of the crystals, but they were empty. He swore, sure that he'd been right, and then another thought struck him. Fighting both revulsion and the returning nausea brought on by the altitude, he pried open the disarticulated skull's locked jaw. Bits of desiccated flesh and skin sloughed off in disgusting flakes. The teeth were loose and a couple dropped out as Mercer prodded, but his fingers found purchase on something that would have been held trapped under the tongue, which was now nothing more than a scaly sac that crumbled to powder.

Mercer's hand returned from its repulsive quest, and into the yellow beam of his flashlight came a nub of crystal the size of an acorn that was the same color, and had the same lifeless dinginess, as a ball of mud. He couldn't help but feel a little disappointment. For no other reason than that treasures are always supposed to dazzle the eye, he'd expected something magical and exquisite, something with the fire of a diamond, or the mystery of a ruby or the spellbinding depth of an emerald. This stone made even the dimmest smoke quartz look luminous.

He decided right there that Dillman had taken just

a small amount of this unlikely gem with him and only returned when told it had value, most likely by Herbert Hoover, and probably on his orders.

Studying the uninteresting lump, Mercer also deduced that Sample 681, the piece Abe had died for, was probably from that first foray into these mountains, but then wondered what happened to the lion's share of the crystals after Dillman came back and wrested them from the geode.

"Shit," he muttered in the empty echo of the chamber. He'd come here to solve one mystery and ended up with another, and one that might well not have a solution because the trail had gone as cold and as dead as the shaman staring at him from his ridiculous stiffened position. Mercer quickly righted the mummified mystic so that he could face eternity without his butt half in the air and then plucked a waterproof digital camera from his bag. He used crisp dollar bills as a reference by placing one on the floor of the geode and sticking another to a wall with a bit of chewing gum and snapped the better part of two hundred pictures. There was a photo interpretation business he knew outside of Washington that did a lot of work with the National Reconnaissance Office and would be able to stitch the pics together to form a three-dimensional composite of the chamber and extrapolate its exact volume. In this way he would know how many pounds of crystal Dillman had removed.

For now, though, his goal was to run a battery of tests on the sample he did have. He slipped the lump of cloudy crystal into a plastic baggie. Sealed it. Slipped that into another, sealed that one, and then finally slipped it into a third before stuffing it into a zippered pocket.

He exited the way he had entered, crawling like a commando on his elbows and the outsides of his boots, slithering inch by inch but mindful of the dust. The initial burst of adrenaline had long since worn off. His head pounded and his mouth felt stuffed with cotton. Using just the flashlight Mercer couldn't tell how much his vision was diminished, but the pressure behind his eyes told him it was fading fast. And he was bone-achingly exhausted. He knew that if he paused for a second while lying on the cave floor he'd be asleep before he could stop himself.

Contemplating the slog out of the mountains drained him even further.

When the cave opened up enough for him to stand, he clicked off his light. Outside, the sky remained murky as more storm clouds moved through the valleys. Mercer heard the distant rumble of thunder, and he purposely touched the crystal nestled in his pocket. He wondered how attractive to lightning it really was.

He clicked his climbing harness onto the rope and gave the line a tug to warn the others he was coming back. He got a quick tug in reply. By the gray-faced TAG Heuer he'd worn for twenty years, he saw he'd been inside the cave for forty minutes. Sykes would be anxious.

He started climbing back across the cliff, certain that the security team would be shortening the line every few minutes to keep him properly belayed.

Another crump of thunder sounded, an odd echoing clap that hit concussively. Suddenly Mercer heard Booker Sykes shout, "Incoming!"

It wasn't thunder, but the hollow whomp of a mortar round being fired from somewhere out in the valley.

Mercer turned to look and saw a puff of smoke being shredded by the wind several hundred yards away. That momentary reflex—to find the source of the danger—cost him his perch on the slick rock. With an irreversible drop, Mercer fell and his body pendulumed at the end of the safety line, arcing across the stone so quickly it was all he could do to keep his legs pedaling and stop himself from getting smeared against the cliff. Above him came the ferocious response to the mortar shot from Sykes and his team. They poured a massive amount of lead down the valley even before the mortar finished its parabola and exploded to the right and below the team.

Mercer came to the end of his Tarzan-like swing along the cliff and twisted quickly before he started arcing back. Rather than let gravity do the work, this time he pushed himself hard, knowing he was as inviting a target as a metal duck at a shooting gallery. From below came another blast from the mortar, followed by the mechanical crash of Kalashnikovs joining the fray. Hooded fighters emerged from cover and started firing. Each long pull on the AKs' triggers blew a jet of flame that looked like rocket exhaust in the dishwater-gray pre-storm light.

The protective detail ducked as the second mortar round came arrowing in, landing much closer as the crew zeroed on their target. The next round would land right where the men defended the ridge and Mercer's anchor point.

With adrenaline once again beating back the symptoms of altitude sickness, Mercer raced across the front of the cliff with the buzz of bullets swarming around him. Bits of rock exploded off the wall when struck by the copper-jacketed rounds, and stung like wasp strikes. He could feel the momentum running out of his arc as he neared its apogee, and he pushed harder, pounding his feet into the rock to gain precious inches, his hand outstretched, and his fingers touching but not finding purchase on the lip of stone ringing the cave.

Like a cat, Mercer reversed himself. As bullets peppered the cliff he ran flat out across its face once again, punishing the safety rope as it chafed against the stone where it was anchored. Sykes and the others tried to provide cover fire as best they could, but twenty native fighters were shooting up from the valley below; no matter how accurate the team was, the Afghanis continued to advance.

The mortar popped again, and this time the Americans had no choice but to abandon their position. The round would likely be coming in for a direct hit.

Mercer was forced to swing back again when the line came up hard against his climbing harness, and for a second attempt he ran across the cliff face at the cave entrance, shouting incoherently, his entire focus on making it to its relative safety. He was almost there when the mortar round impacted with a deafening blast, directly where Sykes had tied him off to a slab of rock. Stone chips and smoke boiled into the air.

Mercer paid no attention to the distraction, and stretched himself like an outfielder going for a pop-up. He had built up so much momentum in his headlong plunge that he was able to hook one forearm into the cave, followed by the other. Mercer fought until he pulled his lower body onto the outer lip of the cavern floor. When he glanced up the cliff face, he beheld a terrifying sight. The thousand-pound anchor boulder was now tumbling from its perch, starting to bounce down the cliff, his nylon line still knotted around its bulk. Mercer only had seconds. His hands were stiff from the cold and hurting from the climb, and yet they flew toward the steel carabiner on his belt. The boulder streaking past the cave opening would tear him from his perch, tossing him bodily down to the valley floor below. With a click the D link opened and was torn from his hands so violently by the plummeting stone that it ripped off his right glove.

Mercer rolled backward, into deeper cover. With his lungs pumping and his heart pounding in his chest, he was on such an adrenaline high that for a giddy moment he actually laughed at the fluke of his escape. Just one quarter second more and he would have been hurled down the mountain.

Bullets from the phalanx of Kalashnikovs continued to buzz and zip all around him, some pinging off the stone and vanishing farther down the cave. He slid back until they were no longer a threat. Several mortar rounds exploded near the entrance and filled the cavern with dust.

Mercer was safe for the moment, but he also knew he was trapped. Equally disturbing, the presence of the mortar told him these men had lain in ambush and waited until Mercer emerged from the cave in order to catch them all off guard. It was only Sykes's quick counterfire that bought Mercer the time to find cover, and his bodyguards a chance to escape. Mercer figured his team would seek high ground and a more defensible position, but the large number of attackers meant eventually they would have to withdraw.

And that left him on his own. The Afghanis knew where he was. These were mountain people who could wait out an enemy for years if necessary. Mercer knew his odds of climbing down undetected were virtually zero, so if he didn't find a way out of this mess quickly, he was going to die in this desolate corner of the globe. The world's anus, indeed.

He really hated Michael Dillman now.

Mercer stayed low and moved deeper into the mountain, abandoning his pack but keeping his camera's memory card and the sample when the cavern walls tightened. The ping and whine of ricochets died off to silence, and the mortar, too, had gone quiet. The Taliban or smugglers or whoever they were didn't have any targets for the moment. He dropped to his knees and began crawling, and then down to his belly to slither when the tunnel constricted further. He passed the spot where Dillman had hit his head. His stomach was knotting up again and his headache was back. His eyesight was narrowing so that a gray halo ringed everything in view, and the halo was growing darker and thicker with each passing minute. On this second trip through the tunnel, however, Mercer noticed evidence that lightning had streaked through the passage, for the walls showed blackened char lines that ran up toward the geode chamber.

He needed a fraction of the time to reach the cave's terminus this trip, and he didn't waste precious moments looking at anything other than the collapsed part of the ceiling that had given way after aeons of being struck by lightning. Mercer felt the air blowing down the shaft from the surface. The going would be tight, but for the first ten or so feet he could see he had enough room to maneuver his body. He hoisted himself onto the heap of loose stone, some slabs as large as automobiles, and reached up and found a handhold just above the ceiling level. Mercer pulled himself up, kicking his feet into the rock to find traction. He pressed his back to the side of the chimney and reached up for another handhold, which broke off in his fingers. He dropped it and groped for another. He pried away several more weak stones before finding one he could use to haul himself up another couple of feet.

At times, the path shaped by the unimaginable force of lightning was so tortured and twisted he had to bend like a contortionist to keep climbing. At others, the chimney tightened so it felt like he had to dislocate a shoulder to work it through. If there was any saving grace, the air was fresher the higher he went, and while it didn't contain much additional oxygen, even an extra little bit gave him strength.

Mercer could discern the pain of his body being pushed too far. Below him, dislodged pieces of stone rattled and pinged as he forged a path up the chimney. When he finally spotted daylight, Mercer could hardly believe his eyes. He was sure the climb would take much longer, and yet the evidence was right above him. The sky was the color of old pewter, but it had never looked better. He fought and clawed those last feet, straining to pull himself from the ground's cloying embrace.

A moment later, all his enthusiasm vanished. It was as if fate had played the cruelest trick. Above him, the very top of the chimney reduced to a hole smaller than his head. A raccoon might have been able to squeeze through it, or maybe a young child, but there was no way a man his size would ever climb free.

Mercer wanted to scream with frustration, and he felt himself sag in the narrow space. With no energy remaining, he wondered if he would become lodged in this tight passageway, unable to free himself.

Mercer took a deep breath, and when he looked up he saw a crack along one edge of the hole. He reached up and worked one finger into it, and then a second. Mercer heaved at the crack, and a small piece crumbled like a rotten tooth. Erosion had weakened the rock, so it had become friable like sandstone. He clawed until more chunks of stone fell away below him, and he was able to wriggle one arm and part of his shoulder out of the hole.

That's when he saw a man pass just beyond a nearby clump of shrubbery. Mercer couldn't be sure in the uncertain light if the man was friend or foe. The man was armed, but it was impossible to see whether the weapon had the distinctive banana clip of an AK, or the boxier magazine for the M-4s. Mercer watched him for a moment and realized the silhouetted figure was stalking another man who was even farther away, and who was angled so that he would never see the approaching hunter.

He had seconds to react, but no idea what to do. He could end up saving one of his own, or giving them all away. He worked his arm back underground and popped the flap for his holster. He thumbed off the Beretta's safety even as he yanked it back out of the earth.

The distant figure didn't move. The stalker was coming at an angle. Mercer decided a warning shot would be the best he could do, and hope his guy had better reflexes than the Afghani.

A wave of altitude-induced pain passed through Mercer's skull, and in its wake he had an instant of clearer vision. He saw the stalker was pulling a knife and that his target's face was too uniformly black for it to be mere shadow.

Mercer drew down his pistol and fired, the bullet taking the Taliban in the throat. The pistol crack echoed for a brief second before the air erupted in the deadly chorus of another firefight.

Sykes whirled, not seeing Mercer, who was half in

and half out of the ground, but he must have spotted another target because his assault rifle came up and he cooked off a three-round burst before dropping to a knee behind some rocks. Tracer fire carved slashing lines through the mist.

Desperate now because he was as much a target as he'd been earlier on the cliff, Mercer fought to free himself. He kicked and pried at the loose stone, chipping away at his rocky prison, until without warning great chunks of earth broke away and the chimney collapsed under him. Had he not lunged for the trunk of a hardscrabble tree, he would have plummeted back down the chute. Mercer pulled himself the rest of the way out of the ground, and found he was ringed by shrubbery, in a depression that had been blasted out by the highly charged onslaught of a million years' worth of lightning.

Twenty yards away, Booker checked out the figure through the scope mounted on his rifle. He let the barrel drop when he realized it was Mercer, ragged and covered in dirt, who had somehow materialized like a zombie crawling out of his own grave to kill Sykes's stalker.

Sykes caught Mercer's eye and motioned to him, then laid down cover fire for Mercer to make a break for the rocks. Mercer didn't waste the opportunity, although his vision was so poor from darkness and altitude sickness that he tripped over a root and went crashing to the ground just shy of the rocks. Sykes had to haul him the rest of the way by his belt.

"Someday you'll have to explain how you managed to outflank us," Book said. Mercer could see that the other team members were positioned to cover each other, even if he couldn't tell which of Sykes's Seven Dwarfs was which.

Mercer gave in to a tearing coughing fit that left him pale and shaking and spitting pink saliva. "Proverbial bad penny. What's the situation?"

"Thirty Talibs ambushed our ass," Sykes said, watching for movement out in the murk. Rain fell in a light haze that swayed with the wind like silvery gossamer. "We got lucky their mortar wasn't zeroed dead nuts or we'd have been swatted like flies."

"The chopper?"

"Airborne but it's too hot and too rugged here. We need to break off and run like hell."

Mercer opened his mouth to tell his friend that he was in no condition to run like hell or any other way, when a lightning bolt shot out of the storm and hit fifty yards away, splitting a gnarled tree in a burst of fire and blue arcing strands of pure electricity. The boom of thunder hit like a cannon shot and came almost instantly. The air filled with the stench of ozone, and a fighter still clutching his AK staggered out from behind the tree, a smoldering hole in the back of his jacket showing where the bolt had entered his body. A bloody stump where his hand had been was the exit. He fell dead before any of the Americans could take aim.

Seconds later another crooked fork of lightning blasted from the sky, landing a little farther away but producing a ball of seared plasma that raced across the ground like a top, swaying and dancing but always coming closer. It hit a stunted pine tree and vanished in a blaze of singed needles.

Mercer realized what was happening and knew he had seconds to find a solution, or risk killing them all. It was at that moment he remembered the copper box next to the ruined cloud chamber in the Leister Deep Mine, and understood its function. Fishing into his pocket he shouted to Sykes because he knew he had been deafened by the thunder and was sure Sykes had been too. "Give me an ammo clip."

Booker Sykes had temporarily lost his hearing in enough firefights to have developed the ability to read lips to a limited degree. His vocabulary was little more than oaths of varying intensity and simple military-themed expressions. Mercer happened to hit on one of the latter, and Book pulled a magazine from a chest pouch and tossed it over, never wondering why Mercer would need ammo to a gun he didn't carry.

Mercer caught the clip and began thumbing the slender 5.56mm bullets onto the ground next to where he crouched. The Taliban fighters recovered from the initial shock of the two lightning strikes and the gruesome death of their man, and renewed firing.

Once he had a pile of shining brass cartridges, Mercer pulled out a field dressing pack from his pocket, and tore it open with his teeth. He scooped up a handful of shells and dumped them onto the dressing. Then he added the lump of crystal and covered it with the rest of the brass shells. He bundled it all together, making sure the dull bit of brown gemstone was completely covered by the ammunition.

The principle was simple; he just didn't know if the physics were the same. He had constructed a Faraday cage around the crystal shard, in order to negate its bizarre electric potential. In theory, the conductivity of the zinc and copper in the brass shell casings should shield the crystal from the lightning that seemed to seek it out, or at the least make the surrounding trees a more appealing conduit. Abe had shielded his original sample in a hinged copper box. He must have discarded the wax paper before leaving his office, after stuffing packing peanuts or bubble wrap around the crystal for its journey to Minnesota.

Mercer used surgical tape to secure the bundle and thrust the whole ball inside his shirtfront.

Another blast of lightning hit close enough to energize all the hairs on his body and make it feel as though every inch of his skin were covered with crawling insects. The accompanying thunder was too much for one of the assaulting Afghan fighters. He broke cover a hundred yards off and started running for the trail to take him back into the valley below the cave. They let him go.

"You good?" Sykes shouted over the ringing in Mercer's ears.

He nodded. He had no choice. As awful as he felt, he couldn't give in, not yet. Not this close. Sykes made some hand gestures to the others and en masse they opened fire in a deliberate attempt to engulf the assault force in sheer weight of shot. Before the last clip ran dry, Booker grabbed Mercer by the upper arm, and together they ran back, away from the valley. Seconds later the others would be following, but they would pause every dozen paces and provide covering fire to slow the Taliban's advance, in this way letting Book, and their client, clear the area.

Mercer's lungs were on fire, and each breath brought up flecks of bloody saliva that ran unnoticed down his chin. His legs were unsteady as well, and without Book practically holding him up he would have collapsed into the dust. Book's meaty hand was digging into Mercer's arm, taking so much of his weight that Mercer felt like a child. Behind them the sound of autofire diminished, swallowed up by the storm. It seemed the threat of a deadly lightning strike had faded because

bolts of twisting electricity were now passing harm-
lessly from cloud to cloud.

They moved forward, from tree to rock to shrub,
finding cover wherever they could. They had to find
someplace where Ahmad could set the chopper long
enough for them to jump aboard, and that meant they
needed distance from their pursuers. But the locals
wouldn't give up. They had the scent of blood in their
nostrils now that the Americans had taken flight, and
would run them to ground the way a jackal hunts
a hare.

The lump of brass in his shirt bobbed painfully
with each flagging footfall. Sykes was taking more
and more of Mercer's weight even as they slowed.
Mercer's body wasn't getting the oxygen it needed to
keep going. He never should have made it out of the
cave, let alone covered more than a mile of uneven
terrain, but he was quickly coming to the end. His
muscles needed rich red blood to function, and his
lungs couldn't provide the needed oxygen.

They ran out from under the storm's edge, the sky
brightening enough for Mercer to see they had been
running toward a prow-like promontory of rock that
fell away several hundred feet on its three sides. They
had raced into a dead end. That was why the Afghanis
hadn't pushed the pursuit too hard. They were merely
shepherding their prey into a kill zone so they could mow
them down in an orgy of hot brass and ruined flesh.

Ahmad must have been waiting for that exact moment, because he rounded a hilltop five miles off and
started in for the only spot he could possibly land.
Sykes knew they hadn't opened a big enough lead, and
that an RPG would blast the Mil from the sky the moment his pilot flared in for touchdown.

Sykes looked behind him. His three men were just emerging from the curtain of the storm. Sleep looked like he'd been hit because Sneeze had a shoulder under one arm and was helping him on. Grumpy had shouldered his sniper rifle, most likely because he was out of ammo, and fired at the unseen swarm of Taliban with his pistol, triggering off evenly spaced, almost unhurried shots that kept the advancing fighters back in the mist.

There were fifty or sixty yards of separation between Grump and the native fighters, and Ahmad determined it was the best he was going to get. He had kept the chopper screened by the mountain's edge and a stand of trees that he'd had to peer through to see his people. He popped up when he thought he could do the most good, and as soon as the wheels cleared the tallest of the trees he fired the contents of a rocket pod attached to the chopper's right side. A dozen unguided rockets almost as slender as arrows streaked just a few feet over the men's heads and hit in a solid wall just in front of the tangos. The concussion knocked the three Americans to the ground, but the wall of fire and blooming vortices of dirt and smoke consumed half the shooters chasing after them.

Unseen behind the curtain of destruction, the remaining natives broke ranks and fled, not knowing the helicopter had fired its one and only weapon and was now defenseless.

Sleep, Sneeze, and Grump hauled themselves to their feet and ran while Ahmad came thundering in, the big Mi-2 kicking up a maelstrom of dust that rivaled the rocket explosions. Sykes all but carried Mercer the last twenty yards and tossed him bodily into the chopper before turning and motioning his men to push it even harder. Sneeze dumped the injured Sleep into the chopper and Book was yelling at the pilot to take off even as Grump, the last man, was still being dragged through the door.

In all it took just seconds. Ahmad threw the helo into the air and as soon as the wheels cleared the ridge, he dropped it down into the next valley, using gravity to build up speed in order to get as far away from the scene as possible.

Sykes grabbed a supplemental oxygen bottle from stores kept in a bin behind the pilot seat, fitted the mouthpiece over Mercer's face, and turned the tap on full. Within just a few seconds, Mercer started feeling the effects. His chest still heaved and his head felt like it had split open, but nowhere near as badly. After a minute he was back from death's door . . . and just felt like he had the worst hangover of his life.

Sykes had turned his attention to his wounded man. Sleep had taken a round to the thigh that hadn't hit the femoral artery, but it would require surgery to remove. The men had it bandaged and pumped him with morphine over his protests. Only when Book was satisfied they were all okay did he look back at Mercer and finally ask, "What was all that voodoo with the lightning?"

"Hell if I know." Mercer pulled the oxygen mask from his mouth. "I've never seen anything like it in my life, but I think that phenomenon is what this whole thing's all about."

15

Roland d'Avejan took to the podium accompanied by a rousing round of applause. This was a sympathetic audience, so d'Avejan wasn't surprised, but knowing a crowd was energized made giving speeches a much less odious task.

"*Merci, merci,*" he called into the microphone, trying to quiet the two hundred or so. "Thank you very much. I am honored to be here today, even if it cost me five million euros just to say a few words." The crowd filling the auditorium laughed at his joke, knowing it was true. On an easel next to the lectern was the oversize mock check he had just presented to the Earth Action League's president.

"I must say that it is I who should be applauding all of you. You are on the front lines of the climate war, fighting the apathy of people who don't recognize the peril that our planet faces. And more importantly, you fight the deniers funded by fossil fuel interests who put short-term profit above the long-term health of the environment."

This remark elicited a few catcalls and hisses, as

though this was some silent film and the mustache-twirling villain had just appeared on-screen. They were like good-hearted children in their naïveté.

D'Avejan continued, "Despite efforts by you and other like-minded campaigners, carbon continues to increase in our atmosphere." He preferred the more evocative sobriquet "carbon pollution," but marketing studies were showing that informed listeners realized it was a bit overwrought and inaccurate, although leaving out the dioxide part of the gas continued to make people think it was something filthy. "The alarm was sounded as far back as the 1980s, but as we know, nothing was done to curb greenhouse gases. Where once the threats were in the far distant future, we now realize to our horror that the future is here. There can be very few in this audience who did not know someone who perished in the terrible heat wave of 2003. France alone lost nearly fifteen thousand people, mostly our elderly. Or what about the terrible summer in 2010 that claimed fifteen thousand Russians. These were some of the first victims of global warming, but they won't be the last when such extreme events become the new normal.

"Sea levels continue to rise, the pace has accelerated, and soon entire Pacific island nations will disappear beneath the waves, adding millions of climate refugees. Hurricanes and tropical cyclones have become stronger and will only get worse. If the United States, the richest nation in the world, could not stop Katrina or Superstorm Sandy from destroying so much property and life, what chance did the Philippines have when Typhoon Haiyan struck and washed thousands of people out to sea? Death tolls are already climbing, ladies and gentlemen, not in fifty or a hundred years, but now. Polar ice is vanishing. Ancient glaciers around the world are in record retreat, and scientists are speculating a catastrophic collapse of some of Antarctica's pristine ice shelves. As thermometers around the globe inexorably rise, it may trigger massive releases of even more potent greenhouse gases trapped in frozen tundra across Russia, Alaska, and far northern Canada."

Roland paused. He had given them the litany of doom and gloom peddled repeatedly by some United Nations scientists and the compliant media. It was well worn and familiar, and for the most part his examples were all either outright lies or localized weather events, or unverifiable computer projections that were little more accurate than darts flung at a board. And yet it had all been touted as evidence of anthropogenic global warming for long enough that people no longer questioned it.

"I need not remind you of the consequences we are experiencing now that Mother Nature has decided to fight back against humanity's wanton disregard for the environment. People who join the Earth Action League understand the crisis we face and have common cause to see it solved. That is why I have pledged such a large amount of money today. I am tasking you with the job of informing the rest of the world of the urgent need for action. We have an ever-diminishing window to save our planet, to stop burning fossil fuels and switch to renewable sources of power. Wind and solar can light our future but only if we start now.

"Many here in Europe have called for a greater reliance on bountiful, naturally produced power"—that was a new marketing term, "naturally produced," and it trended well with the antifracking element of the environmental movement—"but there are still many who don't realize our time is limited. You need to go out and educate them so that they see a wind farm in their town as an asset and not a liability. We must change attitudes from 'Not in my backyard' to 'Please in our backyard.'

"We need the political will to make the hard choices. But that is what you here understand and those out there do not. There are no longer any choices, only inevitabilities. We must stop burning fossil fuels. We must turn to renewable energy or we will simply fail as a sustainable society, and I see by the bright eyes out there and eager anticipation that you will not let that happen. Not on your watch. Not when the EAL has something to say about it. Not now. Not ever!"

That's what this was about, d'Avejan thought as he listened to their thunderous approbation. He needed to get the great unwashed majority off their collective fat asses so they would elect politicians ready to listen to the UN and others and tackle the problem head-on. For the cameras, he shook hands once again with the president of the Earth Action League, a man untroubled by his own body odor, though he had at least put on pressed slacks for the event. Seconds after getting offstage, d'Avejan had his hands slathered in waterless purifying gel as a stopgap until he could properly wash them.

"Thank you once again, Roland," Jean-Batiste Reno said, "both for the extraordinary financial support and for taking the time to speak with us today." A clutch of supporters stood nearby. Roland noted that many were female, and some were not unattractive.

"You are all fighting the good fight," he replied.

"But it gets tougher all the time," the nonprofit's

director lamented. "Just a few years ago climate change was on everyone's mind. Money poured into our coffers, and we could organize rallies of a thousand or more on short notice. We had just a few hundred here today, and many of them are paid staffers."

"When the real estate bubble burst both here in Europe and in America it gave people the excuse to forget problems other than their own immediate situation," d'Avejan said, as he'd opined many times.

"My grandmother used to say that the lighter the purse becomes, the tighter are its strings."

"Wise woman," Roland conceded. "It does not help that current model predictions and the reality of global temperatures are continuing to diverge. We are well into our second decade with no appreciable increase in surface temperatures."

"That doesn't concern me," the environmental crusader replied. "Every few months a new paper comes out to explain away the issue. What does bother me is the way some in the media are reporting that the pause was unexpected, and questioning our excuses for it because for years we said the science was settled."

"That was a mistake from the beginning." D'Avejan frowned. "The *physics* of how carbon dioxide traps heat is well established. The claimed *science* behind all future scenarios relies on a lot of assumptions that are essentially unverifiable. But it is too late to point out that distinction without hurting our cause."

Reno nodded. "I agree. In the beginning things became so alarming so quickly, and now we have little choice but to keep going in that direction. If we attempt to walk back some of our earlier claims we will lose credibility and our planet will surely be doomed."

"That's why you have me." The industrialist had to smile. "I will make sure Earth is here for our children and theirs too, my friend."

Enthusiastic applause broke out among the small group, and d'Avejan ended the conversation, and any opportunity to chat up some of the prettier hangers-on. A few journalists asked him some questions as he made his way from the university auditorium, but he politely declined comment, saying he was late for a meeting. Outside, tables had been set up on the Parisian sidewalk for passersby to take leaflets and study posters on the dangers of fossil fuels in general and hydraulic fracturing in particular.

D'Avejan didn't think any of the young protesters knew fracking had been around for a generation, and had been proven safe time after time. He was again grateful that the youth took so much on faith and never investigated a subject on their own. Often attributed to either Lenin or Stalin, the term "useful idiots" came to mind. A bit harsh, he thought, but not too far off the mark.

The so-called fracking revolution in America had vastly increased the United States' supplies of natural gas. If allowed to happen in Europe, Roland thought, it would devastate his company's financial position in renewable energy. This wasn't about lowering carbon footprints by using gas as a bridge fuel or staving off climate change. It was simple capitalistic necessity. If Europe allowed fracking, energy prices would plummet, and every wind farm and solar array under development would be abandoned, leaving the bulk of Eurodyne in ruin. D'Avejan would do anything to prevent men like Ralph Pickford from scavenging the bones of the company he'd built, and that included financing rabble like the Earth Action League, or being party to violent operations in the States. It was what had to be done.

When the dust settled he'd make sure to plant some extra trees someplace.

In keeping with his well-tended eco-image, his car was a new Tesla S sedan. His chauffeur had been waiting just down the block and was up to the curb even before d'Avejan could hail him. A small crowd of EAL staffers was congregated nearby, and d'Avejan choked when hit by a waft of patchouli oil and cannabis smoke. He opened the rear car door for himself rather than wait for the driver.

"Sorry I wasn't quicker, sir," the man apologized.

"Not your fault," d'Avejan said as the car silently pulled away, watched by a few of the tech-savvy eco-warriors who recognized the sleek car for what it was. "I had to get away from the stench. My father used to complain about how hippies smelled in the sixties. I don't think their aroma has much changed."

"*Non,* monsieur. Or their politics. It's the women, you know."

"The women?" Roland asked, intrigued.

"*Oui,* monsieur. At least that's what my father told me. He said back then the women saw makeup and hair care as signs of male oppression, so they stopped all that and went au naturel. When the odor got too bad they doused themselves in funky oils, not perfume, mind you, but some gunk called—"

"Patchouli. I just got a noseful."

"That's the stuff. Well, since this was how the women were protesting, the guys back then had to go along with it if they wanted to sleep with any of them. The guys stopped shaving and let their hair grow, and before you knew it a whole generation of nonconformists looked exactly alike. And still do to this day."

"So it's all about having sex?"

"Isn't it always, sir?"

D'Avejan smirked. Michel had driven him to his various mistresses over the years and waited in the car while he was in their arms. "I suppose you're right."

"Heading home, monsieur?"

Roland was checking for messages on his two phones. There were several missed calls on his personal phone, most of which he could ignore. The smartphone he treated as disposable showed a missed text. It simply said "Call me." And had come through when he was donating the money to the EAL. "Not just yet," he said and slid the phone into his pocket. "I need to get back to the office for a minute."

"Mais bien sûr, monsieur."

Thirty minutes later, d'Avejan was in his electronically swept office. He poured himself a drink and watched the lights coming on all over his magical city. He dialed out on a new phone to replace the one he'd just fed through the shredder. From up here the traffic-choked streets were transformed into somnolent rivers of light, while the Eiffel Tower shone like a beacon pointing to the heavens.

"Niklaas?" he said when the phone was answered but no one spoke.

"Ja, sorry. I was taking a sip of water."

"How did it go?"

"As we suspected," the mercenary replied.

D'Avejan cursed, but mostly at himself for getting his hopes up. "The American had already come and gone?"

"No. The Pakistani team made contact. They reached the coordinates Mike Dillman provided almost a century ago, but there was nothing there. The Afghan guide was questioned about any kind of mining done in the area. He told them there was an old stone quarry several miles from where they were searching but then mentioned something interesting, a mountain that his grandparents said used to attract lightning. I'll give it to my old friend Parvez to pick up on a possible connection. He and his team headed for this mountain and when they arrived, the American was already there with a group of hired guns out of Kabul. Not sure which company yet, but Parvez thinks one of them was a black man named Sykes who was Delta but now works for Gen-D Systems."

"Get on with it, man," d'Avejan insisted.

"*Ja.* Okay. So the ISI guys we hired made contact when they thought they had the best advantage, but their assault went to crap pretty quick. The Gen-D fighters had a chopper fitted with rockets. Parvez lost six men KIA and another eight wounded."

"I thought you said they were good, these Pakistanis you knew."

"When I met Parvez Najam in Somalia he was part of the Pakistani contingent of UN troops trying to stabilize the country during the whole Blackhawk incident. He was and remains a top-notch soldier, *meneer,* but sometimes combat does not go as planned. Especially when he had no warning that the geologist would have air cover."

"Okay." Roland blew a breath and took a gulp of his vodka soda. "Did they learn anything?"

"Yes. They found a cave. He sent me video. There was an old body in it that looked like it had been there for years and a natural grotto that appeared to have been picked clean, but there were no minerals of any note, at least none he could determine. I have uploaded everything from his report to the secure account you set up."

"Anything else?"

"One odd thing. There was a storm during the firefight, and one of his men was struck by lightning and several more bolts landed extremely close. You told me this mineral might have odd electromagnetic powers. It stands to reason that if lightning was striking so hard and so fast, then perhaps the American managed to secure a small sample."

D'Avejan snapped, "Small? Why small? He could have carried out sacks of the stuff."

"No, *meneer*, the men identified him quite clearly and saw he carried nothing with him but a pistol. He was not the one who looted the cave. That had to have been Dillman years ago."

"So the bulk of mineral is still out there? That is what you are saying?"

"Yes, and I think I know how to find it."

D'Avejan listened while his special facilitator outlined his proposal, nodding approvingly as its chance of success sounded high. Outsourcing contractors from the Pakistani intelligence service had been a gamble that hadn't paid off, but what he heard now sounded like a winning plan to secure the last of the mineral for use aboard the *Akademik Nikolay Zhukovsky.*

"All right," d'Avejan said when his subaltern finished. "Make it happen and I'll give you a bonus large enough to retire on."

The former mercenary started a sarcastic reply but held his tongue. He may have worked for Roland d'Avejan and Eurodyne for the past two years, but being part of a corporation hadn't blunted the rougher edges of a lifetime spent in and around combat zones stretching across three continents.

"Dankie, meneer."

16

Mercer downloaded e-mails to his tablet from a Wi-Fi hot spot in the New Delhi airport. He had been bcc'd on a note from one of Abe Jacobs's office mates at Hardt College. In it, Professor Wotz outlined, as best he knew, what Abe had been helping Dr. Tunis with. Mercer suspected the two schools, Hardt and Northwestern, were still stonewalling direct access, so someone had asked around casually. Judging by the dates, this appeared to be something Kelly Hepburn had set in motion before her accident.

Mercer read with increasing interest. Their work was indeed groundbreaking, and given the right set of circumstances, their research was something any number of groups would never want to see reach the light of day. This made the list of suspects impossibly long.

Wotz's description of Abe's research into Sample 681 had jibed with what little Mercer had learned himself of the odd crystal's electromagnetic properties. Wotz was a field biologist, so he was pretty light on the details, but he said Abe believed the mineral could help deflect deep-penetrating cosmic rays, so scientists could run subterranean cloud chamber tests that were uncontaminated by all outside influences— without having to run those tests in some of South Africa's ultra-deep gold mines. He saw the mineral as a way to vastly reduce the cost of experimental climatology and cosmology.

Mercer thought Abe and Tunis were missing out on something far more important than climate science, although that was Susan Tunis's specialty. If it was possible to replicate Sample 681's properties in the lab, it would help solve one of the problems facing microelectronics products—they are constantly bombarded with cosmic rays, and each strike increases the chance of a glitch. A Qantas flight from Singapore had to make an emergency landing in 2008 when a pair of rapid descents injured more than a hundred passengers. Investigators thought it likely that a cosmic ray collision had interfered with data from an inertial referencing computer, which had caused the aircraft to plummet. Communication and other satellites had their service lives severely compromised because of the constant assault of supercharged elementary particles sweeping across the cosmos. An effective shield that didn't add unnecessary weight would be a godsend to both industries, Mercer surmised. Even PCs on the ground suffered faults that erased unimaginable amounts of data.

Then there were massive solar discharges that have the potential to crash entire electrical grids, as happened in Quebec in 1989. Protecting power supplies from such storms was an expensive but necessary priority to utilities all over the world.

On top of that, doctors attributed a portion of

cancers to cosmic rays hitting DNA at the exact moment of replication. Earth's magnetic field routinely blocked most interstellar rays, but enough got through to cause noticeable trends in cancer rates.

It was laudable that Tunis and Jacobs were pushing the envelope in terms of climate and weather forecasting, but they were missing the true potential of what Abe had somehow inherited from Herbert Hoover.

Mercer's flight was called. He tucked away the tablet and tried calling Agent Hepburn. Her Neanderthal partner, Nate Lowell, didn't pick up, so the phone went to voice mail. He left her a generic message about following a lead, wished her a speedy recovery, and said he would call later. He tried reaching her through the George Washington University Hospital switchboard, but they could neither confirm nor deny a Kelly Hepburn was a patient there.

He called home. Jordan answered on the second ring. "You've reached the home of Philip Mercer."

"Call the police," Mercer said. "There's a strange woman in my house insisting on answering my phone."

"Mercer!" she cried. "I've been so worried. Are you okay?"

"Fine. Tired, actually, but everything went well. How are you doing?"

"Bored without you. My arm's feeling better and there are some things I want to try out with it."

"Really. Like what?" Mercer asked as if he didn't understand where the conversation was going. To his shock and utter delight Jordan spelled out some very erotic and explicit activities she had planned for the two of them upon his return.

"Anything you'd like to add?" she asked with a husky chuckle.

"No, I think that covers the bases, and the outfield and the stands and a good part of the parking lot."

"So are you heading home now?"

"I am," he told her, "but I have to stop in Mumbai."

"Why?" she asked, failing to mask her disappointment.

"I found a body inside a cave near the coordinates. I did some research, and I think he was a guru who died around 1881. The real expert on him is a professor in Mumbai, and since it's a short detour I thought it better to meet face-to-face than to ask a bunch of potentially disrespectful questions over the phone. Apparently the academic is a descendant."

"And you think knowing more about the dead guy can help."

"It's more of a case of it not hurting, I suppose," he replied. "They just called my flight. I'll give you a ring when I get the chance. How's Harry?"

"He's given up smoking, embraced temperance, and has started doing Zumba."

Mercer laughed. "That sounds like Harry, always striving to make himself a better person."

"Oh wait," Jordan said as if giving color commentary at a sporting event. "What's this? Yes, he just shut off the workout DVD, poured a Jack and ginger, and he's fishing in his pocket for his Chesterfields. He was a better person for all of . . . eight seconds, ladies and gentlemen."

Mercer heard Harry over Jordan's teasing chuckle. "I'd give you a spanking, young lady, but your behind's so tight I'd probably break my hand."

"Talk to you soon," Mercer said with a smile. "And watch yourself because he's more than willing to test that hypothesis."

He didn't like lying to her, but if his suspicions were right it would be better for them both that he had. At least in the short term. Long term? Who knew? He boarded the Boeing jumbo jet and took his seat in first class. He was asleep before the plane even left the ground, and only had a vague recollection of being awoken for a meal.

—

It was pouring rain when he finally left the climate-controlled confines of the modern air transportation system, once again stepping back into nature. The sky was pewter colored and blotchy and looked like it hovered just a few feet over the ground. The concrete and asphalt around the terminal ran with runoff that poured through downspouts with the force of fire hoses. The sound of rain muted the occasional honks of taxis jostling for position, the cried greetings of drivers picking up loved ones, and the rumble of shuttle buses as lumbering and ponderous as dinosaurs. Passing cars hydroplaned as they went, kicking up rooster tails that rivaled those of offshore racing boats. The air was chilled and heavy. Mercer's leather bomber was more than adequate, but he ducked back into the terminal and bought the first baseball cap he could find, a black one with a stylized red bird above the brim.

He had to wait with a dozen other passengers for a minibus to take him to the closest rental car lot, but as a preferred customer he found his name on a lighted board outside their office/garage directing him to his vehicle, an SUV only slightly smaller than the beast he'd driven just a few days earlier.

He plugged his destination into the satellite navigation system, thankful for it since he had no idea where he really was. He tried the radio, got a slot of static and something that sounded even more jarring than what had been playing at the Gen-D Systems compound in Kabul, and decided to let the storm be his companion.

By the looks of things he had a couple-hour drive, and once again marveled at the vast expanses of the American Midwest. Iowa in particular, even under a biblical storm, looked like it was nothing but wide-open spaces.

—

Sherman Smithson turned the lock on his front door and sniffled. He was coming down with a cold, which made the past week of rain even more miserable. Despite his somewhat precise nature, what others called prissy, Smithson wasn't a small man. He topped out at over six feet, and for a year back at Iowa State he had been on the Cyclones football practice squad. He was forty-seven now, and what physique he had once possessed had slouched into humped shoulders and a pronounced belly that he couldn't muster enough pride to be ashamed of. What bothered him was the retreat of his ginger hair that had left him just a horseshoe fringe around his shiny scalp. Mrs. Jenkins, one of the volunteers at the Hoover Presidential Library, had rightly dissuaded him from the comb-over several years back.

He would never grace the cover of a magazine, but he had been able to win the affections of Alice Holmes, a childless widow only a couple years his senior. She worked for a lawyer in Iowa City but lived only a few miles from his home near the library in West Branch. He had been looking forward to cooking her dinner tonight, but with all this rain there were flood warnings for eastern Iowa, especially along the Mississippi River and its tributaries. She had opted to stay with a friend in the city rather than chance driving out into the storm.

As a native Hawkeye, he didn't think the flooding was any worse now than when he was a boy, but Alice, a transplant from Chicago, was convinced that each storm was getting worse and that something had to be done about it. He thought she should brave it out so they could have spent a cozy weekend trapped in his house by the rain with some nice wine and Trivial Pursuit, Genus Edition.

He stepped into his overheated house and sneezed.

Maybe it was best she didn't come over. The living room was gloomy, the light coming in through the windows somehow menacing, and the rain cascading off the eaves made it impossible to see more than a few feet into the back or side yards. Smithson reached to flip on the light switch, when a hand clamped over his wrist and he was yanked into his house and tossed bodily to the floor. The front door closed with a solid thunk. He tried to scramble to his feet, his hands coming up in a defensive stance like he'd seen in movies, but an unseen foot kicked out and connected with the side of his knee. He yelped at the stabbing agony and collapsed, clutching the joint and whimpering.

"Eh, enough of that," a voice said in a guttural accent, something foreign—likely European. "If I wanted to break it, I would have."

A light finally went on. Smithson saw two men.

Both wore black leather jackets, like bikers, but without any patches or insignia. They wore dark shirts and jeans with work boots, not Western styled. But what held his attention and weakened his resolve were the black ski masks both men wore over their faces. All he saw were eyes that bulged from the holes in the knitted wool, and mouths that looked too large and too red. Meant just to hide their features, the masks made them look all the more terrifying. Neither man had a visible weapon, but at this point they didn't need them.

The leader of the two, the man who had tossed him so casually to the floor, hunkered down so he could look Smithson in the eye. "We have a couple of questions and we'll leave you alone. Okay?" He slurped as though his mouth was filled with saliva.

Smithson could only nod. He was grateful he had urinated before leaving the library because the small trickle that just ran down his leg was the entire contents of his bladder. The masked man seemed not to notice.

"I couldn't ask you outright, okay, so we had to do it this way. See? I am not a bad sort, really. It's just that I'm asked to do some rough stuff sometimes. Hell, man, I started out as one of the good guys. I used to protect workers in Angola from terrorists. There are a lot of kiddies out in the world today who still have their daddies 'cause of me. I'm telling you so you aren't so scared, okay. Tell me what I need to know and we go. I'll need to tie you up, you understand, but we won't hurt you."

"Nik?" the other man prompted.

"*Nee!* There's no need for more killing."

"What do you want?" Sherman Smithson asked

through gritted teeth. His knee felt hot and swollen. He stayed sitting on the floor, the joint cradled in his hands.

"The same thing your friend Philip Mercer wanted. We found that Sample 681 was once owned by your President Hoover, from a file in Ohio that gave the location where it was discovered. Mercer learned all that from you, *ja*?"

"Yes. No. He knew President Hoover was once in possession of it but not the location. That I gave him from our archives."

"That's what we need to talk about, you and me. What else is in your archives? Because someone went back to Afghanistan a long time ago and mined the rest of the crystals. We need to know who, and where they are now."

"Mike Dillman," Smithson blurted. "He retrieved the rest of the stones. Mercer confirmed that to me in a phone call yesterday."

"And what else did he confirm?" the masked man asked. He was not being overly aggressive, but Smithson could not stop trembling.

"There was a cave, and a grotto he said was a natural geode, and that all the crystals were gone, but he found Mike Dillman's initials written in blood on a wall."

"What did Dillman do with the crystals he took out of those mountains? Did he give them to Hoover?"

Smithson suddenly looked like he was going to throw up. Sweat erupted across his face and ran in rivulets into his already rain-soaked shirt collar. "I don't know," he whimpered. "There was no record of Dillman ever going back to the cave. Not in the official archives anyway."

The second intruder strode across the room and kicked Smithson in the ribs. The archivist gasped and fell onto his side, curling into a ball and trying to reinflate his lung. "He's lying," the man sneered.

The leader stood and backhanded his subaltern so fast and so hard the masked man spun into the Sheetrock wall and almost fell to the floor. He snarled in Afrikaans, "Interfere with my interrogation again, and I will cut off your ball sack and use it to carry biltong."

He switched back to English when addressing Smithson. "Sorry about my young companion. He gets a little carried away, *ja*?" The intruder sucked at saliva that had soaked one corner of his mask. "Now, mate, you just made a bad mistake, and it's going to cost you unless you tell me the whole truth. See, I've been doing this a lot of years and I know things about how people talk and act when they lie. You didn't lie just now, but you didn't give the whole truth."

Smithson looked around, his eyes wild and wide, like a feral animal about to be cornered. It couldn't have been more obvious had he written "guilty" across his shining forehead.

"You said there was no record in the official archive," the masked man said, adding quickly, "and I believe you. But what about the unofficial archive, eh? What's in there about Dillman going back to empty out the cave?"

"I don't know what's in any unofficial archive," Smithson said so unconvincingly that the mercenary didn't bother hitting him.

"Try again, Sherman, or my partner here's really going to get busy on those ribs of yours. And he's still learning the trade, so to speak, so he could very easily puncture a lung by mistake and then we're all jolly fooked, *ja*?"

To his credit, Sherman Smithson lasted thirty minutes. The team leader didn't think the mild librarian had the strength, but he had seen stronger men crack in a tenth that time, so anything was possible. And to the mercenary's credit, he had made certain that Smithson's injuries weren't life threatening, and used two full rolls of duct tape but left enough slack to truss him up and bury him under a mountain of clothes in a closet. In a day or two he'd be recovered enough from the beating to force his way out and eventually get to the neighbor's house.

The two masked men planned on being long gone by then, and the stolen car they were currently driving burned beyond recognition.

17

Judging by the volume of rain sheeting from the plumbic sky, Mercer half expected to see pairs of exotic animals trudging along the side of the road in search of an ark. The deluge reminded him of a tropical cyclone he'd sat through in a small hotel in the Philippines, overlooking a fishing village that was all but wiped out by the time the storm abated. Though the wind now wasn't as strong, the rain forced him to slow the SUV to a crawl. Midwesterners, knowing that this weather could spawn tornadoes, wisely stayed indoors or stopped their cars under overpasses. He had little traffic to contend with as he made his way south and east toward the Mississippi River, and a woman who potentially had another piece of the puzzle—hopefully the last piece to solving why Abe and the others had been murdered.

Mercer had made arrangements while still in Kabul for the shard of crystal. First he'd had a guy in Sykes's motor pool hammer out a copper envelope to sheathe the stone. Not trusting the Afghan postal service, he'd flown it to New Delhi and express-shipped it from there to an acquaintance at the Goddard Institute for Space Studies who was salivating at the prospect of getting his lab equipment on something as fantastical as had been described. Mercer promised him equal authorship of any paper that came out of the discovery.

The woman Mercer was en route to visit was Veronica Butler, and for the last few years of Herbert Hoover's life, she was his personal secretary while he lived in New York's famous Park Avenue Waldorf Astoria. After his death in 1964, Butler had returned to her native Iowa and worked at the presidential library until her retirement a decade ago. In a call from Kabul following their extraction back to the Afghan capital, Sherman Smithson promised Mercer that if there were any secrets pertaining to the late president's life, especially his link to Mike Dillman, then Roni Butler would be the only person to know. Smithson had promised to inform the woman about his interest, and make sure she was up to seeing him.

Mercer had tried to verify with Smithson when he'd landed in Des Moines that the elderly woman knew he was coming, but the library had closed early because of the weather and the archivist wasn't answering his cell. He hit redial as he traveled on through the downpour, but now he wasn't getting any cell coverage.

Mercer tried the radio, and after scanning the frequencies finally found an emergency broadcast alert that discussed the flooding all along the Mississippi River Valley. The monotone announcer rattled off a number of towns' names that Mercer was unfamiliar with that were under mandatory evacuation. Fortunately the one where Veronica Butler lived wasn't mentioned, at least not yet.

Two hours later than the satnav promised he should arrive, Mercer pulled up short of his destination at a police checkpoint near a large complex of buildings that served as the middle and high schools for an entire county. Yellow buses were parked along its front like elephants performing a nose-to-tail parade. A couple of police cars were pulled across the road with enough room to squeeze through if necessary. A cop wearing a poncho and a plastic cover over his wide-brimmed hat levered himself out of one of the black-and-whites and approached Mercer's door.

Mercer lowered his window a crack. The sound of the storm wasn't the sizzle of bacon like a normal rain but the roar of a waterfall. Drops splattered against the glass and pattered his face, so he had to wipe it after just a few seconds.

"Sorry, sir." The cop had to shout over the storm. "Can't let you pass. It's too dangerous."

"Has everyone been evacuated?"

"Near as we can tell. There's about two thousand people packed into the schools."

"Do you know a Mrs. Veronica Butler?"

"No, sir. I'm sorry. I'm from Urbandale, here to help with the flooding. Whoever you're looking for will be in one of the school's gyms. There are people inside to help folks locate loved ones. They'll be able to help you out."

He turned away before Mercer could thank him and strode back to the warm, dry interior of his cruiser. Mercer wheeled through the barrier and turned into the high school's parking lot, which was full. He noted the majority of the vehicles were pickups, and not one of them was foreign built. He found a space near a baseball dugout and ran through the storm to the nearest school entrance. A couple of men stood in the doorway watching the rain and parted so Mercer could dash inside. Just a few seconds outside left his jeans soaked to the skin.

"Mighty brave," one said. He was big and wrinkled but with a light in his blue eyes.

"Just a little rain," Mercer replied.

"Talking 'bout the hat." He pointed a finger to his own black-and-gold baseball cap. "Folks in these parts are Hawkeyes. You're wearing Iowa State."

Despite his gruff tone, the man was obviously teasing. Mercer acted as if he were having a sudden epiphany. "I knew there was something wrong with it. It only keeps a little of the rain off my face."

The big farmer laughed. "That got you a pass. Head on down this hallway and take a left. That's the gym. There are towels, doughnuts, and coffee."

"Thanks."

A moment later, Mercer had a tepid coffee in hand and was explaining to an overworked volunteer coordinator that he was looking for Veronica Butler. The din in the echoing gymnasium was a beehivelike buzz, punctuated by children's shouts and infants' wails. He would have much rather listened to Harry singing falsetto than endure this cacophony for a moment longer than necessary. The air was heavy and smelled of wet dog.

"I'm sorry, she isn't here," the woman said without needing to consult the binders she and the others had compiled of the storm's temporary refugees.

"She's in the middle school gym, then?" he asked hopefully.

"Obviously you don't know Roni too well. She won't leave her home no matter how hard the police try to get her to evacuate. She's as stubborn as a mule, and ten times as tough." There was a trace of civic pride in her voice at how the old woman defied the authorities despite the danger.

"So I'll find her on Water Street?"

"She'll be there all right, but I wouldn't go looking for her just yet or she might mistake you for a deputy and fire off a few potshots."

"Is she . . ." Mercer tried to find words that wouldn't insult the old woman. "All there?"

"Oh yes. She's as sane as they come, just ornery. Her grandfather built the original house where her place is now, and she claims in over a hundred and twenty years that spot has never flooded, no matter what the Mississippi does."

"And she knows that since then there have been hundreds of miles of levees built that change the game entirely?"

"Don't matter to her none. She's sticking by her place come hell or high water." She chuckled at her own unintended pun. Just then some more people came in, a young couple with two children and an infant in the woman's arms. The baby was thankfully quiet but the younger boy sniveled with his face buried in his mother's jeans. "Crystal, Johnnie, how you two holdin' up?" The volunteer produced a lollipop from a bag at her feet, and the crying boy's tears suddenly dried when he reached for it.

Mercer nodded his thanks to the woman, who was already too busy to notice and made his way back to the door he'd entered a few minutes earlier.

"They're chasing you out, eh?" the comedian-farmer asked. "Should have pocketed that cap, boy."

"At least I didn't wear one from my real alma ma-ter," Mercer replied, paused for effect, and told the Hawkeye, "I'm a Nittany Lion."

He was back out into the storm before the older man computed that Mercer had gone to one of the University of Iowa's Big Ten rivals, Penn State.

The cops at the roadblock were busy helping guide a semitruck with a trailer-load of new farm equipment through a tight U-turn so the driver could head back to wait out the storm in a hotel someplace. Mercer ran back to his rental and drove along the verge to get past the preoccupied cops. If they noticed him, they didn't bother to give chase.

The rain continued to pound the earth and rattle off the truck's bodywork like it was taking small-arms fire. The wipers could only keep the windshield clear for half a cycle, leaving Mercer to drive on faith as much as his vision. Fortunately, the GPS was still pinging off the satellites even if his cell showed zero bars.

He passed through a deserted town with roads awash like flat black streams. The power was off, either by accident or design, and it gave the place a haunted feel. There was no one around, no motion other than the downward streak of rain and the froth of water boiling down from the hills. It was barely noon, but the storm cast the buildings in twilight gray that shrouded them like a layer of decay.

He spotted two men with a trailered Zodiac boat standing under a gas station canopy next to their pickup. They were dressed in waders and rain jackets and appeared to be part of a volunteer rescue team. The truck had a modified suspension so it could be jacked up on massive tires and had a magnetic red strobe attached to his roof. The pair pointed at his truck and made waving gestures with their arms as if to warn him off. Mercer tooted his horn in acknowl-edgment but kept on going.

Beyond the town and through some trees he could see a long grass-covered levee that stretched from north to south in an unending wall of compacted dirt. He knew on the other side raged the Mississippi River, one of the world's greats, and one that hated to be contained the way a wild animal fought its captivity. Give it just a chance to escape and the waters would run until the whole miles-long system of earthworks collapsed into so much mud and sludge and this little town was wiped off the map.

Mercer turned right, tracking south out of town. He crossed a spindly steel through-truss bridge whose surfaces were more rust than green paint. Eight feet below the road deck, a once lazy stream coming from a valley ahead of him was now a brown seething mass that raced past like a locomotive. Swirling on the rag-ing water were tree trunks and other unidentifiable flotsam caught in its inexorable grip.

The road to Veronica Butler's home paralleled the stream. It was like a river in its own right and was well over its banks and at various points sluicing across the road itself. Driving in conditions like this was not the smartest thing he'd ever done. Despite the SUV's size and the shallowness of the water careening across the road, the torrent could easily lift his truck and hurl it into the main channel so fast he'd never have time to react.

The wipers now barely made a dent in the rain slamming into the windscreen.

On his left were houses every couple hundred yards with barns in the back, and occasional silos. He couldn't see through the storm past them, but Mercer figured their backyards were fields stretching to the horizon. To the right was the river lapping at the road. Movement in the channel caught his eye, and he saw a large white box shoot past. It took him a second to realize the box was actually the back of a large moving van, and its cab and engine were completely submerged.

"You will reach your destination in five hundred feet," the female voice of his GPS informed him.

Veronica Butler lived in a white single-story clapboard house on a bluff directly above the tributary. When the weather was clear, there would be a long gentle slope down to the water's edge, but today the current was rushing by no more than thirty feet from the back door. She had no garage, so her late-model American sedan sat in the driveway and was being lashed by the storm. Next to the house was a tractor shed just big enough for a riding mower and maybe some gardening tools.

Mercer pulled in behind her Ford four-door and killed the engine. Without the motor noise and the whipsaw action of the wipers, he could hear the stream's passage even over the rain. Roni Butler's grandfather might have picked a great spot for his homestead and it might never have flooded before, but there was always a first time and Mercer feared this might be it.

He took a deep breath and threw himself out of the truck, running toward the front porch as hard as he could go. Just before reaching it he remembered to whip off his baseball cap and stuff it into a jacket pocket. No sense in antagonizing her by wearing the wrong colors.

The porch was only five feet deep but stretched the

full width of the house. A curtain of rain fell from the eaves, so it wasn't until Mercer was through it that he could see the house wasn't white, but a pale blue. The trim was a darker shade in the same family. Flower boxes hung from the windows, but they hadn't yet been planted. The outdoor furniture was all made of either wood or thick-gauge steel and looked like it had been there since the Dust Bowl. He saw no lights and assumed her power was out. Mercer swung open a screen door with a coil spring return and rapped on the jamb. With no answer he hit it harder. But to no avail. Next time he kicked the door with the toe of his boot, and it swung open in a flash. The shotgun barrel came at him with the speed of a striking cobra. He just managed to get a hand on it to deflect it away from his head.

"I told you, goddamnit, that I ain't leavin'."

"I'm not asking you to," Mercer said, still holding the shotgun barrel high and to his right.

Veronica Butler was probably in her eighties by now, but she looked a decade younger. She had her fair share of wrinkles and crow's-feet, but she stood tall and proud. Back in the day she would have been a stunner and even now was still attractive, with dyed red hair that swirled around her neck in permed curls. She was busty and curvy and fiery as hell, and Mercer knew if Harry had been here the old letch would be tripping over his tongue.

"You aren't one of Sheriff Conner's boys." She eased her grip on the Mossberg pump-action, and Mercer let her take it back so it hung in the crook of her arm.

"No, Mrs. Butler. My name is Philip Mercer. Sherman Smithson at the Hoover Library was supposed to call you and tell you I was coming."

"He mentioned it yesterday, but I didn't think anyone would be damned fool enough to drive out in this."

"I surprise myself sometimes with what damned fool things I do," he admitted.

She gave him a critical look. Her eyes were an almost identical gray to his own, and she must have seen something in them. "I don't think there's a whole lot that surprises you, Mr. Mercer. Come on in out of the rain and tell me why you'd risk your neck to talk to an old broad like me."

Mercer followed her into the house. He loved the temerity of women who referred to themselves as "broads." It told him they were comfortable enough in their own skins not to care what others thought.

She didn't ask him to remove his wet boots, for which he was grateful, but waited so he could hang his bomber jacket on a peg next to her coats. She led him through a dim living room to the kitchen at the back of the house. A big picture window overlooked a backyard now dominated by the overflowing stream. They had maybe another eighteen inches of elevation before the water seeped into the house.

She must have read Mercer's mind. "We're one foot higher than Blair Creek's ever crested. My grandfather was an amateur geologist and figured that record goes back well over a thousand years. That's why he built on this bluff."

"I'm actually a geologist myself and I'd agree with his assessment, but that was before they started putting levees along the Mississippi, and God knows what other flood control measures upstream of your house."

She suddenly looked a little less sure of herself and her grandfather's geologic insights. "There's a dam about ten miles from here."

"Concrete?"

She nodded and Mercer relaxed. So long as the dam held, they could drive west through the fields faster than the river rose, so there wasn't any real danger. Still, he said, "I told you earlier that I'm not here to ask you to leave, but I think it might be a good idea."

She set the shotgun in the corner of the kitchen and fired up the gas stove with a wand lighter. "You're welcome to shove off, but I am not going anywhere. The dam's been there since the thirties, and I've seen storms a lot worse than this. Coffee? I only have instant."

"We should drink it fast," he said to prompt her to rethink her position.

"Sherm said you were looking into some rock samples President Hoover once owned."

Mercer assumed wryly that Roni Butler was probably the only person in the world Sherman Smithson allowed to call him Sherm. "That's right."

She didn't let him elaborate and went on, "I hate to disappoint you, Mr. Mercer, but I know nothing about rock samples. When I worked for the president we were living in New York, and he was working on his greatest book, *Freedom Betrayed*. He was a topnotch mining engineer when he was a younger man, but by the time I started as his secretary in the late 1950s he considered himself an elder statesman and historian. Other than a few tales of adventure he'd tell me from time to time, I know almost nothing about that earlier part of his life."

She said this last line looking over her shoulder as she fiddled with the copper teapot atop the blue ring of burning propane. Mercer imagined that her convincing delivery was enough to deter most everyone who ever asked, but not him. Hoover had to have coached her on what to say and she'd likely practiced it in the years following his death, but that had been many, many years ago. With so much time having gone by, she couldn't have expected to be asked about this any longer. She had to feel the secret was comfortably in the past.

Her smile seemed a little forced, and she turned back again to unnecessarily adjust the stove's burner.

"Roni," he said over the rattle of wind-driven rain against the window and shutters, "you knew someone would come along eventually. Hoover knew it too. That's why he told you about it in the first place. It's too big of a secret to have died with him and it's too big to die with you either."

That flustered her, and she stammered, "I—I don't know . . . what you're talking about. I think maybe you should leave me be."

She turned back to him and they looked at each other across the simple kitchen. In the background came the serious voices of broadcasters on an emergency radio talking about the storm. "I've been to the cave, Roni," Mercer said and he saw her resolve start to crack. She'd carried this burden for fifty years, and she wanted so badly to pass it along. "I was in Afghanistan two days ago. I know Mike Dillman went back there and cleared it out, but I found a sliver of Sample 681 he overlooked."

A crack appeared in Roni Butler's decades-long resolve. "That's what the president labeled it for his collection, though he called the mineral electricium. I liked Mike Dillman's name more. He said they were called the lightning stones. I don't know if he made that up or heard it from natives living around the cave."

"A single sample of these lightning stones ended up

with a friend of mine, who was murdered along with several other people when the crystal was stolen."

"Murdered? Stolen? What are you talking about?"

"It's no longer all that secret," he informed her. "But I need to know the rest of it if I'm going to stop the killers."

She sagged further, and in a symbolic gesture of which she herself was probably unaware, she set down a dishrag as if throwing in the towel. "Like I said, President Hoover named the gem electricium, because of how it attracted lightning, and also how it changed the way magnets worked. It had other strange properties, but I honestly don't remember what they were—it's been too long now."

"That's fine. Just tell me what you do recall. Who was Mike Dillman, for example?"

"He worked for the president when Bert was running a mining concern in China. The president called Dillman his bloodhound because he could find minerals everywhere." Mercer didn't point out that minerals *were* everywhere. "He credited Dillman with finding lodes of ore that the Chinese had overlooked for centuries. Dillman would go off prospecting for months at a time without telling anyone where he was going. The president was in his early twenties at this time, young to be given such responsibility, and he said that Mike Dillman was younger still, not yet out of his teens.

"President Hoover said that his protégé was as much an anthropologist as he was a geologist, and would use local lore to help find interesting rock samples. That is what took him so far to the south that he ended up in Waziristan, as it was known at the time. On this particular trip he was accompanied by a young Frenchman who'd been sent to the Orient by his family to avoid a scandal back home. They had some connections in Peking or Tianjin or some such. Anyway, as the president implied when he told me the story, the Frenchman had a particular predilection that wasn't appreciated back home even if they did call it 'Gay Paris.'"

"Ah." Mercer's eyebrow went up. "Was Dillman . . . ?"

"I'm sure I don't have the faintest idea, but the two of them did find something on that trip and they had a bit of a falling-out over it. The Frenchman left Asia soon after they returned to the capital. Not long after that came the Boxer Rebellion and the Hoovers left China for Australia. Dillman went off on his own at that time. No one realized the potential of the few crystals Dillman returned with until many years later, when the president was donating a lot of his possessions. A crate of old geological samples went to a scientist friend at Carnegie Mellon University. President Hoover said after the fact that it was mostly samples of copper ore, recovered from several mines he had worked, and this had something to do with stopping the crystals buried in the crate from showing their true selves. It was the friend at Carnegie who went on to discover all the odd phenomena and actually coined the name electricium."

"So that's how and where Abe got his sample," Mercer said, more to himself than for her benefit. She made an inquiring gesture as if he should elaborate, but he shook it off and said, "Please, go on."

She asked first if he wanted cream or sugar, and when Mercer demurred she handed him a ceramic mug of strong black coffee. After the swill he'd had back in the school gymnasium, this was just what he needed. His body had no idea what time of the day or night it was, so he was awake by force of will alone.

"When President Hoover realized the importance of what had been in his collection all those years, he reached out to his old friend Mike Dillman one more time and asked that he return to the cave where he had first discovered the crystals, to bring back the rest."

The emergency radio cut to static, and Roni fiddled with it until the newscasters were audible again. She added with a dark tone, "It was only later that the president learned Dillman had called upon the Frenchman to help, not realizing this was supposed to have been a secret."

"Do you know the Frenchman's name?"

"No. I was told it once or twice, but I can't recall, and the president forbade me from writing any of this down."

Mercer hid his disappointment. Knowing that could open up other avenues for investigation. "Please, continue."

"The Frenchman refused to return to Waziristan, or so he claimed, and Dillman went off to recover the rest of the electricium by himself. Just so you know, this would have been in January of 1937 when he left California, where he worked as an assayer."

"And they discovered the mineral at the time of the Boxer Rebellion. That was 1900, right?"

"Well done. Yes."

"So Dillman was no longer a young man?"

"He wasn't, but President Hoover had a way about him that almost compelled people to drop everything they were doing and help him. That was why he is credited with saving Belgium from famine during

World War One, and it was his idea to distribute food across Europe after the Second World War. When he asked you for something you did it, because it was invariably the right thing to do. In this country, history has not been kind to him, because he is falsely blamed for the Depression, but internationally he remains one of the most respected presidents this nation has ever produced. He was a great man, Mr. Mercer. Even in his golden years he was so . . ."—she sought the right word—"well, compelling."

"Mike Dillman," Mercer prompted when she became lost in her memories for a few seconds.

"Yes. Mike Dillman. He returned to what is now Afghanistan and recovered the rest of the crystals from the cave. He managed to cable a report from Rawalpindi once he was safely back in civilization. I remember President Hoover telling me that Dillman said there was a dead body in the cave that hadn't been there on his first sojourn."

That made the corpse of the mystic Mercer had seen much newer than he'd lied to Jordan about.

"His next cable came from Calcutta, on the eastern side of the Indian subcontinent. He informed President Hoover that men had tried to rob him of the crystals several times since his return from the tribal areas. He believed they were agents of the Frenchman and said that they had managed to trick him out of a single shard before he realized their nefarious intent."

Roni gave a soft sad smile of remembrance. "Those were President Hoover's exact words. I can still hear his voice in my head. Sorry. When you reach my age all you have is arthritis and memories."

"My eightysomething friend Harry says an enlarged prostate, too, but that doesn't apply here."

She chuckled. "I was going to add 'and boobs down to your knees.' I should meet this friend of yours."

"He'll feel the same when I tell him about you."

She went back to her story while Mercer's coffee went cold and forgotten in his cup and the rain continued to fall. "Dillman managed to stay one step ahead of these dark agents as he hopscotched his way ever eastward by tramp steamer, sailboat, and whatever native craft he could beg a ride on. But by Dillman's own admission to President Hoover, it was a race back to the States that he was going to lose. His health was failing, and the Frenchman seemed to have bought thugs in every country from India to the Philippines. Every time Dillman tried to book passage on a legitimate steamship, corrupt agents informed the Frenchman's proxies. In Singapore Mr. Dillman had to shoot his way off a San Francisco–bound ship and leap over the side several miles from the nearest land. Through cables, President Hoover urged him to find an American consulate or embassy, but Dillman had begun to crack under the pressure of the pursuit and was too paranoid to turn to strangers. By this point he was hiding in the city of Rabaul on Papua New Guinea, and wrote that there were men roaming the streets looking for him. Unknowingly, though, he had put himself in the perfect place. The president came up with an idea to end the chase once and for all, and he called in a favor from George Putnam."

"Who is?"

"I'll tell you in a second because the end of this story is going to knock your socks off." The old woman chuckled knowingly.

"Like everyone else, Putnam couldn't resist the former president's request and he in turn allowed President Hoover to contact his wife. Dillman was given a new final destination, and he agreed to turn over the crystals once he got there. He managed to steal a sailboat and sailed it south to the town of Lae, where on the morning of July second Putnam's wife sent a note back to her husband informing him that the package had been delivered the night before."

Mercer started getting a bad feeling.

"And so she took off with the crystals aboard her Lockheed Electra with navigator Fred Noonan on the longest and most dangerous leg of her round-the-world journey, a publicity stunt so her husband and financier, George Putnam, could sell more newspapers."

He groaned when the names and dates all came together in his mind. Few knew George Putnam, but every schoolchild knows the name of his famous wife.

"You know who I'm talking about?" It was more statement than question.

Mercer wasn't sure whether he wanted to laugh or cry at the cruel irony of it all. "Amelia Earhart," he said dejectedly. "She had the lion's share of Sample 681 aboard her plane when she vanished."

18

In the next moment, Mercer's world went from bad to worse.

A piercing alarm blared from the radio. It was the nerve-jangling sound of the emergency response system, that annoying tone most people switched away from when listening to the radio or watching television. But in parts of the country where residents understood that nature had not yet been tamed, they heeded these signals as life-or-death alerts.

When the awful honking ended, a mechanical voice replaced it and started rattling off county names. They meant nothing to Mercer until Roni Butler suddenly tensed. Whatever was happening was happening here.

The voice then said, "It has been reported that Army Corps engineers have initiated an emergency release of water from the Wilbur Berry dam reservoir on the upper reaches of Blair Creek. Anyone who has not followed the evacuation order and lives in the Blair Creek watershed, the creek is estimated to crest a further five feet above its current level."

Mercer didn't need to hear the rest. "Let's go!"

Naked fear made Roni suddenly look her age. Mercer took her hand and pulled her in his wake as he rushed for the front room. He wouldn't have bothered with his coat, but the SUV keys were in its pocket. He tossed Roni her bright yellow rain slicker and slipped into his bomber. He opened the door and drew her outside. Water cascaded off the eaves but through it Mercer spotted the big bulbous-tired four-by-four with its Zodiac in tow approaching the house. It was the rescue team he'd seen earlier in town, and he was suddenly grateful for its presence. Doubtless the men were locals and knew the best way to avoid the impending catastrophe.

It was only after the truck came to a stop shy of the driveway entrance that an animal instinct struck Mercer. It dawned on him that the red strobe light affixed to the truck's roof was off, and so were the banks of high-intensity lamps running the width of its grille. If they had come to rescue Roni Butler despite her protests, they would have arrived with horns blaring and lights flashing. They wouldn't have crawled up the road in stealth mode.

The passenger threw open his door and jumped out into the rain. Mercer could see just his indistinct outline in the murky light, but he could tell by the way he moved that something was desperately wrong. He couldn't be sure, but it appeared the man carried a pistol in his right hand.

Mercer didn't wait for the driver to exit the tall pickup. He drew Roni back into her house and closed and locked the front door. He was pretty sure they hadn't seen him. He rushed through to the kitchen and snatched the shotgun from where she'd left it.

"Rack it," she said.

He looked at her questioningly.

"You think I greet people with a loaded shotgun?" Roni asked him. "The chamber's empty."

Mercer shook his head at the absurdity of it all and pumped a shell into the short-barreled Mossberg's chamber. "Slugs or shot?"

"Double-ought buck." She gave him a handful of extra shells she'd taken from a kitchen drawer.

"That'll do. Stay down next to the stove." It was an ancient beast of an appliance made out of much thicker steel than a modern range, and it offered her good protection.

He crossed back to the front window. He didn't see the first guy, but the second was now out of the truck and crossing the lawn.

Mercer's heart tripped inside his chest when he got a clear look at him, and an extra dose of adrenaline raced through his veins. It was him. The leader, the top dog, whom Mercer had first spied coming out of the mine chamber following Abe's cold-blooded murder. He moved like a jungle cat, smooth, sure, deadly. He and his partner must have hijacked the rescue team's vehicle.

Mercer brought the shotgun up to his shoulder but held his fire. Without a full choke, the range was just too far for the nine-pellet shell, so he lowered the weapon again, breathing slow and even, trying not to let his emotions cloud his tactical awareness.

"Who are they?" Roni asked in a rasping whisper.

"Killers."

"No shit," she snapped back. "Who? Why?"

"They're after the mother lode of Sample 681, same as me. I just don't know how they found you."

Just then her phone rang. It was a wall phone with a long coiled cord, the kind Mercer hadn't seen in years. She slid up just enough to knock the handset loose into her palm, and went back to cowering behind the stove with the phone clamped to her head.

Mercer heard her talking but paid no attention as he went from room to room checking for targets outside the simple clapboard house. The lawn was a quagmire as treacherous as the no-man's-land between World War I trenches. He spotted one of the men watching the house from behind a tree.

"Mr. Mercer?" Roni called out. He was in her bedroom. Satisfied he had a few more minutes while the pair reconnoitered the house, he moved well back from the window so as not to give himself away and then tracked back to the kitchen.

"That was Sherman Smithson," Roni said. "He called to warn me these guys were coming. They hit his house a few hours ago and left him tied up in a closet. They tortured my name out of him."

Mercer expected they would have just killed him and been done with it. He wondered if their leniency had any meaning, then recalled the wounds in Abe's chest and decided it didn't.

The old woman continued, "He says he only escaped because his girlfriend got over her fear of the storm and drove out to West Branch to surprise him. He says he only saw the two of them and doesn't know if there are more."

Mercer's opinion of Smithson went up a few notches. For an archivist, he seemed to have a pretty good grasp of what was important at a time like this.

"How far upstream is that dam mentioned on the radio?"

"About ten miles."

Mercer estimated the time since the report and the speed of the oncoming deluge and knew they had to chance it. He held out his hand to take her back toward the front door. "We have to make a break for it, Roni, otherwise we'll be trapped in here when the wall of water hits. Can you run?"

"Not as fast as I used to, but just you try and stop me."

"Okay, I am going to open this door and step out onto the porch. One of them is behind a tree about to the right."

"The one outside my bedroom?"

"Yes. As soon as I'm outside I want you to get up a good head of steam and start running for my SUV. The doors aren't locked, so just jump in the backseat and stay down. I'm going to keep them pinned with the shotgun."

She looked uncertain.

"We can do this, Roni. It's not even twenty feet to my truck, and a shotgun blast will keep anyone's head down long enough for us to make it."

This time she nodded, tightening her mouth in a grim line of determination.

Mercer opened the door and was about to step out when the sound of gunfire exploded from his left. The second shooter was at the other side of the house, and had just been about to vault the railing to gain access to the porch. Mercer stepped back, switching the shotgun to his left hand, and swung its barrel blindly around the jamb. He fired. The blast nearly ripped the weapon from his grasp, but he was able to use the recoil to seat the gun so his right hand was on the slide, ready to ram another three-inch shell into the chamber. He fired again and chanced a look outside. The second shooter was gone. He could have taken a full blast to the chest and been lying in the grass dead, but most likely he had dropped back before the shotgun fired.

He looked the other way and spotted the leader running diagonally from his post behind the tree, heading for the road. He appeared to be in headlong flight, his feet gliding over the muddy earth and his arms pumping with the smooth stroke of an Olympian. Mercer turned back the other way again and saw the shooter, too, was running for their stolen pickup like the hounds of hell were at his heels.

He got it. He understood what they'd seen that had frightened them so.

Mercer slammed the door a second time and looked at Roni. When he spoke he couldn't keep the fearful edge from his voice. "Is there an attic or crawl space?"

"Yes. What's happening?"

"The water from that reservoir is coming a lot sooner than we figured. Where's the access?"

"Pantry behind the kitchen."

This time she led the way. Mercer looked out the back window and saw the creek had consumed the last of the back lawn and was washing along the building's exterior. He moved closer still and saw it was actually up almost halfway to the window itself. Once it reached that height, the old single pane would implode from the pressure against it—or if by some miracle it held, it would shatter when struck by any of the debris borne along the runaway torrent.

He strained his eyes to look upstream and saw a wall of water stretching the full width of the valley, its head a foaming crest that curled but never collapsed. For as much danger as Mercer had faced in his life, he had never felt more certain that he was going to die.

"Roni!" he shouted as she was reaching for a pull string attached to a hatch in her pantry ceiling. "Brace yourself!"

The surge struck the house, rising up so that it covered the windows and plunged the kitchen into near-total darkness. Mercer expected the glass to explode and took a deep breath on the off chance he survived the initial blast of water. Instead, the entire house lurched drunkenly, knocking him off his feet. Something tore under the building, where the floor joists met the stone-and-mortar foundation. It had been built to withstand the screaming fury of a tornado, but it couldn't hope to fight the remorseless onslaught of water.

Mercer clutched at the heavy stove as Roni Butler's house was torn off its foundation. He smelled a brief blast of propane from the ruptured line feeding the stove, and heard over the roar of water the metallic shearing of pipes and ducts that rose up through the floor from the basement. It grew suddenly lighter in the kitchen as the wooden house reacted to its positive buoyancy and bobbed up from the depths to begin floating downstream in the somewhat calmer waters behind the initial swell. It spun and weaved and rocked like a piece of cork, but the building had found a way to survive.

But it wouldn't last. Already water was sloshing in from the living room, where it came gushing in from under the front door and bubbled up through the air vents recessed in the floor.

Mercer scrambled to his feet, still reeling from being alive. He had to hold on to the walls to keep his balance as the house lazily pirouetted amid all the other trash picked up in the flood.

"Roni?" he called. "Roni."

"I'm in here." Her muffled answer came from the adjoining pantry. As if he were aboard a ship in the middle of a typhoon, Mercer staggered to her. Roni was on the floor, covered in flour from a sack that had fallen from a shelf and burst when it struck her. Around her prone form were cans and boxes and other detritus that had been dislodged when the house tore free. He helped her to her feet. She was unsteady but appeared unhurt.

He shook some flour from her hair. "You know, it looks pretty good white, should you ever want to go that route."

She was so far beyond the scope of her experience that she glommed on to Mercer's weak joke as an anchor point and gave a hearty belly laugh. "But I bet your friend Harry prefers redheads," she quickly replied.

Mercer looked back through the large kitchen window. The world spun by in a kaleidoscope of water and land and rain as the house weaved its way toward the Mississippi.

The water inside had climbed to their ankles.

"We need to get out of here," he said, bracing her in the pantry and sloshing over to the front of the house. The window suddenly disintegrated as a pair of pistols were unleashed in a fusillade that came with unimaginable savagery.

Mercer had forgotten all about the gunmen. They had avoided the onrush of water by retreating to the Zodiac, and now they were pacing the floating house in the rubber inflatable just waiting for their opportunity. He cursed his stupidity. The shotgun was in the kitchen.

The boat was just a few yards off the front porch, and the only thing stopping one of them from jumping over was that the house still rotated on its axis. On this pass the stoop remained out of reach, but on the next rotation the driver would have a better fix on his angle of attack. Mercer ran back for the gun, sliding across the linoleum floor like a base runner going for home. He snatched up the weapon and rolled in the water to regain his feet. Around him the house spun dizzily, but he was just quick enough so that when the Zodiac was positioned outside the rear-facing kitchen window he was on his feet and ready. The Mossberg roared, and the front of the twelve-foot inflatable erupted in a fluttering burst of shredded rubber when several air cells exploded.

Mercer couldn't tell if he'd hit either of the gunmen but doubted he'd been that lucky. The boat wasn't in any danger of sinking because its hull was compartmentalized, but the driver was going to have a hell of a time controlling it.

He tore back across the house. This time the icy water had risen up to his knees, and he had to bull his way to get to the front parlor. Some furniture had begun to float. Rain blew in through the glassless window frame. He took up a position next to it and peered out. The Zodiac should have reappeared as the house rotated yet again, but he couldn't see it. He saw whole trees blown into the river by the storm, and the pink bodies of several drowned pigs, but no white inflatable boat.

Water climbed up to midthigh while he waited. Roni's house was sinking fast, and he still had no plan to get them out of there. He didn't think he'd be able to lure the Zodiac close enough to steal, so his next option was finding something in the house he and Roni could use as a raft. Mattresses seemed the best idea, and he had seen a queen-size bed in the master that he might be able to wrestle out the front door. Mercer slung the shotgun onto his shoulder and waded down the hallway heading for the bedroom. The gunmen must have peeled off, because he didn't see them out the bedroom window either. He quickly stripped off the hand-sewn quilt and the blankets so they wouldn't become tangled, and wrestled the mattress onto its side. It was bulky and unwieldy, and grew heavy as it absorbed water while he was trying to guide it back down the hall.

Suddenly, Roni Butler screamed. Mercer tried to abandon his makeshift raft but was momentarily pinned against the wall by the sagging Posturepedic. He swore and pushed at the thing before getting free. The river was gushing in through the front window, and the house had begun to fill unevenly and tilt even more wildly.

Mercer fought his way to the kitchen just in time to see Roni being hoisted through the back window by one of the shooters. He must have leapt through the shattered kitchen window and grabbed her from where Mercer had left her cowering in the pantry.

The killer-turned-kidnapper was silhouetted perfectly, but with an unfamiliar shotgun Mercer couldn't chance taking direct aim, for fear of hitting Roni. Instead he lowered his right arm and shoulder and raised the shotgun's barrel, so when he pulled the trigger the gun was mostly pointed at the ceiling over the shooter's head. A single slug fired at the extreme angle would have missed the gunman's head by the narrowest of margins. However, the gun had a shortened barrel and improved choke, so the cluster of shot expanded just enough.

For a terrible moment the man's head contorted like a rubber Halloween mask—and then it came apart and splattered the area where ceiling met wall in an obscene paste of blood and tissue and hair.

The Zodiac's outboard screamed at full throttle even as the nearly decapitated corpse tumbled through the window and into the turgid water. Mercer sloshed to the window, pumping the slide once again and ramming the shotgun to his shoulder, ready to fire. The inflatable, with its sagging nose, was twenty yards away already, drifting farther by the second in the angry current of muddy water and trash. He could see Roni's gaily colored blouse; she was huddled on the Zodiac's floorboards at the feet of the gunman in the black jacket.

Mercer didn't have a shot from this distance—at least, not with a shotgun. In a fit of rage he pointed the barrel skyward and yanked the trigger, and the gunman looked back at the blast. Mercer could have sworn the man smiled crookedly at him, but through all that rain it was hard to tell.

The view changed as the house spun, and the kitchen window began to face downstream. What Mercer saw chilled him more than the frigid water. Directly ahead lay the iron truss bridge he'd crossed when first leaving town on his search for Roni's house. Any debris that piled up against it was quickly pulled under by the force of the river and emerged on the far side, where the tree limbs and whole trunks continued on toward the Mississippi. Judging by the height of the river and the amount the house had sunk, it would strike the bridge's road deck in line with the windows, and the whole place would come apart as if filled with explosives.

Mercer dropped the shotgun and lunged for the

pantry. He grabbed the pull string and yanked open the attic crawl space hatch. Dust fell from the dark opening, but there was also some light filtering down from above. He vaguely recalled seeing a gable window on the side of the house.

There was no ladder, so Mercer clambered up the pantry shelves, kicking loose the few items that hadn't yet fallen to the floor. He levered himself into the crawl space. The roof rafters met over his head, giving him just enough room to stand in a crouch. The ceiling joists were roughhewn into two-by-sixes, but were so old they could barely take Mercer's weight. Between them, strips of ancient insulation lay tattered and compressed, no thicker than carpet.

There was a small window on each gable end of the house. Mercer raced for the one that would be above Roni's bedroom, praying that he hadn't miscalculated the house's slow rotation. He had to dance from joist to joist while bending low to keep from smacking his head into one of the thick rafters. Through the dusty window he could see nothing but the screaming river. An occasional wave even lapped at the glass.

He yelled, channeling all his energy into those last careful footsteps, knowing that if he missed a joist he would crash through the ceiling and end up being smeared against the bridge when they struck. A flash of green whizzed past the window as the house made its last rotation. Bridge girder.

It was now or never.

Mercer hurled himself at the window headfirst, punching through the pane with clenched fists as if he was a little kid playing Superman. Glass exploded all around him as he flew several feet, passing between two steel support girders. He hit the bridge's road deck and tumbled into a ball to protect his head, while behind him Roni Butler's cozy ranch smashed into the bridge with the detonative violence of a chain-reaction crash.

The entire 1,100-square-foot building splintered when it hit the bridge. Rafters, joists, studs, lathe, plaster, clapboard, shingles, and sheathing. It all blew apart in a maelstrom of wrecked furniture, destroyed appliances, and the accumulation of a lifetime of memories. Most of it was sucked under the bridge by the unending current, but some blew across the two-lane span, nearly rolling Mercer over the far rail as he was pummeled with the remains of the house and all its furnishings and fittings. He ended up shielded from some of the deluge when Roni's vintage claw-foot tub tumbled against him and he was able to hold on to it as though it were a turtle's protective shell.

It was over in a violent instant. The house was gone, and Mercer was left lying partially in an over-turned bathtub on a rain-lashed bridge, with a once tranquil little stream raging less than a foot below the span. Beyond the bridge were islands of civilization sticking up from the floodwater—telephone poles like lonely sentries, buildings with water up to their eaves, and some buried even deeper so all he could see were their triangular roof peaks. Great swaths of the levee that had once protected the town from the Mississippi were missing, and the river was freed once again to flow where it wanted.

Unlike the levee, the bridge was one of the high-est vantage points that wasn't in danger of collapsing. Mercer was safe for the moment but was frozen to the core, so undoing his belt and using it to lash himself to the bridge took all his concentration, and many min-utes longer than it should have. Once he was secure he replaced the ball cap from his pocket on his head to prevent a little heat loss, and soon felt his body begin to shut itself down, as he knew it would. He became drowsy, and no amount of anger or need for revenge could prevent his lids from closing and his mind from turning to blackness. Mercer went slack, and would have eventually been washed from the bridge by a surge of water had he not had the foresight to tie himself off.

—

He woke three hours later, when the rain had finally stopped and the Army National Guard had launched a fleet of search and rescue helicopters. It was nearing four in the afternoon. The sun wasn't exactly shining, but the day had brightened enough for the pilot of one of the Blackhawks to see a man roped to the bridge truss. He thought it was a corpse until the man raised a hand and started waving. Ten minutes later the rescue jumper came back aboard with the soaking man secured to a harness.

A paramedic guided Mercer to a bench seat in the noisy cabin as the chopper lifted clear to continue the search. The medic tucked a Mylar space blanket around Mercer's shoulders and said, "Apart from the fact you're freezing and wearing Iowa State colors, are you all right?"

"Let me guess," Mercer managed to say with quivering lips and a shuddering jaw. "You're all U of I fans?"

"Hell no! We're from the Illinois National Guard. We're all Fighting Illini."

They were a more hated rival in the Big Ten for Mercer's Penn State Nittany Lions than even the Hawkeyes. "Out of the frying pan . . ."

He did manage to tell his rescuers about Veronica Butler and the one surviving armed man, knowing that making the report would lead to hours of questioning and the need to write up everything in triplicate—but he needed them to be on the lookout for the old woman and wary of the shooter at the same time.

Within an hour, the chopper had picked up a full load of survivors from various roofs and trees and returned to the Illinois side of the river, where Mercer was soon warmed, hydrated, and settled in a National Guard tent. No trace of Roni or the armed man had been found. The gunman Mercer nailed with the shotgun was fished out of the Mississippi four miles downstream when his body had snagged on a channel marker. The injuries to the body were consistent with Mercer's story, but without corroborating witnesses he was still treated with suspicion. Mercer was not exactly a prisoner in the Guard encampment, but he hadn't been allowed to leave either.

It wasn't until a few hours later that his name was noticed by someone in the D.C. FBI office, and a call was made. A corporal walked into the tent with a cell phone and handed it over.

"What's this?" Mercer asked.

"Get-out-of-jail-free card. My CO says you can now leave anytime."

He took the phone. "This is Mercer."

"Is there always so much death and destruction in your wake?" Special Agent Kelly Hepburn asked.

Mercer grinned, tired and thankful, and said, "Yeah, on most days there is."

19

With the area under evacuation orders, Niklaas Coetzer had had no problem finding a house to break into with his prisoner. He'd motored back almost to where they'd started before he spotted a place that was set far back from the flooding stream. Coetzer had grounded the Zodiac and hauled the nearly catatonic Roni Butler onto dry land. He used a folding knife to slash the inflatable's remaining air cells and dragged the tattered remains of the boat with him to be disposed of later on.

The farmhouse was larger than the one Roni had owned, a two-story with a minefield of children's toys littering the lawn—bikes, miniature tractors, and the wrecked shell of a wading pool. The front door, unsurprisingly, wasn't locked.

"This is Bob and Ellie Loomis's place," Roni said when she finally realized where she was. "They've got kids. What are you planning on?"

"I need dry clothes and transportation, and you need to tell me what you told him."

"I ain't telling you nothing," Roni snapped at him.

He backhanded her so hard that her head snapped around and her lip split. "Yes, you will."

She laughed and thumbed the trace of blood from her mouth. "That the best you got, you foreign prick? I had a husband who would kick my ass for days straight. Gave me black eyes so often people thought I was part raccoon, and more broken bones than I can count. You better step up your game if you think a little love tap like that's gonna make me talk."

"Shut up," he snarled.

"Or what? You'll hit me again, you dickless asshole? You beat up old women? How badly did you screw up your life to end up here? Ever think about that?"

"I said shut up!" Coetzer roared and jammed the barrel of his automatic pistol hard enough under Roni's chin to force her onto her tiptoes.

She saw the madness in his eyes and knew if she so much as swallowed he'd pull the trigger. A tense second passed before the South African pulled his weapon from her throat and pushed her farther into the house. It was dank from the rain and dark from the lack of electricity. Light filtering in through the windows was weak and watery.

He thrust her into a kitchen chair. The table had been cleared prior to the Loomis family's evacuation, but the dirty dishes were left in the sink and the plastic tray attached to a high chair near the table was littered with uneaten Cheerios. Coetzer rummaged through the drawers; he didn't find tape, but a ball of string would suffice.

Roni thought about resisting, but in the end she let him tie her to the chair. The twine was thin, so he had to wrap it around her wrists and ankles multiple times to make certain she couldn't move.

"I am sorry about this," he said as he worked. "It wasn't supposed to happen this way. But hey, your friend from the library? We tied him up just like this—he's fine and you will be too. Just tell me what you told Philip Mercer and I will leave."

He wasn't looking at her when he was talking, but Roni could still tell he was lying. Sherm Smithson had told her that the men who trussed him up and tossed him into the back of his closet had worn masks the entire time. But Mercer's presence at her house had altered their plans, and neither one had covered his face. And this man was so easily identifiable that she knew he couldn't let her live.

"As to your earlier question, about what made me the way I am? That's a story that started with my grandfather, Piet Coetzer. He was an expert marksman who would have represented South Africa at the Olympics in Berlin. When the war broke out a couple of years later, our country narrowly sided with the Allied cause rather than stay neutral. My paps knew his duty. He became famous for training thousands of soldiers how to shoot, so they could join the Allies in defeating the Nazis. He even wrote a training manual. He was a great man, my grandfather, and he inspired me to join the military when I was of age.

"Only problem was . . . I accidentally shot and killed a man during a training exercise. He was a black man, and he outranked me. This was right after the blacks took over my country, and so I was charged with murder. It was race politics bullshit and everyone knew it, but I had to stand trial. They acquitted me, and yet I was forced out of the army anyway. So I became a mercenary. You know what this means?"

"You're a hired gun. A thug."

The man sucked at his teeth. It was a nervous tic she'd noticed since their time in the boat.

He nodded. "Now we're called contractors . . . and we're paid a king's ransom to risk our necks so your soldiers don't have to fight. But back then . . . yeah, we were hired guns. I worked for some good people, mostly as a bodyguard and doing hostage rescue. I never shot first and I never killed anyone who wasn't trying to kill me. I lived by a soldier's code."

"And soldiers slap old women?" Roni sneered.

"One patrol went horribly wrong," he replied with a trace of bitter regret. "We were on a mission to rescue three aid workers who'd been snatched from a bush hospital, when we came across a camp in the jungle. I believed these were our kidnappers, and we were putting the men under observation when the fighting started. I don't know which side fired first, but it turned into a fookin' mess . . . guys were dropping left and right. That's the only time in all the years before or since that I ever got shot. A few of my mates were dead and a couple of us were pretty banged up, me included, so we retreated back to the hospital to report what had happened.

"Turns out they weren't the terrorists we were looking for—just a bunch of zoo types looking for monkeys or apes or some goddamn thing. They patched me up as best they could, but the police wanted to question me about the incident. I had to get out of the country, and by the time I found another doctor to look at my injury, well, there wasn't much he could do. After that, jobs became harder to find and I became a lot less choosy . . . and eventually, as you said, I became a hired 'thug.'"

Coetzer cinched the final knot and regarded Roni with hard eyes. "So, what did you tell Mercer?"

"I gave him my peach cobbler recipe," she replied, without missing a beat.

"Lady, I don't want to hurt you but I will just the same. I work for a very big corporation now, and there's a lot of money riding on the success of my mission. The kind of money even rich people kill over. Billions of dollars. Tell me and I'll go away, and I'll make sure you are never bothered again."

"You start with flour and shortening, and don't dream of using anything but fresh peaches."

"What is it with you pigheaded Americans?"

"I've seen your face," Roni said. "I know your voice. You are going to kill me as soon as I tell you what you want. Sherman's girlfriend freed him already, and he called me when you were outside my house. He told me you and your sick little partner wore masks. Now that I can identify you, you have to kill me. I might be old but I want to keep on living, so I'm going to prolong this for as long as I can. And the whole time you're hurting me, the pain will be my reminder that I am still alive. You'll also need baking powder, ground cinnamon—"

The next slap was harder than anything her late husband had ever doled out, and Veronica Butler realized she wasn't going to make it nearly as long as she'd first thought.

—

Twenty minutes later, Niklaas Coetzer hid the remains of the Zodiac underneath a rusted car in the barn behind the farmhouse. The car itself was covered by a tarp that looked like it hadn't been removed in a generation. The old woman he buried in a stand of trees about two hundred yards from the road. The rain had turned the ground into a soupy mess that made digging difficult, so the grave was much shallower than he would have liked.

On the other hand, he figured that once the evacuees returned, they would care more about rebuilding their lives than searching for the body of their elderly neighbor who had refused to evacuate. If by some miracle Philip Mercer survived, he would suspect what had happened to her, and he might be able to galvanize a search, but ultimately to what end? Coetzer himself would be long gone, and what the Butler woman had told him meant the trail for the last of the mineral had gone cold for them both. The mission was over.

He scoped out another four houses until he found another one that hadn't been destroyed by the flood. There was no car in the driveway, but in the barn he found a small off-road buggy with knobby tires and a fifteen-horse engine. The key was in the ignition.

Coetzer motored out of the area heading west, away from the Mississippi and the rescue efforts that would be launched as soon as the rain let up, and a little more than an hour later he came across a town large enough to have a bus terminal. He hid the ATV and joined a dozen other wet-weather refugees who boarded the next Greyhound, not knowing or caring its destination so long as it took him away.

Tradecraft dictated he switch buses a couple of times before he eventually found himself in Dallas, Texas. He booked himself into an anonymous hotel near the airport, took one of the longest showers of his life, and slept for twelve straight hours. When he woke, he ate breakfast in his room while his clothes were being laundered, feeling very much like a new man.

Only then did he check in with Roland d'Avejan. As expected, his employer wasn't pleased with the news Coetzer related.

"Amelia Earhart?" d'Avejan scoffed after spewing profanities for a solid minute. "She had to be lying."

"That's what she said, and by that point she was no longer capable of holding anything back from me."

There was a pause. Coetzer could sense that the Frenchman wanted to ask how he could be certain but was hesitant to know the details. Instead he asked, "What about the American who has been such a thorn in our side?"

"Philip Mercer? I have every reason to believe he is dead, *meneer.*"

"But you did not see him die?"

"That is correct. The last time I saw him he was trapped in a house that was being swept down a river. Moments after I left him I saw the house smash into a bridge. It was totally destroyed. However, until his body is recovered I will always assume that he somehow managed to survive."

"Your famous caution?" This was said with some snide derision.

"It has kept me alive while so many of my comrades have fallen," Coetzer replied without rancor.

He recognized that his employer was still seething mad and just wanted to goad somebody so he would feel in control again. Coetzer kept regular tabs on d'Avejan and several other key people at Eurodyne, in case he ever needed leverage. He was aware, therefore, of d'Avejan's escalating OCD and suspected that as soon as the call ended, the Frenchman would step into his en suite shower and sear his body with custom-made acidic soap. He supposed this behavior was preferable to beating his wife or mistress, but the fetish unnerved Coetzer.

D'Avejan grunted. "I guess we will have to make do with the sample passed down to me through my family, and the shard you recovered in the mine in Minnesota. Along with the artificial crystal we managed to grow in the lab we can go forward, but it will take a great deal more time for the effects to become noticeable. And that always leads to the possibility that we will be discovered."

"That explains the need for the *Zhukovsky*?" Coetzer knew the true purpose behind the shell company called Luck Dragon had been to shield the stockholders from knowing they had purchased a mothballed Soviet-era research ship. "Because she can remain at sea she will be much harder to detect than a land-based antenna array."

"That is correct," d'Avejan said. "Also, she is nuclear powered, so she is one hundred percent self-sufficient. No one can track her power usage from a grid and ask why we are using so many megawatts of electricity. Once we start operations, the change will be slow but steady, and most importantly the atmosphere will react exactly as the climate models predicted. In ten months or so, the world will once again clamor for Eurodyne's products."

Coetzer allowed d'Avejan's words to echo uninterrupted for a moment. "Beaming energy into the sky to raise the world's average temperature seems dangerous to me, *meneer*."

"The energy itself does nothing. The change is created in the way the energy is channeled through the crystals and affects the magnetic fields around the earth. By marginally strengthening the fields, we will allow fewer cosmic rays to penetrate the atmosphere and help seed cloud formation. Because of their albedo properties, clouds reflect sunlight back into space and reduce planetary heat absorption. Fewer cosmic rays mean fewer clouds, which means Earth's temperature will start to rise after a nearly two-decade-long pause. Scientists have been unable to explain why this happened, but now they won't have to.

"Climate change will once again become a dominant issue, and not just among the Western elites. When the thermometer really starts to rise, everyone will demand their governments do something. Europe, America. China. It doesn't matter where. They will all feel the heat, so to speak. Coal markets will collapse while investments in wind and solar will double, triple even, and Eurodyne will be right there to fill the need.

"But more important than our stock price is the fact that mankind will actually confront the realities of global warming and deal with the issue once and for all. Levels of carbon pollution will actually go down, and the catastrophic rise in temperature so long predicted will never materialize. When enough of the world's energy needs are met with renewables, we will dial back the beam transmitted from the *Zhukovsky,* cloud cover will return to normal, and the excess heat we helped generate will dissipate. Like a vaccine, we will give the world a mild dose of global warming so that nations can build a real defense against it."

"So there is no real danger?"

"I am not a scientist," d'Avejan said. "But I've been told the Americans have a system called HAARP in Alaska that fiddles with the upper atmosphere and magnetic fields all the time to no great detriment. I have been assured our system is not dissimilar. It would have been better if we had been able to find the original cache of gems, but our artificial ones will have to do."

"I tried my best, Monsieur d'Avejan, but the stones have been lost for all time."

"Yes, well, there are things even beyond my control. Take a few days for yourself and return to Paris by week's end."

"Yes, sir. I will be in the office Monday."

"And Niklaas," d'Avejan added, "even though you failed to find the stones, you managed to double the amount of natural crystal at our disposal, and I will not forget that. I will see to it that some sort of bonus is forthcoming."

"Thank you, *meneer*."

"See you next week."

Coetzer hung up the phone and immediately called the airlines. Before returning to Paris he had another destination in mind. He held on the line until a customer service representative asked him where he wished to travel.

"Washington, D.C.," he replied. Hanging around the Midwest to see if Mercer's body was discovered was not an appealing prospect. He planned to confirm Mercer's fate much more directly.

20

Mercer came through the door as tired as he'd ever been in his life. His body was sore from the punishment it had taken over the past week, and the clothes he'd bought at a discount store near the National Guard staging area were as itchy as fiberglass. He wanted nothing more than a shower and some serious rack time. What he got was a blur launching itself at him before he had time to react. A warm mouth was pressed to his and the elasticity of firm breasts was mashed against his chest.

"Don't say a word," Jordan breathed into him. She was panting with desire. "On the pool table. Right now."

"Harry?"

"He's at Tiny's." She had his shirt open and her tongue on his skin while her hands were working on his belt.

His pants loosened, Jordan maneuvered them both so the backs of her thighs were pressed against the billiards table's rail. She thumbed down the sweatpants she'd been wearing and her panties as well. Mercer freed himself of his boots and legged out of his khakis. Their mouths parted for the barest moment it took Jordan to pull the T-shirt over her head. Her arm was out of the sling, but the quick movement made her wince. Rather than pause, the pain goaded her so that she ground herself against Mercer's leg.

Coming off a long winter, her nude body was pale and without tan lines. She was athletic but not too thin, with womanly curves as beautiful as any sculpture. Mercer's hands roamed her body, tweaking and gently pinching in places that made her squirm and moan. Frantic, she guided him inside her and his exhaustion sloughed away. They were not gentle, but ravenous and uncaring about anything but the carnal pleasure of the act. When it was over, Jordan lay sprawled across the green felt, her breasts high, her nipples so stiff they ached, and her lower body quivering with aftershocks.

"Wow," she finally said. "We have to do that again."

He smiled down at her. "I'm not twenty. I need some time."

"I'll feed you oysters . . . and red meat for stamina," she promised, a rapturous smile on her face. He helped her to her feet and she swayed against him, her eyes half closed. "You're good at that."

"I've been practicing by myself since I was about thirteen, and with other women since my senior year of high school."

She slapped him playfully and gathered up her clothes. "I'll meet you in the bar in a minute. Make me a mojito. There's mint in the fridge, and then I want you to tell me everything that's happened since you left."

He gave her more than a minute and used the time to shower quickly and change into some comfortable jeans and a black polo shirt. He was waiting in the bar with a Heineken in his hand when she emerged from the guest bedroom. She had washed her face and applied some artful makeup. She wore the same sweats but had changed shirts. By the way she moved he knew she wasn't wearing a bra.

The oysters she mentioned wouldn't be necessary.

She kissed him on the fly, scooped up her drink, and flopped onto the couch. "I feel like I've been impaled. Thank you."

"No . . . thank *you*," he replied, and saluted her with the distinctive green bottle. "How's your arm?"

"Better, thanks. I should have it in the sling, but I'm sick of it. Tell me all about your trip. Was Afghanistan awful?"

"It's not the worst place I've been," Mercer admitted, and moved to a chair next to her. "But not too far off, either. The rough part was that the men who attacked us at Abe's house were a step ahead; they had deployed a force in Afghanistan by the time we arrived at the cave."

"What? How is that possible?"

"I spoke with Sherman Smithson about that. He told me the terrorists interrogated him the day before yesterday, and they let slip that they had learned about the cave's location and Herbert Hoover's involvement with the lightning stones from documents they recovered from Abe's office."

"Before we got there?"

"I didn't think they had the time to do much of a search. I guess I was wrong."

"Were you ambushed?"

Mercer nodded. "It was a little hairy. Apart from their assault rifles these guys were packing mortars and RPGs. If not for Booker Sykes and his men, they would have killed me for sure."

Jordan had gone a little ashen, but her voice was firm. "Mercer, you have to stop this. You're putting your life in danger. For what? Some rocks? Revenge? Are those things worth dying for?"

"It doesn't much matter now anyway," he told her.

"Why's that?"

"Because I also learned that Mike Dillman tried to have the rest of the crystals flown back to the United States. Only they never arrived."

"How can you be sure?"

"They were aboard Amelia Earhart's Lockheed Electra when she went down over the Pacific Ocean in 1937."

"Whoa. Amelia Earhart? Really?"

"'Fraid so. Unless someone's willing to fund a multimillion-dollar search with no guarantees for success, the crystals, and Miss Earhart, will remain forever lost."

"Hmm . . . so that means you and I have some time to get to know each other a little better. I have to admit I've been mooning about like a teenage girl since you left."

"Mooning? I think I like that."

She smiled shyly. "There's something about you, Mercer. You're . . . different. I find I want to know all about you. Do you have family? What your favorite movie is. Everything."

The doorbell rang.

Mercer stood. "I guess we don't have the time to get to know each other, after all."

Her eyebrows knitted. "Sure we do. Whoever it is, send them away."

He walked to the library overlooking the front atrium and shouted, "It's open." The door swung in and Mercer watched two people enter. Both wore suits. He waved them up and he rejoined Jordan.

"Who is it?" she asked. He said nothing. A look of concern spread across Jordan's face. "Mercer, what's going on?"

"Her story didn't hold up," he said gravely.

"What are you talking about? Whose story?" Jordan had pulled the steamship blanket up to her shoulders.

"The girl whose car hit Agent Hepburn's. Her story. At first it seemed fine—she was a Starbucks employee and a student at Maryland, so the fact that she was on the road and rammed into Kelly's sedan sounded like a plausible accident. But other things have been bothering me, so I phoned Kelly Hepburn's partner yesterday from Iowa and begged him to look a little deeper."

"And I did," Special Agent Nate Lowell said as he stepped into the rec room. He removed his sunglasses and folded them into his suit pocket. Entering behind him, on crutches, was Kelly Hepburn. Her head was swathed in crisp bandages and her leg was in a tall plaster cast.

She smiled at Mercer and said, "It turns out that the girl, Samantha Rhodes, constantly chats with friends on her cell phone while driving from work to school. We pulled those records and saw from the tower pings that she always drives a route to class that's a half mile from where she hit me."

Lowell took up the story. "I leaned on her to explain why she'd taken a different route, and I told her she targeted Kelly on purpose. She said no, but I started yelling and playing all that bad cop shit."

Mercer suspected he loved playing the bad cop.

"I don't understand," Jordan said. "What are you saying?"

"I am saying that Samantha quickly broke down and confessed. She was paid by an organization she works for to target Kelly Hepburn. They even let her borrow an SUV so she wouldn't get hurt."

"What?! What organization is it?"

"Just knock it off, Jordan," Mercer snapped. "She worked for the Earth Action League. You work for them too, I suspect." Jordan looked at him incredulously. "I should have listened to my damned gut at the very beginning, back at Abe's house. I thought I heard footsteps upstairs when I entered, but I wasn't sure. Then I found you asleep—but you'd been casing the house for your buddies, and threw off your clothes and hopped into bed and only pretended to be out. It was all an act. I'm assuming you were picked to search his place in case things went wrong down in the mine because you actually did know Abe when you were young, and he and your father did teach together."

Jordan said nothing.

"The Honda Fit we chased was your car, wasn't it? Who was the driver? A boyfriend or just a comrade in arms?"

She refused to answer. It didn't matter. She was up to her neck with these freaks. Mercer plowed on. "Things got a little dicey at Hardt College with bullets flying everywhere and men holding guns to your head, but you never broke your cover. You played it perfectly. And when it was all said and done, I believed you were as much a target in all of this as I was, and all of a sudden the opposing side had a spy living in my goddamned guest room." He slapped the coffee table and Jordan winced, but she would not meet his eye.

"You told them what we found in Abe's trash. How this linked to Herbert Hoover. You fed them the coordinates I got from Sherman Smithson. That's how they knew to hire the local fighters and have them in position to ambush us when we found the cave. When we escaped, your people then did what I had already planned to do. They went to the Hoover Library to find out if there were any other possible leads that Smithson hadn't thought of. There was. A woman named Veronica Butler. A woman I saw kidnapped, and who I presume is dead right now."

Jordan took that news like a slap.

Mercer went on, coldly dispassionate. "I thought it odd that the team leader let Smithson live. They gunned down Abe and his colleagues, so why not just shoot Smithson too? Odder still was the fact the gunmen told him that they had found a lot of information in Abe's office. They made a point of telling him that, I think, because that piece of information was supposed to get back to me. It was a plant, a plausible explanation as to why they kept in step with my own search. They were making sure I never came to suspect the real source of their information.

"What's funny," Mercer said to the two FBI agents, "is that I remembered Jordan telling me she'd lost her cell phone when Abe's house burned, so I checked my home phone records after the ambush in Afghanistan. I wasn't suspicious of her, just thorough. There was nothing but numbers I recognized. She hadn't contacted anyone.

"Then this morning on the flight from Des Moines I saw in a magazine the same plastic bracelet Jordan's been wearing since we met. I remember it jangling her first night here when she was petting Drag. Only now I know it's the latest-gen smartwatch that doubles as a cell. She's been in touch with her people all along."

Jordan kept her silence.

"What I don't understand is why target me?" Kelly Hepburn asked. "You specifically told them I was lead on this investigation so they would try to kill me. Why? It wasn't like we had any clues. Nate and I were stalled."

When Jordan remained stubbornly mute, Mercer said, "I imagine she was standing just outside of this room that first night when you two burst in here like Rambo and Ripley from the *Alien* movies. We thought she was asleep, but she must have heard something to set off an alarm. Or maybe she figured without you, I'd be completely cut out of the investigation. I think you said something along those lines when we had dinner here."

"And without your help," Hepburn said, nodding at the logic, "the FBI's investigation wasn't going anywhere."

"Why?" Mercer asked Jordan. "There are people dead over this, you were shot at and could have been killed. You asked me if what I was doing was worth dying for. I'm asking you the same thing."

"Am I under arrest?" Jordan asked. Her voice was much harder than Mercer had ever heard it, and he wondered if he was hearing the real Jordan Weismann for the first time.

"Not yet," Kelly said.

Jordan looked at all three of them before saying, "Then I'm not saying a freaking word."

"Fine." Kelly nodded to her partner. "Nate, do the honors."

The big agent crossed the room. He had the presence of mind to yank Jordan off the couch by her uninjured arm. "Jordan Weismann, you are under arrest for conspiracy to commit the murder of a federal agent." She yelped when he crossed her wrists behind her back and slapped on a pair of stainless-steel cuffs.

"You have the right to remain silent. Anything you do say . . ." He rattled off a rapid-fire Miranda warning. "Do you understand these rights as I have explained them to you?"

"Go to hell, you fascist pig."

Mercer shook his head sadly. "I think I know what this is about." Lowell and Hepburn turned to him. "She and I got into an argument over global warming before I left, and I got a glimpse of what a fanatic she is—so certain in her beliefs that dissent can't be tolerated. I've been saying for years that the topic of climate change is no longer about science or policy, but moral imperative. Some believe they're saving the planet, and anyone who doesn't recognize the rightness of their crusade becomes an impediment. This then becomes de facto justification for almost any action. Whenever you read about the climate you see words like *may, might,* or *potentially.* Weasel words that have no place in real science. But soon these caveats get dumped in the name of expediency, and people are left with the impression that climatologists can actually predict the weather in a hundred years."

"The science *is* settled, you son of a bitch," Jordan snapped. "Ninety-seven percent of climatologists agree that—"

Mercer cut her off. "What do they agree on, Jordan? That the earth is warming. The number who agree with that should be one hundred percent, not ninety-seven. That humans have contributed to that warming. Again it had better be one hundred percent, or those three percenters are complete fools who don't understand what the science really says. But what about stating that the current warming is unprecedented? That it is dangerous? That we have to suspend all industries that use fossil fuels or risk the planet turning into a burned-out husk? Do you really think ninety-seven scientists out of a hundred agree in lockstep with what are essentially either points of policy or individual assessments of risk?

"The ninety-seven percent I hear tossed around is as worthless as when someone tells you that a particular year is one-hundredth of a degree hotter than any other because of global warming. That's statistical noise, not proof of the need to decarbonize our society."

"You're just a denier, Mercer," she said. "You patronize me and say I take the truth of climate change on faith, but you dismiss it simply because it stands in the way of all your fossil fuel cronies who want to frack the whole planet."

"I never said I denied anything," Mercer replied. "But you have accepted the climate dogma without question. I was once pretty sure science would win out in the end, and the belief that the planet is doomed if we don't return to the eighteenth century would be reexamined in light of new research. Now? Climatology has been hijacked by politicians and environmental activists, and I'm not so sure sanity will ever prevail.

"And remember, you and your people have been willing to kill others in order to promote a scientific theory . . . one that is still in its infancy. If that's not the definition of blind faith, I don't know what is."

The room was quiet for several long moments, before Nate Lowell finally said, "So what now?"

"Now we build our case against Jordan and the girl who tried to kill me with her car," Agent Hepburn said, "and we investigate the Earth Action League. I'm sure they'll deny direct involvement with these two, but it's worth a shot, I suppose." Jordan just stood near the couch, staring straight ahead.

"And what about you, Mercer?" Kelly asked.

"Me? Oh, I have the easier job, by far. I'm going to find Amelia Earhart's missing plane, and I'm going to do it within"—he looked up as if actually calculating something—"three days."

"Bullshit," Lowell said.

"Watch me."

"Nate, take Miss Weismann to the car. I want to talk to Mercer. I'll be down in a minute."

"Excuse me, bitch," Jordan snarled. "I don't have shoes or a bra."

Kelly replied sweetly, "Sorry, dearie, I hadn't noticed. I'll gather your belongings."

"You can't touch my stuff without a search warrant."

"Well, since Mercer paid for it and it is in his house, it's his stuff, not yours. All I need is his permission." She looked over at him and Mercer nodded. "There. I'll bring it out to you."

"Jordan," Mercer called as Lowell was leading

her out. "For the record I did you a favor by not telling you I was going to Iowa, so you wouldn't report it back to your masters. That's one less conspiracy charge you'll face. I recommend you cooperate with the FBI, and maybe you can avoid going to jail."

"And I recommend you go to hell."

Mercer turned his attention back to Kelly, rolling his eyes at Jordan's obstinacy. "Good to see you back on your feet, so to speak."

"I'm not medically cleared yet, but I wouldn't have missed this for the world."

"What are the docs saying?"

"I'm in the leg cast for five weeks, which already sucks after just a few days."

"And your noggin?"

"Concussion. My vision was blurry for a day and I had the mother of all headaches, but as long as I don't get another tap on the head I'll be fine."

"How much of your hair did they have to shave?"

"Enough that I'll be wearing hats once the bandages come off." She looked at Mercer with a funny grin. "You know it was the boobs, right?"

"Excuse me?"

"Come on, Mercer, it was Jordan's boobs. That's why you didn't suspect her, or if you did, you ignored your gut. It's kind of pathetic . . . but I can't say as I blame you. They are very impressive. Either nature was kind to her or she dropped thirty grand at a Beverly Hills plastic surgeon's office—and if you say which is correct, I will tear off one of your arms and beat you with it."

Mercer grinned, not fully denying her accusation. "I'm sure there was more to it than just that."

"There's a reason it's the oldest trick in the book.

It works. Me, on the other hand, I didn't trust her from the moment I laid eyes on her."

"Woman's intuition?"

"Call it whatever you like, but I knew she was hiding something behind that rocking bod and pretty face."

"And me? Was my little head doing the thinking for me?"

"You're a man, Mercer. The software can't override the hardware." Kelly winced at her own bad turn of phrase. "I did not just say that."

Mercer laughed. "And I didn't hear it."

"Anyway, I truly think Jordan told her handlers to have me targeted because she felt I was onto her. She had you wrapped around her finger, and Nate wasn't a factor since he thought this whole case was a waste of time, but I was a danger to her."

"Makes sense," he agreed.

"Also, if I am being honest, I think she saw me as a rival too, and wanted me out of the picture."

"That's ridiculous, Kelly."

"Don't be dense. You know what I mean—and while you might have just showered, she absolutely reeks of sex, Mercer." Before he could say anything, Kelly Hepburn put up her hands. "I'm not here to judge."

Mercer started to speak, but was at a genuine loss for words. All that came out was a laugh.

Then it was Kelly's turn to laugh. "You're *so* predictable . . . In fact, I think you're already considering asking me out on a date."

"I am?"

"You are, but I wouldn't do it until your house no longer smells like the last woman who was here."

"Duly noted."

"And make sure not to ask in front of Nate. He's a little overprotective . . . which explains why he plays macho asshole whenever he's around you."

"Also noted. Anything else?"

"My favorites are Thai and French, and unless you're triple-jointed or own a Jaws of Life you aren't getting anywhere with me until after the cast comes off . . . maybe. Now I have to go. Walk me out."

Mercer had to admit, she had grabbed his attention.

They started out of the room, and Kelly paused at the top of the stairs, leaning against her crutches. She looked Mercer in the eye. "Nate was right, wasn't he? About it being bullshit you're going to find Amelia Earhart's plane?"

A conflicted look crossed Mercer's face. He held up a finger to his lips to indicate Kelly should be quiet. "Yeah," he said. "It was bullshit. Amelia Earhart will never be found. I like yanking your partner's chain." He leaned in close enough to smell the shampoo Agent Hepburn used on her hair. It was a scent he decided he liked, and he whispered, "It occurred to me that Jordan had the run of my house for more than a week. It could be bugged."

She gave him a look that told him she hadn't thought of that, but should have. She asked casually, "So, what's next for you?"

He led her out, walking in front of her when they got to the stairs. Because of how they spiraled, Kelly had to take them especially slow. "I'm going to scour the Internet looking for a set of Jaws of Life," Mercer replied.

"Funny."

"I thought so." They crossed the foyer and Mercer opened the door for her. From the top of the stoop he scanned the street. Nothing appeared out of the ordinary. His Jag was where it should be. Traffic was normal, and he didn't see anyone sitting in a car watching the brownstone. He did spot Nate Lowell bent over the open rear door of his government sedan, presumably talking to Jordan.

"Do you think it is bugged?"

"It's possible," Mercer said. "She has contacts in the area with enough juice to stage that car accident."

"So, Earhart—are you serious?"

"I am. I'll know roughly where she went down in just a couple of days, tops. Physically finding the plane will probably take longer."

Kelly Hepburn already had her phone out of her jacket pocket.

"What are you doing?"

"Calling Nate. I'm still on medical leave, so I can't call in a team to sweep your house. He can."

"Put that away," Mercer said. "You'll tip our hand more than my gaffe a second ago about finding the plane. Maybe if my place is bugged they'll believe I was bullshitting about the plane in order to irk your partner."

Kelly saw the wisdom in that and slid her phone back into her inside pocket.

"Do you want protection?" she asked.

"No. I don't think it's necessary. For someone like Jordan, or the girl that crashed into you, this is a crusade. A way to prove their commitment to the cause. To the men above, I suspect money is the real motivation. There's no need to waste more on me if they believe the trail's cold."

"Okay," Agent Hepburn said, though she looked a little dubious. "So we'll be in touch in the next day or so, when there's something to report."

"Right-o," said Mercer.

Hepburn was right to be leery of his seeming disinterest in hunting down the remaining killers. Had she known Mercer better, she would have realized that he had been on the defensive for far too long, and was now ready to take the fight to his enemies.

21

Over the next forty-eight hours, Mercer put on an act. He left the brownstone only once, to accompany Harry to Tiny's for a few drinks the second night, but other than that he busied himself at home. He polished all the brass accents in the bar. He caught up on some job offers, declining four and requesting additional information about another. Mostly, he made sure his behavior and conversations gave the appearance that he had given up any hope of finding the remaining crystals of Sample 681. He had indeed found two bugs planted in his house—one affixed under the edge of the bar and the other near his desk in his office, and Mercer was putting on a convincing show for whoever was listening in.

Agent Hepburn had sent him a text offering to post guards, but again Mercer declined, explaining that it would draw undue attention. It was better, he said, that the entire affair die for lack of interest.

That didn't mean he wasn't also making preparations. These he had actually started back in Kabul following their return from the cave. He had instructed one of the Gen-D Systems mechanics on how to build a proper Faraday cage for the sample he'd taken from the dead swami's mouth. The makeshift contraption he'd cobbled together in the field showed he was on the right track, but he wanted to have something a bit better before transporting it.

The crystal had arrived in Washington, D.C., at the same time Mercer was landing in Des Moines. All of the photographs and notes he'd taken on the grotto/geode in the cave had preceded the package and had doubtlessly already been analyzed to death by perhaps the smartest person Mercer knew. Jason Rutland was his name, and he worked in Greenbelt, Maryland, at the Goddard Space Flight Center, a sprawling campus off the Capital Beltway that housed perhaps the nation's greatest concentration of scientists and engineers outside of Silicon Valley. Mercer had met Jason several years earlier, working on a different project, and Rutland had amazed Mercer with his brilliance, both in the laboratory and with his analytical skills. Breaking all stereotypes of the nerdy science genius, Jason was as slick as they came. He wore stylish clothes, drove a classic Ford Mustang, and was currently dating, in Harry's estimation, the sexiest weather girl on any of the local news stations. Even Harry, the aging lothario, had been tongue-tied when the four of them had bumped into one another at Pimlico for the Preakness Stakes.

For the last three days, Jason had been sending Mercer regular text updates on his findings as he followed a hunch Mercer had given him. That hunch now looked more and more likely to pan out. It was on the morning of the third day, long before sunup, that Jason's latest text came through. It read simply: "Found her."

Mercer got the message when he woke at six, and he felt the surge of adrenaline. Minutes later he was sitting on his bar stool, making sure he was positioned closest to the bug Jordan had planted, and he dialed Rutland at home. The machine picked up. Mercer started leaving a message, but Jason's hurried voice rang through the line. "Sorry about that. I wasn't screening calls. I just got out of the shower."

"Even if you were screening, I made the cut, so you don't need to apologize."

"Hey, good point. Never thought of that." Jason was excited and speaking way too fast, a clear indication he'd gotten little sleep in the past few days. "I can't believe you did it, Mercer. I mean, Amelia Earhart . . . after all these years. Are you sure she crashed near—"

Mercer cut him off before he could say anything more. "Not over the phone! You know better than most that the NSA records every call placed in the D.C. area."

"Take it easy. You think the government cares about her?"

"I think the fewer people who know about this the better, because whoever finds her plane is going to become a household name." He then added for the extra ears that might be listening in, "Funding that trip to Afghanistan tapped me out, so it's going to take me at least a year to mount an expedition to the South Pacific."

"Ah. Okay, then. Mum's the word."

"Thanks. Can you meet me?"

"Sure. Where?"

"Someplace public, but safe."

"Pentagon Metro stop."

Mercer knew it. This particular subway stop was right at the entrance to one of the most heavily defended buildings in the world. "Perfect. What time's good for you?"

"I was just about to crash. I'm beat. How about late this afternoon—say five o'clock? No, make it six. That gets us past the worst of the rush."

"Okay. Six o'clock at the Pentagon Metro stop, right by the building's entrance."

"I'll bring all my findings."

"Not that ridiculous man purse of yours."

"It's not a purse," Rutland protested. "Felicia calls it a satchel."

"Felicia can call it a kumquat for all I care, it's still a purse."

"Eff you," Jason said, hanging up. Mercer clicked off his cell with a sly grin.

It was a nice enough day, and the Pentagon was close enough that Mercer decided to walk partway when the time came. There was just enough breeze for him to throw on a khaki Beretta shooting jacket. Holstered at his spine was one of their signature 9mm's, the Model 92. He left his house with plain white earbuds stretching down to the phone he'd stuffed into one of the coat's numerous pockets.

Mercer walked casually, glancing into the glass office windows of the buildings beyond his block of townhomes. In their reflections he saw no obvious signs of a tail, but his instincts told him he was being watched. He could feel the eyes on him.

An elderly man in a fedora and rumpled suit stepped out of one of the office buildings, raising an arm to get the attention of a driver parked at the curb. The two men exchanged a greeting as the rumpled guy slid into the passenger seat. Traffic was snarled enough that they got only a few feet before being forced to stop. For the next two blocks it seemed the car and Mercer were in a slow-speed chase, neither getting much ahead of the other. The traffic lights cycled from green to red so quickly that only a few cars could squirt through the nearly gridlocked intersections.

The two men ignored him on the sidewalk and conversed casually enough for Mercer to put them out of his mind and scan other places for a watcher.

The car turned at the next cross street, the driver accelerating hard to get away from the worst of the traffic in an annoyed display.

Mercer walked ten yards past the Pentagon City Station and turned so suddenly that he almost plowed over a diminutive Chinese woman and her even tinier mother. He paid them no attention, his face the picture of annoyance at himself because he'd apparently walked past his destination, but his eyes were watchful for anyone caught off guard by his sudden reversal. No one seemed startled or upset, other than the two people he'd nearly trampled.

He descended into the city's subway.

He fished a SmarTrip Metro card from his wallet, touched it to the scan pad, and passed through the turnstile. Built in time for the nation's bicentennial, the Metro stations still possessed a futuristic feel that made one think the trains entering and exiting were headed to distant planets, rather than other stops along the Blue or Yellow Line. When the train came, he loitered on the platform until the bell sounded and the doors were about to hiss closed, before jumping aboard.

Once again no one paid him the slightest attention. He began to have doubts. What if the listeners at the other end of the bugs in his house had given up after Jordan's arrest, and he was putting on a performance for an audience that wasn't there? He hated to think his elaborate plan was for naught, but on the other hand, if his adversaries had given up, that opened the door for him to work unimpeded.

It also meant that he'd forever lost his chance to find out who, and what, was behind Abe Jacobs's murder.

That was a personal failure he would not contemplate, and so he refocused on the task at hand. He checked his TAG. He had timed this perfectly. The appointed hour was just a minute away, and the subway was decelerating as it approached the Pentagon stop. The platform was crowded with commuters, many in civilian attire, many others in the uniforms of the four major military branches.

Mercer stepped into the press of humanity on the dimly lit platform, looking for Jason, but also watching for anything suspicious. He figured that of the original five-person team he'd encountered in the Leister Deep Mine, he had killed one in the Lauder Science Center at Hardt College, and another in Roni Butler's kitchen, so he was looking for two perfect strangers and the leader—the man whose posture, walk, and movements he would know in an instant. It was an odd feeling. He'd gotten only a few fleeting glimpses of the guy, but it felt like he'd been studying the gunman for years.

He saw nothing except harried commuters wanting to get home. As he exited the platform, within sight of the entrance to the Pentagon itself, he felt a quick movement behind him. It was the rumpled guy from the car that he'd spotted earlier. He must have phoned in a description to someone already here at the station. The man made a hand signal over the heads of the streaming commuters. Mercer whirled in time to see Jason. The NASA scientist saw him too and raised a hand in greeting.

"Jason! No!"

It was too late. Jason had been spotted, and no sooner did he lower his hand than a shape slid through the crowd the way a shark parts a shoal of fish, and Jason's leather satchel had been cut free of its sling. The shape moved on, leaving Jason in its wake, a surprised look on his face at the audacity of such a blatant robbery. He looked ready to give chase.

"No, Jason. Stop," Mercer shouted as he himself was about to launch into a run to catch the thief. He felt something hard ram into his kidney and dig a little into his flesh. It took no imagination to know it was the barrel of a snub-nosed revolver.

"Leave it be, or I drop you and take my chances in the confusion." The voice was a Brooklyn cliché.

There was no way this old guy had been part of the assault team at the mine. Mercer tried to turn to get a better look at the man's face. His earlier impression was a bad shave, sallow skin, and drooping eyes. As had been intended, Mercer could better describe the hat the man wore than his features. Whoever he was, Mercer realized he was good at this.

"I'm putting a pair of zip cuffs in your hand." Mercer felt the wiry length of plastic press against his palm. "Secure them around your ankles."

When he bent to comply, Mercer felt his Beretta being lifted from its pancake holster. It was a good thing he wasn't sentimental about guns, because that one was about the fourth or fifth he'd lost. The gunman stayed close enough that no one rushing by them saw or suspected a thing.

"Thanks for the piece," the New Yorker said.

Mercer straightened, and he was abruptly shoved from behind. The plastic tie around his ankles meant he fell like a sawn-down tree and took the brunt of the impact on his hands, wrists, and arms. A woman gasped at his collapse. Mercer turned to see the rumpled suit and cheesy gangster hat vanish out of the building lobby. He moved well for an older man.

"Are you okay?" a pretty petty officer in navy camouflage asked. She looked more closely and saw the white plastic band securing Mercer's legs together. She got suspicious. "What's going on?"

"Remember the 'knockout game' from a couple of years ago?" Mercer said, feigning anger. "I think this is similar. I felt something around my ankle, then someone pushed me. Down I went." He fished into his pocket for a folding pocketknife. The blade easily sliced through the plastic.

She helped him to his feet. "Do you want me to get an MP?"

"No," Mercer said. "It was just some stupid kids who are long gone. Thank you for your help."

"My pleasure, sir," she replied and headed off without a backward glance.

By then Jason had made his way over. He looked a little pale. Mercer asked, "Are you all right?"

"Never been mugged before. Don't like that feeling one bit."

Mercer straightened one of his earbuds so the integrated microphone was close to his lips. "Book, you got him?"

Jason's expression registered surprise.

"Oh yeah," Mercer heard over his cell connection to Sykes. "It was a skinny white kid wearing baggies like a gangbanger. Dumbass nearly tripped on those stupid pants coming up the escalator. Wait a second . . . what kind of car did you tag earlier?"

"Six-year-old silver Caddie. That's what the older guy got into."

"Bingo. Kid just dove into a silver STS. Pennsylvania plates, but two'll get you ten it's a rental from Dulles."

"I'm in on that action. The rumpled guy sounded like he's from Brooklyn—bet they came down on the JFK-to-Reagan shuttle. That's where they rented the Caddie." He hadn't even noticed the kid in the Cadillac's backseat. They must have been a professional black bag crew, most likely hired as outside contractors to supply and monitor the bugs, and then tasked today with the robbery.

Mercer was casually scanning the crowd when his blood turned cold.

The team leader. The animal Mercer had vowed to put down.

He was there watching the whole thing, looking down onto the subway from the top of the escalator. The man was mostly shadow from this distance, but Mercer recognized the tilt to his head and the way he carried his shoulders. He must have been waiting for Mercer to recognize him, because he gave a mocking wave and vanished from sight.

Mercer cursed into the microphone. "Book, guy at the top of the escalators." He pushed his way to the mechanical stairs. Normally Washingtonians are conditioned to stay to the right if they intend to stand so others can climb the escalator on the left, but such niceties vanished during rush hour, leaving the entire breadth of the escalator blocked.

Booker Sykes heard the panic in Mercer's voice. "What guy?" he asked crisply. "Describe him. There are dozens."

"My height, white, medium/large build. I don't know hair color or what he's wearing."

Sykes was positioned in a room at the nearby Double-Tree hotel, glassing the Pentagon through some borrowed special-ops binoculars. He wasn't looking for a man who fit the description; there were too many. Instead he looked for someone moving fast through the crowd—and there were none. "No one like that's drawing attention, Mercer. The Caddie is pulling away. You sure you don't want it followed?"

"Positive. But we can end this now if you find that guy." Mercer did his best to bull his way up the escalator, but he was making poor progress, and earning a lot of angry looks.

"I still have no illicit movement. There must be a hundred people out here and twenty buses. He could have jumped onto any of them."

Mercer stopped fighting, sagged a little. He'd been defeated and he knew it. The man wouldn't give himself away by running from the scene. He'd come here to taunt Mercer, show him how big his organization was, to brag that they could get muscle down here from New York, and finally to vanish without a trace as the ultimate insult.

Mercer let the escalator deposit him on street level and he stepped aside so others could get off. Behind him was the massif that was the Pentagon, while ahead were acres of parking and a bus loading/unloading plaza that was still crowded even now. He had come here with a plan, and it had worked. Getting at the leader would have been a coup, but it was not meant to be. He would just have to be satisfied that the trap he had set was sprung so quickly.

He scanned the bus loading plaza. Book was right. There were dozens of Metrobuses, and as three left the terminal two more arrived to pick up the queues of tired commuters.

He looked for the man, peering over the heads of people to see passengers in the window seats on the buses. Commuters swirled around him in a co-ordinated ballet to cram as close together as possible while maintaining personal distance. It was a delicate act. Mercer continued to look as one man to his right clicked off a Bluetooth headset and turned toward him. Mercer was barely aware of the commuter, but then the man quickly spun into him with a powerful jerk of his shoulders, a fist held just below Mercer's sternum.

The knife was a classic killing weapon, with a six-inch blade of blackened steel and a thin handle so it was concealable. A proper strike should slice under Mercer's rib cage, cleave through his diaphragm, pierce a lung, and, with an upward jerk and twist, shred his heart. And this had been a proper strike.

The impact forced Mercer to double over, and his hands instinctively went to the point where he'd been struck. In the first microseconds after the blow he wasn't sure what had happened, only that he felt a dull pain exploding from under his chest. Mercer's fingers found those of the man who'd barreled into him, and something razor sharp, too.

In another instant he figured out what had happened, and Mercer wrapped the man's hands in both of his, and squeezed with everything he had.

Not knowing what to expect on this outing, Mercer had worn a Kevlar vest he'd gotten from Booker. Jason was wearing one, too. Mercer wore his beneath the Beretta shooting jacket. While most bulletproof garments are susceptible to knife thrusts, this one had a double weave that prevented blades from penetrating. The knife had stopped dead and because it didn't have a protective hilt, the man's hand had slipped from the handle onto the blade—and before he could pull away, Mercer clamped his own hands around the knife wielder's fingers and squeezed.

Mercer quickly released his grip and brushed past the guy before anyone around noticed that something horrifying had just occurred. He was fifteen feet away and still striding before the attacker's nervous system registered what had just happened. He raised his painful hand to the air, his eyes going wide while the knife clattered to the ground. A jet of dark arterial blood spurted in a spray that caught one woman across the face and spattered against another's dress uniform.

Like nearly everyone else, Mercer turned back when he heard the woman's horrified scream. He saw his assailant's raised hand through the crowd, his wrist clamped off with his good hand but blood continuing to bubble and drip from the nearly severed fingers and thumb, the digits flopping obscenely as he swayed. The man dropped to his knees. As the crowd closed off Mercer's view, he backed away.

"Book?" he called into the tiny mic.

"You're clean. All eyes are on that dude. What'd you do?"

"He tried to stab me, but that vest you got me stopped the blade. I sliced his fingers against his own blade."

"From here it looked like you practically de-gloved his hand." Booker Sykes was not squeamish, but even he made a disgusted sound at the spectacle down below.

"Watch for their lead guy, Book," Mercer chided. "That was another of his lackeys."

"You're still clean. I'm just a little queasy. That was nasty."

Mercer backed himself against a concrete planter so no one could come up behind him. His heart raced and his hands shook; had he not thought to wear the vest, he'd be dead. As it was, he had been so intent upon finding the leader that he never saw his subaltern until it was far too late. Mercer had gotten lucky ... and no matter how much he'd always depended on it, he still rebelled at the truth that chance plays such a large role in life.

Moments later Jason Rutland approached. He hadn't dashed up the escalator like a bull going after a matador's cape, the way Mercer had almost fatally been goaded into doing. Mercer hated himself for being so easily manipulated. Jason pointed back over his shoulder. "Someone got stabbed back there."

"It was one of them," Mercer spat. "I think it might have been the young guy driving the Honda back in Ohio. Come on, let's get out of here." MPs were already showing up to take control of the situation. Mercer led Rutland to the next bus in line, and the two boarded. It wasn't so crowded that Mercer couldn't check every passenger for the team leader. No one else got on.

Jason held up a flash drive shaped like a *Star Wars* character. "Here."

Mercer took it, smiling a little at the cartoonish face staring back at him. "This it?"

"Yup."

The bus lurched as it pulled away from the loading plaza. After thirty seconds, Sykes came over the radio to tell Mercer that no one was following the bus. They were clear. And he was leaving his observation post.

Mercer thanked him and pulled out the second earbud. He shoved it in his pocket. There was some blood on his shirt and jeans, but the spots were dark enough that no one seemed to notice. He adjusted his coat to better hide them anyway. "Talk to me."

"Are you okay?" Jason asked with genuine concern. He wasn't used to seeing Philip Mercer rattled.

"Fine. Even though everything went pretty much as I expected today, I still feel they pulled one on me, you know."

"Well, you almost got stabbed."

"Not that. The taunt. That effete little wave he gave me—as if to say his weakest effort is better than my best. It pissed me off."

"I'd still go with getting stabbed as the low point of my day, but to each his own . . ."

Mercer shook his head as if to clear it. "On to the important stuff. Tell me what you've got."

"Right," Jason said, unconvinced that Mercer could let the other stuff go, but understanding it was best to move on. "I calculated the volume of the geode from the pictures you took, like you asked. Then I weighed the sample you shipped from India and ran the numbers to come up with a range of weights for the crystals taken from the cave and loaded onto Amelia Earhart's Electra. I cross-matched this figure by examining each individual cell within the geode to get exact sizes for every crystal. That gave me the precise weight of gems. Considering the volume of stones and the need for some protective sheathing, the logical place to put them was in the plane's nose storage compartment. That gave me an approximate distance from the radio equipment as well as the navigational instruments."

"Okay so far."

"This was all pretty straightforward math, something you could have done yourself."

"I would've needed to take off my shoes and socks for some of the longer calculations," Mercer replied. "What next?"

"I modeled the electromagnetic variances induced by the crystal you gave me. That is some weird voodoo juju, by the way. I've never seen anything like it in my life."

"I don't think anyone has," Mercer remarked.

"Did you know it's just shy of a diamond's hardness on the Mohs scale?"

"No."

"And its electrical properties are all over the spectrum. Conductor, insulator, semi—heck, it could be a Josephson junction too for all I know. It also acts as a step-up amplifier in micropulsed applications."

"Meaning?"

"Meaning it can take an electromagnetic signal and amplify it a thousandfold—or conversely, I think, diminish it to nothing. And it could work as a propagating cascade effect. It's hocus-pocus stuff."

"Jason, first . . . slow down. You're talking way too fast. Second, you're using physics on a simple geologist. And third, I am less interested in what it can do now than in what it did back in 1937."

"Got it." The physicist took a deep breath. "In a nutshell, your hunch was right. These crystals would have warped Earhart's radio transmissions, as well as the signals reaching her radio direction finder. Also, with the amount of crystal on board, about twenty-three kilos, it would have messed with the navigator's chronometer. When he took sun and star shots and compared them to his charts, his faulty timepiece would have sent them hundreds of miles off course, and they never would have known it. We know her radio kept receiving signals from the USS *Itasca* anchored off Rowland Island, and they could occasionally hear her, but their communications were distorted by the lensing effect of the crystal stored in the plane's nose."

"Here's the million-dollar question," Mercer said. "Were you able to tell by the amount of crystals aboard just how badly Fred Noonan's navigation was off?"

"I had to run about a million simulations to get a mean that made sense, but I did it. The real trick was estimating how much of the electromagnetic disturbance effect Dillman was able to block with whatever he shielded the sample in. I went by the KISS principle and figured he'd do just enough to keep from getting pounded by lightning, but would not have known to block the effects at shorter distances, wavelengths, and frequencies. This is the stuff that would have messed with the jewels in a chronometer or the crystals in an old radio set."

"That gave you a hard number?"

"No, but solid estimates. That's why I needed so many runs on the Goddard mainframe. You were right. She was nowhere near Howland, their intended destination. I estimated they started flying northeast as intended, but over time they would have arced more east than north."

"Putting them where exactly?" Mercer had already

made travel arrangements covering most of the South Pacific. He'd booked through to Fiji, Tarawa, Nauru, and Majuro in the Marshall Islands, not knowing the aviatrix's final flight path. And if pilot Earhart and navigator Noonan had really screwed up, he also had tickets for Auckland. Jason's answer would narrow that list down to one destination.

"Best I can tell they would have run out of fuel near Wallis and Futuna."

"Who?"

"Wallis and Futuna are islands, not people. They're French. Wallis is more northerly than Futuna, and I think they went down near the latter."

"What's the closest international airport."

"I'd go with Fiji. Samoa is closer to Wallis, but Fiji's closer to Futuna."

"Now for another million-dollar question. Did she get close enough to see the island and attempt to land, or did she run out of fuel short of there and ditch in the ocean?"

"That I can't tell you, Mercer. But the tallest peak on Futuna is about seventeen hundred feet. They could have seen that for forty or fifty miles, depending on visibility. If she had the gas she would have beelined there."

"Populated?"

"What am I, Wikipedia?" Jason asked. "I found the place for you. You want its full history, too?"

Mercer smiled. "I suspect by now you are the world's foremost authority on Wallis and Futuna, even if you've never been there."

Rutland looked sheepish and prideful at the same time. "I like to be thorough."

"Populated?"

"Yes. Today about five thousand, most of whom live in just two towns. Back when Earhart crashed I bet there were half that number. Interestingly there's an uninhabited island just off of Futuna called Alofi. Rumor has it cannibals ate the people who lived there sometime in the nineteenth century, and no one has ever gone back. So to answer your unasked question, yes, it is remote enough to have kept her crash site secret for eighty years."

Mercer paused as he remembered something. He fished out his phone and dialed.

"Nine-one-one. What is the nature of your emergency?" a woman answered.

"There was an incident within the past few minutes at the Pentagon Metro stop."

"Yes, sir, we are aware of it. Do you have something additional to report?"

"Yes. The injured man, the one whose hand was cut up, is a person of interest in the attack at Hardt College in Killenburg, Ohio." The gunfight on campus had been featured prominently on the national news. "Show his photograph to witnesses. They will recognize him as the driver of the Honda that tore through the science building."

"Who is this, please?"

"I was on campus when the attack occurred and saw the same man again today at the Pentagon. It looked like he tried to knife someone, but he was the one who ended up being injured."

"Your phone is coming up blocked on my screen, sir. May I have your name?"

"No. I'm sorry. Contact Special Agent Kelly Hepburn or Nathan Lowell out of the FBI D.C. field office—they'll be able to piece together the chain of events. I'm positive the man wounded today at the

Pentagon and the Honda driver at Hardt College are the same person. Thank you, and good-bye." He slipped the phone back into his pocket, then said to Jason, "That should keep him off the streets for a while even if no one can make the identification. Where were we?"

Jason shook his head slightly at Mercer. "We were discussing Amelia Earhart being on or near either the island of Futuna or Alofi, and how Fiji is your best bet flying from the States."

"Already arranged," Mercer said, grateful that it was one of his preselected jumping-off points.

"Wish I could go with you," Jason said, a bit enviously. "It would be the chance of a lifetime to be in on this."

"You can have all the credit, I promise. The last thing I want in my life is fame. What about the stuff we let them take when they grabbed your purse?"

"Satchel!"

"Kumquat," Mercer parried. "And you wouldn't have used it if you didn't want it swiped. Now you have a legitimate excuse when Felicia asks."

"Touché," Jason conceded. "You mentioned the bad guys have some of the mineral already, so I couldn't fudge its electromagnetic qualities since that's something they can test for themselves. What I did was distort the pictures you sent of the empty geode so that it looks like the amount of recoverable crystals is about ten percent less than what was really there. Even if they rerun my numbers they will come up with the answer I want them to."

"They won't be able to tell the pictures were doctored?"

"Please," Jason said, obviously insulted. "We've got photo equipment at Goddard that Hollywood doesn't have yet. I could make images that show the geode filled with leprechauns, and the best computer analysis in the world would say they're genuine."

"Okay, okay. Where are you sending them?" In case his adversaries had access to airline databases, which was likely given their sophistication and reach, Mercer planned to cancel all his flight reservations except the destination Jason had chosen for his ruse. Of the flights he'd arranged under Booker Sykes's name, he'd keep the two tickets to Fiji.

"They'll think the plane went down at a place called Gardner Island. It's part of the island nation of Kiribati, formerly the Gilberts, of which Tarawa is the most famous. Gardner is more in line with Earhart's intended course than Futuna, and has the added bonus of being an atoll where people claim they've found clues that she did indeed crash."

"Really?"

"Oh, absolutely . . . Earhart hunting is a cottage industry. Bits and pieces purported to be from her Electra have been found all across the South Pacific. Gardner's just the most recent. Before that, one of the prevailing theories was that she and her plane were captured by the Japanese. She was tried and executed for spying, and the Electra ended up in some secret warehouse like at the end of *Raiders of the Lost Ark*."

"Neat theory . . . except the U.S. occupied Japan for seven years following the war and never found any secret warehouses."

"I said theory, not fact."

"Sorry," Mercer said, a little distracted. He was already running equipment checklists in his head. Some of what he thought they would need should be available in Fiji, while some would have to be brought in. "This is all really good, Jason. I can't thank you enough."

"Piece of cake, my friend. All I want in return is the right to keep studying these lightning stones of yours. It is spooky, spooky stuff. Between its attraction to lightning and all its other bizarre properties, it's best that it sits in a nice safe laboratory."

"Let me ask you . . ." Mercer said. "I get that these crystals are unusual, but a lot of people are dead over them—and someone has shelled out a lot of money to lay their hands on the source lode. Why?"

It was clear that Rutland had considered the question already but didn't like his answer. "The short answer is I don't know. There are a ton of possibilities, but for any of them to be commercially applicable, you'd need a lot more of the crystals than have been found—or a way of growing them yourself."

"Susan Tunis and my friend Abe were investigating how cosmic rays affect cloud formation, and how that interaction is likely to naturally regulate global temperatures. If their findings are correct, that could mean the climate is nowhere near as sensitive to man-made carbon dioxide as we've been led to believe."

"Meaning what . . . that global warming won't be as bad as everyone says?"

Mercer nodded. "That's what they were researching. Because the claims of climate change are so broad and so far into the future, many of them are unfalsifiable. They were trying to prove something very specific so that at least part of the hysteria can be put to rest. Abe was using the Herbert Hoover crystal sample to protect the experiment from galactic ray contamination. So there is research potential for this stuff, but any commercial application would need a lot more than has ever been discovered.

"There has to be something else, Jason, something that makes it unique. Do me a favor, and keep thinking about what someone who obviously has no morals could use it for. They've killed to get their hands on it, so I imagine their final intentions are pretty shady. Think weapons."

"Sure," Jason said. "I'll game some potential military applications and see what makes sense."

"I want you to be careful. These bastards are ruthless. There's no way they can trace you to me. I never used your name and my phone wasn't tapped. All the same, keep a low profile for a few days, take Felicia someplace if you can get away, all right?"

"She can't get time off from the station, but I'm heading to Houston for a conference in a couple of days. There's no reason I can't bump up my plans."

Mercer hit the bell to tell the bus driver he wanted off the bus and held out a hand. "Thanks. With any luck in a week or so you can go down in history as the man who located Amelia Earhart's airplane."

"What about you?"

"I'll be the schlub you sent out to do the grunt work." Mercer chuckled. "People remember Howard Carter, not the Egyptian shoveler who actually dug out King Tut's tomb."

22

The *Akademik Nikolay Zhukovsky* was 560 feet of post-Soviet glory. Her hull was painted black, the superstructure white, and all interior passages that particular shade of institutional green that the Russians seemed to love so much, or could purchase at a tremendous discount. Her superstructure was low and almost sleek and would have given her a racy line, especially since she didn't need an ugly soot-blackened smokestack. But what made her functional was also what made her ugly. Forward of the three-story superstructure were two massive dish antennas measuring more than a hundred feet in diameter, which made their outer edges hang far over the ship's rail. Aft was an even larger antenna. They resembled the skeletal dishes used by radio astronomers. The first two were mounted on powerful hydraulic gimbals, so they had some degree of directionality. The aft structure was so large it was permanently affixed to the ship and overshadowed the rear deck like a monstrous upside-down parasol.

The *Zhukovsky* had been conceived and constructed as a mobile tracking station for the Soviet version of the space shuttle, a reusable orbiter they called the Buran. Though the program never got past a single unmanned flight, a great deal of infrastructure was put in place for a time when squadrons of Burans would orbit the earth and ostensibly terrify the West with Russian strength and ingenuity.

And like so many projects the Soviets attempted as their government was about to collapse, most of it was for domestic propaganda. While the American space program enjoyed the hospitality of dozens of nations who allowed tracking stations, the Soviets were forced to build their own floating system because only a handful of countries had strong diplomatic relations with Russia. In that regard, the *Zhukovsky* made sense. What did not make as much sense—and where Soviet bombast came into play—was the fact that the ship and her planned sisters were all atomic powered. There was no functional need for nuclear reactors to power them; the energy needs weren't outrageous. But the Soviet planners simply liked the idea that their latest creation had the most modern, efficient power plants, and that their mastery of the atom was so complete they could employ nukes on civilian research ships. America had gone a similar route with a nuclear-powered freighter called the *Savannah*—until it was realized that propaganda was only necessary when you were falling behind.

While the *Akademik Zhukovsky* never got a chance to fulfill her role in the space race, she did earn another assignment. Rather than being decommissioned, the *Zhukovsky* had been laid up in a naval base near Vladivostok, and her nuclear plant was kept operational as a backup power supply for the base's notoriously unreliable main generators. It was a rather ignoble end, but it had saved her from the scrap heap.

D'Avejan had approached the base commander with an offer to buy his backup power source. The ship needed extensive refit to make her seaworthy once again, and the price was quickly agreed upon. The corrupt admiral had even offered the use of his base facilities to revive the vessel. That took six months, and ate up the better part of the Luck Dragon trading company's slush fund, but the payback was going to make d'Avejan's purchase the greatest investment of all time.

After leaving Vladivostok, the vessel had stayed well clear of established shipping channels—with the exception of a chartered helicopter delivery from Kushiro, Japan, which contained the crystal sample recovered in America. *Akademik Zhukovsky* was now in the Pacific Ocean, approaching the equator in a remote spot north of New Guinea. The irony that the mission had taken them there, considering what had been learned in the last forty-eight hours regarding the remains of Earhart's plane, was not unnoticed. The bulk of the crystals they sought were less than a thousand miles from the ship's current position, and they intended to find them.

Before this new revelation, plans were well under way to use a combination of artificial and genuine stones—d'Avejan had one stone from America and another that had been passed down to him from his great-uncle (who himself had acquired it mysteriously as a young man in the Orient). Professor Jean-Robert Fortescue, a gifted scientist who worked for d'Avejan in Eurodyne's sophisticated labs, had taken d'Avejan's sample and figured out how to coax it to grow, which had led to the discovery of the stones' true potential. Fortescue had synthesized the crystals using a massive press machine that exerted tremendous force, while at the same time heating the seed crystals to 1,000 degrees centigrade. In this hellish place, tiny bits of the original shard were forced to grow once again, adding to themselves the way a lizard regrows a tail. And like the reptile, the new appendage wasn't quite as good as the original. Fortescue was as eager as d'Avejan to obtain a larger selection of real gems, though for him this was an intellectual exercise rather than a quest for profit.

Fortescue had already run the numbers twice and had come up with the same location for the lost aviatrix as the one that had been intercepted in Washington. He was a cautious person and never accepted another man's work if he could do it himself. The measurements of the sample's electrical properties jibed with his own work, and the assumptions seemed reasonable and in line with what he would have done. But he also knew that a minute deviation from the starting point could have profound implications at the end. Whoever the American had used to do the work had been very, very good. So much so that Fortescue would have welcomed the scientist into his own lab as an assistant.

Like many academicians, Jean-Robert Fortescue neglected the passage of time when he was engrossed in a problem. He could spend hours working and forget to eat, or entire weekends and forget to shower. His single-mindedness could be off-putting.

Fortescue had wanted to explore the crystals' remarkable shielding ability. His initial thought was that the crystal could offer unprecedented protection to microelectronics for nano-scalar circuitry, but soon after, Fortescue instead found himself drawn into a geoengineering experiment to try to strengthen Earth's magnetic field. D'Avejan had told him his work would help avert a global climate catastrophe. Jean-Robert wasn't so certain about that side of the experiment, but with d'Avejan's encouragement he was eager to continue.

Fortescue was in his tenth straight hour of work, having stopped only to relieve pressure in his bladder and force himself to swallow some electrolyte-infused sports drink. He was clicking through the images the American had snapped of the Afghan geode that had yielded the amazing gems. Fortescue had seen the geode already, in a series of photos taken by a Pakistani soldier they'd hired to track the American in the dangerous tribal regions bordering the two countries.

Fortescue should have missed the anomaly. The inside of the geode was roughly bathtub size, with a honeycomb surface where the accretion matrix had once held the dun-colored crystals. It was intricate— so complex it became featureless, like looking at faces in a crowd. In their multitude they lost their individuality. An earlier computer match of some of the pictures had shown the topography to be identical in both sets of photographs, but somehow, comparing the two side by side on a pair of monitors, Fortescue now noted a difference. As soon as he did he cursed.

"Oh, you are indeed a clever one," he said to the empty room. "You were so smart and so good that you even fooled my computers. Ha! You did not fool me."

For the next hour, Jean-Robert redid all the work he'd so laboriously produced already, only this time he adjusted his own calculations about the size of the geode. He didn't understand how a filtering program through which he'd washed the American's pictures hadn't detected the difference. The filters analyzed at the bit level, searching for statistical anomalies or signs of infilling, and had found nothing. The technology he was up against was indeed formidable, but sometimes what a computer cannot see, a human can. And after the first hour's work he knew that the pictures sent to him from Washington, D.C., had been doctored.

The size—and yield—of the geode had been reduced by 9.681 percent. That's when Fortescue realized his opponent was making a fool out of him. This was a slap in the face—and Fortescue threw himself into the contest. He ran numbers for another couple of hours, churning simulation after simulation through the mainframe so intensely that the ship's engineer had detected a spike in the nuclear plant's output and called to the control center to inquire if everything was all right.

"Better than all right, Chief, I assure you," Fortescue said into the phone embedded in his workstation. "But you must excuse me. I need to speak to Monsieur d'Avejan right away."

23

The adjacent islands of Futuna and Alofi crouched low on the horizon, clinging to the line where earth met sky, humpbacked and verdant and about as unspoiled as any place on Earth. The larger, Futuna, was on the left as they approached out of the south, and was separated from its neighbor by a two-mile-deep channel. Alofi was craggier from this vantage, with volcanic cliffs not yet pounded flat by the relentless action of wave and tide, but the rest of the island was reef-lined white sand beaches. The forest canopy covering the island looked primeval, though the captain assured his passengers that there were a handful of small plantations carved into the jungle by Futuna islanders to grow tobacco and taro.

The boat was a sixty-footer rented out of Fiji, and no amount of money would convince her captain and owner, an expatriate Australian named Rory Reyes, to let his two clients take her on their own. She had a tall fly bridge for fish spotting, a rear dive platform and compressor for recharging scuba tanks, a small Zodiac for trips to shore, and sleeping accommodations for seven. Reyes had his cabin just off the main bridge below the fly tower. Mercer and Book had flipped a coin for the master suite located in the broad V of the bow under the main deck, and the coin had come up in Book's favor. The second day aboard, Sykes informed Mercer the bed was like a cloud; Mercer told him his was a foam affair stuffed into a box frame that smelled of feet.

Through a combination of accrued vacation days and some successful lobbying by both Book and his girlfriend Stacy, Sykes had been able to spring himself a week early from his final tour in Afghanistan as a civilian contractor. It had cost him the promise to Stacy that he wouldn't go back to Kabul, and the assurance that he and Mercer weren't off to bed native girls in the South Pacific. Stacy liked Mercer, but she didn't necessarily trust him and Booker together. Freely borrowing Aretha Franklin's line from the movie *The Blues Brothers*, she called him Book's "white hoodlum friend."

After successfully staging Jason's "mugging" in D.C., Mercer and Book had driven down to Sykes's bungalow near Fort Bragg in North Carolina, where they'd made lists and then refined those lists until they knew exactly what they would need for their trip. The following morning, Book went on a shopping spree, while Mercer's main task was to get the right kind of charter boat in Fiji. He spent hours on Book's laptop, and more time on the phone, until he found Captain Rory Reyes of the *Suva Surprise,* a nice wide-hulled sport fisherman named for Fiji's capital. The ship was fitted with extended fuel tanks to cover long distances.

Mercer attempted to rent the boat for himself, but that was a nonstarter and the weathered Aussie insisted he come with them. Reyes was in his late fifties, with bright blue eyes held in creased pouches of skin in a broad friendly face. His handshake had been firm when he'd met them at Nadi International Airport. His accent was pure outback, and he had a good sense of humor and an honest laugh. One of the first things he'd said, though, was that judging by the looks of his latest clients he was glad he hadn't let them take the boat themselves.

"Why's that?" Book asked in an intimidating voice.

"Because I know trouble when I see it, and you two are it. In fact, if I hadn't just lost my big summer charter I'd tell you two blokes to get back on the plane for Hawaii and forget you've ever heard of ole Capt'n Rory."

Reyes had studied them both as they stood in the hot sun outside the terminal building. Book had switched into shorts on the plane, but Mercer was in khakis that were beginning to stick to his legs. "I'm not sure what your game is," the boat captain said, "but I don't think it's archaeology like you said on the phone."

"We're looking for a wrecked plane," Mercer assured him. "That's all."

"We'll see."

Before they could leave the airport complex, Mercer told Reyes that he had a package waiting in cargo customs. There he signed for a boxed-up duffel bag that had been express-shipped from the United States. The customs inspector made Mercer open the box and duffel so he could verify its contents against the bill of lading. Suspicious or maybe just bored, the Fijian then ran the box through an X-ray scanner, taking nearly a minute to ensure there was nothing suspicious in the grainy image. As stated, the American *was* picking up eighty pounds of bare copper wire that had been unspooled and repacked in a dense rectangular brick the size of a longish picnic cooler. He forced Mercer to pay a small import duty and sent them on their way. Where the customs man needed an assistant to manhandle the weighty duffel, Book carried it out as easily as if the box were packed with Styrofoam.

The next morning the three boarded Reyes's boat. They motored out of Royal Suva Yacht Club and were soon beyond Fiji's barrier reefs and into the open sea. The *Suva Surprise* could more than handle the ride. The humidity dropped away from land, and the sun and sea conspired to lull the two jet-lagged passengers to sleep for the first half of their four-hundred-mile trip to Futuna and Alofi.

When Mercer woke, he noted the seas had picked up slightly. The sun was still shining, but there was an edge to the wind that even a nonsailor like him could tell meant a storm was coming. He went up to the bridge. Rory Reyes sat relaxed at the helm, a liter bottle of water at hand and a half-smoked cigar clamped between large white teeth.

"Nice nap?"

"I'm like a narcoleptic whenever I get on a boat," Mercer confessed. "We cast off and I'm out like a light."

"Your big friend too?"

"No. He's ex-military. He's been trained to grab sleep whenever and wherever he can."

"So, what are you two really, mercenaries?"

"No. We really are looking for an old plane wreck. The problem is there's another group interested too.

We've sent them searching in the wrong direction, but they are dangerous, capable men."

"Dangerous?"

"I won't lie. They've killed people looking for this plane."

"What plane are you looking for?" Reyes asked. "And if you say Amelia Earhart's Lockheed Electra I'm adding an idiot's tax to my charter fee."

"Tack it on, Captain, because that's exactly what we're looking for."

Reyes threw up his hands theatrically. "Lord save me from fools. It's your money, mate. Your charter. But let me be the first or maybe the last to tell you she's lost somewhere more than a thousand miles northwest of us in about twenty thousand feet of water."

Mercer said, "When she left New Guinea, she was carrying a geological sample that messed with the plane's navigation gear. She and Fred Noonan were off course ten minutes into their flight but kept on going because they didn't know it. One of the most powerful computers in the world ran the numbers for me, and it says she ran out of fuel someplace close to Futuna Island, a place so far off the beaten trail that no one ever looked for her there."

"So you're treasure hunters looking for her plane like all the other blokes mucking about the South Pacific?"

Mercer shook his head. "Two weeks ago Amelia Earhart meant no more to me than she does to anyone else. But a friend of mine died for a sample of the mineral she was carrying, and the men who killed him are after the rest. I plan on denying them that prize."

The two men regarded each other, assessing to see what was real and what was an act. In the end Rory

Reyes said, "Fair enough." He bumped the throttles a little to put on some more speed without jeopardizing too much of their fuel range. The twin Cummins diesels purred.

It took a total of twenty-four hours to reach Futuna and Alofi, and the last eight of them were spent battling rain squalls and wind gusts that would have made it miserable if they were on a sailboat, but the motor yacht had no problems bulling its way through the Pacific chop. Although it was morning when they arrived, the sky was dark and tempestuous. Rain fell in line-straight patches, and over the horizon flashed the electric cannonade of lightning.

"We'll swing around and tuck into the channel between the two islands. It's the best cover we can hope for before the real storm hits." Reyes made to adjust the helm, but Mercer put a hand over the captain's wrist. "Huh?"

"Booker needs to get to shore first. Then we can find cover."

Reyes didn't like that one bit. "What the hell for?"

"We were prepared to wait days for a storm like this," Mercer told the man. "It would be a shame to waste this one."

"What are you talking about?"

"I have a theory that if Earhart's plane is within reasonable distance of the island, there are going to be an inordinate number of lightning strikes over its resting place. To see that, Booker needs to watch the storm from the top of the tallest hill here."

"Mount Kolofau."

"If you say so."

Booker just now appeared on the aft deck below the tall bridge. He had spent a great deal of the trip down in his cabin unwinding the block of copper wire and carefully respooling it around a length of broom handle he'd borrowed from the skipper. He wore jungle combat fatigues under a military-style poncho. His silhouette appeared misshapen, like that of a hunchback, because under his weatherproof cape he'd thrown a rucksack over his shoulder.

"Mercer!" he bellowed up over the sounds of the growing storm.

Mercer stepped out from under the fly bridge and into the warm rain. He descended the exterior ladder in shorts and a borrowed rain slicker, and in seconds his hair was plastered to his head. He had to flick it often to keep water from clouding his vision.

Sykes rubbed his own denuded scalp and grinned. "Bald is beautiful, baby."

"You got everything you need?"

Book patted his hump. "All set. Give me a hand with the Zodiac and wait for my call."

The ten-foot inflatable was stowed on its side along one gunwale. The two men waited for a break in the wind so they could unclamp it and get it into the water before a gust tore it from their grasp. Using the painter line, Mercer wrestled it to the transom while Booker Sykes opened the dive door and stepped down onto the platform. The *Suva Surprise* was bobbing on large swells, so as soon as Sykes's feet hit the platform his legs were awash; no doubt some water overtopped his combat boots, no matter how tightly they'd been laced.

He turned to Mercer and called over the wind, "Next time you can have the cush bed and I get to stay aboard for this part."

Mercer shot back, "You're nuts if you ever think there's going to be a next time. In you go."

Booker leaned one long leg across to the little inflat-

able, steadied himself for a moment, and then bodily
flung himself into the craft. Mercer fought to keep
from being pulled in after him, but he wouldn't let
go of the line until Sykes had started the outboard motor that was attached to the Zodiac's stern. He watched
through the squall as Sykes first primed, then yanked
the starter handle. To Captain Reyes's credit, the one-
cylinder four-stroke fired to life on a single pull.

Sykes flashed him a thumbs-up and Mercer released the line. Booker cut around the back of the sport
fisherman and carved a channel through the heaving
seas for the nearest beach, about three hundred yards
away. He was an expert small-boat operator, so he
had little trouble battling through the surf line and
running the Zodiac high onto the beach on a particularly tall wave. The rain was thickening; Mercer could
barely see Sykes raise the motor and drag the Zodiac
above the tide line, where he could tie it off to one of
the countless palm trees. He threw Mercer an exaggerated wave to tell him he was all set, and vanished
into the jungle.

Mercer climbed the chrome ladder back up to
the bridge. He was soaked and thanked the captain
for the hand towel he tossed him. "We're good to go
wherever you feel it's safest to ride out the storm."

"Like I said before," the Aussie replied, "the channel's safest."

"The channel it is."

Twenty minutes later, the walkie-talkie in Mercer's cargo shorts squawked to life. "Cool to Nerd.
Come in, Nerd. Do you copy?"

"At what point," Mercer asked Sykes, "did people
start telling you you're funny?"

"Day one, brother, day one."

"You in position?"

"Yeah, I've got a good view of the southwesterly approach to the island. I'm at about four hundred meters elevation, so that should give me good range even with the storm. I'm ready to get bearings, and if we get lucky the laser range finder's good to go, but I think the rain's going to eighty-six that idea."

"Do what you can. I'll be sleeping in a comfortable bed tonight, dry, and with a belly full of warm food. Enjoy your MREs and lonely vigil. Nerd out."

The storm raged throughout the day and into the night. Mercer and Reyes played cards for a while, then Mercer helped him tinker with the pair of Cummins in the engine room. Although they were in range, Book kept radio silence more out of habit than necessity. And as much as Mercer wanted to call to find out if their hunch was right, he played the waiting game too. It wasn't until dawn broke clear and sweet, with gentle trade winds and tolerable humidity, that Book finally radioed in.

"Cool to Nerd, I'm ready for extract, over."

"It's not over until I say it's over, over."

"Do I have to tell you over and over that it's over, over."

Mercer laughed. "I take it by your good mood that some balloon-chested island princess found your bivouac?"

Sykes chuckled lecherously. "It wasn't my bivouac she found."

Mercer cut him off, anxious to know whether his idea had paid off. "All right, enough . . . spill."

"One niner five degrees from my position, no more than five miles off the island, is a spot in the ocean that got walloped all last night by lightning.

It was the most amazing thing I'd ever seen, Mercer. The sea seemed to glow for a mile around, like it had absorbed the electricity and fluoresced like neon or something."

Mercer roared with delight. "I owe Jason a case of his favorite Scotch."

"I prefer bourbon, don't forget."

"I might even spring for a bottle or two of that."

"Bottle or two? No respect, I swear to God, none at all. Get your butt into gear and pick me up. We can be diving the wreck in less than an hour."

Captain Reyes had the engines warmed and idling. As soon as he heard they were ready, he engaged the transmission. He eased the boat back around the western tip of Alofi Island and cruised parallel to the southern coast before turning inward to the beach where Booker was waiting.

Booker had stowed his shirt and poncho in his bag, so he stood like a half-naked statue of an idealized male figure, each muscle from beltline to throat etched and edged against his smooth dark skin.

"Jesus, mate," Reyes said, watching Booker on shore. "I knew your buddy was big, but he is bloody ripped."

Mercer said absently, "He can't work out his brain, so he trains his body."

The charter captain shook his head. "You two are a pair. How'd you meet? Military?"

"What?" Mercer dragged himself to the present. He'd been staring out to sea, imagining what they would find on the dive. "Ah, no. Booker was a sort of babysitter for me when I was working on a government contract. I realized pretty quickly that there's no one who I'd want watching my back other than him."

"Good to have a mate like that," Reyes said. "Rare."

"Yeah." Mercer thought about Abe for a moment. He'd been another of those rare sorts.

Sykes dragged the Zodiac into the surf and rolled over the gunwale as had been drilled into him when he took a SEAL training course at Coronado Beach, near San Diego. Like his entrance the day before, he timed his race through the rollers with an expert eye and squirted past the surf's break line without upending the boat or even dousing himself with spray. In a few seconds he'd motored out to the *Suva Surprise*. Mercer was at the transom and ready to catch the line Book tossed up. He hauled the inflatable tight to the dive platform, and Sykes slid across and stood.

"Thanks."

"You can really thank me for the coffee I have for you in the holder at the fighting chair."

"I take back all my earlier nasty comments. You are a good man after all."

Together they manhandled the Zodiac out of the water and secured it to its mounting clamps along the port-side gunwale.

Mercer called up to the bridge, "Okay, Rory, you know the bearing and distance. Let's not waste any more time."

The idling engines burst to life, and a creaming wake grew from the back of the large fisherman. Mercer and Book used the time to start laying out scuba gear. They weren't yet sure of the depth, but they had decided they wouldn't need wet suits in these tropical waters. Reyes's gear was all well cared for and of the finest quality. Even Sykes, who was used to Uncle Sam buying him the best and latest toys, was impressed. Since he had more experience, he would be lead diver, Mercer his backup.

Twenty minutes later, the engines dropped back to

idle and then went silent. Then came a rattle followed by a splash. Reyes appeared above them, his head covered in a big white floppy hat. "We're here and you're in luck. Water's only eighty feet. Shallow enough for me to drop anchor."

"Excellent," Mercer said. "Our plan is to do a preliminary dive and get the lay of the land, so to speak. We might get lucky and you've put us on the mark. If not we're going to have to use the side-scan sonar you rented for us back in Suva."

"You want to tow it with the *Surprise*?"

"Not necessary. It's a small enough unit that we can drag it behind the Zodiac."

"Whatever you fellas want is fine by me. Lay out a spare tank, and I'll monitor you from the surface. If one of you gets into trouble I can lend a hand."

That service wasn't part of their charter deal, and Mercer suspected that Reyes was catching treasure hunter's fever—that most contagious of diseases that compels a sane person to ignore all odds and gamble everything on an impossible dream.

As they donned their gear, Book checked over Mercer's equipment every step of the way—weight belt, buoyancy compensator, his tanks and regulators. He even tested the rubber flippers and the seal around his mask. "Dive partners," he said as each piece of equipment passed through his big hands. "Means that if you're in trouble, I'm in trouble. This goes for our stuff too. You got faulty gear means I got faulty gear. I check it so I don't drown trying to save you."

Mercer recognized that this wasn't a time to joke. Book took his job seriously, and right now he was dive master and that meant his partner understood the stakes. "Roger that."

Once finished with the final checks, they jumped off the dive platform and splashed into the aquamarine world off a volcanic Pacific island. As soon as their bubbles dispersed, Mercer could see their visibility was almost endless. The bottom looked as sunlit as a country meadow, marred only by the wavering shadow of their dive boat. The gin-clear water was bathtub warm and held them in its intimate embrace.

Below, the seafloor was mostly sand, broken up by banks of coral outcroppings and chunks of black and gray rock that had been ejected from the earth during the island's fiery birth. Booker finned down, pausing to adjust his buoyancy and looking back to make sure Mercer equalized the pressure in his ears. He checked his depth when he reached the sandy plain and entered the number into his wrist dive computer. It spat back their bottom time, and he gave Mercer the diver's okay sign of a circle made by thumb and forefinger.

Mercer returned the gesture.

Sykes had the compass, so he set the direction and pace. Mercer, much less comfortable breathing through a rubber tube, forced himself to inhale and exhale only when he saw Book do it. This way he didn't make the novice mistake of gulping too much air too quickly.

Soon they began attracting the interest of some local denizens. Mercer couldn't guess the names of the fish, but he marveled at the fantastic variety of colors and shapes and wondered at the evolutionary niche each one filled. Between the outcroppings, the seafloor showed signs of life as well, tracks and trails left in the sediment from crustaceans and starfish, but it was around the living reefs that life teemed in its multitudes. Sea fans waved gently in the currents. Corals of a million shades and hues burst from the sandy background while schools and shoals and swarms of fish darted and raced, some prey, others predator. Large eyes and blurred shapes peered from some of the deeper crevices, and in one Mercer saw the permanent grin of an eel flushing water though its gills, its jaw open, its mouth a profusion of serrated teeth.

Book roamed back and forth for the better part of a half hour, trying to see anything that would give away the presence of a nearly forty-foot-long aluminum airplane. Though the bottom here was a fascinating and beautiful realm, nothing looked like a target. He shoved off, taking them eastward for a hundred yards so their return to the boat would pass over uncharted territory.

Coming up over a coral head, they saw the bottom on the other side slope away into a narrow valley. The far side of the cleft was only a hundred or so feet away, but the bottom went down a good forty feet deeper than their current depth. It seemed darker down there, more forbidding.

The two men looked at each other. They both felt it.

The trench walls were gray stone, volcanic rock that had been tortured first in the earth's crust and again when it spewed from the depths. Sand had accumulated along the chasm's bottom, but it was an irregular surface of buried boulders and hidden outcroppings. A shadow passed over them, something big enough to interrupt the sun's beam. They startled and looked up, but there was nothing there. They went back to their search.

As a geologist Mercer saw the anomaly. Part of the canyon wall had given way, sheared clean from its base. An avalanche like this wasn't so unusual. What struck him was how the rock above the collapsed section of stone was riddled with cracks. He swam up to inspect it. He lightly brushed the stone, and his finger gouged out a small divot. The rock was fissured, so that it crumbled easily. He looked up. The distance seemed impossible, but the evidence was right in front of him. For eighty years lightning had been striking the ocean's surface above this spot, and the shock of 50,000-degree Fahrenheit electricity—transmuting water into steam with each pulse—had eventually fractured the rock. It was a similar scene to what he'd found in Afghanistan, only here the uncompressible water had allowed the lightning to cause even more damage.

Book drew a question mark in the water.

Mercer nodded and pointed down.

The army vet checked Mercer's air supply, and his own, and then consulted his computer before flashing five fingers twice to tell Mercer they had ten minutes. Mercer gave him the okay sign and let Sykes lead him down into the canyon.

The water temperature dropped as soon as they started their descent. Both men tested the wall as they finned downward to make certain that it wouldn't collapse on them when they reached the bottom. Their hands kicked up some flakes and chips, but nothing larger dislodged. Mercer kept one eye on Sykes's air bubbles to keep his breathing in sync with the dive master's.

The bottom of the canyon was a jumbled mess of rocks, most of them no larger than a man's fist, but a few were boulder size. They began moving some of the rubble aside, being careful not to mix too much sediment into the water around them. There was little current down at this depth, so whatever became suspended would stay like that for a time.

Sykes was the first to discover it. He made a sharp pointing motion to catch Mercer's attention. He'd uncovered something smooth and curved that was covered in a film of scum. He brushed it away to reveal dull metal.

Mercer felt his heart trip. They'd done it on their first dive! They'd found the plane. He helped Booker move more loose rocks, and his elation suddenly turned to dismay—then disappointment. They hadn't found the wing or fuselage of a Lockheed Electra. Instead it was a steel-hulled open boat, like a lifeboat, and judging by its age it had been down here for decades. It took five more minutes to realize it had once been loaded with bags of cement. The paper sacks had long since rotted away, leaving loaves of hardened concrete piled five deep on the boat's flattened keel.

Book tapped Mercer's shoulder and pointed up. They'd reached their limit and would have to ascend. They made two decompression stops on the way to the surface and breached a quarter mile from Rory Reyes and the *Suva Surprise*. He spotted them even before they started waving. He'd already unshipped the Zodiac and jumped aboard it. A cloud of blue exhaust erupted from the motor, and in seconds he was planing across the sea.

Sykes spat out his regulator. "You should never leave a boat unattended like that."

"He must figure it's only for a second and we're close enough to shore that we could swim it."

"Pull that stunt in the military and you're scrubbing toilets on a garbage scow for the rest of your hitch."

Reyes chopped the throttle when he neared them and began to coast. The inflatable lost all headway just as he came abreast of the divers. He helped Mercer over the gunwale with a strong pull to his tank harness, and together they heaved Book into the boat. It was a little crowded with the three of them and their gear, but they made it work.

"How'd it go?"

"We found something promising," Mercer said. "But it turned out to be an old inter-island trader that sank with a load of cement bags, I'd guess sometime in the 1940s or '50s."

"You gonna dive again?"

Mercer looked to Book.

Sykes said to Reyes, "We'll give it a few hours first, but we can hit it again before sunset if you want." Book then turned to Mercer. "Or are we breaking out the side-scan sonar and playing sea sleuth?"

An interesting thought had occurred to Mercer. "That fractured rock has me really intrigued. It makes me wonder if there's something under that old boat, and it also makes me think its captain and crew might have been in the wrong place at the wrong time."

"The boat was sunk by lightning?"

"It's possible. We'd need to see the bottom of the hull, but it seems awfully coincidental that it's in the exact spot where we were looking."

They returned to the *Surprise*, and while Book refilled their scuba tanks, Rory made them a lunch of broiled early-season wahoo he'd caught. He used the perfect amount of spicy piri piri to complement the fruity chutney he'd slathered on the fish.

An hour later there was an anxious moment when Mercer heard the sound of an approaching aircraft.

He couldn't see the propeller-driven plane because the bulk of Alofi Island was in the way, but they could all hear it clear as a bell. The sound suddenly ceased. Mercer shot a look to Sykes, who ducked below. He didn't come back on deck but lurked just out of sight.

"Rory?" Mercer asked.

"Relax, mate. That's the supply plane come down from Wallis Island. Give it twenty minutes, half hour, and it'll take off again."

Mercer strained his senses for the twenty-five minutes it took for pilot and crew to unload the aircraft over on Futuna and pack in whatever meager wares the natives had to sell to the outside world. When he finally did spot it, the plane was a retreating silver flash climbing hard to the north in the otherwise cloudless sky.

"No worries, mate," Reyes assured them.

"No worries," Mercer repeated, uncertain but unable to justify a heightened sense of paranoia.

At four, Book determined that any dissolved nitrogen had cleared their bloodstreams, and the two men got back into their diving gear. Reyes had already moved the boat to the spot where they'd found the sunken dory, so all they'd need to do was follow the anchor chain to the bottom. On this dive, they also brought a pry bar to lever aside the heavy cement blocks.

Mercer and Sykes descended quickly and got to work right away. The light was murkier now that the sun was setting out beyond Futuna Island, but visibility remained excellent. The rounded blobs of cement each weighed close to a hundred pounds, and even with the help of the water's buoyancy, moving them was exhausting. Forty minutes into the job, as Book was giving thought to ending the dive because of the additional exertion, Mercer heaved out one of the last cement chunks and let it fall off the gunwale and into the rocks. He looked back to see a hole in the bottom of the boat, about a hand's span wide. The hole clearly had been blown out of the bottom, as opposed to being punctured inward.

What caught Mercer's attention even more was what lay under the sunken dory. Through the hole, which appeared blackened as if it had been struck by lightning, was another metal surface. This one was as shiny as a mirror. Mercer reached down to brush his fingers on its smooth surface, and he felt the little bumps of aircraft-grade rivets. He motioned for Book to come close, and pointed.

Booker Sykes's eyes went wide when he saw what appeared to be part of an aircraft, either its wing or the top of its fuselage. He shot Mercer a questioning glance. Mercer nodded. They had emptied enough of the cement nodules to be able to move the sunken boat, but with so much debris around it now there was no place to tip it over. Sykes studied the problem for a moment and gave Mercer the okay sign followed by a signal that they should surface. Mercer wanted to keep working, but he deferred to Sykes's experience.

This time when they breached they were able to cling to the dive platform hanging off the *Suva Surprise*'s transom and climb the ladder that Reyes had folded out underneath it.

"Tell me you've got an idea," Mercer said as soon as he'd removed his regulator.

"I've got an idea," Booker said to him.

Reyes helped Mercer off with his tank. "What'd you guys find?"

"There's something under the old boat," Mercer told him. "Something made of riveted aluminum."

"A plane?" the Aussie asked.

"Pretty sure," Mercer said.

"Pretty sure, my black behind," Book said. "The rivets are ground flat. It's a damned plane and you know it. What we're going to need to do is drag the boat off the plane. It's too big for us to move by ourselves, but we should be able to tow it if you've got enough line aboard."

"No problem. I keep about five hundred feet. It's only half-inch line, but we can triple it up. That ought to hold."

"Perfect," Booker said. "We'll dive at first light and with any luck finish this up by noon."

"I've been thinking," Reyes said. "If that really is Amelia Earhart down there, shouldn't there be some experts here, professional underwater archaeologists and preservation people?"

"Tell you what," Mercer said, toweling off his hair. "We just want to get a crate stored in the nose of the plane. We grab that and our interest in this thing is over. Take us back to Suva so we can go home, and you can come back here with a crew and claim you found the plane with the help of an American friend of yours."

Reyes wasn't sure if he understood what Mercer was saying. "Friend? What do you mean a friend?"

"His name is Jason Rutland. He's the NASA egghead who pinpointed this location. I promised him a piece of the discovery. You two can make up some story about how you've collaborated on the search for some time now, and presto you become as famous as Bob Ballard, the guy who found the *Titanic*."

"You two don't want the credit for this?"

"I certainly don't," Mercer said. "Book?"

Sykes thought for a second, and then shook his bald head. "Last thing I need in my life are a bunch of aviation geeks asking for my autograph. Pass."

"There you go, Rory. This ought to be a boon to the charter business. If you want to be really creative, you can probably sell the right to finding the plane." Mercer made air quotes around the word *finding*. "You must have some rich client who would love to be in on this."

"I could name a few," Reyes said noncommittally.

"Bet one of them would pay some serious coin to be able to brag that he was there when Amelia Earhart was finally found."

"I'll have to think about it."

Mercer could already see the gears churning in the Aussie's mind, and he imagined that this time next year, the *Suva Surprise II* would make the current boat look like a pile of junk.

While Mercer and Booker rinsed their dive equipment in freshwater, Rory took them in closer to shore. At a new anchorage, just far enough off the beach that the mosquitoes wouldn't find them but close enough to enjoy the sound of the surf, Rory beer-steamed five pounds of shrimp. After the men ate their fill, they passed around a bottle of cognac. They drank sparingly, since two of them were diving in the morning and technically Rory was on duty, but the spirits helped mellow the mood and they talked about the lure and mystique of America's most famous aviatrix.

In the end they agreed on one point: Earhart would not have been as famous if she'd actually completed her circumnavigation. Dying on the flight made her an aviation martyr, while surviving it would have just made her a historical footnote. Mercer put the final punctuation on that point by asking the other two who was the first female pilot to successfully fly around the globe. His question was met by silence.

24

Mercer and Booker were back in the water by seven o'clock the next morning. It took just a few minutes for them to tie off the nylon lines to the sunken boat and get into position for Rory's attempt to drag it free. They had devised a simple signal system using colored balloons that the divers could inflate with their air regulators. When they were ready they would release a white balloon to float up to the surface. A yellow balloon meant the divers wanted to pause for five minutes before attempting to move the boat again. And if more than two balloons surfaced at or around the same time, the charter captain would stop entirely and wait. Either the maneuver had worked or there was trouble and the divers were on their way back to the boat to rethink their strategy.

Sykes filled a white balloon from his regulator's purge valve and tied it off with a deft twist his big hands seemed incapable of. It floated up to the surface like a jellyfish, and only seconds after release they heard and felt the *Suva Surprise*'s engine ramp up.

Reyes used a careful hand on the throttle. He already knew which bearing to keep to avoid dragging the boat sideways, so it was really just a matter of finesse over the diesels. The *Surprise* edged forward, making minimal headway, and he knew in an instant when she came up against her tether. A touch more throttle and the stern started to bite deep, crouching lower into the sea as the horses fought a half century of muck adhering the boat to the bottom. He kept an anxious eye on the stern bits. They really weren't designed for this kind of strain, but he'd tied off the lines in such a way that the weight of the tow was well distributed.

Reyes opened the taps another notch. That first hit of power had merely stretched the nylon lines to their fullest. Now he was really fighting the sunken boat. The *Surprise* began to slew from side to side. Reyes kept one eye on the compass to make sure he didn't sheer too far off the towline and the other on the water where the first balloon had shown itself in case there was a problem down below.

Mercer and Sykes were well back and to the side of the dory as the sportfisher above exerted its considerable power. Because of water's density there was little danger of a whip-back if the line parted, but it was best to be prudent. They could both look up out of the undersea chasm and note how the *Suva Surprise* was pulling in the right direction. The lines linking the two appeared as taut as rebar.

For what felt like many long minutes but was actually less than one, nothing appeared to happen. The fifteen-foot dory remained stuck in place, and Mercer was beginning to think, pessimistically, that they might need to return with more dedicated salvage gear. He'd never anticipated the plane would be trapped under a sunken wreck.

In a silent burst of silt boiling up from under its hull, the bow pulled free of the ooze and rose several feet. Almost immediately its stern was dragged across the seabed, bouncing and shaking as it jostled over debris that had fallen from above, and the lumps of cement Booker and Mercer had so laboriously heaved over its side. Sykes let Reyes tow the boat well clear of their area of interest before releasing the two balloons he'd already inflated. Mercer might have doubted but Book never did.

The old open boat was twenty yards from its initial resting place when the signal was received topside and Captain Reyes throttled back on the twin engines. Silt wafted around it like smoke coiling from a fire, and it took several moments for the weak current to clear it away enough for them to see the open craft sitting upright on the bottom. It was rusted and banged up and had seen a lifetime's worth of abuse in its day, but it somehow maintained a plucky defiance even here on the ocean's floor.

After that initial look, the two men didn't give the former lifeboat a second's thought. Their attention went immediately to what the boat had so effectively hidden for all these years.

They swam to where the boat had spent the decades. The dory's outline was clearly visible as an area of pure sand in the otherwise rock-strewn canyon bottom. And in the middle of the boat-shaped space was the shining aluminum curve of an aircraft's wing. Other than some scratches where the boat had marred the aluminum, it looked to be in remarkable shape.

Mercer felt a lump in his throat as he looked at it. Normally he wasn't all that sentimental, but he couldn't help thinking what this moment represented.

One of the most enduring mysteries of the twentieth century had just been solved, revealing the final resting places of two brave souls.

Book felt no such reverence. He swam over the wing to orient himself to where the Electra's fuselage would be, and he set about moving more rocks out of the way.

Mercer looked up to see if their actions had disturbed the cliff just above, and he noted that the canyon wall was bulging more than it had. His instinct was to shout to Booker, but that didn't work underwater. Instead he darted forward, kicking hard and pulling with his arms so that he crashed into his friend and spun them both out of the way a few seconds before the bulge of rock gave way. It came down in fractured chunks that trailed streamers of silt, so the whole mass looked like something shot from hell. Even underwater the sound of the crashing rocks was concussive. The downpour crashed onto the plane's wing with enough force to peel away hunks of coral that had used the fuselage as an anchor for a new colony.

Tons of rubble and debris fell away from the plane, disappearing down the newly exposed sinkhole, and all at once the wing wasn't the only part of the plane they could see. From her nose to the wing root, the plane was now exposed. The wing itself wasn't attached to the Electra's hull but had been torn back during its water landing. The big engine nacelle remained in place, but the two-bladed prop had been lost in the crash. They could see the cockpit windows but couldn't see into the cockpit because of marine growth on the inside of the glass.

Most important for them, they had easy access to the nose cargo door.

They waited ten minutes for everything to settle, and for the water to clear enough for them to work. Amelia Earhart's Electra looked to be in far better shape than the old boat that had shielded it for so many years. The broken wing was the only obvious sign of damage. The fuselage, or as much of it as they could see, appeared intact. None of the cockpit glass had even broken, and thirty-odd feet back from the cockpit, they could see the vertical stabilizer part of her twin tail sticking out of the canyon wall.

Book tried to peer into the cockpit from several angles but could see nothing in the beam of his small dive light.

Mercer went to the nose and tried the cargo hatch. Neither the handle nor the door itself would budge. Book came over and together they tried again. Mercer didn't want to disturb the site more than necessary, so he didn't want to rip the hatch clean off, but it seemed they might not have a choice. It was jammed tight.

And then, without warning, the door flew open, sending both divers tumbling. Booker was the first to regain his equilibrium, and he steadied Mercer. Together they returned to the downed aircraft and used Book's light to reveal the interior of the cramped forward hold.

A tin trunk was the only obvious piece of cargo—a trunk that looked like it was ready to fall apart after sitting immersed in the ocean for the best part of a century. Mercer took the light from Sykes and played it around the bottom of the hold. Even in such a tightly sealed space as this, the living seas had encroached. The floor was covered in a layer of brown and green slime. He reached a hand in and felt along the floor. No matter how slowly or carefully he moved, he kicked up tendrils of organic matter. But

Mercer's fingers also felt something else. He grasped it and pulled it out into the light.

The crystal was dull brown, lifeless and uninteresting, and yet it had driven men to kill. It was the size of a banana, octagonal and blunted at both ends. It was something any self-respecting gemologist would dismiss out of hand—and yet it might just be the most valuable crystal on Earth.

Mercer met Booker's eyes and nodded. The African American grinned around his regulator and flashed Mercer the okay sign.

Sykes carried a large nylon bag folded into a pouch attached to his dive belt. He unfurled it and anchored it on the seafloor next to the open hatchway. It was tight confines, but he and Mercer managed to wrestle the small trunk close enough that they could lift it out of the plane and settle it into the bag. The case had cracked during the crash, and a string of crystals fell free as they maneuvered it. Rather than try to deal with preserving Dillman's old steamer trunk, Book tore off its lid and let the whole thing collapse into the bag. He picked out larger chunks of the disintegrating trunk, including sheets of copper that had so dissolved over the years they were little more than a film of verdigris.

Mercer swept the hold for more loose stones and picked out dozens. No wonder, he thought, that the crash site attracted so much lightning. The minimal shielding Mike Dillman had devised was now worthless, and Sample 681's bizarre affinity for electricity could be fully realized. He thought, too, that any curious islander or Western diver hoping to explain why this one spot of ocean attracted so much lightning would have found the sunken boat and deduced it was somehow the reason.

He placed handfuls of crystals into the bag until he'd recovered them all. He backed out of the hold while Booker cinched the dive bag tight. He attached a flotation balloon and inflated it enough so the bag was neutrally buoyant. Book jerked a thumb upward. Mercer held out one finger and finned up and over the cockpit windows. To access their plane, Amelia Earhart and Fred Noonan had to climb in through a hatch cut into the top of the fuselage. Mercer scraped away some bits of stone and sand and found it easily.

He wasn't sure why he wanted to do this. He'd told himself moments earlier that he didn't want to disturb the site, and yet he couldn't stop himself from opening that hatch. The hatch popped loose effortlessly in his hands. Visibility was excellent in the cabin, which had been sealed for eighty years, though Mercer knew if he entered, his movements would stir up the detritus covering every horizontal surface. He rotated his dive light to look forward. Additional light filtered in through the slime on the windows, so he could see nothing but vague shapes and shadow. Aft he could clearly see the remains of a seat that had seen its cushion long ago consumed by some sea creatures. On the floor below it were buttons that had once adorned Fred Noonan's now-dissolved shirt and other smaller lumps hidden in the slime.

Out of respect, Mercer wasn't going to enter the cabin through the roof hatch to determine what remained of the fabled pilot. He liked the images through which the world knew her—a sexy, determined tomboy type, smiling as she stood next to an airplane—and not what he knew was hidden from his view by the tall-backed command chair before him.

Running between the cockpit and navigator's seat was a stainless-steel cable, and he recalled from the little research he'd done since first learning of Earhart's involvement that this was how the pilot and her navigator communicated during the flight. They passed notes back and forth written in grease pencil, on an early form of whiteboard.

Gingerly he reached out and grasped the wire. It was a little slack, but when Mercer pulled it came freely. The board had been next to Amelia during the end of the flight, those frantic minutes before the plane struck the ocean and sank. She had to have known it was coming and would have had time to think about what would be her final words, as the fuel gauges slowly spun down to empty and the Pratt & Whitney starved.

He pulled ever so gently until the board came gliding out of the gloom. He dared not touch it, so he craned his head awkwardly into the cabin and cast his light on the board. Whatever it was made of had repelled the slimes and molds that were flung like cobwebs around the cabin. The white slate was clean except for the following words:

> George, thank you for the adventure that has been my life.
>
> I love you,
> Me

Somehow he knew that's how she signed their most intimate notes and felt like he'd just read the most honest and beautiful thing ever written. He never knew a person could tear up in a diving mask and realized ruefully that he couldn't wipe away their stinging saltiness.

He returned the board to where it belonged next to the pilot's seat and eased out of the plane. He closed the hatch reverently, rethinking his decision to let the world know about his discovery.

Book was there, waiting. Mercer gave him a slow nod, and together they returned to the surface, the bag of crystals in tow.

Rory was on the dive platform when they reached the surface. Mercer spat out his regulator, having used the slow ascent to process his feelings. For the time being he was going to focus on the fact that he'd recovered the last cache of the lightning stones, and he knew now he could use them as a lure to finally flush out his enemy.

"Well?" the Aussie asked in that peculiar twang.

"One Lockheed Electra Model 10," Mercer said, now grinning like the Cheshire cat, "circa 1937 or so."

"It's her?"

"Positive," Mercer assured him. "We've found Amelia Earhart after all these years."

"I'll be buggered," Reyes said. "I had my doubts about you two, but no more."

Sykes handed up the bag, and Reyes had to strain to haul it clear. Water poured out of it until it was light enough for him to lift it over the transom and manhandle to the deck. The stones weighed more than fifty pounds, and the bag still leaked gallons of water. He then helped each man out in turn, giving them the high five and a hearty slap on the back.

While they were shucking their gear, Rory came back with a bottle of Dom Pérignon. "I keep a few aboard so if a charter catches a big one they don't mind shelling out some extra coin for the good champers. This one's warm, but who gives a tinker's toss."

He popped the cork over the side like he was firing a starter's pistol and held the frothing eruption of sparkling wine to his lips before passing the bottle to Mercer. Mercer took a mouthful of foam and gave Book his turn. By the time the bottle had gone around a second time, the carbonation had relaxed enough so they could enjoy the wine's sublime taste and texture.

They finished the bottle and Reyes broke out the Foster's. He gave the men a hand with their gear and asked if they wanted lunch before returning to Fiji, and when they said no he climbed to the flying bridge to start the long haul back south and home.

With the twin engines getting on line, Mercer went below to rinse the salt from his body—but he quickly detected another sound that was distinct from the throaty diesel's roar. It was a higher-pitched note, and he knew what it was. He'd heard it the day before, and it had raised his hackles then.

Mercer grabbed a pair of tennis shoes from his cabin floor and raced back out onto the rear deck. Booker was lolling in the fighting chair, his broad chest rising in the slow rhythms of a man already asleep. But even before Mercer could slap his shoulder to wake him, Sykes's eyes flashed open as he, too, detected something.

"What?" Sykes said, coming alert.

"Not sure," Mercer said, scanning the skies above Alofi Island.

The plane didn't come over the top of the isle. It flashed around the flank instead, barely skimming above the waves. So low, in fact, that its propellers kicked up spray in its wake.

They hadn't heard the regular supply plane out of Wallis Island the day before, Mercer realized. It was a twin-engined flying boat they'd heard land on the far side of Alofi. It had taken off again as part of the illusion, presumably after dropping off an observer to watch the men aboard the sport fisherman that was anchored in the spot where Jason Rutland had calculated Amelia's plane would be. And now the venerable PBY Catalina, a World War II–vintage workhorse that was still in wide use throughout the Pacific, was rounding the island again and charging straight at the *Suva Surprise*.

Mercer already had a good idea how they'd been found out.

"Will you look at that," Rory Reyes shouted down from the bridge, delighted at seeing the ungainly old warbird with its high wings and engines like Dumbo's ears. He didn't understand the danger they were all in.

The PBY was considered a slow aircraft even back in its heyday, but the lumbering plane still ate the distance between itself and the fleeing boat in seconds. Booker was already in motion, dashing down into the cabin space. Mercer shouted for Rory to take cover an instant before the plane rocketed past, no more than fifty yards off their starboard rail and at a height of twenty feet.

A side hatch was open in the aircraft's hull, and from the darkness came the continuous flash of a gun on full auto. Despite the speed and the instability of the shooting platform, half the bullets from the thirty-round clip raked the side of the *Suva Surprise*. Fiberglass exploded with each impact, wood splinters blew free, and aluminum and polished brass were holed by the blast. The plane immediately pulled up into a sharp turning bank, nearly as tight as an Immelmann, to come back for another pass.

Mercer knew Reyes had survived because the engines were suddenly throttled up to everything they had, and he started turning the wheel erratically.

Booker appeared with a bundle wrapped in a beach towel.

"Plan B," Mercer told him. "Just like we talked about."

"How'd the bastards find us?"

"Doesn't matter right now."

Booker left his mystery package on the fighting chair and helped Mercer with the Zodiac. The *Surprise* was running hard, so the wind across the deck was savage, but they managed to get down and tie the crystal-laden dive bag to the Zodiac's integrated oarlock.

"They put a spotter on the island," Mercer said as they worked. "As soon as he saw us heave a bag over the side and start celebrating like a bunch of idiots he called in the cavalry."

"I always thought the cavalry were the good guys."

"Willing to bet these guys see themselves on the side of the angels, same as us." Mercer finished the triple knot. "Make sure Reyes stays out of it. This isn't his fight."

The Catalina finished its turn and started back for another strafing run. There wouldn't be enough time to get clear, so Mercer and Sykes threw themselves flat as the plane came directly overhead. The gunman didn't open fire this time, but he did hurl something out of the door. It hit the deck inches from Booker's head and smashed, peppering him in glass.

Mercer looked up in time to see what had shattered. It was a Mason jar, which had contained a hand grenade whose spoon had now popped free. It was an old Vietnam-era trick used by chopper crews to keep their grenades from exploding before they hit the ground. Mercer lunged forward, grabbed the rounded incendiary, and flicked it over the side. It exploded in their wake two seconds later, throwing up a geyser of water as if they'd just released a miniature depth charge.

"You know what to do," Mercer said and got ready.

Booker nodded, pressed something into Mercer's hand, and climbed up to the bridge while the flying boat came around for yet another attack. Book laid his bundle onto the floor at his feet and shouldered Rory aside. "Sorry, Cap'n."

He chopped the throttles and turned to see Mercer shove the Zodiac over the transom and leap in after it. He kicked the engines back up to speed, leaving the inflatable bobbing in his wake.

Then Sykes started swinging the boat around in a desperate bid to return to the islands and the illusory safety of the town of Kolotai on nearby Futuna.

"What the hell is going on?" Reyes bellowed.

"Apparently our ruse didn't work."

"And what's in the bundle?"

Sykes bent to retrieve it. The towel fell away, revealing a wicked-looking contraption that was a cross between a carpenter's nail gun and a science fiction laser blaster.

"Jesus," Reyes gasped. "What the bloody hell is that thing?"

"It's called a Vector, and it's built by Kriss. It fires forty-five-caliber ACP. This is only a semiautomatic, but I can still lay down cover fire as effectively as a machine gunner."

The weapon was a bullpup design with the magazine behind the trigger assembly to keep it compact but still give it some barrel length for accuracy. It was considered one of the best close support weapons ever built, though Sykes had chosen it for this mission because of its incredible compactness.

They had smuggled the gun into the country by putting it and extra ammo into a metallic pouch developed for American Special Forces troops who needed to smuggle weapons through civilian customs. The pouches were part of an antidetection system that could fool most modern X-ray machines. Book had access to the pouches but not the special carrying cases operators were also issued, so he'd improvised. He'd wrapped the pouch in coils of copper wire. The old scanner back at the Nadi airport's customs house hadn't stood a chance. That first day out of Suva, Book had sat in his cabin peeling back the wire to get at the weapon. The wire would then be repurposed as swaddling to shield the bag of gems once they'd found them.

The plane had straightened out for another run at them, and Reyes eyed it nervously. "Shoot that damned plane!" he yelled.

"Waste of ammo," Sykes replied calmly. "I'd never hit it, let alone anything vital enough to slow their attack. Trust me on this. Mercer and I considered this and have a plan."

Booker looked back and saw that Mercer was racing the Zodiac toward Alofi as fast as he could go. He was still less than a mile off their beam, but the distance was widening with each passing second.

Booker ordered Rory to go below, but the Aussie stubbornly refused. The PBY swooped by their starboard side, flying only a few miles per hour above the plane's astonishingly slow stall speed. The gunner's door was open and the machine gun spat again, a long raking barrage that tore up more of the boat. This time the shooter concentrated on the stern in hopes of knocking out the engines or starting a fire. The combination of engine noise and autofire was a hellish cacophony that filled the air, relenting only when the plane passed by. Book fought the urge to grab the Kriss and return fire. At that slow speed he could have laid in a few well-placed shots, but then the PBY would have just stayed out of range and picked them off from a distance.

The fourth pass was another bombing run, and this time there was nothing they could do about the glass jar that bounced off the windshield, shattering it. The grenade popped free and seemed about to fly over the rail when a wave tipped the boat just enough for the explosive device to catch the railing and drop back onto the aft deck.

—

Mercer was a mile and a half away, pushing the little one-cylinder for everything it had, when he heard the crump of an explosion over the dragonfly whine of the Evinrude. He turned in time to see greasy smoke and torrents of fire rising from the fishing boat's stern. He swore. That hadn't been part of the plan. The attackers should have figured out that the lone man in the Zodiac had the stones, not the big sportfisherman. He and Book had exaggerated their actions for the sake of the guy manning the observation post so that he would then pass on that information to the pilot.

Then he got it. His adversary was as ruthless as they came. He'd forgotten that Sherman Smithson hadn't been spared out of any sense of kindness. He was alive because he was needed to pass on information. There was no way these people were going to leave any witness, innocent or otherwise.

Mercer kept racing for Alofi Island, but he also kept looking back to see the Catalina circling again, like a buzzard waiting for its intended meal to die. He couldn't believe this was happening. Book was supposed to get clear with Rory Reyes, not end up taking the brunt of the attack.

Sixty seconds after the first explosion, a second massive detonation ripped across the ocean's surface. The *Suva Surprise*'s diesel tanks lit off in a towering plume of orange, red, and black. Moments later, the sea was peppered with flying debris—shards of fiberglass and wood and steel that had once been the beautiful sportsfisherman. Anyone left aboard would have been carbonized by such a massive fireball.

Not satisfied with its first victims, the antique seaplane maneuvered around, low to the water, and turned toward Mercer. Its engines were pitched so it sounded like a dive-bomber dropping out of the sky. It wasn't a vulture now, but a screaming bird of prey.

25

It was the end of the first full day of the conference, and Jason Rutland was exhausted—and he still had to get changed for a dinner he would have rather avoided. He got back to his room, threw his briefcase on the bed, and hung his suit coat over the back of the desk chair. It was the same generic mid-price room where he'd stayed dozens of nights in dozens of cities, attending dozens of near-identical symposiums. As a fresh-faced PhD he'd loved these events—the travel, the new places—but after twelve years he found the experience tedious and, worse, pointless.

He thumbed the remote and new age music filled the room while the television screen brightened to display the events currently taking place at the hotel. He had to flick through eight more promotional screens before actually finding a television station. It was the local news, running a story on global warming. He turned the sound down and decided to close his eyes for fifteen minutes.

Rutland lay on the bed, staring at the cream-colored hotel ceiling. He had been thinking constantly about the strange crystal Mercer had brought him and its fascinating electricity-conducting properties. Jason wondered if Mercer had had success in the South Pacific based on the calculations he'd done.

Suddenly an idea jolted him out of bed as if he'd been hit with a defibrillator. Maybe it was the mention of global warming on the local news, or maybe it was just a terrifying connecting of the dots, but Rutland had an ominous thought. He grabbed his tablet and started scrolling through the notes he'd made on the crystal sample.

Rutland worked for an hour, ignoring the buzz of his cell phone from the guys he was supposed to dine with. During the second hour of work, what had begun as a crazy idea was gelling into a likely scenario. Was somebody about to tinker with the earth's environment? Why anybody would attempt geoengineering at this scale was beyond his ability to comprehend, but it was a gamble of unimaginable consequences. If he was right, and didn't find a way to stop it, the world would pine for the days when climate change promised just two or three degrees of additional heat.

Rutland reached for his phone and frantically dialed Philip Mercer.

It was Mercer's old buddy who answered. "H'lo."

"Harry, is that you?"

"Yeah. Who's this?"

"Jason Rutland. We met at—"

"Pimlico," Harry supplied. "You're the young fella dating my future wife, the Weather Lady."

The man sounded drunk but earnest. "Thanks, Harry. She told me if she ever gets tired of me, you're the next on her list. Listen, I need to get in touch with Mercer right away. Is he still out of reach?"

Harry was suddenly all business. "Booker has a satellite phone. Give me a minute to get the number."

When Harry came back on the line he rattled off the string of digits. Jason thanked him, killed the connection, and immediately dialed the new number.

He got a computer-generated request for him to leave a message. "Mr. Sykes, this is Jason Rutland. It's critical that Mercer calls me. I think I know what they're going to do with the crystals if they ever get their hands on them. It could be a disaster if they screw up . . . I mean a real global catastrophe. I'm going to see if I can get some help, but we need to stop them. Please tell Mercer to call me right away." He gave his cell number and clicked off.

Rutland recalled a line from a science fiction movie, saying that in a battle with a sentient computer system, humanity had been forced to torch the sky.

It sickened him to think that someone was playing with the technology to bring that about.

26

Mercer timed his move to the second. The PBY flying boat was coming in low and slow, bearing down on him like a lumbering beast, so the waist gunner would have the best angle, and the longest window, to fire. He watched over his shoulder as it came closer, steeling himself to the growing roar of its engines, knowing he had one chance to get this right and a million to get it wrong.

The plane began to turn, its engines so close he could see the twin brown ribbons of exhaust spewing into the slipstream. The door gunner was doubtlessly in position, though Mercer couldn't yet see him. The pilot twisted the aircraft, and suddenly Mercer was exposed to the open door. He could see the man braced there, an assault rifle to his shoulder, his one arm up in a classic firing stance. Even in the uncertain light of the aircraft's cabin and despite the pitching and rolling, Mercer recognized the shooter instantly—as he knew he would.

Without hesitation, and before the marksman could draw a bead, Mercer hauled over the outboard, and he crossed under the string of bullets that tore over his head and kicked up little fountains from the Pacific's surface. The inflatable was just too maneuverable. The plane made a wide turn and came back for another pass, and this time Mercer simply cut the throttle and the next fusillade tore at the sea in front of him.

He played mouse to their cat the entire way in to shore, with Mercer winning each round. The only time they came close was during the final run-up to the beach. The plane was coming at him at an angle, and until he made his passage through the breakers, he couldn't turn or he'd capsize in the surf.

The rifle barked its repetitive mechanical cracks, and the water around him erupted with the impacts. The Zodiac began to hiss as two cells were hit and started to deflate. Mercer's bare shoulder was singed by a passing bullet, but he made it through without being struck.

The large plane banked off, turning so tightly he could imagine the old aluminum struts and supports groaning at the G-load. They wanted one more pass before he beached the boat and vanished into the jungle. Mercer raced through the pounding waves, even as the plucky little inflatable sagged. He recalled the roles being reversed in Iowa.

The boat burst through one large curling wave, and suddenly he was through the breakers. The Catalina was coming around, slower and lower, and Mercer realized that this strafing run would be parallel to the beach because they were landing just inside the reef line. It was a gutsy move, but one he didn't waste time appreciating. He gunned the boat, and just when he was sure he could feel the cross hairs on his spine he threw himself over the side and into the water.

Bullets shredded the air overhead, while the wave action and momentum shoved the Zodiac on the shelving beach. Mercer stayed underwater for another few seconds, then rose up when the plane had flown past. Standing knee-deep in the surf, he untied the dive bag from the oarlock and tossed it over his shoulder. A quarter mile up the beach the PBY skimmed the water and then alit with the grace of a swan. Spray erupted around the hull and engines as the propellers' pitch was changed to augment the deceleration of planing into the sea.

Mercer wore only a bathing suit and sneakers, so when he took off running into the underbrush bordering the beach, the foliage ripped at his skin without mercy. He ran as hard as he could, because his head start would vanish quickly against armed hunters dressed for the sport.

In order to survive he would have to make it until dark. It was his only chance. Under cover of night he could swim to Futuna. It was two miles away, and Mercer recalled observing a substantial current the first night when they had anchored and Book watched for lightning, but he had no choice. Alofi was only twelve square miles. It could provide cover for a few days, but eventually they would find him.

Mercer knew he would have to ditch the stones. Fifty pounds wasn't the heaviest load he'd ever packed, not by a long shot, but that deadweight would sap his strength in the heat and humidity, making his pursuers' job that much easier.

He continued through the brush, contemplating where he could hide the stones, when he suddenly heard the sound of approaching feet pounding through scrub in front of him. He hadn't expected the encounter, and neither did the man rushing at him. Mercer had the advantage as he was running slightly uphill, while the man they'd posted to watch the marine salvage operation was running down and a little out of control.

Mercer veered just before they collided and threw out a foot to trip up the other guy, who crashed into the undergrowth. Mercer whirled and whipped out the compact Glock 30 pistol they had smuggled in with the Kriss Vector. Like Booker's submachine gun, the Glock 30 packed the .45 ACP, a round developed for fighting in the Philippines after the Spanish American War, in which the Moro tribesmen would all but ignore being shot by the .38 calibers the Americans had been issued.

The guy recovered fast. He'd been running with a pistol in his hand but had landed awkwardly enough that he had to roll over to fire. He was just twisting to aim at Mercer when Mercer leapt at him, crashing his own gun down against the man's temple. The first blow stunned him, but Mercer couldn't take a chance and he slammed the butt into the thinnest part of the gunman's skull a second time. He heard the bone break.

Mercer didn't wait to see if the guy was dead; he knew he was. Nor did he bother looking for wherever the man's gun went flying. He took off running again—but instead of trying to gain safety by gaining distance, Mercer reversed himself and went back toward where the seaplane had landed.

When he was close enough to see the landing spot, he peered out at the ungainly plane resting in the water just offshore, its nose already tied off to a large stake driven into the sand. The pilot and copilot were taking a moment to look over the wings and tail, while on the beach three men in baggy khaki pants and dark T-shirts huddled over a fourth man kneeling on the beach. He was bent over a piece of electronics, and Mercer saw his odds of success plummet.

They had some sort of detection gear. Mercer was almost certain it was a device that sent out radio or microwave bursts and measured for unnatural distortion fields in its proximity. The greater the warp in the field, the closer the gems.

Mercer turned back once again and began running for the interior. There would be no clever ruses or artful dodges. He needed distance from them, and he needed it fast. Sweat ran down his naked torso in rivulets that mixed with blood from where saber-like leaves had slashed at him. There were no large native animals on the island to carve game trails, so Mercer had to move across the terrain, fighting it, while at the same time trying not to leave an obvious trail that a tracker could follow.

He came upon a stream that was still running with the remnants of the storm two days earlier. He palmed several quick mouthfuls of drinking water, and then walked carefully along its course so that he left no tracks. Mercer stayed with the stream for two miles, climbing into the interior of Alofi Island, unconsciously seeking high ground. When the water-course dried up, he moved back into the dense foliage. He decided not to hide the stones just yet, now that he had seen the electronic device being used by his opponents. Mercer knew his best chance was to keep on the move, maintaining enough separation that their detection gear wouldn't home in on the crystals.

The day stretched on and Mercer kept at it, staying in motion in the thick underbrush for six hours. Dusk was still several hours away, so he couldn't let his guard down, but he'd done as well as could be expected. He hadn't seen or heard any sign of the men chasing him. However, he hadn't eaten since breakfast, and his shoulders ached from lugging the bag. He was also severely dehydrated.

Mercer knew he couldn't keep moving much longer, and once he stopped the crystals would act as a homing beacon. He would have to ditch the stones now. During one of his earlier loops around the central hills, he'd spotted the old volcanic vent on a hillock near a ravine. The vent wasn't very deep, about five feet before its passage was blocked by a plug of solidified lava, but he hoped it would help shield the crystals a little. He spent another twenty minutes backtracking to the vent, then jammed the bag into the fissure and began packing loose rocks around it.

Mercer finished piling rubble into the hole and stood. It was an enormous relief to have the weight off his shoulders, and as much as he wanted to take a few seconds to rest, he didn't dare.

"I think we've played this game long enough."

Mercer heard the voice and froze. He recognized the accent as South African, from his many times in that country, but he couldn't see the man. He kept his pistol low and out of sight, turning in place to watch all approaches.

"You're quite the pain in my ass."

"I aim to please," Mercer replied, still not sure where the man was. Not that it mattered—the South African's support team would be surrounding him soon while he kept their quarry busy.

"Not so much anymore, eh, tough guy? I hope you

realize we've been down on the beach the whole time watching you on our detector. We just don't know what happened to the man we dropped off to watch your operation."

"I bashed his head in," Mercer said.

The man chuckled coldly. "No matter. I put this team together on the fly. I knew none of them."

"They're a bunch of amateurs."

"That's true. Hell, I think this would have all turned out a lot different if the greenhorn you killed in that old woman's house hadn't gotten jumpy back there in the mine and started firing. He left me no choice but to finish them all off."

Mercer's hand tightened on the pistol held down by his thigh. The man spoke so casually about Abe's slaughter.

"I've had a bellyful of killing, Yank. I told my boss that there would be no need for violence on this operation. I told him that after it was over, I was done."

"After *what* is over?" asked Mercer, partially to keep the man talking, but also to get some clarity on what this whole nightmare was about. "What's so important about a handful of crystals?"

The man in the bush chuckled again. "You won't live to see it, mate. This is space-aged . . . beyond our pay scales. They say these stones are going to help beam energy into the sky, and play with the temperature on Earth. It's big business—billions. Nothing that concerns you and me."

Mercer tried to comprehend what he had just heard. How was that possible?

"Now toss away the Glock I see in your hand, or I drop you where you stand," the man said, stepping from behind a flowering bush.

Mercer looked up and was again struck by the familiarity of the man's silhouette and the way he carried himself. Then the South African took another step closer, and a beam of sunlight penetrating through the canopy of trees shone across his face. Mercer gaped. Now he knew why the man was so memorable. He knew him. Had known him. In another time and at another place.

The port-wine birthmark had once taken up half the man's left cheek, but a bullet scar puckered and contorted the blemish and twisted his mouth so that the lower lip hung slack. That deformity forced the man to slurp back saliva that tried to dribble through his seemingly lifeless mouth.

Mercer knew he'd gone pale, and the man's eyes narrowed. The killer must have assumed it was revulsion at his hideous disfigurement; he was probably accustomed to seeing that reaction.

The mercenary raised an American-made M-4 assault rifle to his shoulder and snapped angrily, "Lose the Glock or you die now."

In his shock Mercer had forgotten the earlier order. He dropped the pistol to the ground. It was useless now anyway. He had one advantage, and he had to use it now before the merc's backup got into position.

"Who was the other white man with you?" Mercer asked.

"What? What other white man? All the guys with me are white."

"Not here. I'm talking twenty years ago—when we were in Cameroon, and you and a small force attacked my camp. It was the day I used your birthmark for target practice."

Niklaas Coetzer's face went through a gamut of

expressions—confusion, shock, anger, regret, hatred, pain, loneliness. It was the playback of a lifetime of woe brought about by the one defining moment in his past. The disfigurement and poor medical care had changed the trajectory of his life. Prior to that fateful shot he had fought on the side of the righteous, working for clients he could believe in. After that there was little meaning in his life. Children ran in horror from his gaze, and Coetzer only knew love when he paid for it in cash. He was cast adrift by his ruined face and soon found himself uncaringly working for some of the worst monsters in the world.

That shot had wrecked his life. Rarely had a day passed that he hadn't wished the round had killed him, or that he'd get a chance to kill the man who'd cursed him.

Coetzer's brain returned from that fate-filled moment in the African jungle, only to realize that his quarry was in motion, backpedaling quickly for the ravine behind him. His men had express orders not to fire until Coetzer gave the command, so none of the men around him were reacting to Mercer's escape. It took Coetzer another second to process this fact, too.

Mercer spun and launched himself off the ravine's edge. The slope was gentle, but the ground was rocky and he hit hard, rolling over his right shoulder, trying and failing to gain his feet as he continued to tumble out of control.

"Fire!"

He heard the shout behind him, but he was already out of the mercenaries' sight, at least for a few seconds. And that's all he'd really bought himself, seconds, because nothing was going to stop the South African from wanting to kill him now.

The shots came from across the ravine, a hundred yards away, and were fired with pinpoint accuracy. Two of the mercenary's hired goons went down before the sound of the report reached them, and before the others realized that they were under attack. The leader recognized the danger and threw himself flat with his two remaining hired guns.

This was all happening behind and above Mercer, but he could see ahead where the sniper was holed up in the crook of a tree, the boxy Kriss submachine gun tucked hard against his meaty shoulder. He reached the bottom of the ravine and staggered to his feet. Meanwhile, on the opposite rim, Booker Sykes watched the area where the confrontation had taken place through a five-power scope.

The mercenaries stayed well hidden but quickly managed to get off volleys of return fire. Three guns on full auto forced Book to relinquish his post. He jumped down off the tree and retreated back into the jungle. Mercer ran as hard as he could, his body aching from so much abuse. Behind him, the remaining shooters maintained their positions; they had gone from offense to defense in the blink of an eye and now had to protect the bag of crystals since it, and not the men who'd found it, was their ultimate goal.

Book slowed his retreat enough for Mercer to catch up. As soon as they were side by side, Booker picked up the pace again.

"'Bout damned time," Mercer wheezed.

"That's the thanks I get?"

"I circled back half a dozen times to the volcanic vent you told me about from your night of recon, waiting for you to get into position."

"Don't know if you noticed, but they blew up the damned boat about three miles off the coast."

"There was that," Mercer conceded. "You two okay?"

"Reyes is seriously pissed but unhurt. In the time between the grenade going off and the diesel exploding, I gathered my gear and a spare scuba rig and got us over the side. It took us this long to swim in without being detected, and to get to a place where I could surveil the vent."

"Did you place the electronic tracker?"

"Planted that first thing when we reached shore. I stuck it under the old Catalina's outer pontoon. Pilots were asleep, while the armed rabble were watching something on an electronic display on the beach."

"Yes . . . they were tracking me the whole time," Mercer said angrily.

Mercer was actually thankful. Their Plan B had been a hairy idea . . . but necessary. He knew there was a distinct chance his enemies would recognize the flaw in Jason Rutland's deception. They had good scientists backing their efforts, and he and Booker had to prepare for the possibility they would recalculate Fred Noonan's navigation error and arrive at the crash site very quickly.

Thirty minutes later, Mercer and Sykes were approaching the north coast of Alofi, almost directly opposite of where Mercer had first landed. Without warning, a thundering sound filled the jungle, and they ducked their heads as the silver PBY rumbled over the island, low enough to whip the topmost branches but gaining altitude as it flew away.

"Wasn't sure if they were going to leave," Mercer said.

"Why wouldn't they? They got what they came for."

"They did . . . but they didn't get me."

Book looked at Mercer quizzically.

"I didn't tell you this," Mercer said, "but the team leader is a South African mercenary."

"Yeah, so. You know him?"

"Not his name," Mercer admitted. "But I shot him in the face while I was in college, and I really, really think he wants me dead."

Booker whistled. "For a rock jock, man, you sure get around. Talk to me."

"First tell me that you managed to save your sat phone so we can get off this godforsaken rock."

"I left it with Rory. We'll have a charter plane here from Fiji by the time we find our way over to the airstrip on Futuna. And don't worry, no swimming. We found a boat we can borrow. Now . . . tell me how a college puke ends up shooting some badass South African operator?"

Mercer nodded. "First let me tell you about the teacher who invited me on an expedition . . ."

27

The chartered Gulfstream III had taken off from Futuna Island, destined for Nadi International. Philip Mercer and Booker Sykes sat alertly in the plush leather seats. Rory Reyes slept, no doubt dreaming of a replacement for the *Suva Surprise*. Once they were airborne, Book had listened to the voice message left by Jason Rutland, immediately handing over the phone so Mercer could call him back.

Rutland was actually on a discussion panel when Mercer's call came through, and he left it without a word.

"We have a big problem," Rutland had said straightaway, laying out his case before Mercer could even say hello. Rutland talked for ten minutes. Mercer interrupted only to tell him what the South African mercenary had said about the stones being used to beam energy into the sky, which meshed with Rutland's frightening theories. Two minutes later, they signed off.

Mercer immediately called his old boss, Ira Lasko. Lasko had been deputy national security adviser to the former president of the United States, and Mercer had reported to him in his role as special science adviser. Since the last election, both men had been out of government work, but Mercer hoped Ira still had connections.

He had gotten only a minute into his story when Lasko, a retired admiral, said, "Stop right there. I don't doubt what you're telling me is true, but I have zero pull with the current administration. That's what happens around here when the party in power switches. Not only was everything done by the predecessor in the Oval Office wrong, but his staffers were all idiots who can't be trusted. Far from being the loyal opposition, everyone who served in the past becomes persona non grata."

"Ira, this transcends politics."

"Nothing transcends politics to the current occupant of the White House. The national security adviser is a former policy director for a leftist think tank who once opined that Neville Chamberlain didn't appease Hitler enough. I can't go to her with this. I can't go to anyone."

"All right, then keep it with your former family."

"Huh?"

"The navy, Ira. You were an admiral. You still have pull there, don't you?"

"Yeah but—"

"No buts on this," Mercer said. "They just flew off with the crystals, and they're on alert because they know we're looking for them. If my friend is right, they could be used to cause a cascade effect within the earth's magnetic field lines. At best it could cause a reversal of the poles, which is a phenomenon that occurs naturally every few million years, but it's something mankind—a species now dependent on satellites and power grids and all kinds of other vulnerable technology—has never experienced."

"And at worst?"

"Jason isn't sure . . . nothing like this has ever happened. The fields could collapse entirely, leaving the planet exposed to massive amounts of solar and cosmic radiation. In a short time, Earth would become a lifeless cinder."

There was silence on the other end of the line. "You're sure about this?"

"I am staking my reputation and our friendship on the fact that this is deadly serious, Ira. It's why I called you. I need someone who can help me stop this, but there's no time to bullshit with bureaucratic channels. If Jason's right, they're about to pump power through these crystals and attempt to geoengineer the planet's magnetic fields. A slight miscalculation and we're all dead. This needs to stop before it gets started."

"What do you need?" Ira asked. "Your friend said they are likely working off of a ship."

"Yes, a special kind of ship, one that only the Russians ever built. It has massive antennas for tracking objects in space. Jason thinks they can be used to beam radiation upward."

"Where is this ship now?"

"Booker and I put a tracking chip onto the PBY Catalina they're using to transfer the stones. We think it will link up with the ship in the next few hours. I'll give you the coordinating information off the tracker so you can get me the GPS location. Jason tells me that it'll be someplace close to the equator so both north and south polarity will be affected. These guys are ecoterrorists . . . what I'd like is a Tomahawk cruise missile to take out the ship, but it's nuclear powered and I know that's never going to happen."

"Nuclear meltdown at sea because of a navy attack . . . No. That definitely isn't going to happen. Besides, I couldn't get you a cruise missile anymore— even if I pulled in every chit I've got. I can provide some logistical support on this, pass it off as a good-will stunt or something, but I can't get weapons or combat troops."

"I'll take anything you can give me, Ira. Jason is finding out everything he can about this ship, the *Akademik Nikolay Zhukovsky*. Once we're familiar with her layout, Book and I will come up with a plan and get back to you."

"Okay. I'll be ready."

—

Twenty hours later, true to his word, Ira Lasko had pulled in favor after favor, and Mercer and Book found themselves in the rear cargo compartment of a Marine Corps V-22 Osprey aboard the amphibious assault ship USS *America*, the latest in the navy's fleet. The Osprey was a tilt-rotor hybrid of a plane and a helicopter. It could land and take off vertically, but the rotors then translated into a horizontal position to become giant propellers that gave it a top speed of 350 miles per hour at fifteen thousand feet.

Apart from the loadmaster, a young kid wearing an oversize helmet that made him look like a boy playing soldier, they were alone in a space designed for two dozen combat troops. The engine noise was nothing compared to the jaw-shaking thunder of the rotors when they got up to speed. They beat the air over the cabin into a screaming fury. The pilot waited for one last authorization from crewmen on the ship's deck, and he applied even more power to lift the plane into the evening sky.

Out the tiny window next to his seat, Mercer could see the lights of the amphib's control island, and a pair of sleek F-35 Lightning II strike fighters. Like the Osprey, those supersonic planes could also land and take off like helicopters. And then those sights all dropped away in a gut-wrenching climb that was the ultimate rebuke to gravity's reign. The V-22 clawed for altitude, bucking like mad as it rose within an envelope of its own turbulence, but then the rotors started to tilt. They lost a little altitude but gained speed and lift across the wings. In seconds they were flying normally, the turbines cut back since they weren't working nearly as hard.

"First time in one of these?" Book shouted to be heard.

Mercer grinned like a kid. It was all the answer he needed to give.

From Fiji, where they'd left Rory with the promise to cooperate with the insurance inquest, they'd continued on in the hired Gulfstream to Tarawa. There they were met by a Sea King helicopter sent for them from the *America*. The assault ship had just completed a friendly port call and was on her way to Indonesia, where her complement of over a thousand Marines was to hold joint exercises with several regional powers.

Mercer had followed Book's lead on each flight and gotten as much sleep as he could, but he still felt like he'd accrued a sleep debt he'd never be able to repay. Now that they were on the last leg of their odyssey, Mercer was keyed up and ready.

They'd been able to borrow some equipment from the ship's stores—wet suits and dive gear. They weren't, however, allowed to take any weapons from the armory. That was a favor Ira couldn't have called in. It wasn't a problem for Booker since he still had the Kriss and four magazines. Mercer had lost his pistol. The *America*'s captain, William R. Tuttle, had met them in his cabin shortly after they'd arrived. He explained that he'd never served under Ira's command at sea, since Lasko was a submariner, but they knew and respected each other immensely. Tuttle was sticking his neck out for Ira. At the end of their meeting, Tuttle went to his desk and slid out a wooden presentation box with a glass window in it. The case was a beautiful piece of workmanship that seemed too ornate for what it contained, until Tuttle explained the origins of the particular piece within.

"This was my great-uncle's," he said, opening the lid and pulling out a dull M1911 Colt .45 that looked like it had been through the wars. And in fact, it had. "He carried it on Guadalcanal, Saipan, and Iwo Jima. He gave it to me when I graduated Annapolis, and I've illegally brought it with me on every one of my floats to remind me that I stand upon the shoulders of giants.

"Admiral Lasko made me understand how important this is." He flipped the pistol in his hand and presented it butt first to Mercer. "If at all possible, I would like it back."

The antique weapon now hung in a waterproof pouch from Mercer's belt, its two magazines loaded from Booker's stash of ammunition.

The tracking chip Sykes had secreted on the PBY indicated the plane had landed for an hour at a spot directly on the equator, two hundred miles east of Tarawa, so they were heading there now. The PBY had taken off again and was currently sitting just off the island of Tuvalu, presumably its role in the operation complete.

For the first leg of the rendezvous flight, they cruised at comfortable speed and altitude, but the plan Mercer and Book had devised would require some fancy piloting as soon as they neared the operational limits of the *Akademik Zhukovsky*'s radar. The Osprey's copilot kept an eye on the threat board; as soon as they were painted by the tracking ship's radar, the pilot would drop them to the deck so fast the operators on the former Soviet tracking ship would assume they'd seen a false return.

Two hours into the flight, after full night had settled in, that's exactly what happened. Without warning, the engines seemed to die, and the plane fell out of the sky like a brick. The Osprey had such poor lift on its own that without constant thrust from the engines it went into free fall. They dropped fourteen thousand feet so fast that Mercer felt weightless, and certain they would never recover. Booker was actually whooping like a cowboy, and even the young loadmaster seemed to be having the time of his life.

It was only at the last possible second that the engines began to take the strain, only this time they were partially translated for vertical flight. When the big rotors began chewing into the air, the express ride to hell came to a gentle end, with the Osprey just fifty feet above the waves and cruising along at a mere thirty knots.

A minute later the pilot spoke to the loadmaster over his intercom helmet, and the young man unclipped from his seat and approached Mercer. "Pilot says we have the fuel to make it to your target flying low and slow like this, but after you jump we can only fly this way for another ten minutes before we're going to need to transition back to normal flight. Egg-beating like we are right now sucks up the JP-8. There's a chance we'll be back on their radar then, and your cover will blow."

"Understood. Once we're aboard the jig's up anyway."

The kid gave him a thumbs-up and went back to his seat.

A few minutes later, the young Marine cocked his head like a dog hearing a piercing whistle while he listened to another report from the pilot. He nodded as if he could be seen and unstrapped himself once again. "Pilot says we just got a radio query from a boat calling itself the *Jarwyne*. Our gear tells us it's your target. Anyway they bought our line about us being a cargo ship. We're moving at the right height and speed that we look like a ship's superstructure on their radar. Pretty slick, huh?"

Mercer didn't tell the kid that it was his idea to approach the *Zhokovsky* at night like this. "Very slick," he said over the racket.

They would fly about four miles west of the Russian ship, supposedly as they were making their way to Hawaii with a load of containers. It was far enough to suppress the distinctive echoing thrump of the rotors but not so far that Booker and Mercer would be floundering around the tropics.

Since they had arrived in the Pacific, days ago, Mercer had kept his mind focused on putting an end to this. Abe's ghost was about to find, if not peace, then a little justice. Now, as they were almost at their target, doubt began to creep up on him—doubts about himself, his ability to carry out his self-assigned mission, and doubts about his right to mete out punishment as judge and executioner. And like other times when these feelings surfaced, he crushed them down. No sane person would question the need to protect himself from a rabid animal, and that's what these fanatics had proven themselves to be.

He thought about the mercenary and about how that chance encounter had changed their lives. For Mercer it was the beginning of a lifetime of service to his country, in ways he'd never thought possible. Since that first firefight, he'd taken up arms a hundred times to defend the defenseless, and he did so without question or need for recognition. That day had made him a better person, someone willing to step in when others stepped back. It had been a momentous point in his life. He imagined it had altered the South African too. He had seen the pain in the other man's eyes, and the savagery with which he had pursued the lightning stones. A lifetime of physical disfigurement had clearly had psychological ramifications. That one shot was a single act of both creation and destruction . . . of the good Mercer had perpetrated, and the evil from which the South African hadn't turned away. Mercer knew the final echo of that bullet's journey was about to die out. Soon one or both of them were going to die. There was simply no other alternative.

A red light flashed next to the rear cargo ramp.

"Game time," Book shouted.

Mercer purged all thoughts of the past, and he stood with Book against the bulkhead.

A minute later, the young loadmaster lowered the rear cargo door. A wash of humidity and spray whipped into the cargo bay. They each picked up one of the car-

rying handles of the used Jet Ski they'd bought in Fiji.
Mercer struggled. They shuffled forward until they
were standing over the precipice. Fifty feet didn't seem
that high, and thirty knots didn't seem that fast, until you were looking backward out of an aircraft from
which you had to jump. Then the ocean looked miles
below and flashed past in a dizzying blur of speed.

As the aircraft came directly abreast of the distant
tracking ship, the pilot slowed almost to a stop and
dipped the Osprey thirty feet closer to the sea.

The two men were grateful for the courtesy. They
leapt in perfect synchrony, and just before they crashed
into the phosphorescent water, they both pushed off of
the Jet Ski so they landed well clear of the 250-pound
watercraft.

Mercer came up spitting water and swam over
to the bobbing machine. Booker reached it a second
later. They checked that the duffel strapped to the old
Kawasaki was in place. Running without lights, the
Osprey was just a distant drone that quickly faded to
silence.

"Ready?" Sykes asked.

"Let's do this."

While the Jet Ski was capable of speeds in excess
of thirty knots, the two men clinging to it kept it humming at just about five. They didn't want to generate
excessive noise, and they certainly didn't want to be
noticed on radar. "Slow and steady" was how Book
proposed they reach the *Akademik Zhukovsky,* and
that's just what they did. It was awkward for the two
men to cling to the slender little craft, designed to
be ridden by one person standing on the rear deck,
but they made it work. It rode so low that occasional
waves broke over its bow and doused the duo, but

with dive masks in place it was nothing more than an annoyance.

It took a little under an hour to cover the distance, and Booker checked his wrist compass constantly. With the former Russian ship running as dark as their Osprey had been, they only realized they had arrived when they were almost on her. There was no moon, and while the stars were bright, the big ship seemed to have been swallowed whole by the night.

They were less than four hundred yards away before Mercer could see that the slight disruption of the star field along the horizon was actually their target. He pointed it out to Sykes so he could adjust their bearing slightly. With its three giant dish antennas pointing skyward, the ship looked massively top heavy. As they drew closer, they could see bits of light leaking from a few portholes. Book killed the Jet Ski, and for another ten minutes they watched the *Zhukovsky* from a distance, looking for any movement that gave away the presence of roaming guards. They saw nothing except a shadowy figure in the darkened wheelhouse who twice walked out onto the wing bridge. At one point another man had opened a hatch and stood at the rail to enjoy a late-night cigarette; when he was finished, he pitched the butt into the sea so it looked like a tiny meteorite that winked out when it hit the water.

It was clear that the Osprey returning to her operational altitude hadn't been noticed by the radar operators aboard the ship.

"Half hour?" Book asked.

"If we're not done by then, we've screwed the pooch. So yeah."

They had borrowed a waterproof tablet computer

from the *America*'s XO that had an alarm clock app that lit up the screen and played Sousa marches. Sykes slid it from the pouch along with some other gear. Once he'd set the alarm, he duct-taped the tablet to the Jet Ski's steering column. With no way to secure the little machine to the towering side of the ship so that it wouldn't bang against the hull, they would have to let it float free. They would be able to find it easily after they were finished with their mission and the alarm had gone off.

They closed the last few yards by using their legs to flutter-kick the Jet Ski across the surface. Mercer put out a hand so they didn't ram into the steel side of the *Nikolay Zhukovsky*. He held them steady while Booker laced special pads over his dive booties and then fitted his hands into oddly shaped paddle gloves that were the size of cookie sheets. He placed a palm on the side of the ship and it stuck fast.

He whispered, "Those DARPA weenies never disappoint."

DARPA was the Defense Advanced Research Projects Agency, the U.S. military's very real version of the fictional Q Branch from the James Bond movies. They are credited, among other things, with creating the Internet, building the predecessor to the GPS system, aiding in the development of driverless cars, and running the secret X-37B space plane program.

This latest toy was called Geckskin. DARPA-funded engineers had studied how it was possible for geckos and other lizards to support their weight while climbing up walls and across ceilings. Eventually they'd cracked the interplay of tendons and muscles and hit on the right combination of stiffness for strength and softness for maximum surface contact.

The result was an adhesive that could hold a large amount of weight for its size while also being very easy to peel back off again and reuse an infinite number of times. Their goal all along had been for a man to be able to perform one of Spider-Man's greatest feats, and they had more than succeeded.

Once Mercer had slid into his own set of Geckskin pads, Book unstuck his hand, reached a little higher, and restuck the pad to the ship. He did the same with his feet, and just like that he was stuck to the side of the ship, perched like a housefly on a smooth wall. They'd received some instruction on using the Geckskin from the DARPA rep who was field-testing it with some Marines aboard the *America,* so Mercer and Book knew how to properly peel off the adhesive pads, reach slightly higher, and reattach. They'd originally planned to use good old-fashioned rope and hooks to reach the deck, but the Geckskin method eliminated virtually any chance of being detected.

Mercer followed the ex–Delta raider and was soon fifteen feet above the abandoned Jet Ski drifting below his feet. The sensation was a little different from traditional rock climbing, but no more stressful on the body. It was even easier in that you made your own handholds and didn't have to expend energy looking for them.

The *Zhukovsky*'s main deck towered twenty feet above the waterline, and the two men climbed it in just a couple of minutes. Even where the hull plates were wet, the Geckskin stuck as surely as a magnet.

Mercer noted something anomalous as he climbed. Half-inch-thick braided wire had been welded to the hull in parallel rows about five feet apart. The wire ran from below the waterline up to the deck and then continued onward until it vanished into the darkness surrounding the main dish antenna. He couldn't tell if the wire was a recent addition or had been added years earlier, but it certainly appeared to be some sort of retrofit.

They stopped climbing just below the ship's rail, listening hard for a few seconds. They heard nothing but the lapping of waves and the hum of auxiliary equipment and other electrical gear on board the ship. They rose a little higher and peered onto the deck. As before, there was no movement.

Mercer and Book completed the climb up and over the rail, huddling in the shadow under a lifeboat to remove the pads and stow them where they wouldn't be found.

"Too quiet," Booker whispered as he pulled the Kriss off his shoulder.

Mercer agreed. These guys had been in possession of the crystals for almost a full day. They should be getting ready to use them, but there was no indication anything was happening. He removed the antique .45 from its pouch, cocked it quietly, and lowered the hammer.

"I don't get it," Mercer said. "It's a perfectly clear night—why aren't they at least running a test on their gear?"

Book shrugged, and they pressed in tighter beneath the lifeboat. Other than the sound of an occasional door closing within the hull of the ship, there was no movement on deck.

A lyrical ping broke the silence, and a moment later a voice erupted from the vessel's integrated PA system. *"Votre attention s'il vous plaît,"* a male voice intoned in French.

Because he had spent the first twelve years of his life in West Africa, French was the only foreign language Mercer spoke comfortably, even if actual Frenchmen thought his accent atrocious.

The message continued and he translated for Booker. "This is it ... they started a ten-minute countdown for their first experimental test with the actual stones. All personnel who have not cleared the decks must do so immediately. All nonessential electric equipment must be powered down. All reactor technicians must be at their stations."

The message ended and Mercer said to Book, "You had to jinx it by saying things were too quiet, didn't you? We could have just snuck aboard, stolen the stones, and been done with this."

The big man shrugged. "You know I like things dramatic ... with lethal countdowns and shit."

28

There hadn't been time to find design schematics of the *Akademik Zhukovsky*, but they had studied plans for the general cargo ship on which she'd been based. They knew in which hold the original control room had most likely been constructed, and they figured in this latest incarnation it would be where the ship's nuclear power plant's output would be directed and converted to some form of emitted radiation. Jason believed it was the likeliest spot where the crystals would be stored so the energy could be channeled through them and finally beamed into the atmosphere.

Booker led Mercer through the door where the cigarette smoker had stood earlier. The interior of the ship was dimmed down to red battle lights to conserve energy, and even as they stood waiting to hear any movement, the air-conditioning system shut down with a sigh of slowing fans. The other thing they didn't know is how well protected the ship would be. Just because they saw no guards on deck didn't mean there weren't any aboard.

They started down the dull-green-painted hall.

They weren't interested in sweeping the entire ship, so they ignored any closed doors they passed, only checking the rooms they could look into. They found one person on the main deck, a ship's maintenance specialist who was working in a bathroom. He was on his knees surrounded by plumber's tools torquing on an open pipe fitting. He turned in time to see the men loom up behind him but never got a word out before Booker clocked him on the back of the head with the Kriss's retractable stock. It was a well-measured blow that rolled the plumber's eyes into his skull and collapsed him over his wrenches.

Sykes tied his wrists behind his back with plastic zip ties, and they moved on.

Moments later the PA system chimed again, and the same voice came over the speakers. *"Huit minutes."*

Mercer flashed eight fingers for Booker's benefit. They were seriously running out of time.

A door opened behind them. Mercer turned to see a man emerge from a cabin followed seconds later by two more. It was too far and too dark to tell who they were. He watched them for a moment longer, trying to determine if they were a threat, when one of the men spotted him in the hallway. There must have been rules in place about where personnel should be during the final critical moments before the experiment, because he shouted and suddenly the three were reaching for their weapons.

Mercer fired two quick shots that forced the other men back into the cabin.

"Go!" he shouted to Book. "I'll hold them. Stop the test."

Sykes took off running, presenting a remarkably small target for such a big man. Mercer flattened himself against the wall behind a six-inch pipe stanchion, his pistol extended and ready.

The corridor exploded in a riot of hot lead and muzzle flashes as a machine pistol on full auto was unloaded in his direction. The onslaught was terrifying, and ricochets careened down the passage, but nothing came close to hitting him. He loosened another pair of rounds to tell the guards they'd missed, but his position was untenable and so he withdrew. Mercer ran through a door that led to a ladderway. He scrambled down as fast as he could and jumped into another hall one deck down.

An alarm started to wail.

Mercer hoped the commotion would make them postpone their experiment until the threat had been assessed and neutralized—but at the moment he wasn't even sure where it was being conducted. The hallway in which he now stood was more utilitarian than the one upstairs. Not designed as living or recreational space for the crew, the hall was a steel tube with a metal-grate floor that looked down over some machinery. It was sweltering. Steam hissed through a relief valve somewhere. To Mercer it felt like he was in some mid-twentieth-century factory.

He took a second to swap magazines, even though the first one was only half used up. Then he passed through the veil of steam. A shadow moved at the limit of Mercer's vision, and he fired a snap shot. Ducking and then peering back, he saw he'd holed a plastic sign hanging on a string from some overhead piping.

But that mistake attracted the attention of one of his pursuers, who'd taken an alternate route to this deck. Lead filled the air, and Mercer dove flat behind an unused generator. He slid across the hot deck, dropped down an open section of grating to a subdeck below, and doubled back to a spot below where the gunman stood. Mercer raised his pistol so the barrel was between the grating slats and fired twice. One bullet entered the man's thigh, tearing through the femoral artery so that a dark pulse of blood erupted out of the exit wound. The other bullet went straight up through his groin, emasculating him before ripping into his gut and eventually pulping his heart.

Mercer had to jump sideways to avoid the rivulets of blood that dropped through the floor grating.

"Sept minutes."

Mercer swore. They weren't stopping the test.

He climbed back up and out of the machinery space and saw a figure farther down a dim hallway. The figure ducked around the corner. The steel passageway curved as it wrapped around the enormous structural pedestal supporting the main receiver dish that dominated the *Zhukovsky*'s stern.

Mercer aimed at the concave wall and triggered off four quick shots. One of the heavy slugs gouged into the steel bulkhead, but the other three ricocheted around the corner and kept going until they hit something. Mercer could hear the slap of one bullet striking flesh.

He ran after his shots and saw one guard lying on the deck and another farther down the passage. That guy was running away but he was still armed, and Mercer wasn't in a forgiving mood. A single shot caused the guard's back to arch at an almost impossible angle, and he fell flat.

Mercer flicked his attention to the first guy he'd hit. He, too, was facedown, with a bullet wound to the back of his thigh. Rather than reach down to turn him, he kicked at the man's hip with everything he had. The guard had been expecting a cautious flip and had his pistol ready to come around when he was rolled onto his back. The kick caught him by surprise, exposing the weapon before he could shoot at Mercer. Instead, Mercer fired one quick shot that put him down.

Mercer took off running. Now that he had his bearings once again he knew how to reach the control center. He passed several open rooms where men in lab coats or crewman's overalls loitered in the doorways, looking confused about the continuing alarm bells. Mercer shouted in French that they must remain at their posts, pretending to be one of the guards for their benefit. No one challenged him.

"*Cinq minutes.*"

He ran around a corner and almost got cut in half by Booker with the Kriss.

"Shit, man. Don't scare me," Sykes whispered.

"I'm the one who needs to change his shorts now, Book. What's going on? We've got five minutes."

"Other side of this door is the control room," Booker said. "They got it closed up just as I got here. I managed to get a few rounds in before they locked me out. We need to find another way."

"There isn't time."

Mercer looked around the antechamber. It was a dead end. He checked the walls, the floor, the ceiling . . .

He took just a moment to consolidate his two half-empty magazines before turning to Booker. "Give me a hand." Mercer pointed to a large ventilation grille embedded in the ceiling.

Sykes shouldered his weapon and made a stirrup with his hands. Mercer stepped into it and was nearly crushed against the roof when Booker lifted.

"Easy!"

"Sorry."

Mercer pulled off the large grille, pulled his sidearm, and wriggled up and into the duct. It was filthy and, he assumed, laced with Legionnaires' disease and God knew what else, but it passed through the bulkhead separating them from the control room.

The thin metal buckled and popped with even the slightest movement, so all Mercer could hope was that the sound was hidden by the klaxon's shrill cry. There was light in the floor of the duct just ten feet ahead, which meant there was another vent. He slithered to it and tried to peer down, but the louvers were angled so he couldn't see anything but the control room's wall directly beneath him.

"Trois minutes."

Mercer was going to have to do this blind, and there was no point in waiting. He hammered at the vent with the heel of his hand, and when it popped free he dove through it headfirst, widening the stance of his legs so his outer thighs caught on the duct's sharp edge and stopped him from falling all the way to the floor.

He hung upside down from the ceiling, supporting himself with his knees, and must have looked like a half-formed moth emerging from its chrysalis. His inverted position meant his head was beginning to fill with blood and in seconds his vision would dim.

The control room on the old Soviet vessel was vast, with banks of computer stations designed for a time when the machines were the size of shipping containers. And it was tall. Mercer was suspended at least twelve feet from the sunken floor. One wall was dominated by massive display screens with the continents shown as a Mercator projection. These would have traced the paths of the Soviet space shuttles. Another wall was mostly a large glass partition. There were only a handful of people there, most in lab coats. They were already on alert because of the alarms and the reports of gunfire, although someone had had the sense to mute the klaxon in this space. As a group they startled at the bang of the metal vent grille hitting the deck, and they were all turning to see what had fallen.

The first to spot Mercer was the man Mercer feared the most.

It was the South African, and he moved as fast as a mamba from his native land. His weapon was already in hand even as he began dropping into a kneeling position that would give him the best stability for an overhead shot.

Somehow Mercer knew he was going to take a knee, and he adjusted his aim to lead his target as he swung the barrel of the .45.

The mercenary's gun was just a few arc seconds from zeroing in on Mercer when Mercer fired. His first shot missed by a millimeter and he fired again. Dead on center, and the South African was punched back by the .45 slug.

Mercer curled his torso up, grasped the edge of the vent with his fingers, and flipped his legs out. He dropped from the duct and landed squarely on the floor below, absorbing the shock in the long muscles of his thighs and calves. The scientists and techs moved back in a herd reflex, eyes wide with fear. Moments ago they felt secure in their fortress with an armed man to look out for them; now they were terrified. Mercer swept the gun so he covered them, and they all moved back until each was pressed against a workstation.

Mercer kicked aside the unmoving mercenary's pistol. He saw that he'd hit the man in the narrow spot just below his rib cage. The angle meant the heavy slug had torn through his intestines. It was a killing shot, only the man wasn't yet dead. It could take a long time to die from being gut-shot. He had one crimson hand pressed to the wound, but more blood was oozing out from under him where the grisly exit wound leached out his life. He looked up now at Mercer, and a sickly smile spread across his scarred visage.

"Can't even finish me off proper, eh? Going to make me die slow so you can watch."

"Not going to watch at all," Mercer said, thinking about Abe.

Mercer moved to the sealed door and opened the latch. Booker came in with the Kriss high and tight. He took in the tactical scene in an instant and quickly moved to keep the scientists covered.

"Who is in charge here?" Mercer shouted. No one spoke, so Mercer fired a round into the largest display screen. The sharp blast of the pistol's discharge was enough to loosen tongues.

A middle-aged man in a lab coat stuck a tentative hand in the air.

"You're not in the bloody classroom. Put your hand down and tell me how to stop this experiment before it's too late."

"Professor Jean-Robert Fortescue is the project leader," the man said, his voice shaking. He pointed to the large glass window on the far side of the room. "He's in there. That's where the crystals are rigged to the antenna relays. This is just the monitoring room."

Mercer saw there was a thick door, like that of a bank vault, separating the two spaces. He peered through the massive slab of glass. Beyond was a bright space nearly as large as the control room with towering machines straight out of a mad scientist's fervid imagination. They were sleek and high tech, their function completely unknowable. He imagined that somewhere in the tangle of power cords as thick as trash barrels, and featureless metal boxes wreathed in frigid clouds of super-cooling gas to keep them from overheating, were the fifty pounds of stones Amelia Earhart had lost her life trying to return to America.

Mercer couldn't begin to guess how to stop the experiment once it came online. He only knew from Jason that once energy from the ship's atomic power plant was flooded through the crystals and into space, the planet's magnetic fields could show the effects within moments.

There were a couple of people in the room. Mercer guessed that the tall and balding man with a smug look on his face had to be Fortescue. Booker tried the vault handle and shook his head at Mercer.

"Can you communicate with them from here?" Mercer asked the tech.

"Yes." The man pointed to an updated workstation with a modern headset.

Mercer strode over. The mousy scientist backed off, his eyes darting to Book, who stood with his wicked-looking weapon at the ready. Mercer slipped the headset over his ears and adjusted the tiny microphone. "Fortescue, you need to listen to me."

Beyond the glass, the professor slipped on his own headset. "I believe I know who you are. Roland warned me a while back about someone interfering with our plans, but poor Niklaas there said you were abandoned on a desert isle just a day ago."

Mercer recognized the voice from the PA countdown. "Please, you have to stop what you're doing immediately."

"Why would I do that?"

Mercer knew there was no time for discussion. "Listen to me. Whatever calculations you made are wrong. You ramp up that reactor, and there's a good chance you will severely damage the earth's magnetic field."

"I do not think so."

Mercer ground his teeth, thinking momentarily about Abe Jacobs and this long nightmare that had started back in the mine in Minnesota. "Okay, asshole, how about I start killing your team out here one by one if you don't shut this down now?"

A momentary silence greeted Mercer. The Frenchman gave a shrug and said, "I do not know what it is you think we are doing here, monsieur, but the power output will be negligible. The effect will be tiny, though cumulative over many months. The field will not be harmed—slightly fewer clouds will form in this region, and the earth will get a degree or two warmer."

Mercer wasn't sure what the man was talking about. Jason was convinced this was an experiment to somehow use the earth's magnetic field to reduce the amount of warming, given the amount of carbon dioxide that had been released into the atmosphere.

"You're trying to make it *warmer*?"

"*Oui.*"

Mercer and Book exchanged puzzled glances.

Over the PA system, Fortescue said, "Zero."

A palpable hum grew in the distance, nothing deafening, nothing really more than a background sound. Mercer had expected a torrent of power from the reactor to funnel through whatever apparatus they'd devised for the crystals, or to make a commanding high-tech tone while blinding light shot to the heavens from the main antenna dish. The vapor from the cooling system didn't even show the tiniest perturbation.

Monitors hooked to the ship-wide CCTV system showed that nothing at all appeared to be happening.

"You see, monsieur," Fortescue said condescendingly over the headset. "My machine and my calculations are flawless. Once I demonstrate I can warm the surface of the planet, I will then be able to cool it once again."

"Mercer . . ." Book was pointing at another desk-mounted monitor. "Check it out."

The camera showed the main satellite dish, which looked just as it had a few moments earlier. That's not what had caught Booker's attention. Above the ship, the night sky, which had been filled with stars, was now darkening with clouds that pulsed with lightning. As they watched, they realized the clouds were moving—spinning slowly, but accelerating visibly like a cyclonic eye with the *Zhukovsky* at its center.

Sykes added unnecessarily, "That can't be good."

Mercer shouted through the headset at the French scientist. "Look at your own cameras—you're causing an atmospheric disturbance that looks like it's building. Shut it down, Fortescue. Shut it all down!"

Mercer singled out the man who'd spoken earlier. "Can you scram the reactor?"

"Not from here. And the reactor room is better sealed than here. You cannot get in unless Dr. Fortescue lets you."

"Book?"

Sykes swung the Kriss toward the window and moved as close as he dared. He fired as rapidly as the gun would cycle, keeping his shots to such a tight group that each divot in the thick glass overlapped its neighbor. He mechanically switched out the magazine once it was depleted and kept firing until the weapon ran dry again. Glass dust and powder blew back from the impacts, but the heavy .45-caliber bullets gouged only a fraction of the way through the armored window. It would take high explosives to get into the next room, something they didn't have—or have the time to improvise.

Fortescue had ducked for cover behind a pair of computer blade servers at the first violent blasts, but soon righted himself when he realized the window wasn't going to shatter. He wasn't brave enough to move closer to the dinner-plate-size spot where the rounds pummeled the glass, though a contemptuous smirk crossed his lips at the bullets' impotence.

Mercer checked the monitor again. The storm looked like it was growing exponentially, and a hellish blue-green corona was forming like a halo thousands of feet above the ship. The light was otherworldly. Soon tendrils of energy were arcing out from it on north-south vectors as they followed the planet's magnetic lines.

"Look, for Christ's sake!" he shouted at the Frenchman.

Fortescue seemed less sure of himself but said with some defiance, "That is nothing but a quick rebalance. The storm will blow itself out quickly."

Mercer didn't know how much time he had. Jason had been unsure of the effects, but he knew it would be minutes, not hours. The storm raging around the ship continued to grow in ferocity, while at its center the invisible streams of energy were being beamed up from the *Admiral Zhukovsky*'s main antenna. Mercer wasn't the type to surrender to panic. He was logical, methodical, and generally found a solution to any problem, but at that moment he was completely blank. He stared in horror as the sky became a dome of tortured clouds and polarized ions.

He scanned the nearest workstations. Much of the original equipment was still in place, old analog switches and dials labeled with indecipherable Cyrillic letters. The newer stuff was secured onto the workstations rather than embedded into them, and was labeled in French. He ignored all the old stuff. That would do him no good. Mercer thought about finding cover, but no place would afford protection, not during a pole shift.

And that's when it hit him.

Protection.

The stones had to be protected to prevent them from attracting lightning, and with the monster storm surging overhead, the ship should have been attracting strike after strike. The machines beyond the glass barrier appeared fragile. They were delicate electronics, not industrial shielding. The room, too, didn't appear to have any kind of system to counter the effect, and suddenly Mercer understood the wires welded to the hull and strung up to the antenna. They had encased the entire ship in a countermagnetic field, almost like they were degaussing the hull to prevent a static buildup. Unlike Abe Jacobs's copper box or the handful of brass bullets Mercer had cadged together, this was an active Faraday cage–like system protecting an entire ocean-liner-size ship.

He scanned the workstations again and found exactly what he'd expected. One was dedicated to monitoring the ship's electromagnetic shielding. He moused open the dormant computer monitor, and when it came to life he quickly found an override to shut off the protective layer of shielding.

"What are you doing?" Fortescue asked from behind the glass.

Mercer ignored him by yanking off his headset and tossing it on the console. He said to Booker. "How are we on time?"

Sykes checked his watch. "We're still a few minutes early for the Jet Ski's alarm, if that's what you're asking."

"Discretion is the better part of valor," he said to Booker. He then turned to the technicians and scientists and shouted, "Everyone get off this ship as fast as you can. Tell the rest of the crew. They must evacuate now! All your lives are in danger."

The storm had worsened, now an angry spinning gyre that was filling the heavens from horizon to horizon, seething with the unimaginable force of a magnetic field gone awry.

Mercer double-clicked an icon on the computer to depower the shield. When he saw the status bar change to "stand-by," he raised his pistol and put three rounds through the computer wired under the table that controlled the system.

Fortescue pounded on the glass in rage when he realized what Mercer had deduced and then destroyed. The vessel was now vulnerable to lightning strikes, and the most powerful thunderstorm in the planet's history was raging overhead.

"Let's go ... now," Mercer said to Sykes, and started running for the exit.

"No!" Fortescue screamed. The French scientist began working the lock to gain access to the control room in the vain hope of somehow reestablishing the protective shield, but it was a useless gesture. The computer was ruined, and he had no idea how long it would take to jury-rig a backup.

Mercer turned to follow Book, and the headlong rush out of the control room. A hand grabbed his ankle. He'd forgotten about the South African, Niklaas.

"I just want you to understand something ..." he gurgled, blood and saliva on his lips. "All those years ago in Africa, we were sent out to look for some kidnapped missionaries. It was a rescue mission. When my men saw your white faces, they believed you were victims, and they shot at the armed blacks they thought were holding you. It was an accident ... call it friendly fire."

"Call it whatever you want," Mercer said without mercy as a flood of anger poured out of him. "A good man named Paul died that day ... and his death is just as much your fault as the death of a saintly man named Abraham Jacobs, who you killed in the Leister Deep Mine two weeks ago. You've made choices, and so have I. Don't think that scar made you the rotten murderer you are. That happened long before I shot you. I'll tell you this, I'm going to sleep easier tonight knowing that you're dead, and Abe and Paul and Roni

Butler and God knows how many others have been avenged."

Mercer began to turn away, but he pivoted back toward the South African. "I'll give you a shot at some redemption you don't deserve," he offered.

"What's that?" the South African choked, his eyes rolling in his head.

"Give me the name of the man who paid for all this."

The mercenary grinned at Mercer and started coughing. He struggled to get words out, until he finally convulsed and went still.

Mercer stared down at him, then turned and jogged over to join Booker outside the control room doorway. That was the moment the first searing fork of lightning struck the ship. The blast of electricity overwhelmed the power stream that pulsed up through Fortescue's apparatus, and the relays exploded at the onslaught. Drawn to the heart of the equipment where the dun-colored crystals lay, the lightning bolt shot through the wiring in an instantaneous flash that burned everything in a blinding white flash. When it subsided, Professor Fortescue was just a shadow outline of carbon dust left on the glass.

Side by side, Sykes and Mercer ran through the ship, climbing where they found stairways. The handful of people Mercer had warned were now scattered, trying to get others to listen to them about the danger. It appeared none of the crew were listening. No seaman would dare abandon ship into such a tempest, and the scientists couldn't convince them the real danger was still to come.

Mercer and Book burst out on deck and saw they were on the opposite side of the ship from where they'd abandoned the Jet Ski. There were no others outside, no one prepping the lifeboats to abandon ship, no one even standing in life jackets. And if Mercer and Book hadn't had an inkling of what was coming, they would have remained within the protection of the ship's superstructure, too—because far above the vessel a vortex was forming, a miles-wide toroid of clouds that was whipping up to hurricane strength. Lightning arced from side to side like the ethereal net inside a dreamcatcher. What made the effect even more unearthly was that the clouds were so high that the winds didn't so much as riffle the ocean's surface.

Down on the ship it was a calm, tranquil night . . . while overhead the sky looked like a fissure had been opened up to the depths of hades.

They wasted no more than a few seconds in awe of the atmospheric disturbance before taking off running. They had to round the aft section of the superstructure, dashing in a narrow space between the accommodation block and the main antenna pedestal. The air there was supercharged with so much static Mercer's hair went on end.

They reached the starboard side. They couldn't see the Jet Ski at first glance, but at this point it didn't matter. Mercer and Book vaulted the rail, plummeting twenty feet and striking the water. They surfaced at the exact same time and started swimming away from the doomed ship. High above, the maelstrom was intensifying. Lightning was growing stronger, and its booms of exploded air were starting to reverberate across the ocean's vastness.

Their only consideration was gaining distance, so they swam hard. For being so muscle-bound, Book moved like an otter and was soon outpacing Mercer stroke for stroke. Ahead and about two hundred yards to their left, a light began to flash in a dazzling display of colors, while below the storm's rumble, "Stars and Stripes Forever" began to play. Their alarm had finally gone off.

Book reached the Jet Ski first and had it started even before Mercer arrived. They positioned themselves as they had before, and this time they opened the throttle to the max. Mercer kept looking back. The magnetic storm clouds were now so saturated with electricity they glowed an eerie green, while forks of lightning kept probing out from the doughnut-shaped anomaly. A few smaller bolts brushed part of the ship, their arcs so blindingly white that even several miles away they were painful to look at. He felt certain the storm was building to an electric potential many times that first strike.

In astonishment, Mercer watched as the toroid suddenly puffed out, as though it were taking a breath, an instant before it unleashed a barrage of lightning many times thicker than anything he'd ever seen. It was as if every lightning strike hitting the earth at that moment had concentrated above the *Nikolay Zhukovsky*.

The massive discharge struck the ship like a fist from above. For a blinding instant, Mercer could actually see the deluge of power ramming down through the main antenna, and then it came blasting back out of the hull in a searing white ball of plasma that tore plate from frame. The entire ship came apart like an exploding grenade.

Mercer had to look away, his vision marred by the afterglow of such an intense display. Moments later, they were struck by the heat of the blast, a hot ozone-laced wind that filled their lungs and made them cough.

The atomic-bomb-style dome of light finally faded, and when Mercer looked back again there was no evidence that anything extraordinary had happened. The clouds had been blown away, and the night sky shone clear again.

"Jesus," Book said when he, too, looked behind them. He throttled down the Jet Ski to idle.

"To paraphrase an old TV commercial that was more prophetic than it knew: 'It's not nice to fool with Mother Nature.'"

29

Mercer and Booker spent close to three hours on that Jet Ski before being rescued in the middle of the night by a Sea King helicopter flown off the USS *America*. The explosion had been detected on monitors all over the planet, and it was at first believed to be nuclear in origin. In response, the navy had tasked their closest ship, one that was actually closer than some top brass had expected her to be, to investigate. Captain Tuttle and his crew searched the area for any sign of what had happened. Nuclear detectors aboard ship found no traces of fallout. As far as the world was concerned, the explosion had been a large meteor strike.

It would be several months before another navy ship would be dispatched to the region. They would use ROVs to scour the seafloor for any wreckage. Of special interest was the containment chamber for the *Zhukovsky*'s reactor core, which was eventually found intact and clandestinely salvaged from eleven thousand feet of water.

Mercer and Book were taken aboard the USS *America* that night—where Mercer returned Tuttle's beloved .45—and eventually flown to Tarawa, for their commercial flights. Sykes was heading home to North Carolina. Mercer had one stop to make before allowing himself the luxury of going home. He flew first to Hong Kong on a connecting flight to his final destination—Charles de Gaulle International, just north of Paris.

In the world of backroom deals that was Washington politics, the real story of what had happened in the Pacific began circulating as soon as the magnetic storm had destroyed itself. Ira Lasko was widely credited with helping to prevent what could have been the greatest catastrophe to strike humanity since our ancestors climbed out of the trees. No one yet knew where to point the finger, but investigations were under way about the ownership of the *Zhukovsky* and the identity and most recent employer of a South African mercenary, first name Niklaas, last name still unknown.

Mercer let Ira take the lion's share of the credit and couldn't have cared less about the legitimate investigations being ramped up in the Hoover Building and at Langley. The only thing that interested him was the name the mercenary had coughed up as he lay dying on the floor of the ship's control room.

Mercer had called Ira by satellite phone while he was still aboard the *America* and given him the name. Within hours, Lasko had called back, and they had pieced together the full picture.

"Roland d'Avejan and Eurodyne . . . I know of him," Ira responded. "But the guy's loaded—why would he do something like this?"

"His chief scientist aboard the *Zhukovsky* alluded to the basics, and it makes perfect sense—in a warped

way," Mercer said. "Until recently, Europe was en-
amored with green energy schemes. Windmills and
solar panels were going up from the coast of Spain
to Germany's eastern borders, and governments were
subsidizing it all with taxpayer money—billions of
dollars per month."

"This was all about global warming and saving
the planet."

"To some, sure. But to business, it was a cash
cow. People were so passionate about it they were
willing to fork over huge sums of money. Companies
like Eurodyne were more than happy to supply the
windmills and solar panels and gobble up the subsidy
money like pigs at a trough.

"Fast-forward a few years, the world economy is
in the crapper and suddenly Juan and Johan Q Public can no longer afford expensive green energy, so
the public spigot closes. This also corresponds with
a time when global surface temperatures were shown
not to be rising as fast as everyone had feared. This
put climate change hysteria on the back burner for
everyone except those with vested interests: environmental NGOs who need funding, the media, which
needs good scare stories, and a handful of companies
heavily invested in green tech. Some of those simply cratered, like Solyndra and A123 Solar ... but
d'Avejan didn't want Eurodyne to end up on the same
scrap heap. So he came up with a plan to save it."

"By causing more global warming?"

"Yes. D'Avejan intended to use the crystals to deflect a little more of the cosmic radiation that strikes
Earth, which would cause fewer clouds to form in the
atmosphere. And once a planet loses a portion of its
shading, it warms ever so slightly."

"I get it," Ira said. "He makes global warming come back, people start to panic again, and suddenly the governments lavish billions on solar and wind."

"And on Eurodyne," Mercer concluded.

"I assume you're not laying all this in my lap out of the kindness of your heart."

"Not at all," Mercer assured him. "You can take the accolades for all this, Ira ... we both know I certainly don't want them. But I do need one thing from you. There's an errand I have to do before I head home."

—

At nine in the morning on the day after his arrival in Paris, Mercer received a visitor in his hotel room. The man had a package, and the address of a plumber not far from Eurodyne's headquarters building. The man and Mercer headed out, and fifteen minutes later they were at the modest shop of the local plumber. The French plumber, a dour mustached man who smoked like the surgeon general had never existed, graciously accepted his fee of five hundred euros and handed over uniforms and two boxes of tools.

At exactly ten o'clock, Mercer and the CIA contact, now both dressed in authentic uniforms, were in Roland d'Avejan's secretary's office. The agent was explaining to her that he'd received an emergency call from the tenant below her boss's office, and there was water leaking through his ceiling. She replied that Monsieur d'Avejan was not to be disturbed, to which the agent replied that he would call the building manager and have the terms of the lease read to her because he had emergency access to all parts of the building, day or night, and Monsieur could go screw himself.

She finally relented, buzzed d'Avejan, and explained the problem.

"Fine," he'd huffed over the intercom.

The lovely executive assistant opened the inner office door and stood back so the plumbers could lug their toolboxes inside.

Roland d'Avejan didn't even look up from his desk, and Mercer dared not look at him in case the man could sense his hatred. He followed the CIA agent into the bathroom and closed the door. The agent cocked an eyebrow as an invitation for Mercer to do whatever it was he wanted. Mercer opened the heavy toolbox. He donned a pair of rubber surgical gloves he'd been given earlier, followed by a pair of thick rubber gauntlets. Only then did he remove the wrapped block that had been formulated for him by a retired chemist who did occasional work for the CIA, as well as France's own DSGE. Mercer removed the bar of soap from the tiled shower stall and replaced it with the new cake. The colors matched, but Mercer's was a little too large, so he pared it down with a knife.

He put the heavy gloves in the box and snapped off the latex.

"C'est tout? Fini?" the agent asked.

"Oui."

"D'accord."

They exited the bathroom, and the agent said to the uninterested executive, "Pardon us, monsieur, but the water does not appear to be coming from your bathroom. Sorry for the inconvenience."

They paused for a second, but d'Avejan didn't

bother looking up, so the plumbers walked out. They smiled at the pretty secretary and left the building together.

It wouldn't break on Bloomberg News until nine hours later, while Mercer was reclined comfortably aboard a Boeing 777 somewhere over the Atlantic. Roland d'Avejan, the wealthy president of one of Europe's most well-respected and environmentally conscious companies, had hurled himself naked through his office window and plummeted to his death. His body showed signs of second- and third-degree chemical burns. A rumor out of the medical examiner's office was that d'Avejan's body continued to melt even on the autopsy table. The subsequent investigation would reveal a pattern of self-abuse using stronger and stronger soaps in a masochistic spiral that obviously got out of control. His latest attempt to expunge whatever sins he thought these soaps could clean had gone terribly wrong. A sliver of the fateful bar had been recovered by investigators in his shower, and tests had revealed its active chemicals became more caustic when exposed to water. An experiment on a piece of pork revealed that when d'Avejan tried to rinse away the painful soap, his skin would have started smoking, then disintegrating. It was universally agreed that the only way d'Avejan could have ended his excruciating agony was to jump. Death by misadventure. Case closed.

———

Mercer arrived home early evening, Eastern Standard Time, to find Harry and Special Agent Kelly Hepburn sitting in his bar. Kelly's leg was up on a coffee table, her crutches leaning on the sofa next to her. Drag was on her other side, his tail going like a slow-tempo metronome while she scratched his ears.

"Well, hello," Mercer said, taking in the scene.

"Hello yourself," Kelly said with a warm smile. "If you don't mind me saying so, Mercer, you look like crap. Where have you been . . . chasing terrorists around the globe?"

"I'm taking Drag out for a smoke," Harry announced, passing Mercer and giving him an affectionate slap on the back.

"I've spent quite a lot of time here in the last week, recovering and chatting with Harry. You've got a real friend there."

"Well, he's certainly not shy . . . or sober," Mercer replied. "How's the leg—did Harry take good care of you?"

Kelly laughed. "Regaled me with stories of your heroics, Mercer. I was a captive audience."

"Never believe everything you hear. And in Harry's case, never believe *anything* you hear."

"Okay, here's the deal," Kelly said quickly as she levered herself off the sofa. "You're probably dead on your feet right now, so I'm going to get out of your hair and let you get some sleep. But I do plan on coming back when you're rested."

"Absolutely not," Mercer replied. "I have to atone for past mistakes and ask a lady for a proper date. Just give me fifteen minutes to shower and dress, and I'll whisk you away to wherever you want." Mercer started walking toward his bedroom, but he turned back when he reached the doorway. "You mentioned French and Thai. I happen to be off all things French for a while, so Thai it is."

—

After dinner, Special Agent Kelly Hepburn came home with Mercer. Despite her earlier warning, they did not need the Jaws of Life, only a carefully placed pillow and a burning desire to find comfort in the arms of another.